# Curtsies & Consequences

Melissa Constantine

*Advanced Reader Copy*
*Uncorrected Proof*

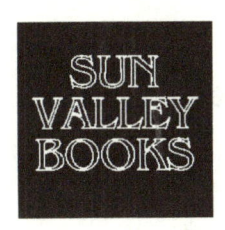

SUN VALLEY BOOKS

Copyright © 2024 Melissa Constantine

All rights reserved. No part of this publication may be reproduced, distributed, or transmitted in any form or by any means, including photocopying, recording, or other electronic or mechanical methods, without the prior written permission of the publisher, except in the case of brief quotations embodied in critical reviews and certain other noncommercial uses permitted by copyright law.

This book is a work of fiction. Names, characters, businesses, organizations, places, events, and incidents are products of the author's imagination or are used fictitiously. Any resemblance to actual persons, living or dead, events or locales is entirely coincidental.

Printed in the United States of America


Book design by: Melissa Constantine
Cover design by: Melissa Constantine

ISBN Paperback: 979-8-9911871-0-7

First Edition: October 2024

*Dedication*

*To Carissa,*

*Who read every book I wrote and never told me they were cringe, even when I knew they were.*

# CHAPTER ONE
## Kira

*When she was Queen, chocolate would be served at every meal.*

Kira bit into her last bar, savoring the sweetness, and its subtle hint of berries. Not her favorite, but still excellent. A bit of the gold wrapper fell to the forest floor, and she kicked over a mound of leaves to cover the evidence. She let the chocolate melt on her tongue as she decided on her next move. The Palace's schedule had noted that the Duke of Lower Miser was due to arrive before noon. Given the threat of the Beast, she'd assumed the Duke would try and make the last few miles to the Palace an early morning journey.

*Probably best to get a bird's eye view.*

She tucked the remainder of the chocolate into her messenger bag and swung up into the nearest tree, scrambling along the branches, her hands digging into the soft spring bark. She needed to get high enough to see the carriage before it hit her trap. From the last branch she dared step on there was a surprisingly good vantage point. The fog had settled into the nooks and crannies of the forest, although the sun was coming up quickly.

She squinted, trying to find the twisty Royal Route. The road snaked out through the miles of the Palace's hunting grounds, doubling back on itself a handful of times because of the natural features of the land. If the Duke was bringing the ceremonial carriage of the Misery Islands, it was too large to take the shortcut paths that cut off the curves. The driver would have to wind through the dense fog and could easily lose their sense of direction for a stretch where the trees were thickest.

Confident she'd chosen her spot well Kira took the cloak from her bag. She had learned the hard way never to try and wear it before climbing. Her shoulders ached with the phantom of falls past, of which there had been many. Becoming the Beast had not been seamless. She absently rubbed at the non-existent pain, before pulling the magnificent many-furred cloak of the Beast of Barlow over her head. The heavy fur settled on her shoulders, along with the familiar tingle of magic.

Honestly, whomever made th3 thing was a true craftsman. The furs covering it were a hundred or more colors — from rich cream to deep-dark night — all blended seamlessly. She didn't believe for a second that it came from the real Beast. Legendary monsters so rarely matched with the stories about them. And this cloak was nearly perfect to the tales she'd heard as a child. The mismatched ears on the hood had clearly come from different animals — one high pointed like a lynx, the other the rounded shell of a bear's ear. No, there were no tusks, no claws extending off the arms, but otherwise, it was exactly like the stories.

What the cloak lacked in animal verisimilitude it made up for in magic. It didn't glow or levitate or any of that nonsense, but Kira could feel it all the same. She sometimes imagined she'd felt the cloak calling to her, summoning her down to the dusty archives where it had been for a generation or more. She'd felt a pull, like an invisible cord in her chest, and knew that it was destined to be hers.

Well, *obviously*, it was hers. Everything in Corlea Palace belonged to her.

But it was more than that.

Wearing the cloak was the first time in her life she'd felt powerful. With it on she was stronger, faster, and her eyesight sharper the moment she pulled the hood over her face.

No one could make her feel small or insignificant when she was the Beast of Barlow. Not the Palace staff who gave her furtive, side-eyed looks as if they expected her to have one of her dead father's legendary outbursts at any moment. Not the visiting royals who ignored her and handed the crown to her stepmother because of her alleged need for "training." *As if every moment of her life hadn't been spent with the knowledge that she was to rule?*

The plan for how to use the cloak had come to her almost without thinking. All year, there had been reports of something roaming the forests. Most of them were nonsense, wild claims that travelers saw the Beast running through the trees or that animals had gone missing from farms. Complete nonsense. Yet notices had gone out to every town, village, and crossroads warning of the threat. Really, Kira thought she should find a way to say thank you to whoever started the rumors. It was a built-in atmosphere of danger that allowed her to graduate from petty theft to something bigger.

Which she would do once again, as soon as the Duke of Lower Miser's carriage came around the bend.

Kira surveyed the surrounding forest. Light barely touched the horizon, nothing more than a thin line of pink breaking into the cloudy gray sky. A bit more visibility would have been nice. Even with a magical assist in her eyesight, it was pretty dark. This particular stretch of the Royal Route was narrow and the trees were full enough that at times their branches would brush the sides of any passing vehicle. Kira would have to scout more locations before the Festival of the Flower. All the major houses would travel the Royal Route on their way to the celebrations in neighboring Dunlock, and she wasn't going to let an opportunity like that pass her by.

Kira shut her eyes, listening past the natural chatter of the forest. The magic pushed restlessly against her chest, spurring her forward. Kira tried to ignore it. She stayed still and focused until she picked up the sounds of a buoy bell tolling mournfully. Corlea was too far from the sea for that to be accidental. It had to be mounted on the Misery Islander's carriage.

If only every royal family would be so kind as to give her advanced warning. She moved closer to the trunk, letting the cloak blend into the foliage, her heart beating furiously.

The buoy bell grew louder as the duke's ostentatious gold carriage came into view, that bell rocking back and forth as if it were caught in a storm. The duke's poor driver must have had a monstrous headache by the time they got anywhere. Hopefully, they were smart enough to stuff their ears with cotton.

Kira willed away that image and every other stray thought she'd collected. It was time to go to work.

A successful robbery had three elements; atmosphere, brevity, and profit.

Thank the Fairies, the atmosphere was sorted. Early morning, and a shadowy stretch of forest. For the second part, well, getting the job done fast was Kira's specialty. She was small and quick, able to dash out of the brush and grab her spoils before anyone knew what was happening. It didn't hurt having the element of surprise on her side. No one really believed they were going to get robbed. Especially not by the Beast of Barlow.

The wild card was profit. The kingdom's elite might be arrogant in their fancy carriages, surrounded by their teams of outriders, but they weren't all that stupid. No one carried all their worldly possessions with them. What they did carry was generally small but sentimental — rings passed down from generations, watches given on a grandfather's deathbed. Little things that meant a lot.

And that suited Kira fine. It wasn't like she needed the money.

She edged out on the branch until she reached the point where it overlapped with the next tree, waiting for a beat before easing onto the new one. It was as thick as a knight's thigh, but zipping through the trees fifteen feet off the ground wasn't something that she'd learned from her governess.

Her heart thumped in triple time until she found her footing, and moved toward the tree's massive trunk. The view of the road wasn't as good as from the old oak. The branches had not yet shed last year's leaves for new spring buds, but the wide and flat nature of the limbs had made it a better place to stage her devices.

Perhaps she didn't need them, what with the cloak's magic swirling around her, but Kira liked to be prepared. A potion that when uncorked filled the surrounding forest with opaque, gray fog, and a collection of old pots and pans tied together with a rope that made a horrendous sound when rattled. Simple but effective.

A lot could go sideways during a robbery. Partly it all depended on how many outriders came with the party or the bravery of the occupants of the carriage. But rob them of their sight and their hearing, and the chances of pulling it off were substantially higher.

As soon as she uncorked the potion, the billowing fog began to tumble out of the bottle like a troupe of acrobats. It settled along the forest floor and the craggy surface of the road, hiding the dangers. She didn't have to fight so much as foster the unknown. She had to be the suggestion of the Beast of Barlow more than anything. Rustle the branches, and growl a time or two. Make great, unexplainable noises and those fools that had been so busy jockeying for power while her father succumbed to his mania would be shaking in their boots.

Top it off with the barest glimpse of the Beast — Kira in her fur cloak charging through the brush — and the deal was done. Most times the travelers threw their gold and ran in the opposite direction. Which was ideal because robbing people was exhausting.

The buoy bell's clang was soon joined by the approaching sound of the Duke's outriders, the clop of the horse's hooves, and the lurch of the slow, gaudy ceremonial carriage. Although she couldn't see them from the oak, she knew exactly when they fell into her trap, as they got deeper into the fog and their voices rose to a pitch that suggested worry. Kira scrambled down the tree, waiting with hitched breath until the whole caravan was enveloped by the fog.

The Duke traveled with four outriders. Two of them were young knights in bold blue and yellow tunics. The other two were grooms perhaps, or footmen conscripted for the journey. There was no one riding post behind the driver, and from the Palace's schedule, Kira knew the Duke traveled without his wife and sons. Five altogether. It was a reasonable showing for the smallest of the Known Kingdoms and a much easier job for her.

Kira watched from her hiding spot behind the oak, squinting her eyes against the gathered fog. One of the outriders, she couldn't tell which, let out a piercing whistle, and the party came to a thudding, ungraceful stop.

"Trouble," said one of the men to another.

The high whine of the horses agreed.

"I'll see what's up ahead," volunteered one of the knights, urging his horse forward. Kira recognized him from the knighting ceremony last year. Sir Robert Shiny Hair. Well, no, the Misery Islander's last name was something else, but Shiny Hair worked both as a nickname and an active description. Too pretty for his own good.

"Sir, no. They say the Beast has been seen here." This from an older man sitting on a comically small pony. Kira smiled under her hood. The man's words were anything but convincing. Shiny Hair urged his horse down the road out of Kira's line of vision. The other three outriders gathered close together, their horses still dancing in agitation.

"I don't like this," said the other knight, this one blond and shaggy.

The maybe-footman made a grunt of agreement. The older man was too busy trying to control his horse.

Kira grabbed the rope line she'd laid between the trees and gave it a dozen hard pulls. The horses reared and the riders again fought to keep them under control as Lord Julius, Duke of Lower Miser, made his first appearance. The blue sash covering the carriage window opened with a snap. The duke stuck his bewigged head out. "What in the Fairies is happening?"

Kira yanked the rope again and the resulting clatter sent the Duke's towering wig to the ground.

"I will not have it!" the Duke said. He pushed open the carriage door and by the oomph he made, stumbled before getting to his feet.

Kira giggled and then tried to cover it up with a low, breathy growl.

"Your Grace," said the shaggy knight, "Please, return to the carriage until we find our way through this fog."

Kira let the rope line go still, and the silence in its absence was enough to raise the hair on the back of everyone's neck, including her own. She added another long roar, using all of her breath to push out the sound. She had perhaps five more minutes with the dense fog. The bank would burn off quickly but that was all the time she needed.

Horse hooves clipped along the road until Shiny Hair Sir Robert returned. "I can't see an end to the fog, the road takes too many turns ahead."

"This is unacceptable, " the Duke said. "What is happening here?"

Kira pitched her voice to the lowest octave she could before speaking into a long funnel that amplified the sound. "It's simple, Your Grace. You've come to my toll."

"Uncle," said Shiny Hair, "get back in the carriage."

"I will not," Lord Julius said, and then raising his voice added, "Whoever you are, stop this at once. I am a royal of this realm and I am on important business with the Queen."

*Queen Regent*, Kira silently corrected. Her stepmother, Isadora of Zinnj, would never be the true Queen of the Known Kingdoms.

"Pay my toll," Kira said in her deepest growl. "Or not even the Fairies will know you."

A hawk – flying high above the trees – added a shriek and the Duke squealed. Kira smiled. It was always nice when the forest gave her assistance.

"Is that what you are, a Fairie? We are friends with the Fairies in The Misery Islands."

"I care not," Kira said. "I am the Beast of Barlow and you will pay my toll."

"Uncle, please, get back in the carriage," urged Sir Robert.

"I do not pay heed to bullies pretending to be…"

"I AM THE BEAST OF BARLOW," Kira wailed. Her voice went unintentionally higher, and to cover it she added another rattle of the pots and pans. "PAY OR BE CURSED."

The Duke screamed, and from his perch on top of the carriage, the driver called. "I can't hold the team much longer, Your Grace. We need to go."

That was excellent. It was always best when the outriders stayed on their horses and the driver on his perch. No knights on their feet meant there was no one to catch her when Kira dashed from her cover. Lord Julius certainly wasn't going to do it.

The fog was already starting to dissipate, the sun breaking through the thick tree cover. It was time.

Kira growled and ran full tilt toward the Duke. A surge of power from the cloak sang through her and she ran faster. It radiated through her limbs, and the weight of the heavy fur cloak on her back was a part of her rather than a burden. She was not the petite princess, the passed-over heir to the throne. She was the Beast of Barlow and she was unstoppable.

Her objective came into view as the fog broke. The Duke screamed as she got close enough that he could see the whites of her wide eyes in the two slits in the cloak's hood.

"Your gold!" Kira growled.

"Anything, anything," the Duke whimpered. He fumbled pulling a small leather pouch from his cloak.

Kira ripped it from his trembling hand, as well as the wig that sat lopsided on his head. She continued her mad dash into the woods, making guttural screams as she avoided the agitated horses.

There would be time to pick up her devices later. She would come back and clear the site of her tricks, and remove any evidence that the Beast of Barlow was a princess in an unwieldy fur cloak. First, she had to outrun the disappearing fog and the approaching sun. She ran, dashing through the brush, the stiff and thorny branches tearing at her fur hide and the legs of the trousers she wore underneath. Her hands sweat and ached from clutching the wig and the pouch of gold.

She ran until there were no voices behind her and no horses in distress. She fought for her breath, enjoying the thrill of a job well done.

When she reached one of the hidden entrances to the Palace tunnels she threw open the door. It slammed behind her, blending back into the surrounding forest. Only with it closed did Kira relax, leaning against the wooden planks. She took a deep breath, willing her heart and her lungs to slow down, and laughed as the magic drained from her.

*Melissa Constantine*

## Chapter Two
### Kira

**The footman sent to fetch her looked rather ill as he handed her the note.**

Kira raised her eyebrows, but Pollock was too engrossed in his own suspicions about the forest to notice. Every snapped twig and rustle of the branches was making him jump out of his livery.

Isadora's precise, yet elegant penmanship graced the outside of the letter. It was addressed simply to *The Princess Royal*.

Kira yawned as she broke the wax seal. Outings as the Beast left her tired in a way she'd never imagined. She'd planned to sleep the whole day, and it wasn't even lunchtime. She'd been hiding under the thick feather coverlet of the stone cottage's single bed when her carriage pulled into the yard. She'd barely had time to hide her cloak in the wardrobe before Pollock's insistent knocking began.

Her stepmother hadn't bothered with pleasantries, she'd simply written, *You are expected by eleven o'clock.*

"Your Highness, we should go. The Beast was near here this morning." Somewhere in the distance an animal called, and Pollock's normally tan face went ashen.

Kira took a deep breath, willing the heavy feeling of needed sleep from her body. "If that's true, we're perfectly safe. They say the Beast never strikes in the same place twice."

The footman was unconvinced. "The Beast of Barlow is nothing to take lightly. The Queen would kill me and John if anything were to happen to you."

Kira bit back a sigh. She was rather fond of Pollock and John, the driver, but really they were grown men scared of a mythical creature. She'd hoped her servants would be made of sterner stuff. "I'll make my own way back. You can inform the Queen Regent that I will be on time."

Pollock shook his head. "Ma'am was very clear we were to bring you back."

"I will be fine, I promise." Kira fought another yawn and lost.

"Highness, if you're tired the trip will be nothing."

"I shall be back at eleven as summoned." Kira hadn't meant for the words to come out so harshly, but Pollock jumped. He was particularly scandalized when she shut the door on him.

Guilt ebb inside her chest. Pollock was a good man. He didn't deserve to be treated unkindly. But going straight to her stepmother wasn't something Kira could make herself do. Pollock would survive. Kira was tired enough that she couldn't say the same about herself.

As powerful as she'd felt dashing through the woods she was twice as exhausted in the aftermath. Sometimes she thought she could sleep for a week, although gnawing hunger always drew her out of bed. Neither the chocolate bars she kept in her leather satchel nor the meager stores she kept in the cottage were ever enough after a robbery. She usually ended up back in the Palace for meals.

Kira pulled out her watch from the bedside table. She had at least an hour. That was plenty of time. As soon as Pollock and John got the hint that she wasn't going with them and left the yard, she would hide her stolen items from the morning and slip through the tunnel entrance behind the wardrobe. Disappearing while they were still nervously pacing in front of the cottage like anxious puppies would raise too many eyebrows. Kira knew that at least some of the Palace staff were aware of the tunnels, but as far as she knew the shortcut from the old gamekeeper's cottage was her secret. As much as any of the tunnels did, it led directly to the Palace. That would put her on the lower ground level of the East Wing, and from there she could zip up the stairs to her own apartments. In all probability, she'd be back before John pulled the carriage through the gates.

She would have to change before seeing her stepmother. She'd fallen asleep in her boots and trousers, both of which were forbidden for a royal audience. Not even the highest-ranked princess in the Known Kingdoms was exempt from that rule. If she hurried, she might also have time for a bath. The simple shirt and tunic she'd worn under her cloak were badly wrinkled and smelled none-too-faintly of sweat.

Kira watched through the single window as the blurry specter of John finally pulled the horses back onto the forest path, away from the cottage. She took her cloak from the wardrobe and moved it to a trunk with a sturdy lock. The bottom of the trunk was lined with the items she collected. She had a dozen handkerchiefs, a few dented gold rings, even a spectacular pair of eyeglasses with pink alabaster frames she'd taken from a countess, or perhaps a courtesan, she wasn't sure.

Kira hadn't planned to keep these things forever, but disposing of them in the woods seemed unnecessarily cruel. When she took things at the Palace, it sent the royals searching every sitting room, salon, and corridor to find them. For a few hours, they felt helpless, until Kira discreetly dropped the necklace or the stick pin or whatever it was in public spaces, as if the royals might have carelessly dropped them. At some point, she would have to decide what to do with the things she'd collected as the Beast. Perhaps she'd take a big batch of them and drop them in the post. Although, really, that was going to be an awful lot of trouble. The Beast of Barlow couldn't turn up at the royal mailroom. *A problem for another day.*

Kira closed the trunk and returned the key to the ribbon around her neck.

****

The tunnels weren't cooperating.

A trickle of brackish water along the dirt floor gave way to large puddles until the way forward was flooded at least two feet deep. Kira searched her memory for a decent enough curse word and barked out a few, but nothing said, "I should like to get to my room without seeing anyone, thank you," in such a short amount of syllables.

The Zephyr lamp she carried only cast enough light to see a few feet behind her, to where the tunnel split between three different routes. The pitiful dark made it too difficult to tell which way she'd come. She'd have to take the nearest exit until she found an entrance to the kitchen.

There were dozens of passages that led from the Palace, coiling out like snakes in chaotic, backtracking loops as if the point weren't to get anywhere quickly, but to get as dizzy as possible. Kira wouldn't put it past a few of her ancestors to have done exactly that. The Vineland Kings had ruled for over a thousand years, and there was more than enough evidence in the Corlea archives to suggest a half-dozen or more might have been politely cracked.

A ladder of sorts was carved into the hard-packed dirt, out of the reach of her lamp. She moved closer, the pale pink light of the Zephyr blinking, as if objecting to being shone on such an ugly sight as a few handholds dug into a wall. Kira flicked the glass with her finger, urging it back to life.

"Enough," she told the Zephyr. "It's not like we have a choice."

The lamp sputtered, red sparks exploding inside the glass, which was no help at all.

"That's quite rude." Kira turned down the gas knob to extinguish the lamp. She didn't need it anyway. She had to be close to the Palace. She might emerge close enough to walk back, tunnels be damned.

Kira secured the lamp in her satchel, and although she fumbled a bit with the totality of the darkness, she managed to find the handholds once again. She was strong from her time in the forest. Blinding sunshine met her as she pushed the heavy wooden door open. She blinked, rubbed her eyes, and willed them to adjust to the light. The area where she emerged was eerily quiet. She had to be near the Fairie chapel. It was the only place in the forest without the chirp of birds and the rattling hum of bugs in the brush.

Sure enough, the little burned-out chapel sat not a dozen feet from where she exited the tunnel. It was little more than a stone shell. The bones remained, but the Fairie portraits that would have once decorated the interior had gone up in flames long ago. Vines as thick as Kira's forearm crawled up the sides and over the roof in the twenty years since the fire.

The last time Kira had been here was the day before her cousin Bertie left for the Royal Academy.

"Can't convince you to come with me?" he'd asked for probably the tenth time.

Kira would have liked nothing better, but her father had definitive ideas about the Academy from his own inglorious time there.

"Father won't change his mind."

"They never should have kicked him out. He was always going to be the king."

Kira sighed. It was no good. Her father would refuse. He had not left the Palace since her mother's death, and therefore she did not leave the Palace. "Whatever, you're going to write to me and tell me all about it."

Bertie made no promises. "Classes and such," he said as if he needed a built-in excuse for the lackadaisical correspondence to come.

Over the years the chapel had been a playroom and clubhouse for the two of them. It was a place to be when Corlea Palace was crowded with royals, all vying for the attention of the King, and those who wished the younger generation wasn't underfoot.

Bertie had paced the room, hands in his pockets. He carried a great deal of tension in his shoulders, and he hadn't looked her in the eyes all day. Kira wanted to grab him in a hug and tell him it was going to all be okay, but she'd sensed that Bertie was too fragile to touch.

"I'm not coming back," he said, as if it were incidental and not devastating.

Kira didn't have to be told why. "Uncle Gore is a jackass. When I'm queen, I'll banish him. And then you can come back."

Bertie nodded. But they both knew that even then; he probably wasn't going to come back. The last fight with his parents had been the final straw. Bertie had refused the match they'd set up with the daughter of a marquis from Spire. It had been an ultimatum, a demand that their wayward son do right by the family. Neither of his parents had spoken to him since.

"I'll miss you." The look in his eyes had gone a little far away as if he weren't seeing Kira or the burned-out building at all.

Kira wondered if he was seeing what the place should have been. She'd never seen an active chapel — her parents had banned any notion of Fairie worship — but she often imagined what the place would have looked like before she was born. She didn't know if the portraits of the various Fairies would have been stacked side by side or end to end, or what the Fairies even looked like. Bertie had been born in the Unknown Kingdoms where their Courts reigned so maybe he could better imagine them. Maybe his eyes found the offering plate that should have stood in the middle of the room, brimming with food and flowers and whatever else might please the Fairies. Kira didn't ask, afraid too many questions would break her cousin.

And really, what was the point of speculation? The fire that destroyed this place had been set deliberately. Black shadows ran up the stones and even after two decades, Kira had never left the chapel without bringing the smell of smoke back in her clothes.

Kira didn't want to dwell on bad memories, but they had a way of creeping over her when she wasn't prepared for them. Seeing the chapel was like a slow, syrupy pull in her chest. She'd never thought of the day Bertie left as a bad memory, but she supposed it must be. Bertie had finished at the Royal Academy months ago and he true to his word hadn't come back. He and his boyfriend, Prince Xavier of Dunlock, had taken over the management of the Dunlock Charity Orphanage together and were living happily ever after. The Palace had felt especially empty ever since.

Kira physically shook to expel the melancholy. She needed to get going to get back in time. She was already trying the Queen Regent's patience, no doubt. Isadora had a way of tightening her lips and staring her down that made Kira want to stick out her tongue and make rude gestures as if she were still a child and not a grown woman. The summons that Pollack had brought to her cottage had said quite plainly that she was expected, so Kira supposed she ought to get on with it.

She skirted the clearing where the chapel stood. Most of the doorways were disguised by some kind of flora, although with her luck this chapel was surrounded by bramble bushes full of sharp, unforgiving little bastards. Her boots, already damp from the tunnel, were covered within minutes as she felt her way through the brush. She stopped to dislodge a particularly sharp barb that had dug its way into the leather when movement inside the chapel caught her eye.

Maybe movement was too strong a word. A fast shadow. A blur seen through a partially covered window opening.

The small hair on the back of Kira's neck stood on end. It might be nothing, but as far as she knew, no one in Corlea had broken the law and used any of the Fairie chapels, least of all one this close to the Palace.

"Hello?"

There was no answer, not even a footstep in the surrounding forest.

"You're not supposed to be in the chapel." That bit was probably unnecessary, but filling the silence seemed more important than saying something intelligent.

What remained of the chapel's wooden porch croaked under Kira's weight as she approached. She listened but there was no sound from within. Her own breath was slightly too loud, and her heart practically boomed in her chest, but there was nothing so helpful as footsteps to be heard.

She used her shoulder, pushing at the door until it gave way.

The chapel was the same. The stools she and Bertie had once carried down from the Palace were tipped over. Enough dirt covered the stone floor to allow for the growth of grass and a dozen stunted tree saplings, but otherwise, it wasn't much changed.

She was being foolish. Clearly, she was alone. She'd been spending too much time in the woods if a shadow was giving her the creeps. Perhaps it was time to go visit Bertie in Dunlock. Kira let out a breath and turned to go.

A doll sat to the left of the door. It was matted and filthy and about 18 inches tall. What creature it was supposed to be, Kira couldn't say. The doll sprouted two curling horns and shaggy white fur like a goat, although it stood upright. It needed cleaning, and perhaps delousing, but it was perfect. It was at once utterly horrifying and yet somewhat adorable.

Bertie was going to love it. He had a collection of gruesome dolls. This one would fit in perfectly.

Satisfied that her detour hadn't been in vain, Kira picked up the doll and tucked it into her satchel. According to her watch, she still had 40 minutes or so to get back to the Palace. She needed to find another entrance to the tunnels.

Her chances of finding one that led to the East Wing were slim, and given the amount of water in her usual route, probably best avoided. Most of the tunnels she'd explored led to the kitchens in one way or another, and from there she could sneak up the servant's stairs, change, and be in front of her stepmother at the appropriate time. Isadora could save her lectures on tardiness for another day.

Back in the sunshine, Kira found the nearest door quickly. The little burnt impression of a bulbous soup pot confirmed that the tunnel led to the kitchens. Assuming no one was about, that was fine. The door slid open fairly easily, and she slipped into the dark once more.

*Melissa Constantine*

# CHAPTER THREE
## Robert

**Robert would have paid money — if he had any — to know why his** family's visits to Corlea Palace often ended in humiliation. His parents, the Duke and Duchess of Greater Miser, had long ago given up making appearances. Perhaps they realized the futility of trying to win influence or favor from the Crown. They stayed at their castle — with its leaking roof and inconsistent crane flower crop — and avoided the politics of the royal court. His uncle Julius, however, was undeterred.

Undeterred and, in fact, absolutely determined to make the whole family a laughing stock in his quest to sever his title, Duke of Lower Miser, from the main line of the Misery Islands. His title was a courtesy, which meant he couldn't pass it down to his oldest child. That fact must have burned in Uncle Julius's gut like acid. As far back as Robert could remember he'd been on a campaign to split the title and get a writ of royalty he could pass to his oldest son.

There had been some chatter that he'd even tried to corner the Queen Regent last year when the family had come for Robert's investiture of knighthood. And this time Uncle Julius had built extra days into their traveling schedule for the Festival of the Flower to once again make his case.

The morning's robbery, however, seemed to do what nine other rejected petitions had not — it had driven the purpose of their visit, if not completely out of Uncle Julius's head, at least to some region in the back.

His uncle was in a lather. No sooner had they arrived at the Palace than Uncle Julius had sought out Queen Isadora in the royal presence chamber.

Robert and Jordaan hadn't even had time to get settled into the visiting knight's quarters over the stables. Thus, the three of them stood in front of one of the most important women in the Known Kingdoms looking like they'd been run over by a dozen carriages.

"Your Highness, my carriage was robbed! Along your road!" The Duke's face and neck were red with indignation and his second-best wig was sliding back on his head.

The regal woman in the queen's crown nodded but did not offer sympathy. She seemed content to let Uncle Julius dig his own verbal grave.

"Something must be done!" the Duke emphasized his words by gesticulating wildly.

Jordaan leaned close to Robert, his voice low and hoarse, "Do you think he's mad about the gold or the wig?"

Robert rolled his eyes and tried to concentrate on standing silent in front of the Queen Regent.

"I'm guessing it's the wig. That thing was a work of art. So many curls." Jordaan laughed and tried to cover it with an audible cough as Queen Isadora noticed them. She gave them both a significant look before turning back to Uncle Julius.

"Your Grace, I do apologize for any inconvenience you've suffered on the Royal Road," the Queen Regent said in a neutral and even tone. Her face was as serene as her words. She did not seem perturbed nor surprised that they'd been robbed. It was as if she'd reached the point in dealing with the Beast of Barlow that no amount of outrage was going to move her.

"Yes, well, thank you. But let me say that the conditions of the roads were abysmal. The Misery Islands pay our fair share in taxes, the least we can expect is good roads when we visit the mainland. No wonder that… that creature was able to ambush our traveling party."

Robert internally cringed but kept his face blank. Sir Timmons, the Squire Master during his training had often said, *"A master will make a fool of himself. Your job is to serve, so keep your mouth shut."* Jordaan had trained alongside him, but apparently, he didn't remember that lesson, because he was shaking with silent laughter.

"You were advised, Your Grace, to limit travel until the threat of the Beast was under control. A royal proclamation was issued, was it not?"

The redness in his uncle's jowly face took on a new shade akin to a summer plum. "The Islands are quite far," he said. "Must have missed it before we left."

He hadn't. Robert had brought him the proclamation as soon as a scribe had copied it over from the official herald. Uncle Julius had dismissed it with a wave of his hand, his many rings clinking.

"And you saw none of the notices in the port when you brought the carriage off the ship?"

Before the ceremonial carriage had been yanked from the bowels of the Miser yacht the Harbor Chief had come with a fresh copy of the proclamation and an apologetic tone. Men could not be spared to unload the carriage, nor to accompany them to Corlea. If the Duke was willing to wait in port, help would be available when the contract workers arrived in preparation for the Festival of the Flower travelers. Uncle Julius had not been willing to wait. Robert could still feel the pull in his shoulders from heaving the carriage from ship to land.

Undefeated, even in the face of Queen Isadora's sensibility, his uncle continued. "I sent word that I would arrive in the ceremonial carriage! That I had to do so at all is beyond the pale. The roads of this kingdom should be safe!"

Queen Isadora gave one incline of her head acknowledgment, but no more. "On that, we are in agreement."

Robert tried to keep his sense of unease in check, but his uncle wasn't making it easy.

"You see, this is why I need my title to be elevated. I need a place among the high royals so that we can all work together to make this kingdom safe again. I could do that, but I cannot with a courtesy title."

There was an audible, amused murmur in the room at Lord Julius's statement. Robert bit back a groan. Jordaan cleared his throat covering more laughter. He wasn't the only one. The assembled royals and staff dotting the throne room might have hidden them behind paper fans and handkerchiefs, but the sound was unmistakable. This was neither the time nor place to bring up matters of succession.

Uncle Julius was determined. "It's enough to make a man go to the Fairies!"

*What in the Fairie Hells?* Of all the things that weren't supposed to be said in the Palace.

The collective gasp from the audience didn't go unnoticed by the Queen Regent, but it did go unacknowledged. How finely the woman on the throne threaded that needle was something Robert had to admire. Her eyes closed for the barest second, and she turned her head toward where the Palace's big, hulking majordomo, Vendell, stood at the ready. He seemed to interpret the unspoken command and nodded before departing, unhurried.

"Lord Julius, it is my honor to have you as a guest of the Palace, should you wish to stay. I do understand, however, if you feel your business will take you elsewhere."

It was about as efficient a takedown as Robert had ever heard, so sharp Robert was going to have to check his own throat for the cut of an invisible blade.

Jordaan's cough didn't cover his snicker, so Robert elbowed him for good measure. "Shut it," he hissed.

Jordaan clapped a hand over his mouth, his eyes watering.

"But if you would like to stay," Queen Isadora continued, "the palace majordomo has gone to prepare chambers for you."

Uncle Julius colored, seeming to realize what he'd said. If bringing up a matter of succession in the middle of a rant was bad, threatening to get the Fairies involved was worse. Fairies and the Crown didn't mix.

"Yes, well, no point in leaving so soon. We've only arrived, and we're traveling on to Dunlock for the Festival," said the Duke.

The Queen Regent nodded. "As you wish, Your Grace."

Robert was almost sure she wanted to smile but her face remained impassive.

On the outside, Corlea Palace was an elegant building clad in shimmering pink stone. The standard of Corlea, the twined crane flowers on a pale blue background, waved in the breeze from the top of no fewer than two dozen turrets. On the inside, the palace was a series of long corridors filled with portraits of all of the kings and queens of the past in perfect alignment. Unlike the castle on Greater Miser Island where Robert had spent his childhood, there were no hidden corners or oddly shaped rooms or places where the paint abruptly changed color three-quarters of the way along the wall. Everything here was precise. Even the furniture lined up exactly with the black and white floor tiles.

After their hasty meeting with the Queen Regent, Jordaan and Robert made their way to the stables. Visiting knights and other outriders found some of the best accommodation in the Known Kingdoms at Corlea Palace. The stables were as beautiful as the Palace, if not more so. On the ground floor, a hundred stalls with gold nameplates housed the best horseflesh money could buy. Each horse had its own groom, all of them scurrying between tack and hay and horse. The upper floors held a large dorm that had wide, comfortable beds, each partitioned off by curtains that offered enough privacy to get a good night's sleep. Robert was looking forward to collapsing in the first one available.

Jordaan felt the same. "Getting robbed takes a lot out of man," he said with a yawn.

"Are you sure it wasn't trying not to laugh at Lord Julius?"

His fellow knight shrugged. "Hey, it is not my fault! I love my job, but sometimes I swear, the duke is missing a few things. He threatened to go to the Fairies! He might as well have stripped naked and asked the Queen to dance."

"Don't remind me."

Uncle Julius likely wasn't serious about asking the Fairies to intervene in his quest for the title, but the threat of it was badly done.

"You think after this, the Duke's going to be able to pay us? The first day of the Festival is Quarter Day."

Robert could only shrug. Although his Uncle always came up with the funds to pay his knights, losing any gold, even a handful of coins, wasn't ideal. Robert's own pockets were all but empty. He'd been looking forward to Quarter Day to buy some new gloves. His were worn through.

They found the stablemaster, a small man with a great deal of black, curly hair not quite contained by the flat cap pulled down over his ears. Durrin was never seen without that hat, and there was some speculation around the stable that he was hiding a fair bit of Fairie heritage.

"Sir Robby, Sir Jordaan, back so soon?" Durrin asked.

"It's been almost a year," Robert said, setting his belongings down. He wanted a bed and a bath more than he wanted anything in his life but for a knight, part of staying in any castle involved keeping in the stablemaster's good graces. At Corlea, that was Durrin, and Durrin liked conversation. Robert could only hope it would be short. This wasn't the first time, nor the last, that the men from the Misery Islands would impose upon the palace staff. It wasn't naive to assume that until his uncle got his way, trips to Corlea would be done regularly.

The stablemaster shrugged. Time didn't seem to mean much to him. "Heard you hit some trouble on the road."

Jordaan smirked. "Robbed by the Beast himself."

Durrin's nose twitched as he scoffed, "Beast of Barlow, *pashaw*. Some twat in a costume is more like it."

Robert wasn't so sure. When the Beast had appeared at the edge of the woods he'd believed they were face to face with a mythical creature. But the creature had spoken. It knew exactly who they were, or at least who they were robbing. No animal knew unimportant royals.

Jordaan yawned and said, "It was at least as tall as a bear. Mismatched ears. I don't know what it was, but no human looks like that."

"Did they get much from you?"

"The Duke's best wig. A little money. Not much else," Robert admitted.

Durrin laughed. "What would a beasty living in the forest want with a wig?"

Robert shrugged. "It knew who we were. Maybe it was personal?"

"The Duke is still driving about with that obnoxious bell? Every gnat in the forest knows exactly who's coming."

Robert smiled, but he wasn't reassured.

"No, I wouldn't worry about the Beast. Now his threat to go to the Fairies, that I would worry about."

Jordaan scoffed. "Word spreads fast."

Durrin gave them a cheeky smile. "I keep my ears to the ground," he said with a tap on the side of his cap. He laughed at his own joke and then fished in his pocket. "Before I forget, Sir Robby, I got a letter for you. Came a couple of days ago."

He handed over a tightly folded letter addressed to Robert, care of the Corlea Palace stables. Xavier's writing. Xav wasn't much of a correspondent. Letters from his best friend were few and far between. Robert broke the thick wax seal.

"*Rob,*" the short missive read, "*If you've got a day or two to spare, come to Dunlock. I'm in some trouble. Yours, etc., Xavier.*"

"Something wrong, Rob?" Jordaan asked.

Xav didn't usually exaggerate. He also never asked for help unless something was wrong. "I have to go."

"Go? We spent two days on the road and you're going to turn around and leave?"

"A friend needs me. I have to go."

"I swear, Rob," Jordaan said, rubbing a hand through his shaggy hair, "you gotta stop trying to save the whole world. It makes the rest of us look bad."

Robert had no time to explain to them that a knight never turned his back on someone who was in trouble. For one, Jordaan should know that. And two, they were trained to do whatever was needed, whenever it was needed. Robert would never shirk that duty. Especially not when the person in trouble was his best friend. There was no waiting until the morning or until he managed a good night's sleep.

"I have to go see the Duke and let him know I'm leaving."

Durrin's eyes twinkled with amusement. "I heard the Queen put him up in the East Wing. Take the hall past the kitchen, you'll get there quicker."

Robert gave his thanks and hurried to find his uncle. If all went well, he could explain his need to be in Dunlock quickly and be on the road in an hour.

*Melissa Constantine*

## Chapter Four
### Kira

**Kira eased open the door between the tunnel and the lower kitchens, careful** not to let the hinges squeak. This time of day, most of the servants should have been in the upper kitchens, preparing for the midday meal service, but the broad, flat vowels of a pair of scullery maids in conversation filled the cavernous space. One of them was scrubbing pots over a large vat of steaming water, while the other swept idly at the hearth. She wasn't so much gathering the cinders as spreading them around like gossip.

"The Queen herself said my trifle was the best she'd ever had." The smaller of the two women preened like she'd been given an award.

Kira rolled her eyes. As if the *Queen Regent's* praise meant anything. She needed to slip past the chattering duo and get to the East Wing. She guided the door to a soft close, and then ducked behind a large stack of flour sacks, trying to keep her footsteps light.

"She's a beauty, ain't she?" said the second woman.

The first made a hum of agreement.

"I'll be sad when they pass her over for the Princess."

Every nerve in Kira's body tensed. She was the one passed over — not her conniving stepmother — but that didn't seem to matter to the scullery maids.

"She's an odd one."

"Someone ought to remind her that her only job is to find a rich, good-looking man. Instead she's hanging around a shack in the woods like an old hermit. I tell you, if I were a princess all I'd do is live the life of luxury."

"Fat load of a chance you have of that," said the scrubber. "Help me with this, would you, Bess?"

Kira watched as the two hefted what looked to be a stockpot as large as a cauldron from the water, and set it on the table, where toweling had been laid out to. Satisfied that they were done discussing her, Kira stepped into the kitchen in time to hear the first scullery maid say, "I'm sure the Princess isn't right in the head. Look at the parents, eh? Crazy as loons."

Kira cleared her throat. The two maids went wide-eyed and dipped clumsy curtsies, repeatedly bobbing up and down like wind-up toys.

"Beg your pardon, Your Highness," the pot scrubber said, cheeks blazing.

"Forgive us, My Lady," said Bess.

Kira bit back any words she might say because she didn't trust herself to speak. She kept her gaze leveled at them, and the two had the sense to look deeply embarrassed before scurrying off to wherever it was that servants went.

Kira ran from the kitchens to the East Wing, shame boiling in her gut in a way that threatened to scald her from the inside out. Those women had no right to talk about her that way. She was the future queen! That should mean something.

Kira kept her head down through the Palace's long, marble and mirrored hallways. She needed to get back to her apartment to change so she could answer Isadora's summons. But the words those women had said nagged at her.

*"Look at the parents, eh? Crazy as loons."*

That was so unfair. Her father had been sick. That wasn't his fault. And her mother, well, Kira didn't care to speculate. She'd been gone for a long time. It didn't lessen the sting, though. She didn't choose to spend her days listening to the Known Kingdom's royals stand around sucking up to the Queen Regent. That didn't mean she was anything like her parents. Her cottage was her private space.

Kira took the corner to the East Wing at a sharp clip, and knocked full force into a wall. Dizzy, she stepped back to catch her breath, only to realize that what she'd run into wasn't a wall at all.

It was one of the knights she'd robbed on the Royal Route.

The incredibly handsome one. Sir Shiny Hair.

The *incredibly bewildered, staring at her like she was as crazy as the scullery maids had made her out to be, mouth open like a fish,* Sir Robert of Greater Miser.

Recognizing her, the knight dipped into a bow. "Your Highness, I am so sorry."

"No, don't apologize, I'm sorry, I wasn't watching where I was going."

Sir Robert stammered. "No, I…"

How was a man that tall, with a jaw that could probably crush rocks, so flustered? Granted, she's barreled into him and gotten what looked to be a good deal of mud on his bright blue tunic. Kira's face burned.

Sir Robert bowed again, as if once weren't perfectly enough. The massive corridors were somehow tight, and Kira was all too aware of the state of her person.

In addition to taking twice as long as she expected, the tunnels sent her through a thousand puddles and she'd brought back a particularly moldy smell.

"Stop that," she chided Sir Robert. "It's my fault and I am sorry but I'm in a great hurry so if you'd step aside please."

"Of course, Your Highness." Sir Robert moved to his left, but as he did, Kira ducked behind him once again.

Heavy footsteps echoed through the corridor. There was only one member of the staff who walked like that. Vendell. Isadora's henchman. And if he had strayed from her side, he was on the hunt. As she was late for their meeting that could only mean he was looking for her.

If he saw her, she'd be hauled in front of the Queen Regent looking like something that came out of the Palace's drains. Which she had, technically, although no one needed to know that.

"Don't move," she said through clenched teeth.

"My Lady?" Sir Robert, bless his shiny hair, didn't wear confusion all that well.

"Hide me, and stay quiet, please." She grabbed him by the front of his tunic, steering him toward one of the East Wing's hidden closets. Vendell was getting closer and the urge to use Sir Robert's height to her advantage was instinct.

"Of course, but…"

"He can't see me!" she said in a harsh whisper.

A majordomo was supposed to glide through the Palace like he was on ice skates, but apparently no one had told that to Isadora's lapdog. Vendell's stomps echoed like death knells.

Kira gestured with her head behind her. "Open that door."

Confused as ever, Sir Robert reached his long arm out and opened the door to the maintenance closet. Kira stepped back into the confined space, pulling Sir Robert with her. The only light in the closet was a dim Zephyr lamp which sputtered to life with the barest flicker. For a half a moment as her eyes adjusted she was all-too-aware of the position she'd put herself in. Sir Robert took up an incredible amount of space. He was built like one of those stone walls surrounding an old keep — broad and solid.

And he was so close. More than close, actually. She was surrounded by him. His chest with all those muscles was right there in front of her face.

A long, uncomfortable silence filled what little space was left among the cleaning supplies. Kira tried to listen for Vendell but found that all she could hear was the frantic beating of her own heart. She willed it to calm down, straining to hear if Vendell's heavy footsteps had finally passed.

Nothing. No sign of impending doom. Kira exhaled, the dizziness of their earlier collision catching up with her. And she realized, a heartbeat too late, her hands were tangled in Sir Robert's tunic from when she'd grabbed him.

She should have let go but her hands had a mind of their own.

With effort she pried her fingers loose one by one. Pins and needles shot up her arms.

"Thank you," She managed, her tongue thick as though she'd been eating something to which she was allergic. "Vendell is…"

Well, it wasn't worth explaining, was it? This was already awkward enough.

Between the little dribbles of light the Zephyr lamp put out and the pathetic sunlight that dared to leak under the door jam. It was enough to confirm what she feared.

Sir Robert was ridiculously handsome.

His hair was a rich dark brown, even in the dimness. And his face, Fairies take her, was the epitome of male beauty. Strong jaw, long, straight nose, cheekbones for days.

"No thanks needed," he said, in a voice that was somehow one of the deepest things she'd ever heard, and yet smooth, like a river of molten chocolate. "I'm sure you had your reasons."

"I don't make a habit of pulling strange men into closets." The words leaped from her. He'd as much as given her an out, but like her rebellious hands, the words seemed to happen of their own accord.

"I know," he said.

No sarcasm, no snark. A simple phrase.

"I'm late for a meeting with the Queen Regent."

No doubt Vendell was already impatiently standing outside her apartment door, giant foot tapping like a metronome as the seconds ticked on.

Kira knew she was staring at him. She needed to get a grip on herself and leave the closet, but she couldn't seem to look away. He was just so damn pretty. His eyes were blue. A deep-dark shade of blue. How was that even an eye color? Most of the blue-eyed people she knew had watery, grayish eyes.

He moved, just a subtle arc of his arm, but Kira jumped, her heart beating furiously.

"You just have something here," he said. He plucked a leaf from her hair and held it out to her.

Heat flared in her face, and she snatched the leaf away. This was all so silly. She was the heir to the throne!

"Thank you. Sir Robert I realize this is all extremely awkward. I do appreciate your assistance but I would prefer it if you never, ever mentioned it to anyone."

"Of course, Your Highness." He spoke too assuredly, as if being pulled into a small space was something that happened every day.

Perhaps he sensed her skepticism, because he added, "You have my word, I shall say nothing."

"I suppose we should go," she said.

Without comment, he turned to open the door and peered out into the sun-flooded hallway. "The coast is clear."

Kira wasn't sure why her legs felt like noodles, but she followed Sir Robert out of the closet, unconsciously grabbing his arm again for support.

He put his hand under her arm. "Are you alright?"

Kira tried to shake off the feeling of being off-balance. It was likely Sir Robert's fault. As they stepped back into the light, she was stuck again by his beauty. There was no other word for it. He was too much. The broad shoulders, the dark hair, the piercing blue eyes. No one should be allowed to be that handsome.

"I'm fine, Sir." Kira said, but as she spoke, the floor seemed to turn to jelly underneath her. The black and white checked tiles wobbled.

"Let me escort you to wherever you're going. It would be my honor."

Well, of course it would be his honor. She was the future queen. But no, she needed to get away from him as soon as possible before she embarrassed herself anymore.

"No! Let me…"

Kira slid past him, almost sorry when she no longer had his hand to steady her, but determined to escape.

"My lady, if you are unwell please let me help you."

"I'm fine. I'm fine. I'm filthy and I need to get cleaned up and forget I ever made a fool of myself."

Kira cursed whomever had chosen the slick marble floors. Clearly they'd never had to run from a handsome man like a coward.

## Chapter Five
### Kira

**For an appointment with the Queen Regent, Kira knew she should have** put on a more elaborate gown than a simple navy day dress. She should be dressed for court — something satin and probably with a ridiculous cape — but Kira hadn't been able to bear the thought of the restrictive dress chosen by her maid, Pamela. The navy dress was made of much sturdier fabric, woven from the stems of crane flowers, but it still had a pleasantly twirly skirt. As far as armor went, it was better than satin any day. Plus, it had pockets.

When she was queen, all dresses would have pockets.

Vendell, who as expected had been waiting for her outside her door, cleared his throat with a significant, phlegmy rumble. "Princess, the Queen Regent has requested that you join her in the Morning Salon."

"I thought we were meeting in the throne room?"

"It is not my place to question the sovereign," he said in a droll voice before turning, expecting her to follow him.

Kira snorted out her irritation. She wasn't all that late for the audience. There was no way the royals who traveled to the Palace for it were done complaining already. It couldn't be more than…she checked one of the massive grandfather clocks that lined the corridor. Almost noon. Fairies damn her. She had meant to hurry, but after her embarrassing run-in with Sir Robert — and the realization that she had brought half a swamp's worth of muck back to the Palace, she'd taken the time to bathe and at least make herself presentable.

Kira turned and headed for the Morning Salon, which was one of the eight dozen sitting rooms around the Palace. Kira had never figured out why the long Vineland line of Corlea kings had needed so many places to sit. Likewise, why would they call a room that was all but unusable before noon — thanks to giant floor to ceiling windows that faced east — the "Morning Salon."

Vendell held open the door, and stepped aside to let her in. Isadora was not alone. Kira swallowed a bitter mouthful of distaste at Sir Roderick Rift, head of the Kingdom Council, sitting across from the Queen Regent and calmly sipping tea as if he were making a social call.

"The Rule of Two is clear, Your Highness," Sir Roderick said. "No titles may split from the line of succession."

"The law is on our side, but if he does take up on his threat, I'm afraid of what might happen."

Sir Roderick lifted one bony shoulder. He leaned toward her as if settled in for a good gossip.

"We cannot prevent him from going, if he's of a mind to go."

Isadora frowned. "No one is speaking of preventing him, merely… dissuading."

Kira cleared her throat, as neither the Queen Regent nor Sir Roderick seemed inclined to notice her. "My apologies for being late," she said, although she wasn't really sorry.

Sir Roderick went to stand and bow, but Kira waved him off. She'd rather not see the ancient old man try and rise. His knees would likely give out.

"Your Highness," Sir Roderick said, "It has been too long."

Not long enough as far as she was concerned. Sir Roderick had done little to help when her father was ill, and Kira had no desire to spend any more time with him than she was required to by law. He was the longest-serving member of the Kingdom Council and a good argument for term limits.

She inclined her head and turned to Isadora. As she always did, the Queen Regent wore a sleek black dress that played up the red of her lips, smooth dark skin, and the blue-black of her hair. She had foregone the Regent's crown that Sir Roderick and the rest of the Kingdom Council had placed on her head, but other than that she had the wicked stepmother's attire down to a fine point.

"A pleasure you could join us." As always, Isadora spoke in a languid, calm voice that got on Kira's last nerve. How the woman managed to be so critical with so few words was a mystery.

"You're welcome." It was a petulant response and Kira knew she ought to be better than that, but she couldn't help it.

Isadora said nothing but glanced at the delicate watch on her fine-boned wrist. Kira's cheeks flush. "Please sit."

Kira stuffed her hands into her pockets to hide her balled fists. She dropped into a chair opposite Sir Roderick.

A soft knock on the door behind her brought a servant with a fresh pot of tea. While the servant fussed with the plates of refreshments, Sir Roderick filled the tense atmosphere with idle chatter.

"Are you looking forward to the Festival of the Flower, Princess?"

Kira groaned inwardly but tried to keep her face impassive. The Festival would be held in Dunlock, which meant a chance to see Bertie, but the rest of it was likely to be torturous. It was supposed to be her official debut in "good society." She'd be spending the whole two weeks being paraded around and introduced to people she already knew, all while the royals pretended to harvest flowers.

"Not particularly," she answered, reaching for a cookie on the tea tray.

Isadora shot her a look, but otherwise refrained from comment as there were the servants in the salon.

"In my day the Festival of the Flower was something young people looked forward to all year."

Kira couldn't stop the snort that escaped her. "And when was that, exactly, Sir Roderick?"

"Do not answer that," Isadora said sharply. "We have much to discuss."

*Oh, what could be so urgent?* Kira stuffed the last of the cookie in her mouth to keep from saying anything else she might regret.

"Yes, Princess, you'll have heard about this business with the Duke?" Sir Roderick said, not quite able to shake off his perturbed expression.

Kira hurried to swallow, wiping crumbs from her mouth. "About the robbery?"

"Unfortunately, yes," Isadora said, serene as always. Kira wanted to scream and run about the room to break the woman's composure. It was maddening how she managed to be so unruffled. Kira wasn't sure she had a day in her entire history where she felt one-tenth of that kind of calm.

"But," she continued, "In addition to having been yet another victim of the Beast, the Duke of Lower Miser has brought a matter before the court. While the law is very clear to disfavor the petition, it is important you are aware of the matters that your people bring forward."

"That's it? People petition every day."

Isadora took a visible breath and let it out slowly as if she were about to explain something to an unruly child. "This is not a mere land dispute or squabble over water rights. The matter before the crown concerns succession. It is a good learning opportunity for you to be versed in the law."

"I have known the laws of the Known Kingdoms since before I could walk. Should I recite them?"

Sir Roderick looked uncomfortable at her insolence, but Kira didn't care. She leveled her gaze at Isadora. Sadly, her stepmother was immune to her stare down and continued on.

"The duke has made an allusion to seeking out the Fairies to attain his writ of royalty."

*Oh. Well. That was...* Kira had no comment. Fairies weren't allowed in Corlea Palace.

"I suspect you haven't had much dealings with either of the Fairie Courts."

"No, but Fairies can't change our laws."

Isadora shook her head. "What Fairies can or can't accomplish is not for us to speculate. What we must do is dissuade Lord Julius from seeking them out in the first place."

"Remind him that…"

"There is no law that prevents our subjects from going to either of the Fairie Courts for favors. Only cautionary tales, I'm afraid."

Kira knew the stories. Girls who wandered into the woods, got lost, and made a deal with a Fairie for a map. Only instead of heading home, they ended up following the map for a decade, because Fairies had no sense of time. Which, she supposed, wouldn't be a big deal if you could live for hundreds and hundreds of years. Books were full of stories about Fairie deals gone sideways.

"But my parents banned them," she said. "Practically right after I was born."

Sir Roderick laughed. "Twenty years is nothing to a Fairie. They're likely just getting around to reading the late king's decree. Why I would bet…"

Isadora held up a hand to stop whatever flippant thing Sir Roderick was about to say next. "King Callum's ban was hasty and ill-advised. Fairies lived in the Known Kingdoms long before humans. We could no more ban them or their worship than we could stop the sun from rising."

If Isadora needed a reminder, Kira could show her a burned chapel not a mile from the Palace. "So what's the point of talking about it if there's nothing we can do. If Lord Julius is going to the Fairies, let him. He'll probably end up with goat hooves or hair in his ears."

Isadora actually looked perturbed, although only for a moment. Petty as it was, Kira felt marginally better for scoring that win.

"The Crown is responsible for its people. We must guide him, gently, away from potential danger."

"I have no interest in lecturing my people," Kira said. "When I am Queen that is not how things will operate."

Sir Roderick had a distinct smirk on his face that irritated her. The Kingdom Council had chosen to install Isadora after her father's death on the grounds that Kira "needed time to learn," and "wasn't yet of age." Which was ludicrous because her twenty-first birthday was only a handful of months away.

"Be that as it may, when it comes to matters of succession, the families can be touchy. You will need to be able to clearly and succinctly understand the nuances to keep the peace. Whether or not Lord Julius, or any other noble house visits a Fairie Court is another matter. What you must do as the Sovereign is show your subjects the benefits of taking the right course of action."

"So lecture them?"

Sir Roderick didn't do a good job of covering his scoff. Miserable old fool. When she was queen, no one over the age of 30 would sit on the Kingdom Council. Old men gave themselves too much credit.

This time, Isadora's calm didn't falter, as if she'd caught on to Kira's petulance far too quickly. "You have a responsibility to the realm to rule fairly. That may sometimes mean telling your subjects things they don't want to hear."

Kira rolled her eyes.

Isadora continued on. "I've asked Sir Roderick to go over a few crucial points of law with you. I'd like you to be well-versed in the applicable laws before we meet with Lord Julius again."

Unable to keep silent, Sir Roderick added, "I'm sure you will find it all fascinating, Princess. I have always encouraged my sons to study the law extensively so that one day they may serve the kingdoms. They do so enjoy it. And it is my honor to share it with you."

"How... wonderful," Kira said, before turning to Isadora. "Is it really necessary?"

"Yes. It is part of the education you must have to take the throne one day."

"I will take the throne regardless. I am the Vineland heir."

Isadora merely rose, signaling to Vendell that she would leave the room. "Sir Roderick, if you would please begin. I'll see you at dinner."

Sir Roderick smiled at Kira like he'd won something. "I'm sure you'll find this enlightening."

Kira gritted her teeth. She would do what was required of her. But she had a strong suspicion that sometime soon Sir Roderick was going to have an appointment with the Beast of Barlow.

## CHAPTER SIX
### Diana

**Outside the carriage window the North Sea churned itself into bubbling** white foam and inky waves. Beyond the beach the fog had gathered like a thick blanket around the castle on Greater Miser Island, obscuring the towers. Diana suppressed a fissure of disappointment.

*It didn't matter.*

She didn't need to see his home because in a few days they would arrive in Dunlock and she would see him. She and Robby would be in the same room for the first time in three years and then she'd be sure. Her heart took a happy little skip.

They weren't kids any more. He was a knight. She was a lady. *It was perfectly reasonable.*

Diana took a deep breath and regretted it almost immediately. The close confines of the carriage — and the small, musty pug on her mother's lap — didn't provide the most bracing air.

"I've written the majordomo to ensure we get one of the nicer suites. I adore Margo, but she's too busy thanks to all those children. She'll have handed off the duty of assigning rooms." Her mother stroked the little dog's head so hard its eyes bulged. If it minded, not a peep came out. A vast improvement over her mother's other pugs.

"How many children are there now?" Diana asked.

Mother didn't remember. She thought the Moorelows might have nine, but she'd lost count in the last few years. There might have been more. "Too many. I much prefer a reasonable number of children."

Diana knew her mother had wanted a dozen children, but much like the bulbous little dog, she never complained. Diana sometimes thought it would have been nice to have a sibling, but that was neither here nor there. "I'm looking forward to the Festival. It's nice that the Moorelows are hosting. I feel like we haven't seen them in decades."

"I wish we could have convinced your father to come along."

"Father is happier at home."

The Countess of Wills didn't complain, but she could sigh like a champion. "It would be nice to have him here. You could very well be engaged by the end of the Festival."

"Mother, it's two weeks!"

"You're of age, Diana. This is the year."

Her heart beat a little harder. If at the end of two weeks she found herself engaged to him, well, that was….

She'd known him all her life. It wouldn't be as if they were strangers who would be introduced on the dance floor. And so perhaps two weeks was enough time to realize what they might be to each other.

"Wills needs a good marriage alliance to continue to thrive."

Of course. The needs of the land she would inherit trumped all. And third son, unlanded knights did not provide good trade opportunities. Still, if she were in love, her parents would never object.

So the plan was to see him and find out if she loved him or if she'd built him up in her mind since they'd last been together.

*A perfect plan.*

The carriage lurched as it hit a particularly nasty patch of the road. The dog tumbled off the Countess's lap, but didn't so much as yelp. Diana swooped him into her arms to keep him from harm. He panted loudly and attempted to lick her. She reared back. Dog slobber was one of the more repulsive substances in the Known Kingdoms, she was sure.

"Oh, give him here." Her mother snatched up the dog.

"He smells like Great Aunt Donna's mothball-ridden closets."

The Countess covered the pug's ears. "Diana, Fritz is sensitive."

Diana rolled her eyes. Her mother's love of small, ugly dogs was only second to her love for her only child.

"How I raised a child who doesn't like dogs, I will never understand."

"I had to have some flaws." She smiled, and the Countess scoffed.

Diana opened the window, hoping for some much needed-fresh air. Unfortunately, they were riding along the Coast Road. The air smelled of salt and dead fish.

She shifted in her seat, unable to get comfortable. Either the cushions in their carriage needed replacing again, or Diana needed to find better traveling clothes. Her skin felt too dry, despite the early spring humidity.

"How much longer until we're there?" Diana asked, feeling petulant.

Mother wasn't sure. Word had been sent ahead to arrange accommodation for at least two nights, but if the roads were heavily trafficked, they might extend it to three.

"I'm not sure I can sit that long."

Mother's eyebrow raised. "You're not usually a restless traveler."

Diana had no explanation, but it was as if the carriage were far too small. Potentially marrying Robby was a big idea, she supposed. He was one of her oldest friends, and that was the kind of change that required room to think. Shutting it out of her mind was probably for the best.

Another excellent plan.

She would not think about him. At all. Not even a little bit.

At her mother's suggestion to pass the time, Diana took out the book she'd brought for the drive. *Dramatics of the Dark Court, Volume 12*. She'd been looking forward to getting her copy for months. The first 11 books in the series were a delicious history full of magic, intrigue, and backstabbing. But for some reason, nothing in this one was keeping her mind occupied. In the early volumes, Fairie disputes ended in the building of great cities or the creation of magnificent art. But the stories had moved toward the modern age, the results of their infighting were less productive. In fact, most of the stories were decidedly petty. The first two chapters were all about the feud between Barbra the Belter, noted Fairie entertainer, and someone named Ant the Argument, who was known to show up at concerts and heckle her. Although she'd read the same words a dozen times at no point did the story have a satisfying resolution.

"Diana, stop frowning. You'll get forehead lines."

*Heaven forbid.*

She tossed the book aside. "I don't know what's the matter with me. I can't seem to concentrate on anything."

The Countess opened her mouth as if she were going to say something, but thought the better of it. She settled back against the carriage seat, scratching absently at Fritz's head. "If there's something on your mind, you can tell me, Darling."

Diana waved away the idea. It wasn't worth mentioning. Not until they were in Dunlock.

"No?"

Diana shook her head. She wasn't going to think about it. Not about the way her hand felt in his as he'd helped her up. Or how he was always so nice to everyone, or how he smiled with a little twinkle in his eyes.

*Nope. No. She wouldn't do it.*

An hour or so passed before they turned off the Coast Road via the bridge that connected the Upper Territories. Although Mother claimed not to believe in Fairie curses, she made a little crooked finger symbol as they passed over the waterway.

"Seriously?"

"It never hurts to be cautious, Diana Michelle."

Diana rolled her eyes, and took another stab at her book. She flipped through the pages, looking for anything that might hold her attention. Unlike previous volumes, this book did contain pictures. Small woodcut drawings, but similar in style to the Fairie portraits that decorated the chapel near Wills Castle.

As a whole, the Fairies were...scary looking.

She supposed that a human, recently arrived on a new continent, might have seen these tall, pointy-looking beings for the first time and been awed. Add in the fact that they could do magic, and no wonder they'd been worshiped. But clearly, those early settlers to the Known Kingdoms hadn't been bored to tears over the story of "Greta Greenhands and the Unrepentant Toasting Fork."

They joined the far reaches of the Royal Route that they would take most of the way to Dunlock. With it came the expected crush of carriages flying a variety of brightly colored standards of the royal houses. Diana recognized many of the banners, although none of them were the sea green standard from Greater Miser. "Are Lord and Lady Lycette going to attend?"

"No, I thought I mentioned. The family is staying on the island to begin the harvest."

"So I'm to be married off, but not any of the Lycette boys?"

Her mother stilled, and then said carefully. "The Misery Islands have been on shaky ground with their crops for some time. I think Lady Lycette wants to wait until their prospects are better."

Robby didn't need to be rich. She had plenty of money. Plus, if they married, someday he'd be the Earl of Wills. That ought to be incentive enough, beyond their history together. Although part of her acknowledged that it wasn't going to entice him. Robby Lycette wasn't the kind to marry for money or title. From what she'd learned from his family, he'd taken to knighthood like a duck to water. He wasn't one to sit around and bemoan the fact that as a third child he wasn't considered royal. He was making a life for himself. Which was admirable and frankly, extremely attractive.

"With Queen Isadora and Princess Kira in attendance, every royal family will send someone. You'll have the chance to meet so many potential partners."

Diana didn't want many potential partners. She wanted one. She wanted the heady rush she'd felt when they'd last seen each other, when she'd looked at him and realized that he was kind and intelligent and so bloody beautiful she'd almost stopped breathing.

She wasn't sure how it had happened. When they were young he'd just been Robby. His ears had stuck out too far and his hair was usually matted because he refused to let his mother brush it. He always had jam on his shirt.

No self-respecting future countess was going to fall in love with that.

She herself wasn't entirely sure of the exact moment, but, sometime during their last visit — between the night of the ball and the final evening — she'd looked at him, the boy she'd known her entire life, and it was like seeing a brand-new person. He was so much more than she'd expect. More mature. More self-assured. There was no way he'd once eaten a worm on a dare or glued one of her braids to her pillow while she was sleeping.

Diana had left that trip to the islands half in love. She needed to see him again to be sure.

"Diana, are you listening?"

"Sorry, wool-gathering."

Her mother kissed Fritz's head, as if she needed a moment before speaking. "My Darling, I know you may be anticipating seeing a certain someone."

Diana cursed her pale complexion, knowing that she couldn't hide the embarrassed flush that filled her cheeks. "It's natural to want to see an old friend."

"You know I adore him, Diana. He's a wonderful young man. And if he is your choice and you are his, I would welcome him to the family. But I urge you not to put all your hopes in that direction. You're the sole heir to the County of Wills. You have a responsibility to make the best match, not only for yourself but for our lands."

Diana tensed. She knew that. She'd always known that. Having no siblings and no first cousins meant that her duty was to marry and rebuild the royal family of Wills. She didn't need the reminder. "I know."

"I know you do. So please, promise me you'll keep an open mind about the potential suitors you'll meet. You never know what kind of person will make you happy. If anyone had told me when I was your age that I'd marry an Earl and go live on the edge of the North Sea, I would have rolled my eyes and told them to seek help. And yet, I can't imagine my life without your father."

"But it might be that I've already met my person." Diana knew the argument was weak, but it was the only thing she could think to say.

The Countess sighed. "Yes, that is possible. All I ask is that you don't go into the Festival with tunnel vision."

Diana let out a breath. "I will do my best."

Her mother reached over and took her hand, squeezing her fingers. "Thank you. You are the best of daughters. Even if you don't like dogs."

Diana gave Fritz a scratch behind the ear. "Oh, it's not just dogs. It's all pets really."

# Chapter Seven
## Robert

**Dunlock Castle was an imposing collection of towers that rose out of the** trees. The large courtyard in front of the castle was guarded by an ornate iron gate at least twelve feet tall. The surrounding walls were patrolled by a dozen knights, both on the ramparts and on the ground. In a few days, the inner yard would be filled with the carriages of those arriving for the Festival of the Flower, but for now it was a working area, a busy hub of servants, gardeners, and others doing the work that kept Dunlock running.

Robert handed Amzi off to one of the stable hands, and made a small effort to brush the travel dust off of his tunic before entering the main house. He gave his name to one of the footmen, who hurried off to find Prince Xavier. Nothing seemed to be amiss at the castle, there was no eerie feeling, no ominous sense of something wrong. Whatever Xav had called him here for had to be personal or secret.

"You could have waited until morning," Xav said, coming down the central stairs.

"You said you were in trouble."

Xav had deep shadows under his eyes, as if whatever burden he carried had already taken its toll. "Thanks for coming, Rob."

"What's the trouble? Is anyone hurt or…?"

"No, no, it's nothing like that. Come on, if I don't bring you to my mother she's going to kill me and make it look like an accident."

He followed Xav to the Moorelow family's personal sitting room, a large, cozy room dominated by a fireplace, and a collection of mismatched and worn but comfortable chairs. The eleven other Moorelows were gathered in little groups, the younger kids playing an elaborate board game, except for Baby Jenny, who was being held by her father.

When Princess Margo saw him, she gasped and came over to envelope him in a hug. "Robby! Oh my you've grown so tall! Brandon, will you look at who has grown up? He's a butterfly."

She fussed over him, wiping dust from his face and straightening his tunic. He'd known her all his life, and thus she treated him as she would any of her children returning from their travels.

"Xavvy didn't tell us you were coming so early. The festival doesn't start for a few days."

Robert looked toward Xav, who simply shrugged. "Lord Julius has him up at the Palace. Figured it couldn't hurt to have him around."

Prince Brandon passed the baby off to one of his older daughters and came around to shake Robert's hand. "We're glad you're here, Robby. We've missed you."

"Thank you, Sir."

Prince Brandon turned to his son, "Lord Albert hasn't made an appearance today. Make sure he's here for tea."

"Bertie, is um..." Xav stuck his hands in his pocket, as if he were searching for the answer his tongue couldn't give. "I think he's still at the orphanage."

"Well he's family now, he needs to join us," Princess Margo said. She crooked her finger at Robert, until he bent down so she could kiss his cheek. "And that goes for you too, Young Man. I will expect you at family tea while you're here. Every day at four."

"Yes, Ma'am," Robert said.

Xav sighed. "Mother, stop badgering my friend."

"How is it badgering? Brandon, can you believe your son would say that?"

Prince Brandon, a tall, lean man, only shrugged, and kissed his wife on her poof of thick, black hair.

"Come on, Rob, let's take a walk," Xav said, heading out before either of his parents or siblings could object. Robert bowed to his hosts and hurried after Xavier.

Although Xav had seemed like he was carrying a great weight, he was surprisingly fast in his escape. By the time he caught up, Xav was halfway to his own apartments.

"Are you going to tell me what's going on or force me to guess?"

Xav took the steps two at a time. "I'll tell you when we get to my room."

"Are you sure no one is dying?"

"Not that I know of?"

Xav's apartments were a series of interconnected rooms on the castle's fourth floor. Everything was the same as the last time Robert had seen the place more than two years prior — a profusion of blue bedding, green wallpaper, and over-stuff brown leather chairs. It was comforting to be in a familiar place after so long, especially after the emotional toll of the last day. Robert could feel the exhaustion brought on by the travel and the robbery — not to mention his deeply unsettling collision with Princess Kira — like a stone that had settled on his chest. He followed Xavier's example and slunk into one of the soft leather chairs by the fire.

Xavier groaned as he discovered the decanter he hid in the end table was empty. "Sorry, mate, one of my brothers must have been snooping again."

Robert shook his head, and had to confess that a drink would likely put him to sleep.

"Really, it's for me. Things have been weird."

"I'll do what I can to help you. Whatever it is."

"I'm grateful, really. It's hard to explain." Xav rubbed his face with his hands, as if he needed to wake himself up. "About a week ago, something started happening at the orphanage."

"What kind of something?"

Xav blew out a breath. "You know all that nonsense about the Beast of Barlow being back in the forest?"

"It's not nonsense. My uncle's carriage was robbed by the Beast this morning."

Xavier's dark complexion turned ashen. "Are you all right?"

"I'm fine. It was over before anyone was hurt. Xav, you're getting off topic."

Xav shook his head, his expression turned toward the fireplace, where the flames danced over the freshly-laid logs. It was probably too warm an evening for a fire, but with the weather so unpredictable in the spring, sometimes it was better to have a fire laid in case the wind blew from the North Sea.

Robert was wondering if he should fetch some whisky from the castle stores to loosen his friend's tongue when Xav finally began to speak. Although that didn't make the sense of foreboding any clearer.

"You know, Bertie and I, we've been trying to reform the orphanage. Give the kids the best education and I don't know, whatever it is kids need. And it's been hard. Because apparently people think we're too young to do the work. But like no one else was doing it? Bertie was really upset when he found out. And he's so cute when he gets something he cares about."

Robert cleared his throat. He was glad Xav had found someone to love, but he suspected that wasn't the point here.

Color momentarily filled Xav's cheeks and he sat up a bit straighter. "Anyway, it's going… not badly but close to it. And then last week something happened."

There was another significant pause. Frustrated, Robert prompted his friend, "So there's something wrong at the orphanage?"

"Not so much the orphanage, but with the children."

"Are they ill?"

Xav shook his head. "No. Not ill."

"So what is it?"

Xav put his head in his hands. "Fairies take me. There's so much."

Xavier was one of his oldest friends, but Robert's patience grew short. He tamped down his irritation, trying to focus. "What is going on?"

"They... poof... and then they run. And there is so much running. We've had to catch them."

"The children ran away?"

"Some of them. They came back, mostly."

"So you can't keep the children in the orphanage. And you're worried about them encountering the Beast?"

A yes would have been an answer that made sense. If the children had been running into the forest where a potentially dangerous creature was on the loose, then Xav would have the right to be worried. But that was not what Xavier said. After muttering, "I need a drink," he said, "Look, I can't really explain it. But I think... I think the children might be the Beast of Barlow."

\*\*\*\*

Robert picked up the curry comb, rubbing large circles into Amzi's white coat. The Dunlock stable hands had brushed and put away his stallion into one of the numerous stalls available for castle visitors, but Robert found that the ritual of caring for his horse was a good way to sort out his thoughts. He wouldn't have been able to sleep anyway, not after spending the evening watching Xav pace and stress.

It felt like they'd gone back and forth for hours, as Robert tried to get all the details of what was happening. But the more they'd spoken the less he understood. Xav talked in circles about puffs of smoke and how he and Bertie were never, ever, going to take up running as exercise.

"It's exhausting. They run so fast."

Robert used the comb, looking for non-existent dirt. Amzi gave a great shake, enjoying the grooming. Robert patted his neck before changing out the comb for a brush.

"It doesn't make any sense," he whispered.

Amzi turned his head briefly, as if agreeing.

"I tried to tell him. I told him! The Beast has been around for weeks. And what we saw in the woods was definitely not a child."

Robert kept his voice low. He wasn't a particularly prideful person, but he drew a line at the servants of Dunlock gossiping that he talked to his horse.

Although Amzi might have been one of the better conversationalists that Robert knew. He listened.

Xavier hadn't heard him, no matter how many times Robert tried to tell him Durrin's theory about the Beast being a man in costume, or any of the logical, reasonable explanations that he could dredge up.

"I don't know what to do to help him. It feels so much bigger than anything I can do."

Amzi neighed softly.

"You're right. I have to try. I wish I knew how."

He traded the brush for a hoof pick, and urged Amzi's back right leg off the ground. The stable hands had done a fine job, clearing out any of the debris and small stones that the horse might have picked up from the Royal Route. There was nothing left to pick out but a few strands of straw from the stall floor. If only helping Xav would be that easy.

Maybe Jordaan was right. Maybe he did want to save everyone, and maybe that was a bit much. But Xav was almost a brother. Robert would do whatever he could to help. It wasn't a question.

Robert put away the tack, giving Amzi an extra helping of oats, and securing the door to his stall. He needed to find a bed, and let the supremely odd day end. He had an ache in his back that made him feel much older than twenty-three.

Princess Margo had set him up in a suite in the family's quarters, and Robert made his way out of the stables for the walk back to Dunlock proper. The cool air that the castle fires had been lit against early in the day had come in with a vengeance. Zephyr lamps around the courtyard flickered with the force of the icy wind.

It was the kind of weather that made him miss home. In the Misery Islands, where Spring always came later, it wasn't unusual for cold nights this time of year. Robert was almost sure he could smell the brine of the far-off sea, although it was impossible. Dunlock was land-locked, and the nearest port where the seagulls swooped above the waves was on the other side of Corlea.

An unusually strong gust rattled the trees, causing the Dunlock banners on the ramparts to snap so loudly Robert startled. A second, stronger gust blew open the tall, iron gates with a wrenching creek.

Because of the late hour, there were no servants about, but the carriage that lumbered through didn't seem to need the assist. In fact, it wasn't even pulled by a team of horses. The carriage — painted a brilliant shade of blue trimmed with diamond-shaped panels in a dozen other colors — waddled like a chubby baby into the inner yard.

It stopped two feet from Robert and its door opened with a pop, a cork released from a bottle. A set of steps tumbled out, and a small figure dressed in billowy blue trousers and a short, red cloak descended.

The woman pulled back her hood to reveal long, shiny purple hair. The Zephyr lamps around the courtyard as one changed their flames to a faint lavender, as if they knew exactly whose way they were to light.

Robert wasn't sure he trusted his eyes, but he was fairly certain the most notorious witch in the Known Kingdoms — Fairies be, the entire world — had arrived in Dunlock.

"You're Caris Mourne." The words had tumbled out before he could stop them.

The woman turned to him, an indulgent smile on her thin lips. "Yes, the last I checked."

Robert remembered his manners enough to bow hastily. As children, Robert, Xavier, and their friend Diana had once been obsessed with Caris Mourne. She was an extremely powerful person. Most witches could brew a potion to cure the sniffles, perhaps use a transformation spell to repair a castle's leaky drainpipe. Caris Mourne's powers put those little miracles to shame. Some said she had Fairie blood, or hinted that she'd stolen her magic from the Fairies. No matter what was said, it was always said in a hushed whisper. No one wanted to risk getting on the bad side of someone so magical.

"You don't happen to be Prince Brandon?" she asked.

"No. I'm Sir Robert of Greater Miser." He bowed so low his forehead was in danger of touching the courtyard stone.

The witch waved away his words. "It's late and I find I don't really care." She took off with a surprisingly long stride for such a tiny person. He doubted she was more than an inch or two taller than Princess Kira, in fact.

In no time, she'd reached the door, and disappeared inside. She never so much as touched the knocker — the door simply opened for her. When she was gone from the courtyard, the Zephyr lamps returned to their normally warm, yellow flames.

Perhaps he should have bedded down in Amzi's stall instead of making his way back to the castle. Yes, he'd wake up smelling like the stable, but that could be taken off with strong soap. This night was never, ever going to wash off.

# CHAPTER EIGHT
## Kira

***Kira liked the woods.*** It surprised her how much she did. She was more comfortable in her own skin here, even when she was covered by her magical disguise.

Unlike the hushed silences of the Palace, the woods were alive. There was movement — the wind through the pine boughs, the birds soaring overhead, and things that scampered over the dried leaves. Everything here made itself known. Nothing was sad. Nothing was formal to the point of being ridiculous. She never felt small here, despite the height of the tree canopy.

If she could figure out how to take that feeling with her without having to grow trees in the Palace ballroom, that would be something.

She moved with an eye for what she needed. The taller trees worked best. Preferably tall enough and full enough to provide the cover she needed and with some accommodating low branches for scaling. At the first sturdy branch, she stopped to look out for a better hiding place.

Nothing suitable. She should have gone down the road a little more. She jumped from the branch but misjudged the distance. Rather than landing neatly on her feet, she fell hard, hitting the ground. Pain shot up from her feet to the top of her head and knocked the air from her chest.

"Son of a Fairie." Kira spat out several of the foulest curses she knew, trying to take in great gulps of air.

She didn't have time to get farther away. Sir Roderick was due to leave the Palace at five o'clock. That gave her an hour. She was tempted to use the same spot that she'd used to rob the Duke of Lower Miser, but that was a good way to get caught. She lay on the forest floor for several minutes, trying to calm her heartbeat and stop her lungs from spasming for air. She almost missed the hoofbeats because the blood was pounding so loud in her ears.

Kira cursed again. It couldn't be. The quick and steady sound grew louder, drumming their rhythm on the packed earth of the Royal Route.

She picked herself up but struggled to get to her feet. Her cloak was unnaturally heavy as if it were weighed down with rocks in the pockets. For the first time it was an unwelcome weight on her shoulders. It smelled like death and it itched something fierce. By the time she pushed herself up, she barely had time to dash behind the evergreen's giant trunk before Sir Roderick's whole company — two carriages accompanied by six outriders — thundered past. The pink and blue lacquered carriage was traveling at a fast clip as if Sir Roderick was in a great hurry. Why had he left early? The Kingdom Council wasn't supposed to meet until three, and none of those old codgers were short on words.

A prickle of unease ran up her back. She needed to get back to the Palace. Something was off. No one gave up the pleasures of Corlea Palace early. If it weren't for Vendell and his extremely effective methods of getting royal families back in their carriages, the whole complex would be overrun. So why would Sir Roderick leave before he needed to be gone?

Kira picked up her walk to a sprint until she reached the tunnel entrances. She pulled back the fallen timbers covering the door and yanked at the handle.

It wouldn't budge.

She had come out this way not half an hour ago. There was no lock on the door, nothing that should have stopped the door from pulling smoothly from the jamb. She tried again, but the door would not open.

Voices, indistinct, but loud enough to announce that she was no longer alone in the wood carried through the trees. Who the hell was out in the forest when a mythical beast was running around? Didn't anyone in this kingdom have a sense of self-preservation?

She would have to run.

"Sir Roderick looked pleased as punch to be asked to stay another day," said a man's voice. Kira recognized it as Durrin, the Palace stablemaster. What was he doing this far from the stables? As far she knew, Durrin had spent his life walking between the stables, the barns, and the kitchens.

Kira threw the branches back over the tunnel door and scrambled for cover. Reluctant as she was to climb another tree, it was safer to be hidden up above rather than to try to hide at ground level. She grabbed for the lowest branch of a pine tree and hoisted herself up, all of her muscles crying out. The cloak was of no help. It was nothing but an added weight. As strong as she was, pulling herself up was no easy feat.

The two voices drew closer, accompanied by the slow clop of horse hooves. Unlike Sir Roderick's carriage, they were clearly in no hurry.

"A suite to himself in the same wing at the Queen Regent? Of course he's going to stay. Hell, it might all be worth being one of those old farts on the council to get that kind of perk."

"I've been around royals all my life," Durrin said. "Never seen a queen do that."

"She isn't the real queen. Just a regent."

*Damn right.*

"King married her before he died. Put the crown on her. Makes her a queen."

Kira clung to the central trunk of the tree she'd climbed, watching the two men pass. Durrin rode Gollum, the biggest horse in the Corlea stables. Kira recognized the young, blond man who accompanied him as one of the knights who'd come with the Duke of Lower Miser. The one who was not Sir Robert. He was almost as good-looking, but not quite. His chief feature seemed to be a pronounced slouch, as if despite having attained knighthood, he couldn't be bothered with much else.

As they passed, both horses pulled and whinnied.

Durrin leaned his whole body forward, patting Gollum's neck. "Easy boy, nothing to scare you out there."

Gollum and the knight's horse did not agree. The knight's horse danced sideways, threatening to buck. Durrin reached out and took the reins, guiding both horses back to the path.

"You've got to learn to ride, Sir Jordaan," Durrin said. "It's damn embarrassing."

"Oh, shut up you half-Fairie bastard," said Sir Jordaan, laughing and grabbing back his reins. "I ride fine."

Durrin's merry laugh floated up to Kira, clinging to the tree.

"Is Lord Julius thinking of getting on the road soon?" Durrin asked. Kira was almost sure he'd deliberately slowed his horse so that she could hear them more clearly.

"Not unless the road to Dunlock is paved with writs of royalty."

Kira bit her lip to keep from laughing, despite her anxiety.

Durrin scoffed. "Smart folks will be getting on the road. Beat the traffic to the Festival."

"Excludes my employer then," Sir Jordaan said, spurring his horse forward.

The two men moved out of sight and Kira was able to exhale.

Sir Roderick was still at the Palace. The carriage tearing by at full speed had been a ruse. Now that was something. She couldn't help but be a little thrilled that Sir Roderick had gone to so much trouble to avoid being robbed by the Beast of Barlow.

Climbing down, rather than risk jumping, Kira made her way back to the tunnel entrance. The door was still jammed.

"Open up!" she commanded, but the door remained stubbornly closed.

"I AM THE BEAST OF BARLOW!" she yelled, and then ducked down in case the riders circled back.

No one came. In fact, nothing but birdsong answered, which was rather infuriating. Something should have been scared and gone running at her outburst. A bunny or a groundhog at least.

She wasn't going to be able to take the tunnels, not today. She'd have to head back to her cottage on foot to put her cloak away before going back to the Palace.

Kira listened, but no other carriages or riders seemed to be coming. She kept to the tree line as much as she could. Her cloak dragged on the ground, slowing her down. It rustled the leaves and pine needles. The sun seemed to disappear, as if a spring storm was coming. It was hard to tell though, because as she picked carefully along the wild undergrowth, the trees were dense, blocking out any light from above.

A prickle of fear walked up her spine, but Kira did her best to ignore it. She'd take off her cloak, stash it in her bag, and forget this little outing ever happened.

Except that when she tried pulling the cloak over her head it wouldn't budge. Her muscles strained, and her arms shook as she tried to lift it from her body. Fighting with it, she lost her balance, and the weight pulled her down to the forest floor. She wrestled, trying to pull the furry garment from her body. It was like a lead blanket, pinning her to the ground.

Kira's heartbeat thumped hard in her chest. She cried out in frustration and finally, finally when it seemed impossible the cloak gave way. Kira lay beside it trying to catch her breath. Empty, the cloak inched toward the base of a pine tree, until it was a good five feet away.

Kira took another moment to steal her courage. She got to her feet and approached the cloak slowly. It rumbled with a deep vibration.

Even filthy it was beautiful. Its fur was soft as a newborn chick's down. The many colors of it swirled into patterns that almost looked like flowers. Crane flowers, if her eyes weren't playing tricks on her.

"Easy," she whispered, as she gathered up the heavy garment, "Be easy."

Whether she was talking to herself or the cloak, Kira couldn't say.

****

Sir Roderick was at dinner, sitting at Isadora's right hand in a seat normally reserved for visiting high royals. There were some three dozen families in attendance at dinner, but because of the way the head table had been set parallel to the rest, there was no escaping the old man.

"Well, Princess, I can say I'm pleased to see you again," Sir Roderick said. "I was hoping we could continue our conversation about the history of laws." He smiled wide as a footman snapped open a napkin and set it on his lap. He was practically drooling over the food already, and the butler hadn't even instructed the staff to lift the covers off the first dish.

"I'm surprised you're still here, Sir Roderick," she said. "I saw your carriage leave."

Sir Roderick chuckled. "It did. That was our Queen who came up with that. Throw the Beast off."

From the head of the table, Isadora signaled to the butler. The roast duck was presented to her with a flourish. For all her parents' formality at dinner, they'd never employed such theatrics. Perhaps at Isadora's home in Zinnj they made dinner into a theater, but that wasn't the case in Corlea. Or shouldn't be. Kira wouldn't be surprised if Isadora called trumpeters in to present the eggs at breakfast.

"Why, may I ask?" Kira said to her. "If the Beast were to stop the Councilor's carriage, surely the deception would be noticed."

Isadora crossed her knife and fork over her plate. "Really, Kira, we should not discuss such things at the table."

"I find it fascinating. The threat of the Beast seems to have taken on a new dimension. I believe that is something I should know about the Kingdom," Kira said. She smiled into her cup as she took a sip of her wine and then had to school her features not to wince. The substance in her goblet was heavily watered down. Rather than any of the excellent vintages that Corlea Palace had in its cellars, the stuff tasted and smelled of brackish well-water. She raised her glass and a footman trotted over, offering to refill it. "Take it away," she said, handing it off. The footman quickly took the cup and replaced it with a new one. One that was, sadly, full of cold milk.

Kira hadn't drunk milk with her dinners since she ate alone in the nursery.

"It has. I've asked Sir Roderick to stay this evening and called the rest of the Kingdom Council in for an emergency meeting. Thus far our measures to stop the robberies haven't worked and it is time to discuss more stringent measures."

"Such as?" Kira asked.

"That is to be decided," Sir Roderick said. "The Council will want to have considerable input on the quest to capture the Beast."

Kira nearly choked on her portion of duck. "Capture?"

"Likely," said Sir Roderick. "From all the accounts we've gathered, there is but one Beast. It stands to reason that if we remove him, the robberies will stop."

"Forgive me," Kira said, trying to gather her scattered thoughts, "but if the Beast is truly the creature of legend, it stands to reason that they are a magical creature. It might not be as simple as capturing anything if there's sorcery involved."

Isadora's lips pursed. "Really, I do believe this is a subject for the Council and not the dinner table. Let us drop this subject and move on to the next course."

The plates of duck were whisked away and replaced with tiny crystal bowls of lemon sorbet. Kira took a spoonful and let the cool tartness melt on her tongue.

Capturing meant hunters. Hunters meant men in her woods. The Crown had thousands of armed men at its disposal. Kira was confident in her ability to remain undetected, but perhaps she would take Durrin's advice and leave for Dunlock a bit early. Let the Beast of Barlow lie low until the hunt was declared a waste of time. If nothing else, she'd see Bertie for a few extra days.

"Oh my," Sir Roderick said, as the dainty cups of sorbet were taken away and replaced with bowls of asparagus soup. "I do enjoy a good soup." He took an over-full spoonful, popped it into his mouth and then grinned. As if that weren't bad enough, Sir Roderick made a noise of what Kira could only assume was appreciation as he slowly withdrew the spoon, and that sound definitely did not belong at the dinner table.

"I am glad you are enjoying our humble offering," Isadora said.

Kira had considered her stepmother to be many things — chiefly an opportunist and evil hag — but never so brave as to call a planned ten course meal 'humble,' and keep a straight face.

"My only regret is that my Margaret is not here to enjoy this bounty with me," Sir Roderick said.

"Your wife?" Kira asked.

"Late wife," Sir Roderick said. "Margaret would have loved such a meal."

For a fleeting moment, Kira felt awful for not knowing that Sir Roderick had lost his wife. It was hard, sometimes, to remember that grief wasn't only something that happened to her but to everyone.

"My current wife, Margie, now, she's not much for fancy meals. But she does set a nicer table than my first wife, Peggy, bless her," Sir Roderick added.

Kira did a mental inventory. *Margaret. Margie. Peggy.* "My apologies, Sir Roderick, have all your wives been named Margaret?"

Sir Roderick nodded. "The rest of the Council joke that it is my only requirement. Breath in the body, and Margaret on the birth certificate." He laughed at his own joke, which echoed dully through the cavernous dining room.

Kira's mouth hung open as she struggled for anything polite to say.

Isadora waved away the current course, and the footmen scurried to swap out the mostly-full soup bowls for a course of cheese and bread.

"I say, I am surprised that the Duke of Lower Miser hasn't joined us tonight," Sir Roderick said, happily moving on from his collection of Margarets. "Trying to drum up some support for his petition, no doubt."

Isadora sipped her wine. Kira suspected that it was to hide her grimace.

"He'll fail, of course. Can't have you splitting titles up willy-nilly."

"Of course not," Kira muttered.

Undaunted by her rudeness, Sir Roderick fixed his watery eyes on her. "In all things, it behooves royals to listen to the Kingdom Council. We are elected to keep order, after all."

Kira bit into a hunk of cheese to keep herself from saying anything. Not that Sir Roderick would have noticed. He was busy tucking into his food once again, leaving no doubt as to his enjoyment.

*Melissa Constantine*

## CHAPTER NINE
### Kira

*Arriving for an official royal visit was as much spectacle as it was the logical* conclusion to a road trip. There were niceties to observe. Pollack and his team had sent a rider ahead to notify Prince Brandon of Dunlock of Kira's arrival. A dozen knights, who'd ridden along with her carriage, had to line up in formation for her official entry into the courtyard. The Prince, along with Princess Margo, all ten of their children, and every servant in and around Dunlock Castle, save the Castle Witch, had lined up in the yard according to prominence and height. And finally, as she stepped from the carriage, assisted by the Prince, a herald had shouted, "Citizens of Dunlock, please welcome Kira Sabrina Stephanie Vineland, Princess Royal of the Known Kingdoms," to a round of tepid applause.

Kira would have preferred to slip in unnoticed, but that wasn't done when it came to an extended visit. Officially, this was her first Festival of the Flower as a representative of the Crown. That meant pomp and circumstance. Kira felt bad that the castle's occupants would be forced to do this all again when the Queen Regent arrived in a few days' time, but not enough to have hung around the Palace and traveled with her stepmother.

The Prince walked her into the castle. He was a stately man with iron-gray hair and a perpetual babyface. He smiled as he spoke, as if everything amused him "Welcome, Princess Kira! We are so pleased you're joining us for the Festival."

His princess, Margo, was a tiny, buxom lady in yards of purple satin. She echoed his welcome. "Your Highness, we are so pleased that you accepted the invitation to join us for this year's Festival. We have some excellent events planned."

Kira smiled. "I am humbled to have been invited."

The Prince beamed. "It is my family and I who are humbled."

The fuss continued, with the servants scurrying from their lineup in the courtyard to a new lineup in the castle's great hall. Kira was introduced to everyone, from the scullery maids, to the governess for the younger Moorelow girls. Kira smiled at them all and repeated each name.

She curtsied to the housekeeper, who blushed furiously at the compliment. In Corlea, the servants saw her every day. Many of them had known her from the day she was born, and none of them were impressed with her attempts to butter them up. She was determined that the Dunlock servants would see her as elegant and royal to a fault. If she didn't lose her temper. Or get an itch on her nose. Or get annoyed that the whole business was taking forever.

After the lower servants were dismissed and sent back to their posts, Bertie took her aside, whispering, "After the dog and pony show is over, meet me in my suite."

Kira nodded, continuing the rounds. Finally, Princess Margo and an army of upper servants walked her to her suite. Princess Margo took great care to show her all of the amenities, from the new Zephyr lamps to the running water tap in the washstand. The rooms themselves were beautiful. Wide-striped paper in mossy green and cream, cut with a border of painted pink roses. The bed had a matching pink canopy overhead and a down coverlet. Attached to the bedroom was a sitting room and two smaller, plain rooms where her maids might sleep.

"It's lovely," Kira said. "Thank you so much."

The Princess blushed. "I'm glad you like it. It was so difficult to decide where each guest would go, and of course with the Queen Regent attending, the Royal Suite was taken."

Kira gritted her teeth and smiled. It was a room. It was probably identical to the one she was to occupy. It did not matter. "I had half-expected to share a room with my cousin," she said. "Bertie and I used to love a sleepover."

Princess Margo didn't seem to know what to do with that information. She laughed, nervously, and continued pointing out bits about the carpets and the pulley bells that would fetch various servants.

Finally, after an eternity, the Princess departed and the suite was turned over to Kira's own array of maids.

"That was some welcome," Pamela said, helping her into a fresh day dress of pale green. That kind of treatment, I can't imagine what the rest of the Festival will be like."

Kira smiled, tightly, praying it wouldn't be as suffocating. Although that was possibly her corset. She could swear Pamela was getting overzealous in tightening the strings.

"I'll spend the rest of the day with my cousin, but I should be back before dinner."

Pamela nodded. "Tell Lord Albert I said hello. He's been missed at the Palace."

Kira couldn't help but agree. When her carriage had pulled through the castle gate, and she'd noticed him among the Moorelows, she'd felt a surge of relief she hadn't expected.

Besides that, she had the gift she'd found for him and she was looking forward to his reaction.

# Chapter Ten
## Bertie

**Bertie's doll collection was the stuff of nightmares.** Hundreds of glossy, dead-eyes staring out from the darkened confines of his closet. As he always did, before lighting the Zephyr lamps, Bertie picked up a rather menacing looking doll in a ragged dress, cradling it like it was a sleeping child.

"Daniella is not pleased you've taken so long to visit," he said.

"You're a red-headed liar," Kira said, as the swirling light from the lamps cast sickly green shadows over the collection. "First of all, Daniella can't stand me and you know it."

Bertie smiled and said, "In her old age, she tolerates you and expects appropriate tribute, as is her due."

"Secondly, you haven't exactly invited me. I had to take it upon myself to show up early, and then I practically had to beg Isadora for a day off from royal lessons. As if I needed instruction on how to be the heir to the throne."

Bertie raised his eyebrows, but said nothing.

"What?" she demanded.

"Granted, I don't know her, but…."

"If you want your gift, say nothing."

"Fine, fine. What have you brought Daniella and me?"

From her bag, Kira took something white and furry and set it on one of the few remaining spaces on the shelf that ringed the closet. Bertie's eyes went wide.

"What in the world is that?"

Kira fluffed the new doll's thick white fur. "Honestly, I've no idea."

"It's hideous and adorable," Bertie murmured, taking in the sight of the doll. It looked at first like a goat on its hind legs, but maybe it was meant to be some kind of horned bear? It's rough coat looked to have been cleaned — but time had clearly done some damage to it. "So how did I do?" she asked, stepping back so Bertie could get a good look at the acquisition.

"Horrifying. Daniella and I adore him. Where did he come from?"

"I found him in the abandoned chapel a few days ago."

"Taking treasures from a chapel," Bertie said. "Naughty. The Fairies will get you."

"No one has been to that chapel for years," Kira said. "Besides, the poor thing was a mess."

Bertie held Daniella up to the horned doll. He used his hand to nod the doll's head. "He can stay."

Job done, he extinguished the Zephyrs, casting the closet back into darkness. He lovingly put his old doll back in her miniature bed and then crossed himself with the motion to ward off evil Fairies, as one did with a collection like that. For good measure, he turned the iron lock on the closet door.

He'd carried Daniella in his arms when his family had arrived back at Corlea Palace after his father's disastrous turn as Ambassador to the Unknown Kingdoms. Kira, all of 5, had taken one look at the doll and curtsied low. "That's a mean Fairie," she'd said. They'd been best friends ever since.

"Before we leave, we'll have to stop in and see the family," he said, between the last bites of a sandwich he'd carried with him from their tea. "Apparently they care about me enough to want to know when I come and go."

Kira made a face. "Seriously?"

Bertie lifted one shoulder. "I guess families do that?"

Neither of them would know. The Vinelands weren't known for their closeness.

"So why do I have to?"

"Well for one, you need to know how hard all their cheerfulness is on me," Bertie said. "You need to see it and sympathize with me. It's exhausting."

"Oh, fine," she said. "But if you're exaggerating I will tell Daniella."

"Fair enough," he said.

They made their way to the palace's great hall, where the Moorelow family, rulers of Dunlock for twelve generations, were gathered.

"Please, come and sit, tea is ready."

The table was laid with what might be called tea if the Moorelows were a poor, struggling family of cottagers from the borders of the Unknown Kingdoms. The scones were exceedingly small. They looked nothing like the sumptuous ones he had delivered to his suite from the village. Kira's eyes went wide. Bertie wanted to say something about having gotten used to the Moorelows's version of tea, but he couldn't bring himself to lie. Besides, those tiny little scones were flecked with raisins. And that was as close to a crime as anything.

Aside from the one platter of scones, there was one pot of tea, and a collection of tiny, almost child-sized cups. Kira cast Bertie a sympathetic glance. Bertie shook his head. He loved tea like some people loved their children, and Kira was one of the few people that understood that.

"We can't stay, Xav is expecting us at the orphanage," Bertie said as politely as he could manage, given the offering on the table.

"One of these days I will get you to join the family for tea," Princess Margo said. "You're one of us now."

Bertie's cheeks turn red. He pulled at his collar. "I will, I…"

"Bertie, come sit with us!" One of the little Moorelow girls demanded. The children erupted in competing offers for his attention. Eight of the Moorelows were gathered around the table, all of them some tiny version of their parents at various ages. Only Xavier and the baby were missing. As a whole they were cute, but always overwhelming.

Bertie had to wonder if he'd ever stop being uncomfortable around his boyfriend's family. There were so many of them and all of them were so exceedingly nice. It was unnatural.

Or it might have been perfectly normal, but either way it was awkward for him. Bertie's only brother was more than a decade older, and had married young, well before he and his parents had gone back to live at Corlea Palace.

"We have to go," Bertie said, taking Kira's arm and pulling her toward the parlor door.

Prince Brandon nodded. "Of course, Son."

Bertie's pale cheeks burned all the brighter. Kira saw, and bit her lip.

"We'll be back before dinner," Bertie said, directing Kira toward the door.

He was waylaid briefly, as Princess Margo fussed over him, adjusting his tie and, licking her fingers and smoothing down one of Bertie's unruly red curls. They promptly stood back on end.

Bertie did not remember if anyone had ever fussed over him the way Princess Margo did. His mother had not been particularly interested in being a mother, and none of the nannies or governesses were allowed to be so familiar. He held himself still until she was satisfied her ministrations had done something.

When they were free of the castle and ensconced in the carriage, Bertie loosened his tie and ran his fingers roughly through his hair until it made a big red nest on his head.

"You see what I'm dealing with?"

She made a noncommittal noise. "I mean, if you think that's bad, try dealing with Isadora."

"Is she really that bad?"

"Yes!" Kira snapped. Bertie could practically see the indignation written all over her. It was nice to know some things never changed. Kira was one of the only people he gave a damn about, but she wasn't the most rational creature.

He sighed and leaned back against the carriage's plush leather seat. "Xav will be happy to see you."

"Why wasn't he at tea with his family?"

Bertie started to answer the question and thought better of it. He didn't want to scare her. *Not yet.* "We've been trying to keep one of us at the orphanage during the day."

"Is that necessary? I thought being a royal patron meant designing uniforms and curriculum and such."

"It's more than that I'm afraid."

The carriage pulled up to a large but plain stone residence set among a handful of vibrantly green trees in early spring bloom. A lazy creek trickled alongside, and past there sat a large open field where a dozen wooly black sheep grazed. It was idyllic until one looked at the massive arched oak door to the orphanage, secured with a comically large lock. Seeing Bertie descend from the carriage, two guards set to open the lock, which was almost as tall and wide as the two men put together.

"Afraid the orphans will escape?" Kira asked, watching one of the liveried guards wrestle the key into the lock.

Bertie sighed. "Yes."

Kira clasped a hand to the back of her neck, as if she was trying to fight the hair rising. "Is there something you haven't told me, Bertie?"

"I meant to write, but, well, you'll see," he said, as the guards were finally able to disengage the lock and the door swung open.

Chaos erupted from inside. A dozen children ran full tilt at the opening screaming in high pitch like shrieking animals. They were all of various sizes and ages, all dressed in the same uniform of blue and purple. When the first child, a small, skinny boy of about six, crossed the threshold there was a burst of blue smoke that produced an opaque cloud. What emerged from the fog was not the small blonde boy, but a creature of indeterminate origin. It was small like the boy had been, but rounder. The hair all over the creature's body was speckled in a dozen colors, from white to black. One ear stood tall, pointing skyward, the other ear smaller and rounder. The little creature snarled, sharp, pointed teeth emerging from a squashed muzzle.

A handful of additional children turned miniature beasts tumbled out of the smoke, all close to the same size. They lined up in a row, each of them snarling, drooling, and ready to pounce.

Bertie bent down to scoop up one of the creatures and hoisted it up on his hip, "We think they might be related to the Beast of Barlow."

"Bertie, they're kids," Kira said. One of the little beasts had advanced and sniffed at the embroidered flowers on the hem of her skirt. "Don't you dare," she warned. The only response was a pair of large brown eyes that blinked at her.

"Be careful," Bertie said, striding into the orphanage, "they definitely bite."

The remaining little beasties trailed after him like puppies following an alpha dog.

## CHAPTER ELEVEN
### Kira

***Once inside the orphanage proper, the children scattered.*** Back through the enchanted doorway, they shrieked and screamed with joy and headed off for parts of the orphanage in little hoards. An army of weary-looking staff did their best to shepherd the children into various rooms. Each of them looked as worn as a well-read book.

Bertie did his best to hastily explain as he led Kira to an airy, light-filled sitting room off the main corridor.

"It started happening about a week ago and we haven't been able to figure out why."

"Bertie, why did you show me that? What am I supposed to do?"

He rubbed his eyes with his palms. "I don't know. Xav said we should get some help, and you were the first person I thought of."

Kira didn't know if she should be pleased that she was the person he trusted, or horrified.

Her gut churned. Children didn't turn into mythical beasts. Especially not the exact same mythical beast that she was pretending to be on a regular basis.

"Couldn't you have told me earlier?" she asked.

"Would you have believed me if you hadn't seen it for yourself?"

Kira honestly had no idea. "Have you and Xav been dealing with this on your own? Have you asked Prince Brandon and Princess Margo?"

"No. It's complicated." Bertie said. "Xav has a bunch of reasons. Mostly related to all the work his parents are doing for the Festival."

"They had better be good reasons."

Bertie bit his lip, and Kira groaned. "Have you told anyone else?"

"Xavier has a friend of his here, he thinks he can help us figure out what to do."

Kira's palms itched and she flexed her fingers to dispel the irritation. Bertie and Xavier needed help, but inviting other people into this problem meant more people were out looking for the Beast of Barlow.

"I don't feel good about any of this," she confessed.

Bertie's brow rose. "Try living it. Anyway, Xav has been friends with Sir Robert since they were kids. He trusts him, so it can't hurt to have him here too."

"Sir Robert Lycette?"

"Do you know him?" Bertie asked.

Other than when she'd robbed his uncle on the Royal Route? Or when she'd dragged him into a closet for some unfathomable reason?

"I knighted him. That doesn't really mean I know him."

She slumped on a small, plush sofa. During the knighthood ceremony, Sir Robert had stood so still it was like looking at a statue. The ceremony had gone on for hours and he'd barely blinked. Someone who could do that was not going to rest until he got answers. He might be perfect for figuring out what was going on here, but how close would that lead him to her?

Kira willed her heart to calm down, but it seemed to insist on beating in her chest with a noticeable flutter. How was she supposed to explain without sounding selfish? She couldn't tell her cousin what she'd been doing. He'd be so disappointed in her. Bertie was the one person in this world who loved her. She let out a breath and went with the only truth she could say out loud. "This is some kind of magic, Bertie. That makes it dangerous."

And it was simply too much of a coincidence for comfort. Why would the children turn into little versions of the Beast? It was impossible and improbable. But she'd seen it with her own eyes. Panic grabbed at her, sinking into her chest. Kira turned her face into one of the silk-striped pillows. Her breath seemed to come out in short bursts as if she couldn't get enough air. "I think my corset is too tight." She was loosening the back of her dress to get at the laces underneath when there was a significant throat clearing.

Kira peered up. Two young men — both exceedingly tall — stood over her, and they'd heard her remark on her undergarments. *Fairies Be.*

Xavier Moorelow smirked. Beside him, Sir Robert Lycette had the grace to keep his face blank.

"Your Highness," Sir Robert said, bowing as if there were nothing unusual about seeing the future monarch face down on a sofa.

Considering they'd last met in a closet, maybe it wasn't.

Xavier couldn't contain a snort and bit his lip. "Good to see you again, Kira."

She glared at Xav and then sat up slowly, tossing the pillow behind her. "How do you do?" She inclined her head to Sir Robert.

Good Lord, how in two days had she'd forgotten he was that handsome? Did he actually glow, or did the light find all of his good angles? It was baffling. His dark hair was short, but one lock fell ever so fetchingly over his forehead in a way that made Kira want to brush it back. He had the sleeves of his shirt rolled up to expose strong forearms that made her a little more *wobbly* than she would care to admit.

"I'm pleased to see you again," he said. His voice was low and deep, and Kira fought off the urge to shiver. Which was ridiculous, because she was going to be Queen. She didn't need to be mooning over a knight from an island smaller than her bedroom. Not when there was so much at stake.

She stood, and then really did feel woozy. Perhaps her corset actually was too tight. "So, now that we're all acquainted. I supposed, we should figure out what we're going to do," she said.

Sir Robert turned to Bertie and Xav. "The children aren't harmed when they turn?"

Bertie shook his head. "They seem fine when they're not monsters anymore."

"So the enchantment is only when they're outside?"

"They're okay in the open courtyard, but that's totally enclosed within the building."

Well that was something. It meant that the spell or whatever it was that caused the transformation might be based entirely on the building itself. Or the children. Which was good, it meant no association at all.

"But outside they become exactly like the Beast of Barlow," Sir Robert said.

Kira squared her shoulders. She needed to drive this conversation before it went anywhere near her. "We don't know that. No one actually knows what the Beast looks like, because it's a story, not a real thing."

Except, when she donned a magical cloak and ran through the woods, but that was beside the point here.

"The robberies are real. Rob was in one. Plus, I've heard the Beast has hit five carriages in the past few weeks."

*Six, but who was counting?*

"Well that is neither here nor there," Kira said. "We don't know that whatever that is, is in any way connected to what's happening."

Bertie's eyebrow quirked up. "It's a little hard to ignore the connection, Ki. They've got all the hallmarks — the mismatched ears, all the colors. You saw them, they look like the stories."

"But they are stories! There's nothing real out there."

Sir Robert looked as if he might say one thing, but then changed his mind. Instead of whatever he intended to say, he said, "Master Durrin, in the Corlea stables, thinks the Beast is probably someone in a costume. And I think I agree."

Well, that was infuriating on a level Kira did not care to think about. She was finding it hard to maintain the balance between outrage that anyone wouldn't be scared of the Beast and reality. Although, Sir Robert's statement was useful for getting the conversation back where she needed it to be. "Exactly. So whoever is doing all those robberies is not who we need to look at. There's magic here. We know that. So that's what we need to focus on."

Above them, there was a thunder of footsteps, as if all of the children were running all at once. All four of them looked upward.

"It's almost dinner time," Bertie remarked. "Before this started happening, the children had free reign of the grounds, and this is when they'd be outside playing."

"After the first few times they ran away, we haven't been able to let them out," Xav added. "They're going to pull this building apart if they don't get some fresh air."

As if on cue, there was a loud crash.

"And that would likely be the mirror in the dining room," Xav said. "I'd better go check it out. Mrs. Banes is going to be beside herself."

"Who is that?" Kira asked.

"The house mother," Bertie said. "She's... well, she's taking all of this hard."

"I can't say I blame her," Kira said. "What does she think is happening here?"

Bertie shook his head. "She won't talk about it."

Well, that was extremely odd. Perhaps the woman was the reason for the enchantment? Kira floated the idea, but both Xav and Bertie shut it down fast.

"It's that she's protective of the children. She's been with the orphanage for years."

Okay, time to find another avenue. Except she really couldn't think of one. She paced the length of the room and back. "So we're back to figuring out what kind of magic is here."

There was another crash, this time of what sounded like splintering wood, and Xav and Bertie exchanged stricken looks.

"Well, go, go," Kira said, shooing them away. "Before the ceiling comes down on us."

Only when they were gone did Kira realize that left her alone with Sir Robert.

****

Maybe she was wrong but Sir Robert seemed to be watching her intently. It was unnerving. *Was he judging her? Would he dare?* Kira sat up straighter. One of her great-great-grand-somethings had issued an edict that no one in the kingdom ever looked directly at him under threat of death. Perhaps it was time to bring that back, less impertinent knights get ahead of themselves.

"Do you believe the children are in danger?" she asked.

He did. "Even if the Beast is a common thief, a lot of people are looking for him. If one of the children gets out and is confused for them, they could be killed."

Kira paled. She hadn't thought of that. Children — orphans — weren't her intended target. They weren't the ones who'd ignored her father's illness and jockeyed for power in the Palace halls. They weren't the ones who'd agreed to forgo her coronation. They were kids.

"When my uncle's carriage was robbed by the Beast I'm not sure I would have said it was an actor. It was genuinely eerie and it all happened so fast."

Kira used every muscle in her body not to beam with pride.

"But then, the more I thought about it, I wasn't sure. It didn't feel mystical, but more like a crime of opportunity."

*That was disappointing.* "I think for the safety of the children, we should start looking at possible magical angles to this problem."

"I agree."

He did? Well good, she was the future queen. More people should go with her suggestions.

"I think we should start with a visit to the Dunlock Witch," he added.

Kira knew it was a practical way to start, but she wasn't entirely comfortable with the idea. She'd been thinking more 'visit the library and figure it out with books.' "I wasn't aware that Dunlock had a witch."

A strange look briefly crossed Sir Robert's face. "She arrived last night."

"What is she like?"

"It wouldn't be right for me to say. She's a well-known magical practitioner."

They were silent for another moment, before Xav and Bertie returned, both somehow looking like they'd been through a battle, despite being gone only a few minutes.

"They're small, but so strong," Bertie said, flopping down on the sofa next to Kira.

"And you're sure they really are children?" Sir Robert asked.

Kira cocked her head to the side. That was definitely an angle she hadn't thought about.

"Maybe," Bertie admitted.

Kira turned to her cousin. "Maybe?"

He and Xavier exchanged guilty looks. "Well, when we took over the orphanage, we were told there were some unusual children in residence."

"Unusual children eat paste and bore you by reciting the territory capitals," Kira said. "This is quite different."

"Look, nothing weird happened for the first few months," Xavier said. "This is all new. And it's weird."

Kira took a bracing breath and tried to keep the focus on the most immediate problem. "I doubt very much that finding one person — pretending to be the Beast or not — is going to help. You need to find out what the real problem happens to be. Sir Robert and I have decided we should start with bringing the matter to the Dunlock witch."

"I think we should also look for what we can find out about the Beast," Xav said. "The story has to start somewhere, and maybe there's a connection we need to know about."

"There's no need to limit ourselves," Sir Robert said. "We can divide and conquer. Princess Kira and I will start with the witch, and you and Lord Albert can research the Beast."

*Did he have to be so practical?* When she was queen, practical people would only be allowed to speak on Tuesdays. Every other day of the week they were too irritating.

"Thank you both," Xav said, "I know this is a lot all at once. Bertie and I really appreciate the help."

Bertie took his hand, and Kira was struck by the care in the small gesture. Her cousin loved Xavier. He was the only person she gave a damn about, and he and the man he loved were genuinely worried. No matter what, she would do whatever she could to help him. Plus, if she stayed close, she had a better chance of protecting her secrets.

She summoned her best, most imperious tone. "We will do everything we can to help you, Sir Robert and I," she said, giving the knight no chance to object. He looked as if he might say something, but his knightly vows held him back from contradicting her.

Good. She was the future queen. She would take control of the situation and help Xavier and Bertie figure out this problem. *How hard could it be?*

# CHAPTER TWELVE
## Kira

**Sir Robert was perhaps the most infuriating person she had ever met.** From the minute they'd gotten out of her carriage at the Dunlock Witch's Tower, he'd kept jogging ahead of her to open doors and offering her his arm when they ascended the steps.

"I am not an invalid." She was tempted to jog up the steps to get away from him, but his legs were so long it was possible he'd keep pace with her even if she took the steps two at a time.

"A knight always offers a lady his assistance." His voice was flat as if he were reciting from a rulebook.

"A knight also should not annoy his queen, so please walk like a normal person. If you can manage that."

"As my lady wishes," Sir Robert said, which was perhaps all the more frustrating. How was it possible that Xavier's best friend was such a stick in the mud? He was pretty but wound much too tight. She wanted to ask him if he ever got tired of being so polite, but even to her that sounded a bit petty. Although if he rushed ahead to open one more door for her, her pettiness was the least of his problems.

The steps to the tower spiraled up to the chambers of the witch, a series of several hundred steps that spun upward until the climber was dizzy.

"Your highness, you needn't go in," Sir Robert said. "It is natural to have hesitation when dealing with the occult."

Kira fought off an eye roll. "I am going in," she said. "Cowardice is not going to help Xav and Bertie."

She went to wrap on the door with her bare knuckles, but Sir Robert shook his head. He took off a glove and offered it to her.

The black leather was warm from his skin and much too large for her hand.

"Thank you," she said, realizing he'd saved her from the possibility of sprouting horns or breaking out in polka dots. Her gloves were in Bertie's sitting room where she'd stripped them off. It was a bad habit in mixed company, but Kira did it anyway. She covered her hand in Robert's absurdly large glove and knocked on the door.

For several long minutes, there was no answer, only the subtle clink of glass and the thud of light footsteps. Kira went to knock again but Robert stilled her hand, his fingers still warm on her wrist when the door swung open.

Kira hadn't met all that many magical people. With both Fairies and witches banned from Corlea, there were few in her sphere and she had no idea what to expect. The woman who answered the door to the Dunlock Witch's quarters was small and skinny, in baggy blue trousers held up by suspenders over a fitted white shirt. But it was the great quantity of shiny purple hair, iridescent as mother-of-pearl, that grew from her head that caused Kira's eyes to go wide.

Sir Robert broke the awkward silence, bowing low in front of the witch, who inclined her head. "Ma'am, we beg an audience."

Realizing she was staring a touch too hard, Kira curtsied quickly. "If you would see us," she added.

The witch took several beats, looking over the two of them before saying, "I don't practice love spells."

Sir Robert colored; his mouth slightly agape. Kira fought off the urge to giggle at his fluster and then wondered if she should be insulted. She turned to the witch.

"I am the future queen of Corlea, I do not need love spells."

The witch smiled, and stepped aside, gesturing them into her inner sanctum. The round room was flooded with light from high windows all around, most of them open to the cold spring air. A great fire roared in the stone hearth, which was easily large enough for a grown man to stand upright. There were three large, overstuffed armchairs and a small tea cart, but the rest of the room was given over to books. They spilled from boxes and tumbled from tabletops. Great piles of them teetered and threatened to fall, and take the assorted abandoned teacups stacked atop them to the ground.

"Please, come sit by the fire," she said. "I was about to summon fresh tea."

Kira hesitated. Taking tea with the witch was all part of the ritual. She had read that somewhere, but knowing that didn't make it any less uncomfortable. *What if she was poisoned?*

The witch noticed that neither of them moved and said, "Oh, I suppose you need this to be a bit more official, hm? Very well. We'll start with something red." She took a small silver watch from the waistband of her trousers, turned the small gear at the top, and muttered a spell. A gauzy red shawl floated down from the ceiling, though Kira was sure nothing had been there before. The witch wrapped the shawl around her shoulders, despite the blazing heat from the fire.

"Better?"

"No," Kira answered bluntly.

"I can appreciate that," said the witch. "Come, sit, you have nothing to fear."

She gave the tea cart a small push, and it zoomed off, though where it went Kira couldn't say. In moments it appeared once more, bearing a silver teapot and a plate of scones.

Kira and Robert sat, though neither of them lounged in the chairs, but sat bolt upright.

"Kira, the Princess Royal of Corlea. I must say you are not as snot-nosed as I would have thought."

*Snot-nosed?* Kira gritted her teeth to keep from snapping at the woman. Who was she to insult the future queen?

"It was a compliment," she said as she poured fragrant black tea into dainty cups, passing them to Kira and Robert. Robert took his cup, which looked small in his hands.

"Now, that leaves you, Sir Handsome," she said to Robert. She raised her thick, dark eyebrows, which were noticeably not the same color as her hair.

"Sir Robert Lycette of Greater Miser," he said.

"Oh, the Misery Islands, I should have known. The smell of salt and sea is about you, isn't it?"

Kira couldn't say if that was true, but she had the sudden urge to lean over and sniff Sir Robert to find out.

"I'm sorry if I offend," Robert said carefully.

"No offense. I spent much of my early life in Fairie City, looking out at the ocean from my room at the coven. I miss it." She took a sip of her tea, in no hurry to allow them to get on with the reason for their visit. Her chatter gave Kira the chance to notice that while the witch's face was quite young, her hands betrayed her as much older. They were as dry and rough as sandpaper, the skin stretched tight over delicate bones.

"Now that I know you, I must ask if you know me?"

Kira shook her head, but Robert nodded. "You're Caris Mourne."

The name meant nothing to Kira, but the witch seemed pleased that Robert knew her.

"It is the hair that gives it away, isn't it? I should really wear more hats."

"We've come to..." Robert started to say, but the witch stopped him.

"Drink your tea first."

Kira sipped at her tea, which had a strong taste of peppermint sweetened with honey. It wasn't bad, but if she spouted feathers or started chanting nonsense, someone was getting a very strongly worded letter.

"Drink, and then we may get on with the business at hand."

They drank as instructed. When they had each drained their cups, Caris Mourne took out her watch again, and in less than a moment the cups flew back to the tea cart, which then zoomed out of sight. Kira was a little depressed to see the scones disappear.

"You don't want them," the witch said. "The kitchens here make terrible scones."

"My cousin Albert has some wonderful ones delivered to his suite."

Caris Mourne smiled. "Does he? You must have him send me the name of the baker he uses. The prince is most generous with my salary but that same attitude does not extend to his baked goods. Now, where were we? Oh, yes, you've come about...?"

Kira tried to think about the best way to describe what was happening at the orphanage. She understood now why Bertie had let the children come tumbling out the front door. Saying, "The children are turning into animals," wouldn't have the same impact as seeing it. She settled on, "There seems to be a problem at the orphanage." She was about to say more when Caris Mourne cocked her head to the side, her eyes intent on Sir Robert. She stood abruptly. "Come with me," she said, standing up. "Hurry please."

Kira stood too, but the witch shook her head. "Most pressing needs first," she said, making a little shooing motion until Kira sat down again.

She practically pulled Robert to the middle of the room, so that they were partially hidden by a tower of books. The witch said something indistinguishable, followed by, "Oh, no, *tisk-tisk*."

"What are you saying?" Kira asked, but neither the witch nor the knight answered.

"There's only so much I can do," Caris Moure said to Robert.

"My lady, I don't know what you're talking about," Robert admitted.

"Of course you don't," she said.

Caris Mourne took out the watch again and returned to the chairs in front of the fire, as if nothing unusual had happened.

"You were saying?" she prompted Kira, her gray eyes piercing.

"There's a problem happening at Lord Albert and Prince Xavier's orphanage. The children might be under some kind of spell."

Caris Mourne's eyes seemed to twinkle for a moment. She looked amused, of all things. But then the witch frowned and said, "And why isn't the young prince here to talk about that?"

Kira twitched, trying to stop herself from saying something she'd regret. "Sir Robert and I have offered to help. It was our idea to visit you."

Caris Mourne nodded. "Among other things," she said, in such a way that Kira had to shake off a shiver running down her back. It seemed that the witch knew something that hadn't been said.

"We were hoping, Ma'am," Sir Robert said sincerely, "that you might know what we can do to find out if there is a spell on the children, and what we could do to break it if there is one."

"What exactly is happening to them?"

"When they leave the orphanage they turn into little furry things," Kira said. "Mismatched ears and all."

"They're the image of the Beast of Barlow," Sir Robert added.

"But it's clear they're under some kind of magic," Kira said.

Caris Mourne whistled, and sat back in her chair. "Tall order." She asked a few more questions, and Kira was struck by how straight-forward her questions were, despite her flippant attitude. In fact, they were much like the ones Sir Robert had asked. And yet, as she asked, she fidgeted and fussed with the red shawl until finally she wadded it up into a ball and pitched it into the fire. "Oh, that's better. Red is not my color."

"Can you help?" Kira asked.

"Yes. Likely. I will need some time. I will contact you when I have something to say."

Sir Robert stood and held out his hand to Kira. She was too mixed up by all that had happened in the witch's chamber to be annoyed at his cloying manners.

They said nothing else as they were ushered out of the room and back to the winding stairs. Kira was too woozy and actually glad of the arm Robert offered her as they descended the corkscrew stairs. "What happened there? I know I was in the room, but it was exceedingly confusing."

Sir Robert didn't know either, as he said, "Caris Mourne has a strange reputation. No one is really sure where her power comes from or why she's so...."

"Odd?"

Sir Robert increased their pace. "I wouldn't say that. At least not where she might hear."

*Melissa Constantine*

# Chapter Thirteen
## Robert

**Robert's ungloved hands were stiff from the cold.** Thankfully, Amzi was a smart horse. He made up for Robert's clumsy handling of the reins with a smooth gait.

Kira had never given him back the glove he'd lent to her when they'd knocked on the witch's door. He'd felt silly, riding out with one glove and so he'd left off the one he still had. He should have put it on. Losing fingers to frostbite was not a great move for a knight.

It would serve him right. He should be wearing gloves. And he definitely should have stayed put in Dunlock. The road to Corlea Palace was one of the more well-traveled parts of the Royal Route, but night was coming and the track narrowed in places to no more than a carriage-width thanks to the forest's ancient evergreens. His mind spinning from the events of the last two days, he'd set out for the sight of the robbery hoping that looking for a practical explanation might help him figure out what was going on.

Robert usually didn't let his imagination get away from him, but it was too easy to picture someone or something running through the trees alongside him. The wind whipped through the branches and threw shadows the height of a man onto the road. Whether Durrin was right, and the Beast of Barlow was a real person or not, the carriage robbery was a fact. There was nothing to say that it couldn't happen again.

Xav believed there could be a connection between the appearance of the Beast and the children. Robert wasn't so sure. What did a bunch of parentless children have to do with robbed carriages? It had to be magic.

But until the witch Caris Mourne had something to say, there was little they could do. Which brought Robert back to the idea of checking out the scene of the crime.

Unfortunately, he was losing the sunlight. There wouldn't be much he could do by the time he reached that section of the road.

"We won't stay out here too much longer," he crooned to his horse.

Amzi whinnied, and kept moving.

Robert didn't want to think about meeting Caris Mourne, but it was either that or let his imagination sabotage his ride. What she'd said had left him more confused than before they'd gone to see her. He knew she was powerful, but how had she known about his wrist?

"The magic that made that mark was innocent but strong," the witch had said, her thin finger circling his arm.

"It's a scar." Robert was surprised that his voice came out in a whisper. He'd had the round, slightly irregular marks since the age of seven.

"It's a claim," Caris Mourne had said. "And it will not be easily broken."

A chill spread from the crown of his head and down his arms. "My lady, I don't know what you're saying."

The witch had looked up at him with a surprising amount of pity. "Of course you don't."

When he'd met up with Xav afterward, he'd left out any mention of it. He told himself that it wasn't relevant, that nothing in that exchange was going to help them solve the problem of the children. But really it was because the story of how he'd gotten the scar was too embarrassing.

When he was seven, the castle on Greater Miser started leaking. Every time it rained — and it rained a lot on the Misery Islands — the cellars filled with water and the whole family ran around placing buckets and stuffing their outgrown trousers into the chimney flues. Not that it helped. Every step was a squishy, moldy mess. All anyone talked about was the ruined crane flower harvest and how bad it had been. And that meant there was no money to fix the roof, or the foundation, or the drainage ditches. In short, the Lycettes needed an awful lot of money awfully fast.

Mother had decided to get it the old-fashioned way. Marriage.

"Are you sure this is the best idea, Maggie?" Father asked. He puffed on his pipe, filling the carriage with sweet, acrid smoke.

Mother waved away the clouds before inhaling sharply and straightening her spine. "The Lycette name is one of the oldest and most distinguished in the Known Kingdoms. That means something."

Father made a general noise of disapproval and sent up a series of smoke rings into the already stuffy interior of the Duke of Greater Miser's traveling carriage. "There are plenty of rich…"

"Start at the top, Charles. You start at the top or else people think you're not worthy of the top."

"Of course, Dear."

Squeezed between his two older brothers on the rear-facing seat, Robert squirmed. He was trying to dislodge his coat tails from underneath Denny's backside and simultaneously avoid the wet willies Charlie kept sticking in his ears. He wanted to take off the itchy starched collar on his suit and he wanted to go home.

The mainland didn't smell right. There was no salt in the air or sand plums getting ripe in the sun. It was roads and carriages and terribleness.

"Robby, sit still. You'll wrinkle your clothes."

"Why do I even have to wear this thing? I'm the third, I'm not going to marry the princess. I'm not even a royal."

His mother's cheeks filled with heat. "You may not be technically a royal, but if the princess is going to marry one of you, it is because we will have successfully traded on our family name. And that requires all of you to stop making a nuisance of yourselves." She grabbed Charlie's hand before his grubby, wet finger could lodge itself in Robert's ear.

Charlie sneered at him. Robert might have escaped now, but he knew there were dozens more wet willies in his future.

"It's not fair."

His mother rolled her eyes. "Get used to it, my love. We live in an unfair world."

They had been traveling at a good clip, shaken by the speed of the horses, but otherwise going along fine when the carriage jolted and the whole rig was pulled to a rough halt. Denny was thrown forward, and Robert took the scramble that followed to yank his coattails back. The force propelled him backward into Charlie, who fell forward onto Father. Tobacco embers spilled out of Father's pipe and before they'd all managed to pick themselves up, they were scrambling out the carriage door to escape a small fire on the carpet.

The groom who went in after them was able to put the fire out, but the damage was done. Robert's suit was crusted in mud, and all of them smelled like smoke — both pipe and small carriage fire.

The driver was apologetic about the abrupt stop, but there was nothing to be done. Most of the Royal Route through the town of Barlow was torn up. Ahead of the horses, a sinkhole had opened up in the road. And with the way the woods crowded the road in both directions, it was going to take some time to get the carriage around.

"Barlow is a few steps up the road, with a nice inn," the groom said. "The Hyde and Hare. Driver and I can get this fixed up and come fetch you. Give you time to get freshened up before we get to the palace."

Mother got a look that said she was ready to spit fire. It was the same look she got when the butcher wouldn't extend any more credit or the governess demanded yet another raise after Charlie and Denny put frogs in her bed. She kept her mouth shut tight and nodded.

"Charles, children. Come along."

Charlie gasped. "Do you think we'll see the Beast?"

Not to be outdone, Denny said, "I heard the Beast is twelve feet tall and has legs like a wolf and a head like a bear."

Charlie nodded. "Yeah, yeah my buddy Peter said it has like a million teeth that stick all out of its mouth. And if you see it you'll die the next day."

"There's no such thing!" Robert said.

"What?" Denny laughed. "You scared?"

"I'm not scared. I'm saying there's no such thing. Father, tell him."

Father had gone back to smoking his pipe, and said, "Of course, Dear."

"All of you, please stop talking," Mother said. "You're giving me a headache."

But Mother's headache didn't stop Denny from jogging alongside Robert the whole way, taunting him with, "Watch out, baby Robby. The big bad Beast will get you."

They were in sight of the squat little collection of buildings that comprised the entirety of Barlow when they heard a blood-curdling scream. It seemed to come out of the woods all around them, echoing and bouncing off the trees. Denny and Charlie tried to take off after the sound, but Mother caught them both by the backs of their jackets.

"There is no such thing as the Beast of Barlow," she said with barely contained fury. "Now we are going to get to the inn and get cleaned up and then we are going to the palace and getting one of you engaged to Princess Kira. End of story."

Except that it wasn't the end of the story. By the time the carriage had been fixed, and they found a way around the sinkhole it was hours after they expected to be in Corlea. The subsequent visit was a complete — but thankfully short — disaster.

For one, although his parents had come on the important business of trying to arrange a betrothal, no one had told the King and Queen. They weren't in residence at the Palace, and no one was quite sure when they would return. The majordomo had done their best to accommodate them, but with the majority of the Palace staff traveling with the King, he was forced to admit they were unprepared for company.

"Princess Kira is in residence," the majordomo had said, looking down on the delegation from the Misery Islands from his impressive height. "I am sure she would be delighted to greet you."

Apparently, however, no one told the four-year-old princess that they were there on important business. She's come flying across the throne room like a ball shot from a cannon. Whatever nurse or nanny was meant to mind her was lost to her trajectory. She'd dashed up to Robert, blonde hair matted, and a streak of thick, black dirt smudged across one cheek. Across her tiny shoulders, she wore the butchered remains of a bear-skin rug. In all his seven years, she was the most terrifying thing he'd ever seen.

"Do you know I'm a bear?" She'd demanded, poking him in the chest.

"You're the princess," he'd said, although only after his mother had elbowed him into speaking.

"Princess Kira," mother began, "We're delighted to…."

But his mother never got to finish her hopeful greeting. Instead, Princess Kira had puffed up her cheeks and let out a scream that echoed through the throne room.

"I am not a princess! I am a bear!"

And then, she grabbed Robert by the arm and planted her surprisingly sharp teeth into his wrist. She'd seemed to hang there for an age, teeth digging into his flesh, until blood pricked the surface.

Denny and Charlie had nearly pissed themselves laughing. As long as he lived Robert was sure to never forget the string of curses that his mother let out. The diatribe began with, "I wanted to save my home, is that too much to ask?" and ended with a few inventive phrases of which he didn't know the meaning.

What little staff remained in the Palace in the King and Queen's absence was able to get him bandaged up and his entire family back into their carriage and on their way in a surprisingly short amount of time.

Robert had been back to the Palace a dozen times since, but nothing was ever as memorable as that first visit. If he ever forgot it, he had the scar to remind him.

He let Amzi slow to a walk. Even his knighthood ceremony last year wasn't that memorable. It had been a lot of standing around and his interaction with Princess Kira had been minimal. When she'd touched the sword to his shoulders she'd leveled her gaze at him in a way that warned she was likely to cut off his ear if he moved a muscle. That was most distinctly not personal. There were a dozen young men knighted that day, and she'd given them all the same look.

But ever since he'd run into her, literally, something had been different.

He wanted to look at her and keep looking at her until he understood exactly why he couldn't stop. There was something about her that was captivating. He had no idea what. She was lovely, yes, but it had to be more than that. Didn't it?

Robert was fairly certain he'd never made quite such an ass of himself as he had around her. Maybe it was because she would be his queen? As a knight of the Known Kingdoms, his first duty was to the ruling monarchs above all others. But a knight did not ogle, or leer, or make a lady feel uncomfortable. He'd done all of that to Princess Kira without saying more than a few words to her. She refused to take his arm and rolled her eyes when he opened doors for her.

And now, Caris Mourne, the world's most famous witch was telling him that the scar she'd given him was a claim? What did that even mean? Was he being a magnificent idiot about all of it?

Possibly.

"What do you think?" he asked his horse.

Amzi stopped, turning his head toward Robert, but otherwise he had no response.

"You're right, I need to focus."

Amzi let out an impatient snort.

Robert looked up, realizing that they'd arrived at the sight of the robbery. The last of the sun saturated the road in the area where the fog had been so heavy. It was much darker in the bend. The trees taller, the brush denser.

All in all, a great place to stage a robbery. There were plenty of places to hide.

Robert once again cursed his lack of gloves as he searched the area around the road. Leaves. Brambles. Thorny bushes and fallen branches. Unhelpfully, not a single sign welcoming him to the home of the Beast of Barlow.

The carriage stopped at the curve that led into the darker area of the forest. It seemed as if the Beast had run at them from the back, on the northern side of the road. The undergrowth wasn't as thick, which meant the Beast had definitely been here.

There seemed to be nothing. No strange smells or tracks or helpful bits of fur stuck to tree bark. Dark was coming on, the sun all but disappearing around him. He was about to give up, when a glimmer of gold caught his eye.

Something the Beast had dropped on his escape?

No, the Beast ran past them, into the brush on the opposite side. Which meant it was possibly something that the Beast had dropped before the robbery.

Crouching down at the base of a low-branched oak, Robert tried to catch sight of the gold object again. The earth had definitely been disturbed here. Not much, almost as if it had been kicked. Before the dark totally swallowed him, he found it.

Glittery gold paper.

A scrap, no bigger or wider than his thumb.

Which as a clue was utterly useless.

Amzi stamped his foot and snorted out a hot breath.

"Okay, we're leaving."

The horse shook his head.

Beyond the bend, light still touched the road, but it was fading almost as fast as it had where he stood. He'd be on the road two hours back to Dunlock from here, but that wasn't safe. Not with the Beast running about, and not for his half-frozen hands.

Corlea Palace was closer. He could bed down in the knight's quarters, and check in with his uncle in the morning, before heading back.

*Melissa Constantine*

## Chapter Fourteen
### Kira

*Kira made her way to Bertie's suite, only to be met with shouting.*

"They're toys, Bertie. *Toys!*" Xavier said.

"They're collectibles," Albert shouted back. "And they're gone."

"You're paranoid, the girls have probably…"

"Who let your sisters into my closet?"

Kira cleared her throat, but neither Xav nor Bertie flinched. Her cousin held the shaggy, horned doll she'd brought him when she was last here. The jaunty little ribbon she'd tied to one of the curling horns had come loose and slipped to the floor. Kira picked it up and handed it to Bertie, who didn't so much as look at her. He and Xavier were locked in battle.

"I don't ask for much, just that no one gives away my possessions when I'm not around," he said. His pale face had turned a shade of purple that clashed badly with his orange-red hair.

Kira surveyed the damage. The doll closet had been emptied. Even Daniella's little bed was missing. That was bad. Most of the dolls, however creepy, were harmless. Daniella was different. Kira wasn't sure she still believed the doll was an evil Fairie vessel, but it certainly was Bertie's prized possession.

Xavier was wide-eyed, his normally tanned complexion ashen. "They're toys, and you're a grown man, why do you care if my sisters play with them? My parents gave you a home, the least you can do is share your silly '*collectibles.*'"

And that was Kira's cue to step in. Bertie was silent with indignation, blowing out short breaths through his nose like a bull about to charge.

Kira took the horned doll from him and pushed it into Xav's hand. "Take this to your sisters and trade it for Daniella, the ugliest, oldest doll. Do not come back without her."

"Not you too," Xavier said.

"Go! I am your sovereign and order you to retrieve Lord Albert's doll."

Xav rolled his eyes, but took the doll and left. His heavy footfalls were halfway down the corridor before Albert let out a string of indignant half-formed phrases about privacy and respecting boundaries. When he caught his breath again, Kira pointed to the sofa and made him sit.

She called for a maid and asked for tea service, careful to instruct, "Bertie's tea service, not the Moorelows."

The maid bit back a giggle, and scurried away.

"You think I'm being stupid too, don't you?" He leaned against the back of the sofa, utterly exhausted.

"I said nothing."

Albert shook his head. "But I am being stupid, aren't I?"

"I think you are rightfully upset," Kira said, trying to keep her voice neutral.

Bertie groaned and closed his eyes. "Why doesn't he get it, Ki? I love him. And I've told him a hundred times how important that stupid doll is to me. You know why."

She did, and she knew exactly why Xav didn't. Prince Xavier Moorelow of Dunlock had grown up cared for and loved by his parents. Anyone who met his family could see how much they loved their children. As far as Kira knew, Prince Brandon was the only royal who'd ever brought a baby in arms to a Royal Audience. Xav didn't understand what it was like to grow up the way she and Bertie had, perpetually overlooked and ignored. Their parents were too busy to bother with them. Xav didn't know what it was like to be an afterthought. As different as she and Bertie were, their shared experience bonded them. That was something that no amount of time could guarantee

Xav would come to understand. Bertie clung to his childhood toy because it was more real to him than anything else.

"He was wrong to say to you what he did."

Bertie reached out and took her hand, pulling her down to the sofa next to him. "I know. Is it wrong that I might forgive him because he's so damn handsome?"

Kira giggled, and relaxed against his side. "Handsome men are the worst."

"Is that why you treated Rob like he was something on the bottom of your shoe?"

Kira's back went up. "I did not!"

Bertie laughed. "You have no poker face, Ki. None. If you could have seen yourself? Yikes."

"Objectively, sure, he's mildly handsome but he was also infuriating. He kept treating me like…"

"Like he's a chivalrous knight and you're the heir to the throne?"

"Like I was fragile. I'm stronger than I look. I don't want people to walk around me like I'm made of glass and I might shatter. It's bad enough with the rumors about my parents, he probably thinks…"

Bertie raised one red eyebrow so high it melted into his curly hair.

Kira flushed. There was no chance for a retort because the maid returned with a whole cadre of footmen in the pale lavender livery of Dunlock. They brought in three different tea carts brimming with scones, tiny sandwiches, and eclairs that glistened with sugary perfection in the afternoon sunshine. A pot of tea, wrapped in a velvet muffler and fragrant with vanilla, was carried in and placed in front of Kira and Bertie on a mother of pearl table that had been brought along with the treats.

When they had the room to themselves again, he handed her a cup of tea. "I know you haven't had any suitors yet. Why not think of Rob as practice? I mean, unless you're planning to be a virgin queen and let one of my brother's terrible children succeed you."

"Ugh, no. Especially not George. He's always sticky."

"He's five. And when I met you, you were so covered in dirt my mother thought you were the pig boy. Stop changing the subject."

"How did we go from talking about your love life to mine?"

"You mean your utter lack of one? You obviously like him, Ki. Flirt. Sneak a snuggle or two behind a potted plant. Live a little."

"No. All I want is for us to figure out what is happening to the orphans and to get through the next two weeks unscathed. Besides, I am the future queen. I can't act like that. Nor do I want to."

"Liar."

Kira threw her half-eaten scone at him.

"Don't!" Bertie said in mock horror. "Have you seen what they do to scones in this place?"

\*\*\*\*

Kira excused herself when Xavier came back with Daniella and an apology, knowing the two of them needed time alone.

"I'm going to get some sleep. I'll see you both tomorrow," she said as she excused herself.

Xavier had his arms around Bertie, his chin resting on his shoulder. "Rob should be back by then anyway."

Bertie wiggled his eyebrows at Kira and made a kissy face. Kira made an indecent hand gesture as she left.

Back in her suite, a small cluster of maids were gathered around one of her trunks. One of them, a Dunlock maid in pale purple with her cap askew, was attacking the lock with a letter opener.

"I think I have it," she said. She brushed back a braided lock of hair that had come loose from her bun. Next to her on the carpet sat a small dagger, a kitchen knife, and what looked like a hoof pick fetched from the stables.

"Excuse me," Kira said, realizing what was happening and exactly which trunk they were desperately trying to pry open.

All four of the maids kneeling around the trunk sprang to their feet and dropped hasty curtseys.

One of Kira's maids, Pamela, added, "Sorry, Your Highness, but we can't find the key to this one and the lock won't give."

Kira pulled the key from around her neck and held it up to the light. It was a heavy, ornate skeleton key that she was hoping had passed as jewelry. She'd strung a ribbon through it and hung it around her neck for safe keeping. "I have it with me."

Pamela held out her hand. "I'll take it, My Lady."

Kira shook her head and dropped the key back to its hiding place in the bodice of her dress. "I don't need that one unpacked. It's merely some sentimental items I did not wish to leave behind."

Pamela went white as a ghost. Failing to unpack her mistress's belongings was up there with regicide, apparently. "My Lady, I don't mind, really. I can find a place to display anything you've brought with you."

"No, thank you," Kira said. "Tuck it into one of the closets, please."

Two of the maids made side-eyes at the trunk, but nonetheless, they picked it up. It took all four of them.

Kira dismissed the maids, asking Pamela to return in an hour to help her dress for bed. Alone, she stepped into the closet where the trunk had been placed. Perhaps it was a trick of the light, but she could have sworn it was moving. There was an uneven glow from the Zephyr lamps. That could explain the trunk appearing to tip every so subtly forward and back. And anything could explain the noise. Dunlock Castle was probably drafty. The pipes that brought water to the tap Princess Margo was so proud of were probably full of air or...mice.

There was no reason to be scared.

## CHAPTER FIFTEEN
### Robert

**Deep shadows pulled across the road as Corlea Palace emerged from the** trees. Amzi slowed and Robert relaxed. The pink stone facade of the Palace was lit by a particularly bright moon. If he could see the Palace, he was on the grounds. And if he was on the grounds, he could claim a bed in the knight's quarters over the stables, and sleep until everything made sense.

Tired as he was, the stables were wide-awake. Although most of the grooms worked the day shift, the evening had its share of comings and goings. Horses were being brushed and curried by the light of a dozen Zephyr lamps, the kind that shone in a warm, welcoming glow the color of buttermilk.

Robert dismounted and led Amzi toward the stall he'd been assigned. Someone had affixed a sign, noting that the occupant was to be one of the horses from the Duke of Lower Miser's traveling party. Everything he needed to settle Amzi for the night was laid out on a low shelf. Fresh hay and a bucket of oats had been left as well.

"A late night for you," Durrin said, appearing at the stall door.

"Dunlock is close, but not close enough," Robert said.

"Any more run-ins with the Beast?"

Robert shook his head. Durrin laughed anyway, a merry chuckle that rang through the wide hallway of the stable.

"I have a theory about the Beast of Barlow," the stable master announced.

Knights did not roll their eyes. They did not sigh and say they were too tired to listen or disrespect their hosts. As the stablemaster, Durrin was as much his host as the Queen Regent or Princess Kira. Hard, cold ride be damned.

"I believe you mentioned it was a man in a costume," he said.

Durrin scratched at his ear, although the flat cap, and thus any hint of Fairie heritage, remained firmly in place. "Sure, yeah, but no."

Robert drew his eyebrows together, not sure what to make of that. He moved through the motions of taking Amzi's saddle off and getting the tack placed on the thoughtful shelves and pegs around the stall.

"I said it was a twat, and sure enough it is," Durrin said. His elvish face was split with a grin. If the late hour bothered him, he didn't show it. "But no, I don't think it's a man at all."

"You think it's a woman?"

Durrin nodded. "You said the Beast took your uncle's fancy wig, no?"

"Yes, and gold."

"But the wig, yes? And the Duke of Trevelyn came through saying his fancy piece lost her eyeglasses. All upset she was. Everyone who comes through with a story about having lost something small. Maybe something that means a great deal to them. Nothing big, but something they like to have. Only a woman would be that cruel."

"Jordaan swears the thing he saw was at least 8 feet. That's a tall woman."

"Pshaw," Durrin said. "Your Sir Jordaan exaggerates. I wouldn't be surprised if what he saw was nothing but a bunny rabbit."

Robert forced a smile to answer Durrin's laugh at his own joke.

"Something to think about," Robert managed to say.

"Isn't it?" Durrin said.

The stablemaster began to whistle as he turned to go. "Good night, young Sir Robby. Sleep well."

Robert gave his horse one final brush and freshened the water in the trough. He did not remember a time when he was so tired. Exhaustion has swept into his bones. It was especially heavy on his shoulders. He gave his horse one last scratch behind the ear and made his way up to the sleeping quarters.

Knights valued cleanliness, but Robert was too tired to bother with much besides swabbing the dust from his face and shucking off his coat and boots. He fell toward the little bed.

He landed face-first on the stone floor of the Dunlock Witch's Tower.

Robert groaned and pushed himself up. The floor was cold under his bare feet.

"Oh, I do apologize, Sir Handsome. My timing must be off," Caris Mourne said.

Robert blinked, trying to clear his vision. It was as if he looked at the witch through a murky layer of glass. He rubbed at his eyes with the palms of his hands, but that only superimposed fireworks over the blurry, moving image of her. Her purple hair was loose, and she wore some kind of floral dressing gown and fuzzy slippers.

"Are you alright?" she asked. "Astral travel can be dangerous."

Robert tried to open his mouth to say that he was tired but otherwise fine, but no words came out. Around the circular room, most of the towers of books had been pushed to the walls, and all of the teacups that had sat atop the piles were now being used as candle holders. A large four-poster bed had been dropped in the center of the room. Robert had stared at it a beat too long, wondering who'd been tasked with carrying that bed up the stairs when he realized he was not alone with the witch. Another figure was moving toward him. Instinctively he reached for the sword at his side, only to realize he'd left it in Amzi's stall.

"Easy," said the second voice. The voice was rather low in pitch, but impossible to tell if it belonged to a man or a woman. Robert's vision was too impaired to see a face and much beyond that the person wore the same flowery dressing gown as Caris Mourne. "No fast movements. You'll make yourself sick."

"I'm sorry about stealing you away from your bed," Caris Mourne said to Robert. "But I had a thought."

"Darling," said the second person, "I've told you before that sharing your thoughts can wait until morning."

"Not this, I'm afraid," said the witch. "I will need to see you tomorrow, Sir Robert. Do not stop and greet your friends. You must come straight to this tower."

"My lady, I..." Robert swayed on his feet.

"The boy needs a chair," one of them said, but Robert could no longer tell them apart.

"I have duties with my uncle," Robert said, stumbling as a chair came floating toward him.

"He'll let you come. I'll make sure of it."

"Caris, Darling," said the other person, "Either tell the boy your thoughts now or let him go back to his sorry little bed."

"Oh, yes, well. I will need to run some tests to be sure, but I believe what is happening to the children is a matter of *Referred Magic*."

When Robert could do little more than look confused, she added, "Do you understand what I'm saying?"

"Referred from whom?"

"You see, he gets it," said the witch.

"He doesn't, Love," said the second voice.

Robert did not get it. The room around him seemed to be moving at a speed that didn't allow him to focus.

"Send him back now," said the second voice, in a rather fatherly way.

"First thing, Sir Handsome. Keep it to yourself. No excuses."

Robert found himself back in the room over the stables, sunlight beginning to peek through the windows and the chorus of grooms rising for the day shift. When he pulled himself out of bed several hours later, he felt as if he hadn't slept at all. He hadn't stayed in bed past noon since he was ill as a child. It made the day feel as foreign as if he'd woken up in a new country. He dressed and dragged himself in the general direction of the Palace kitchens, only to run into Jordaan, hurrying back to the stables.

"You missed a morning," Jordaan said. He passed Robert a heel of bread and a mug of coffee. "The Duke wants to leave as soon as we can get moving."

Robert gratefully ate some of the bread, squinting against the too bright sunlight. It was hard to imagine that Uncle Julius was prepared to leave so soon, not unless the Queen Regent had agreed to his petition. And that seemed unlikely.

"What happened?" Robert asked, taking a sip of the hot coffee. It burned going down, but that helped shake some of the lethargy from him.

"He wants to head to Dunlock early. He got a special invitation from Prince Brandon."

"Why?"

"No freaking clue," Jordaan said. "Middle of breakfast this morning, a messenger came in and handed him an invitation. Next thing you know, he practically lost a second wig running around trying to cancel all the appointments he made. So we're headed to Dunlock."

A knot formed in Robert's chest. Caris Mourne must be behind the invitation. He could only hope that whatever they were being summoned to Dunlock for, it didn't give his uncle any false hope.

****

"I'm to be an honored guest at the Festival of the Flower," Uncle Julius said. He took an armful of clothing out of the wardrobe and passed it to his waiting valet, who bowed under the weight of brocade and fur collars.

"What about your petition to the Queen Regent?"

Uncle Julius hesitated but then continued pulling objects out of the wardrobe. "Robby, Prince Brandon's letter said they were interested in buying the entire harvest of the Misery Islands. Think of it!"

Uncle Julius threw the half-dozen pairs of shoes he was holding to his overburdened valet. "Prince Brandon's invitation stated that we should arrive as soon as possible," he said, beaming with pride. " If we can sell to Dunlock this year, we'll be able to repair the docks!"

Unlike the flowers that grew in other regions, the Misery Island crop didn't have many medicinal or other practical uses. Mostly, the cranes were pretty. Despite all of his father and Uncle Julius's best efforts to have the flowers cross-pollinated with other varieties, there wasn't much that could be done with them. A slug of dread settled in Robert's chest. Uncle Julius's hopes were too high. Caris Mourne might not think enough of the duke to make sure the sale of the flowers went through in all these magical manipulations, but he had no wish to see his uncle disappointed.

"Uncle, I worry that we're leaving Corlea before the Queen Regent has a chance to consider your petition."

Uncle Julius added his two remaining wigs to the pile in the valet's arms. "Robby, we both know that's not going to happen. Not this time. My fault. I was angry after the Beast attacked us, and I made a poor showing."

Robert had no answer to that, and his uncle plowed on as if talking to himself more than his nephew. "But, if the Queen Regent can see my success in Dunlock she'll understand that Lower Miser is a viable, thriving place. She'll understand why it is so important to split the titles."

That was a lot of supposition, and Robert did not like the chances. "What will she think if we rush off?"

"I'm going to meet with her before we leave and make my apologies," his uncle paused in the act of searching through his jewelry. "Jackson, what time are we meeting with the Queen Regent?"

The valet handed off his sartorial burden to several housemaids recruited to help. "Within the hour, Your Grace."

Uncle Julius's hurry took on a new dimension. "The crops, Robby. Think of selling the crops! I want to depart for Dunlock as soon as we can. Only good can come from this, my boy."

# Chapter Sixteen
## Diana

***The gates of Dunlock opened, and their carriage led the parade into the*** courtyard. The banners of all the major territories adorned the top of the ramparts ringing the drive. The flags of the smaller territories, including the pale pink of Wills, were represented on lower posts. Servants in Dunlock's lavender livery were positioned at each place where one of the carriages might stop. And everywhere there were crane flowers from all parts of the Known Kingdoms. It was only the beginning of the harvest, which meant that the flowers were hothouse grown and costly. It made the gray stone courtyard a riot of color.

"Well, I suppose the rumors are true," the Countess said as they climbed out of the carriage.

"What rumors?"

The Countess stepped into the sunlight, eyes scanning all of the decorations. "Prince Brandon hired Caris Mourne to be his castle witch. I'll bet my favorite handbag that all of this is her work and likely to be gone by morning."

Diana gasped. *Caris Mourne?* "How could you not tell me!"

The countess sighed, "Really, Diana, I would have thought you'd outgrown your obsession with her."

"Mother, it's Caris Mourne! People write books about what she's done. There's like nine songs that people actually sing that are about her."

"She's a witch, Diana. That doesn't make her particularly special. Fairies, witches, all of them are people. Magical or not."

Diana's mouth opened several, long seconds before words came out. "Caris Mourne rebuilt Millstone Castle with nothing more than a three-word spell!"

Mother raised a skeptical, immaculately sculpted eyebrow. "That's likely not true."

"Maybe she used a few more words, but..."

"Diana, you are a grown woman. Please, I beg of you, never ever bring any of this into conversation."

"I am not the only one who is going to want to talk about her. It's Caris Mourne! Once she builds something, no one can undo it. That's amazing."

"Please, I beg you. If you see her, do not start listing her accomplishments to her. It's rather tacky. She's well aware of what she's done."

Diana ignored her. Caris Mourne and Robby Lycette in one place. It was incredible.

Diana and her mother were swept with the crowd into the castle proper. Although the Festival wouldn't officially begin until the Queen Regent arrived for the ceremonial harvest, most of the royal families were already streaming into Dunlock Castle.

Her mother held Fritz as if she were afraid to lose him in the crowd. "Let's find our suite. I want to give Fritz time to calm down."

Fritz was impassive as always. "Mother, if that dog gets any calmer he might actually be dead."

"Diana Michelle Yarborough, don't you dare say that."

She held her tongue. Fritz did not, letting his tongue droop out of his mouth with a significant amount of drool. Diana bit back her revulsion.

It took almost an hour to find the castle majordomo and confirm which wing of the house they would reside in. Dunlock didn't have the finery of many castles in much smaller territories, but it was exceedingly large. By the time their maids had unpacked, and helped them change from their traveling clothes, and Mother declared that Fritz was significantly rested, a maid arrived to tell them that dinner was to be served in the Great Hall, which meant another change of clothing.

"I had hoped to take Fritz out for a walk," her mother said. "There never seems to be enough time."

A maid or a footman could have taken Fritz out without her accompanying him, but Diana knew that the Countess of Wills preferred to take the miserable little thing out herself. *To protect his nerves.*

Diana's dinner gown for that night was not as elaborate as her mother's, and so with a reluctant sigh she held out her hand. "Give me his leash."

Mother hesitated. "You will be careful. And make sure the footman cleans up after him?"

"Yes, Mama. My furry little brother is in good hands I promise."

Her mother handed over the leash. Fritz trotted along, as vacant as ever. The two of them, and one of the footmen, made their way through the crowded halls and out toward the crane fields that began at the backside of the castle.

The Dunlock crane grew in tall, graceful clusters, their purple petals ranging in shades from pale lilac to nearly black. She knew, thanks to her last governess's obsession with the cranes from each territory, that the Dunlock cranes were harvested for their stems, more than their blooms. They were one of the hearty varieties so they could be broken down and the fibers woven into cloth. The Wills cranes — so pale pink they were nearly white — had a much less practical use. They made perfume. Luckily, they only grew in the cold, northern climate of Wills, and so they were rare enough to keep their lands wealthy.

"What do you think, Fritz? Are these prettier flowers than ours?"

The dog did not answer.

Neither did the footman, who stayed a respectable distance behind them as they made their way across the first field, scooper at the ready.

"You're right," she said to Fritz. "Wills cranes are much, much prettier."

A small laugh echoed through the flowers. Diana stared at Fritz for half a beat before realizing he wasn't the source of the laughter.

A young woman about Diana's age waved from a row over. "I like the cranes from Spire. They're a lovely shade of chartreuse."

"Chartreuse?"

The blond nodded. "It's a very garish shade of bright green. I wish they would grow around Corlea, but apparently the soil isn't good for it."

"So they're garish and lovely?"

"Exactly."

Her companion in the fields was petite, her long hair tied up in a messy bun. Her dress was made of a heavy pink satin, but she didn't seem to care as she knelt down to scratch Fritz behind the ears. "He's darling."

"My mother will be so pleased to hear that. She adores him."

"I take it your mother is the Countess of Wills?"

"She is, yes."

"I'm Kira," said the girl.

Diana was startled. "As in Princess Kira?"

"That's me. But call me Kira."

Words died on Diana's tongue. She had a thousand questions, but all of them seemed a bit rude. She settled for, "I'm Diana Yarborough."

"It's nice to meet you."

Princess Kira got to her feet once again, neglecting to wipe the dirt from her dress. "I suppose I should go. I'm probably needed for something. Although, to tell you the truth, I'm ready to give up being royal all together. It's exhausting."

Diana laughed uneasily. "Really?"

"No. Of course not. I'm going to be queen. No one gives that up."

Diana couldn't hold back a snort of laughter. No one ever said the Princess was funny. Mostly they said she was 'opinionated for one so young.' It wasn't a sparkling recommendation.

"I guess I should head back in too. My mother will be apoplectic if I don't bring Fritz back in a timely manner. I hope I see you again."

The Princess's smile seemed genuine. "I hope so." She waved and set off through the cranes with a determined gait.

Diana was too stunned to do more than watch her go. The footman shared her astonishment, his mouth hanging open slightly.

****

The Countess wasn't ecstatic at her new acquaintance. She passed a comb to the maid working on Diana's hair, a worried look on her face.

"You met the Princess?"

Diana nodded and one of her thick red curls popped free from the elaborate style the maid was attempting. She tucked it back behind her ear to the maid's barely contained irritation.

"She was in the crane fields. She is really nice."

They had a rather large suite on the fourth floor, which boasted several mullioned windows that overlooked the main courtyard. It was a warm and comfortable room full of heavy wooden furniture that seemed to invite lounging. The Countess would never. She sat bolt upright in an overstuffed armchair, as if she might need to spring out of it at any moment. Fritz, panting heavily despite his lack of movement, clasped in her arms.

"Well, that is neither here nor there. I've heard some odd reports about her."

Diana winced as the maid pulled the brush through her hair. "Like what?"

Mother sighed. "Bits here and there. She hasn't made much of an impression on the Kingdom Council since the death of King Callum."

"Her father died right after remarrying. And then they wouldn't crown her. That's not small."

The Countess shook her head. "Be careful of appearing too friendly with her. We don't want to limit your pool of potential suitors based on people's assumptions about her."

"No one really knows her; how can they have opinions?"

"Have I taught you nothing, my child? Among the royals, everyone has an opinion on everything."

"Even me?"

Mother's nostrils briefly flared. "Yes. That is why I don't want you chatting up anyone about Fairies or magic or any of it. The whole subject is passé."

"I promise not to bring it up. However, if it slips into the conversation…"

"Diana!"

She smiled at her mother, only to regret it when the maid gave another great yank of her unruly hair. The maid murmured an apology barely louder than a whisper.

The Countess turned the conversation to what she considered the more pressing issue — the list of eligible suitors Diana might encounter. She was running through the children of Dukes, Earls, and Viscounts as if they were a shopping list prepared for the housekeeper.

"And of course, the youngest son of Baron Park is in attendance. Plenty of money of his own, but his older sister will take the title to her marriage."

"Marcus Park used to eat paste in the schoolroom. I can definitely do better than that."

And that, the Countess had to concede was true. "There is the daughter of Countess Ambleside, I hear she is quite pretty."

Diana didn't have much interest in a female partner, as much as her mother loved the idea of building that connection. In truth, despite her earlier promise to her mother, the only person she wanted to consider — at least at first — was Robby Lycette.

"Mother, can I meet some of these people before we dissect them completely? I can't imagine anyone else is going to be this mercenary."

The Countess scoffed. "I have failed you as a mother if you believe that."

*Melissa Constantine*

## CHAPTER SEVENTEEN
### Robert

*Prince Brandon had come to the Dunlock Castle courtyard to greet them.* Uncle Julius, who'd been beaming since the carriage had left Corlea, was incandescent as he climbed down.

Robert wanted his uncle's welcome to be genuine. He hoped that in her machinations to get him back to Dunlock, Caris Mourne had actually made some plan for the purchase of the Misery Island crane crops. Uncle Julius was a stubborn, vain man but his love for their islands was genuine, and Robert loved him. His uncle's sponsorship meant he'd been made a knight immediately on finishing his training. No lingering as a squire, but going straight into the five years of service he would need to retain the title of Sir.

"Your Grace, a pleasure," said Prince Brandon.

The prince offered a slight bow, to which Uncle Julius's smile widened as he bent low.

"The pleasure is mine, Your Highness. I was so pleased to receive your invitation."

"Well come in, come in, both of you. My wife is waiting to greet you inside." Prince Brandon led them through the main entrance to Dunlock Castle.

Although the kingdom of Dunlock was prosperous, with some of the best crane flower crops in the Known Kingdoms, the marble tile in the entrance hall was worn from a few hundred years of footfalls. Everything was spotlessly clean, but the well-made furniture had gone shabby and the tapestries that hung along the corridor walls were faded. All in all, it felt more like home than any place Robert ever visited.

The princess and the children were all gathered in the family sitting room. Three small girls in pigtails and flouncy dresses were playing with a tea set by the windows, and two of the boys, James and Gregory, were tossing a ball between them.

"You'll pardon the informality," Prince Brandon said. "We try to spend at least a few hours together as a family every day, a tradition my beautiful bride is unwilling to break."

"Oh, yes, of course," Uncle Julius said with an apprehensive look around the room before settling his gaze on the smallest Moorelow, Jenny, who was propped up in an infant seat with a great deal of drool running down her chubby face.

Princess Margo once again commanded him to bend down so she could kiss his forehead. "Stay this time. We've barely spent any time with you."

She then turned to his uncle and greeted him with her typical warm smile. "It has been too long, Lord Julius. We are so pleased you decided to accept our impromptu invitation."

"I was most honored to receive it."

"Mummy!" bellowed one of the girls, "Violet isn't sharing!"

"Then play with something else, Lissa," Princess Margo said. "There's a whole castle's worth of toys, and you fight over one ugly doll. *Honestly*."

"Your Highness, I don't wish to interrupt your time with your children," Uncle Julius said. "Perhaps I should see my men settled."

"I was rather hoping to get to the business I wrote to you about," Prince Brandon said. "We've learned some rather exciting things from our new castle witch. And I believe that could create incredible business for us both."

Robert saw the gleam in his uncle's eyes that meant once again he thought he was going to sell the crane crop. "Uncle, I am familiar with the staff quarters, I will see to the arrangements."

Although Uncle Julius cast another furtive glance at the drooling baby as if the little girl were a ticking time bomb, he agreed. "I'll see you at dinner."

Robert excused himself and he headed for the Witch's Tower.

Caris Mourne welcomed him with yet another cup of tea thrust into his hands. "Drink quickly, we have much to do."

The bed and the companion from last evening were absent from the circular room. The stacks of books were back, their teacup crowns replaced by dozens of mortar and pestle sets, some as large as a small child. Many of them were filled with thick, colorful pastes that gave the room a strong smell of medicine.

Robert drank his tea, which had the tang of citrus and a sweet finish. As he did, Caris Mourne dashed about the room, randomly opening books and muttering to herself when the answers she sought didn't jump off the page.

"Most annoying," she said, shutting a leather-bound tome that sent a cloud of dust into the air. "These books have a mind of their own."

"My Lady, I can come back another time if this is inconvenient."

"You're a sweet boy, Sir Handsome, but no, there's little time to waste."

"What can I do to help?"

The witch smiled, the lines at the corners of her mouth crinkling. She handed him a large book with a bright orange cover. "I'm looking for a picture of a bird. Large, bright, bombastic."

Robert turned the pages. He did not know what the point of flipping through the books was supposed to be, but he shuffled through the pages as instructed. "Only black and white illustrations," he told her.

She motioned to a stack close to the fire. As with every other time he'd been in her presence, the fire was roaring despite the warm day. Sweat gathered under his tunic. Because he hadn't taken the time to change after traveling, the heat and the dust of the road made his skin itch and made him keenly aware of his own discomfort. Although that might be more for the strangeness of the afternoon. He wanted to ask Caris Mourne about his uncle and the potential sale of the crane flowers, but the time didn't seem right.

The witch hummed as she discarded one book after another. Her shiny purple hair caught the sunlight. Everything he knew about the witch was based on rumors. She had caused the mudslides that took down the walls to Fairie City. *Allegedly.* She had cursed the head of her coven and taken all of the powers of her fellow witches for herself. Probably mere speculation, but mind-numbing all the same. How one person could have accomplished all of that was a mystery, especially one who was small and slight, and almost comical.

In the third book, Robert opened to a richly detailed print of a bird in flight. It had black-tipped wings and multi-colored feet. "My Lady?" he said, holding up the open book.

"Excellent. Put the book on the floor, if you would."

Robert placed the open book to the spot she indicated.

"Best move," she said. "About nine feet away."

Robert was half the distance when the witch took out her silver watch and turned the dial. The bird, a massive creature with at least an eight-foot wingspan, emerged from the book. He fluttered his wings in an indignant fashion as if highly offended to be taken from the comfort of his book.

"So sorry to bother you, Sir," Caris Mourne addressed the bird. "Have you a name we can call you?"

The bird puffed his chest and said, in a surprisingly cultured voice, "I am called Maurice by my acquaintances."

"A pleasure, Mr. Maurice. This young man is Sir Robert of Greater Miser and I am Caris Mourne."

"I know who you are," said Maurice. "I've been in your books for some time."

"Yes, sorry about the hasty transport the other day."

The bird nodded his many-colored head in acknowledgment of the apology. Robert blinked hard, trying to make sure he wasn't having a stroke. The bird had come from a book. And it talked. Birds did not talk. *They were birds!*

"Sir Robert and I believe we may be dealing with a matter of Referred Magic," Caris Mourne said to the bird, who was definitely standing at the hearth, the flames from the fire causing opalesce patterns to dance over his feathers.

"Nasty business," said the bird.

"Yes," Caris Mourne agreed. "At the moment, we have no idea where it might be coming from."

"Animal, mineral, or vegetable?"

"Animal. No dodgy carrots about, right, Sir Handsome?"

Robert shook his head, unable to form words. He knew Caris Mourne was powerful. She had a reputation in both the Known and Unknown Kingdoms for exactly that. Pulling a talking, fully realized bird from a book wasn't only beyond what he'd imagined she could do, it was staggering. Witches usually made a few potions or listened to the troubles of the castle occupants. Some, depending on their powers, could cast a spell to fix a dodgy rain spout or repair a castle foundation. What she had done made all of that look petty.

"Well, if it is Animal in nature, then it must come from a person," said the bird.

Caris Mourne let out a growl of frustration. "I was afraid of that."

"Nasty business, as I said. Animal effects have a wide range. They can travel miles. Assuming, of course, it is a matter of Referred Magic. You've done the usual tests, I presume?"

"I have."

"Then I'm afraid you have an arduous task ahead of you. Find the source, find out why the magic is referred from them, and what kind of magic was used to begin the whole mess."

"Any tips on how we'd identify them?"

Maurice puffed out his feathered chest again. Robert could almost swear he was smiling, although his bright orange beak hadn't changed. He was proud to know the answers.

"A source can't escape magic. It follows them. It builds up."

"Rather like a bad odor," Caris Mourne said.

The bird inclined his head. "A crude metaphor but yes. Magic clings and when it is being pushed away, it lashes out."

"Thank you, Maurice." Caris Mourne checked a small watch attached to her suspenders by a long silver chain. "About an hour's worth of magic left. Care for a flight?"

The bird bowed and hopped toward the wide-open windows. "Be so good as to leave some tea by the book, would you?"

"Of course, happy travels," said the witch.

Maurice spread his wings and pushed off from the windowsill, disappearing into the clouds.

The witch turned back to Robert. "That was productive. We now have our marching orders. Close your mouth, Sir Robert, out-of-water fish is not a good look for you."

Robert snapped his jaw shut, only to open it again when a question came unbidden out of his mouth. "What in the Fairies happened?"

"Magic is a science, not an art. This particular science needed a dose of incredulity to work. I can't manufacture that myself."

Robert's temples throbbed, a headache for the ages building between them. "I need to go lie down."

"I suspect you do. I shall be in touch," she said, ushering him back out of the tower to the stairs.

Although his head pounded, Robert still had to see to his duties for his uncle. He found Jordaan at the stable, the horses already ensconced in their stalls.

"You look as if you've seen a ghost," Jordaan said. "You didn't look this bad after we got robbed."

Robert had no words to explain what he'd seen and fewer still when he noticed a large, multi-colored bird soaring in the skies over the stable.

## CHAPTER EIGHTEEN
### Robert

*Although the Queen Regent wouldn't arrive until the next day, the* Festival's first unofficial event was a feast in the castle's sprawling dining room. Princess Margo gave a welcome speech, and a team of footmen spiraled through the great hall presenting each course under silver domes. Uncle Julius was at the head table, while Robert was seated among the knights attached to the various royal households. Many of the younger knights had trained with him in Spire, so it wasn't a hardship to be seated in the back.

Neither was it a hardship to have his seat face Kira. She wore a light purple dress, the same color as the Dunlock standard, in deference to her host. Her hair was swept up high on her head, and the mix of Zephyr lamps and candles made it shimmer like a spill of gold coins.

Sir Jordaan, never at a loss for something to laugh at, noticed his rapt attention. He leaned in and said, "You might want to look somewhere else, Robby. You don't want to go anywhere near that kind of crazy."

Robert flinched. Jordaan's breath was already heavy with alcohol. "You shouldn't talk about her that way. She's our future queen."

Jordaan smirked. "If the Kingdom Council has its way she won't be."

"She's the rightful heir."

Jordaan shrugged and took another drink. "Don't get on my case. All I know is that a friend of my dad sits on the Council. He says they're not sure she's up to the job. Probably cuckoo like her old man. That's why they put Isadora in as regent."

"Princess Kira isn't crazy. She's not twenty-one yet, that's a lot to handle."

"Tell yourself that." Jordaan slapped Robert on the back so hard he jerked forward and had to catch himself against the edge of the table. "All those high royals are nuts. Look at Travers. Couldn't even negotiate for his crane crop this year. You don't have to do anything to sell those stupid flowers. Literally grow them and stick your hand out for the money."

Robert didn't have time to tell Jordaan how wrong he was about that. Jordaan was a Van Dine, a family so well connected in the crane trade all over the continent that he probably couldn't imagine how fragile the crops were, nor how hard it was to make money on them when your territory produced a single variety. Robert had no wish to continue the conversation, so he excused himself to go speak to his uncle.

He made his way through the crowd to the head table. Uncle Julius was all smiles from his spot at the front. If anyone from the Misery Islands had ever made a head table at a royal gathering, Robert had never heard about it.

"Robby!"

"Uncle, I wanted to check in."

"No need, go enjoy yourself, my boy! The Festival of the Flower is all about fun."

"Is there anything you need?"

Uncle Julius was beaming. He leaned close to Robert and whispered. "Dunlock bought the whole crop."

"All of it?"

Uncle Julius's wig threatened to tumble to the floor. "This year and next!"

Robert was stunned. What possible use did Dunlock have for the Lower Miser Crane? It was beautiful but useless. "That's wonderful."

"Wait until the Queen Regent arrives. I'm sworn to secrecy, but apparently there's a new use for them. Something important."

Robert couldn't help but wonder how much Caris Mourne was involved. While he was glad that the crop was sold, how much had Prince Brandon and Princess Margo paid for it? It was a tangled web, and he wasn't sure he was up to unraveling it.

"Go. See your friends. Enjoy the night."

Reluctantly, Robert turned to go back to his seat. He was making his way through the throngs of people when there was a tap on his shoulder.

"Don't you dare take another step without saying hello to me, Robby Lycette."

Robert smiled. He'd known Diana since they were children. At three, Diana had been chubby and freckled with a puff of orange hair. Although she'd changed since the last time he'd seen her, there was no mistaking Diana Yarborough. Like her mother she was tall, only a few inches shorter than himself. She owned her height by the elegant way she carried herself. Her red hair had been half-tamed to an elegant waterfall that traveled halfway down her back. At one point, he'd wondered if the two of them might end up together, but he'd known her so long that she was almost a sister.

He bowed to her. Diana cocked her head to the side. "Really? You're too good for this world." She leaned in and wrapped her arms around him.

Embarrassed, Robert stepped back quickly. "It's good to see you, Diana."

"Knighthood looks good on you. It's hard to believe you finally grew into those ears."

"About the time you grew into your feet."

"I am happy to report my flippers remain as elegant and enormous as ever." She raised her foot. Beneath the hem of her dark blue dress her shoe was the same color. The bit of her stocking she exposed was stripped in bright, vivid purple.

"Nice socks," he said.

"Don't tell my mother, but you'll never guess who they are in honor of, Robby. Never."

Awareness prickled over his scalp. "Caris Mourne?"

Diana nodded. "She's here! Can you believe it?"

Unfortunately, he could. He hesitated telling Diana he'd not only met the witch but witnessed her magic. When they'd first learned of the infamous witch as kids, they'd spent hours speculating on what her power could do. Neither of the witches at their castles had anything like the reputation of Caris Mourne. Mostly they were old women in red who could brew cold remedies.

"She doesn't come down much," he said.

"It's the Festival of the Flower, is she really going to miss it?"

Robert could only shrug. He wasn't so sure it was wise to have gone to see the witch, even if his intention to help Xavier and Lord Bertie had been genuine. The kind of power Caris Mourne wielded was too great. He wasn't sure he'd ever be entirely comfortable around her. Nor was he sure he'd ever be able to look at a bird in flight ever again and not see that great, colorful bird emerging from the pages of a book.

"You know I do expect you to dance with me at the Heir's Ball," Diana said. She batted her eyelashes in an exaggerated fashion, and then laughed at her own joke.

Robert smirked. "It would be my honor to dance with you in the opening set."

"How gallant. I accept."

A new fleet of servants entered the hall, bringing in the large platters of the dessert course. They wound through the long tables, dropping delicate plates of iced cake in front of the diners.

"That's my cue. I refuse to miss dessert," Diana said. "Find me tomorrow so we can catch up." She leaned in and kissed his cheek before dashing away.

Back at his table, the other knights had already eaten the portion of cake left for Robert.

"We *should* feel bad," Jordaan said, "but we don't." He made a point of licking the last of the icing off his spoon and then laying it over Robert's plate.

"The fact that you're thinking at all is remarkable, Van Dine."

The night passed far too quickly. When the food and wine finally ran dry, someone brought in a cask of ale, and a round of songs began that lasted into the early morning hours. By the time Robert left the great hall, his steps were erratic and his vision blurry. Although he'd spent plenty of time at Dunlock through the years, with the number of families visiting, he wasn't 100% certain of the best way back to the knight's quarters.

A handful of wrong turns and he found himself in a corridor he recognized, but sadly a long way from his bed. Pale, early morning light crept into the hall from the far end, where a mullioned window faced east. The family suites were in the eastern section of the castle, while most of the guest rooms were in the west and northern wings. He turned to go and tripped over something small and fluffy.

Robert caught himself from falling in time to see what looked like a familiar, towering wig roll down the hallway. Dizzy from all he'd drunk and the hours he'd been awake, he blinked hard. It could have been a child's toy, certainly. A doll of some kind. It couldn't be his Uncle's wig. It couldn't. Whomever lost the wig was probably right around somewhere looking for it. That the wig rolled on with a surprising amount of momentum, reached the end of the hall, and executed a neat turn to disappear out of sight was certainly the result of the ale sitting in his belly.

A wave of nausea washed over him, and the floor pitched forward. He stumbled back the way he'd come, desperate for his bed. He was never going to drink again. Ever.

# Chapter Nineteen
## Kira

**Kira bit her bottom lip as she read through her list again.**

*Item one, discuss with Dunlock Castle Witch.* She put a black strikethrough with a little flourish of the pen. The daffy purple-haired witch may have been unhelpful but a to-do list required items to be marked completed.

*Item two, consult with Mrs. Banes.*

Kira considered crossing that one off the list, but as Xav and Bertie were currently ensconced in the house mother's office, technically that wasn't done.

*Item three, talk to the citizens of Barlow.*

Kira had her doubts about the effectiveness of that one. Barlow was a town of no consequence, a few miles past the reach of the Corlea Palace. Beyond the nice alliteration that it offered, she doubted they'd find out anything from the townspeople. They certainly wouldn't know she was the Beast.

Which was probably a reason to go talk to them. No one in the tiny town would point too pretty for his own good Sir Robert toward her activities on the Royal Route.

She'd noticed him watching her during dinner. He did that thing again where he was looking at her as if he knew something about her. Kira had been annoyed, even from across the room. She might as well send him to Barlow. Let him run around in circles. After all, it wasn't like the heir to the throne could go knocking on doors asking, "By the way, have you noticed any children turning into small to medium-sized hairy monsters?"

If that got back to Isadora, Kira would spend the rest of her natural life sitting in policy meetings with insufferable Sir Roderick and his ilk "learning her duties." As if she wasn't endowed from birth to rule the Known Kingdoms! She was the rightful queen.

Kira tried to think of other items to add to the list, but the answers wouldn't come. Restless, she put down her pen and stretched. She'd come to the orphanage with Xavier and Bertie to restart their investigation since they had nothing else to go on, Sir Robert's suggestion of going to the witch having come to nothing. They'd heard not a word from her yet.

*Good.* Going to a witch was an old and antiquated way to solve a problem.

She, Xav and Bertie could figure it out. If they let her talk to anyone. Xav had been scared to have Kira speak to Mrs. Banes.

"She'd got enough on her plate, let's not throw any more royalty at her," he'd said.

Kira felt silly for coming. If she was going to be left in a sitting room, she might have stayed back at Dunlock Castle and done some poking around there. If nothing else she could keep people away from her trunk.

Kira had no idea how long it took to get information from a peasant woman in charge of magical children, but surely it couldn't take too much longer. It was getting late in the afternoon. Her driver would return to fetch her soon and it was beginning to seem like a wasted day.

For lack of anything else to do she paced the small sitting room. It was exactly thirteen steps from one end to the other. Kira tried shortening her stride, taking small, mincing steps as she did when trapped in her court dresses. Thirteen again across the well-worn carpet. It could have been a coincidence. Perhaps she'd miscounted. She started again, this time from the door to the wide bank of windows. Thirteen steps. She increased her stride, stretching her legs as far as they would go on the return. Thirteen steps. No matter how short or long the steps, or which side of the narrow rectangular room that she began, it was always thirteen steps.

Kira felt a spurt of optimism. She'd solved it. Or at least, she had a real clue. If it was the orphanage itself that was cursed and not the children, then Bertie and Xavier could move the orphanage and the problem was solved.

Kira rushed out of the room, before realizing she had no idea where to find the house mother's office. The hallways of the orphanage were silent and empty, with the exception of a small girl sitting on the steps, head in hands. She was skinny and possessed a great deal of brown, tightly curled hair, but it was the expression on her thin face that drew Kira. She recognized the look of simmering fury about to burst out of the little girl like confetti from a cannon.

Kira said nothing as she sat down next to her. Endless nannies had tried to coax the Princess Royal to talk about her feelings and that always made things worse. Kira had bitten most of them.

The little girl gave her a scathing side-eye as she sat down beside her. Kira wondered if she gave lessons. Even knowing the girl couldn't be more than six, and that she was both fully grown and the future queen, the child's expression was intimidating.

"Do you know where I can find Mrs. Banes?" she asked.

One shoulder lifted, accompanied by a long sigh.

Finally, the girl said, "Have you got any chocolate?"

Kira took a bar of milk chocolate from her bag and tore off the wrapper before handing it over. "I always carry chocolate."

"Why doesn't everyone?" said the girl, as she tore into the treat.

"Mostly because they're idiots," Kira said.

"Are you allowed to say that? Mrs. Banes says it's rude to talk like that."

"I can say whatever I want, I'm going to be the queen."

The girl scoffed. "Mrs. Banes says that's not true. She says everyone has to be nice, even royals."

Kira lifted her shoulder, mimicking the girl's shrug. "I can take the chocolate back."

The girl let out a low, guttural growl.

Kira smiled. "What's your name?"

The girl crossed her arms over her chest. "Why should I tell you?"

"You don't have to," Kira said. "I used to say I was a bear and my name was Great Ginzer the Great. Two greats. On purpose."

"That's a lie," said the girl. "Mrs. Banes says lying is a sin that will get you thrown to the Fairies."

"You seem to like Mrs. Banes."

It was the girl's turn to shrug. "She's okay. She's always, *'Daisy, stop playing with that. Daisy, eat dinner first! Daisy, stop making a mess!'* But she tucks us in at night."

Kira felt a pang in her chest. No one had ever tucked her in at night. "Daisy is a nice name."

Daisy fell quiet and sullen. There was a smear of chocolate on her cheek, and she wiped at it with her hands, making it worse.

"My name is Kira, by the way."

"I know."

They sat in silence for another long moment, before Daisy sighed and said, "Do you have any more chocolate?"

"That was my last one, I'm afraid."

"Are you lying again?"

"Something tells me that lying to you would be a big mistake."

Daisy smirked. A warmth spread through Kira. She smiled back at the girl and put her arm around her. Daisy leaned into her side.

"Why were you all by yourself?" she asked.

Daisy stiffened a bit, but said, half into the bodice of Kira's dress, "I want to go outside. But we're not allowed."

Kira realized that she and Daisy weren't alone. Sir Robert had apparently arrived and was watching from a door a few feet away. Once again, his deep, dark blue eyes bored into her. Kira shook it off.

"Do you know what happens when you go outside, Daisy?"

The girl nodded and snuggled into Kira's side.

"Does it hurt?"

Daisy's head shook back and forth, her great cloud of hair tickling Kira's chin.

"Do you like to change like that?"

Daisy stayed still for a long second before she nodded again.

Well, that was interesting. Kira wondered if it was anything like the surge of power she felt putting on her cloak. She looked at Sir Robert, who seemed to be most interested in what they were saying.

"Can I come back and visit you, Daisy?"

The little girl wrapped her arms around Kira's waist. "Bring chocolate."

She gave the girl a hug and then got up. "I'll see you soon. With chocolate."

Daisy got to her feet and disappeared up the stairs. "That better not be a lie," she called as she ran off.

Sir Robert held out a hand to help Kira down from the step. Kira waved him away. "I can walk by myself."

"You were good with her," he said.

"Bribery never hurts," Kira shrugged.

Sir Robert's gaze didn't leave her face, and Kira flinched. "Is there something you wanted, Sir Robert?"

He shook his head. "No, I wanted to thank you."

Kira's eyebrows contracted. "Thank me for what?"

"You got us a valuable clue."

Kira looked down at her shoes. "Yes, well, I'm glad we know." Why was she sputtering? She was the future queen. She straightened her spine as she pushed past him on the stairs.

"Princess Kira, I'm sorry if I've offended you somehow," he said. "That has never been my intention."

"You think too much of yourself if you think you have any influence on me."

Kira quickened her steps and shut the door to the sitting room behind her.

## Chapter Twenty
### Robert

**The discarded shred of gold paper sat on the stairs, calling out to him like** a beacon in the dark.

*It was a coincidence. It had to be.*

The paper Princess Kira had torn off the chocolate bar she'd shared with Daisy was a thin strip, a few inches long, about as wide as his thumb. She'd torn it from the candy in a quick, practiced motion, as if she had been doing it in the same way for years.

It was about the same size as the piece he'd found in the forest.

Suspicion crept up his back like an unwelcome spirit. *Durrin said he thought it was a woman committing the robberies. But that would mean...* No. No. He refused to think about it. A candy wrapper was a candy wrapper, not proof of the impossible.

A high shriek came from the sitting room. Robert's heart thumped so hard his chest hurt as he yanked open the door.

"Kira, are you alright?"

The princess was walking the length of the room, placing one foot directly in front of the other.

"Thirteen," she said with another shriek.

"What?"

A wide smile broke out over her face. "It's thirteen steps, you have to try it."

"Pardon?"

She laughed, and her blue eyes shone. "I tried it again. it's thirteen steps, no matter which way you go, end to end."

Robert cast a skeptical glance around the room, which was at least doubly long as it was wide.

She pointed to the door. "Start where you are. I know it sounds crazy, but well, the children are turning into small beasts, so all the rules are out the window."

Bottom lip between her teeth, expectant expression, she waited for him to comply. He didn't want to contradict her, but she was the future monarch and she was asking him to test her theory. Robert placed his left foot directly in front of his right, and started carefully from the door to the window. Princess Kira fell into step beside him, so close the ruffled part of her skirt brushed against his leg.

"You see!" she said, as he reached the windows, "thirteen!"

"My lady, I took twenty-seven steps."

"What? No, I must have counted it a dozen times. It's thirteen."

He turned to retrace his steps, careful to line up his boots in the same way as when he'd crossed the room. It was still twenty-seven steps.

"No, I'm telling you I…" she trailed off and then started to count her own end-to-end steps. Her feet were considerably smaller, and she counted over thirty steps aloud.

Her face flushed. "How could I miscount so many times?"

Robert had no answer for that.

Kira muttered something indistinct, and then slumped into one of the sitting room's dozens of spindly chairs.

"My Lady, I'm sure it was a…"

"I thought I found the answer. I thought maybe the building was cursed, and Xavier and Bertie could pick up the children and move."

She put her head in her hands.

Unsure of what to do, Robert took a chair near her. "You tried, that's important."

She shot him an incredulous look. "Do not try to mollify me, Sir Robert, I am not fragile."

"I seem to say all the wrong things around you."

She exhaled. "Well, try to stop."

He wanted to explain to her that he was only trying to follow his training. Being a knight meant being considerate and respectful and always, always adhering to protocol. Except that as he formed the sentence, he knew that those words could easily sound like excuses.

He had no wish to make the situation worse.

"I'll try. Because I would like to be your friend."

For a long moment, she looked at him as if she had never seen him before. Her eyes searched his face, and Robert couldn't stop the blush that pooled in his cheeks at her close scrutiny.

"Oh don't do that. It's really unfair."

"Don't try to be your friend?"

"Don't blush. You're much too handsome already."

Any reply died in his throat. He pushed the bit of gold wrapper farther into the reaches of his pocket. He was being irrational, and clearly it was affecting his judgment.

"Let's go find Bertie and Xav."

She stood and held out her arm. He rose and tucked her hand into the crook of his elbow. He couldn't be sure, but he thought she stood closer than she had before.

They left the sitting room, heading for the office. Xav and Bertie were hunched over their desks. The office's heavy drapes were pulled over the windows, but it wasn't hard to pick out that Xav had his head in both hands. Lord Bertie was alternately chewing on the end of a pen and rapidly tapping it on his desk.

"Maybe we fire Mrs. Banes?"

Xav offered them a wave as they came into the office. "Maybe we do."

"You absolutely cannot do that!" Kira said, aghast.

"Ki, she won't talk to us." Xav sat back in his chair and folded his arms across his chest.

"She won't tell us what's going on with the children. We have to have a House Mother who reports to us."

Kira's grip on Robert's arm tightened. She turned to her cousin. "Bertie. The children love her. She tucks them in at night."

Bertie let go of the pen, as if this were extraordinary news and not something that any parent, real or temporary, would do and agreed with her.

Robert turned to Xav, who was likewise unable to explain what was happening.

"That's not a reason to keep an employee who won't work with us." Xavier's dark eyebrows drew together.

"You don't understand," Bertie said.

"Oh enough with the *You wouldn't understand!* You can't blame everything on that."

"I'm not blaming anything."

"Xav, have you actually spoken to any of the children?" Kira asked. "Because Daisy adores Mrs. Banes. And I'm sure if she's evasive it's because she might think she's protecting them."

"Who?"

"Daisy. One of the children you're currently trying to help?"

Xavier looked slightly ashamed, but said, "Regardless. Rob, back me up here."

"I'm not sure I understand the argument," Robert admitted.

He nearly missed the slight smile that Kira gave him, before she charged back into the fray. "Xav, for all the things Bertie and I had growing up, getting tucked in at night wasn't one of them. Our nursemaids weren't allowed to be that familiar with us. And our parents were busy. Bertie's were gone most of the time, and mine..." she trailed off, leaving an open-ended unknown in the conversation. "I don't imagine anyone but Mrs. Banes has ever done it for these children."

Robert knew in his bones that Kira didn't want his pity, but he couldn't help it. That terrifying little girl, wrapped in a makeshift bearskin and running wild through Corlea Palace made much more sense.

"Well what are we supposed to do then?"

"I'll talk to Mrs. Banes. As I should have from the beginning."

"What makes you think she'll talk to you and not the person who pays her salary?" Xav asked.

Beside him, Kira drew up to her full five-foot height. "I am her sovereign. She has no choice."

Xav laughed, but the sound was hollow. "Have at it."

"Sir Robert will accompany me. You two should head to Barlow and start asking questions."

Robert tried to kill the spurt of hope. She wanted him to accompany her. It wasn't much, but it was something.

"Fine. We'll go tomorrow after the Queen's arrival."

Kira cleared her throat imperiously. "The *Queen Regent* arrives tomorrow."

Albert rolled his eyes, "Honestly, Ki, she's not *that* bad."

"She's on my throne."

\*\*\*\*

Robert and Kira snaked through the orphanage; the long halls punctuated with hazy streams of sunlight from the haphazardly placed windows. A chorus of whispers and giggles accompanied them toward the offices, although the doors on either side were locked tight.

No one answered their knocks on Mrs. Banes's office door.

Robert pressed his ear to the door. "She's in there, I can hear movement."

Kira tried again. "Mrs. Banes, Mrs. Banes, will you open the door please?"

Finally, the door creaked open the barest amount. Only a sliver of her tired face appeared in the gap. "Your Highness, please. You must go."

"Ma'am, I am here to help you."

"There's nothing you can do," Mrs. Banes said. She made to shut the door, but Kira stepped forward, forcing her way inside the office pulling Robert in tow.

The house mother had the pale, ashen look of the overworked. Much of her brown hair frizzed away from the upswept style she wore, and there was a suspicious stain that might have been dried tea on the front of her dress. She dropped a hasty curtsey.

Kira let go of Sir Robert's arm, as if embarrassed that she'd been holding onto him "Mrs. Banes, I know Prince Xavier and Lord Albert tried to talk to you, but I'd like to see if you would speak with me. I promise I'm worried about the children. The only goal is to help them."

Mrs. Banes shook her head. "No, I'm afraid, no."

"I must insist, Mrs. Banes," Kira said. Robert had to admire how she kept her voice so steady, her gaze never leaving Mrs. Banes' lined face.

The House Mother shook her head frantically. "No, the children… it wouldn't be right."

Kira put her hand on Mrs. Bane's arm and the woman startled and drew her arms tight to her chest. "You shouldn't be here," she said. "Princess Kira, you should go."

"Ma'am," Kira said, "I am here to help."

Mrs. Banes blew out a breath. "No. I can't guarantee you're safe here, Your Highness. I know how to care for the children. I've been keeping them safe for their whole lives. But I can't keep you safe. Not Lord Bertie and the prince, either. I've told them they need to go."

It was obvious that the woman was firm in her decision. Robert held his tongue. He wasn't sure they were taking the right tact, trying to speak with the woman, and so it seemed best not to say anything at all. Kira, however, was not deterred.

"Please," Kira said. "I spoke with Daisy, and she mentioned some things that I think might be significant to understanding what's happening."

Mrs. Banes's voice ticked up to a more imperious tone that suggested she was an efficient wrangler of children - beast or royal. "No. This is Fairie magic and I will not discuss it," she said. She stepped forward, forcing Kira and Robert to step back out of the doorway. As soon as they were over the threshold the door was shut in their faces.

"Well, that was a disaster," Kira admitted.

Robert chose his words carefully. "I think we've already learned what we're going to get from Mrs. Banes."

"She thinks it's Fairie magic."

He nodded.

"Well, do we go find a Fairie and ask them? It's not like they make themselves known."

"We can try," he said. "There is a Fairie chapel not far from here. We can bring an offering."

The look on Kira's face was skeptical, as if she were imagining something improbable. Robert's own family wasn't devout, but he'd spent enough time in Fairie chapels. Some good could come of it, if he could convince her. "It's worth a shot," he said. "Maybe one of the Fairies will be listening."

Kira let out a huff, and drew back her shoulders as if she needed courage. "Fine. I'll find a way to get away from the Queen Regent, and we can go tomorrow."

*Melissa Constantine*

## Chapter Twenty-One
### Bertie

**Bertie had never been much of a rider, but Xav had insisted that the fastest** way to reach Barlow was on horseback. However, because of his lack of equestrian skills Bertie had been given a slow, plodding animal by the Dunlock stables, which meant that they didn't reach town until well after midday. Barlow was situated midway between Corlea Palace and the Dunlock border. It was a place of low, timbered buildings all squeezed in together along one cobbled street. It was quaint but that was about all.

"Not much here," he said, to have something to say. Xav had gone sullen at their lack of progress. Sadly no amount of amusing chatter on the road had changed that.

The north and south sides of the road met at a fountain. The figure in the center was a man holding a large knife high over his head, and some kind of cloth in his other hand. Whoever he was, he was awfully proud of himself.

They handed their horses off at the blacksmith's shop, and after getting directions, headed to the town lending library.

The interior of the Barlow Free Library was much the same as the street that housed it. It was a small room with a high ceiling crisscrossed with heavy dark beams. There were a few dozen shelves bursting with books, and one main desk where an elderly librarian in thick spectacles sat reading.

Xav crossed toward him, steps full of purpose, but before he could speak, the librarian cleared his throat and spit into a bin hidden somewhere at his feet.

"Sir, we've come looking for…"

The librarian coughed, holding up a hand to stop Xav from speaking.

"How about you point?" Bertie said. "Information on the Beast of Barlow."

The coughing spasm stopped, and the man's eyes narrowed. "You must be from out of town."

"Amazing you sussed that out in a town this size."

Xav elbowed him gently in the ribs to get him to shut up before addressing the librarian again. "I'm Prince Xavier of Dunlock."

Unimpressed, the librarian sniffed, and picked up his book again. "Barlow is in Corlea, not Dunlock."

"Well, I'm from here," Bertie said. "Lord Albert Vineland, at your service." For good measure Bertie stuck out his hand.

The librarian eyed it, but declined to shake. "Haven't much use for you either. Royals aren't much welcome in Barlow."

Frustrated, Xav slapped his hand against the desk, causing the librarian's tea to slosh, and his book to absorb the liquid. "We need information on the Beast."

"Don't have any," the librarian said sharply, moving to shake the water out of his book.

"This is Barlow, isn't it?"

The elderly man nodded. "It is."

"The town known for the Beast of Barlow?"

Again, a nod, this one infuriatingly more condescending the last. "Used to be."

Xav gave up, gesturing for Bertie to take over the questioning. As they weren't going to get anywhere with the librarian, Bertie decided to take another tactic.

"Any place around here to get a pint?"

Xav scowled at him, but Bertie ignored it. If they were here, they might as well eat, have a drink, and eavesdrop on the locals to see what they might know.

"Past the Fountain. The Hare and Hyde."

Bertie took a gold coin from his pocket and slid it across the desk to the librarian. "To replace your book."

"This man has information we need!" Xav said.

"No, he doesn't. He told us so. Let's go get a drink."

He took Xav by the hand, practically pulling him out of the library. In the seven steps it took them to be outside again, Xav had worked himself up with a head of steam.

"How dare he! I am a prince of the realm."

Bertie gritted his back teeth, even as he maintained a neutral face for his boyfriend's sake. Xav had led a life of privilege. And not that Bertie hadn't, but his early childhood in the Unknown Kingdoms had taught him one crucial lesson.

Not everyone loved royalty like they loved themselves.

In the Unknown Kingdoms, where his father's title as Prince of Corlea meant absolutely nothing, he'd seen it. His parents, despite being the brother and sister-in-law of the King of the nearest continent, had been shut out of the social whirl, which was mainly made up of rich merchants and those humans adjacent to the Fairie Courts. The Unknown Kingdoms had no royal families and didn't care to treat any who showed up as anything special.

His parents had been livid, and yet they spent years chasing invitations. Bertie had been too young to articulate it then, but if he could go back in time he'd have told him the same thing he now found himself telling Prince Xavier of Dunlock.

"It's not worth getting upset."

"Are you kidding me? Have you forgotten what we're doing here? We're trying to help children and protect the kingdom from a dangerous predator. And that old fool can't be bothered to even look me in the eye and answer a simple question?"

Which, Bertie reckoned, was about how his parents might have reacted. Not that they would be advocating for anyone but themselves, but he imagined that their indignation would be as palpable.

"This is a small town. It's not on the Royal Route, so it's unlikely that any of the noble families ever come here. And people have free will, they don't have to like us because we were born with titles."

Reasoning didn't help. Xav was offended and determined to be mad. "I know that."

"Okay then, let's go to the pub and get a drink."

"Bertie, we don't have time."

"Well what do you suggest we do? I'm saying, let's go to the pub and regroup."

"Are you even taking this seriously?"

Xav let out a bit of a growl, and started walking back to the blacksmith's hut, forcing Bertie to jog after him.

"Hey, where are you going?"

"I'll ask anyone I see," Xav said, charging ahead.

"What do you think I'm saying we do?"

"The same thing you do every damn day — give up and have a cup of tea."

Bertie stopped chasing him. It wasn't their first fight. It probably wouldn't be their last, but he'd be damned if he'd be his parents, shouting down the rafters for any and all to see. He turned and headed back toward the Hare and Hyde.

That Xav continued on in the opposite direction stung a little more than he would like to admit. They were supposed to be a happy couple. Happy couples did not fight in the middle of dinky little towns with suspicious-looking men standing in fountains.

The pub was roughly the same dimensions as the library, a large open room with a high ceiling. It was as if the builder had found one basic set of architectural plans and said enough was enough. Really, it was remarkably efficient. Presumably the bath rooms would all be in the same place, no hunting when the need was urgent.

The pub's open space was ringed with high booth tables with plush leather seats. Bertie signaled to the barmaid before dropping down in an unoccupied one.

She brought over a menu board, eying him as if he had grown an extra head on his shoulder. "You're not from here."

"No, but how could I resist such a welcoming town," he said, taking the small menu, and passing it back almost immediately. "A pint of ale, and whatever's hot."

She tucked the menu in her apron pocket, but didn't move back to the bar. She was a plain woman perhaps a few years older than himself. Her face was long and narrow, and her dull brown hair was pulled back tightly, making an unfortunate showcase of her ears. "What brings you here?"

"You wouldn't believe me if I told you."

"Try me."

"Runaway orphans. A witch with purple hair. And the Beast of Barlow."

The barmaid laughed. "There's no such thing as the Beast of Barlow. It's a myth."

"A myth named after this town."

She shrugged. "Take a look at that fountain out in the square. That's Jedson Barlow, the founder of the town. He was supposed to have killed some kind of animal and taken its coat. Claimed he was keeping everyone safe because he was the only one who could beat the big scary thing in the woods. Jump up about 50 years and when he's dying, he admits there was never any such thing. The fur he used to parade around was a fake."

Bertie wished she'd brought him that ale already, because he could use a drink. He sagged back into the leather seat. "So there was never any Beast?"

She shook her head. "Not even a funny-looking rabbit."

"Good to know."

The barmaid went to put it in his order. He'd made up his mind to get up and find Xav when he came into the pub.

He held out a weedy-looking red flower. "I'm an ass, I'm sorry."

Bertie made no objection when Xav slid into the booth. He sniffed the flower, only to reel back at the strong stench. "What kind of flower is that?" he said, dropping the bloom.

"No idea. It was all I could find."

"I guess it's the thought that counts."

Xav gestured to the barmaid for an ale. "The blacksmith wasn't in the mood for questions."

Bertie repeated what he'd learned as they drank. "It looks like this place is a dead end."

"There's got to be something."

But there wasn't. When the barmaid brought them bowls of beef stew, she picked up Bertie's discarded red flower, tucking it behind her ear. "These ward off bad luck."

Bertie scoffed. "Is it because bad luck has a sense of smell?"

"Maybe so," she said, placing their bill on the table.

Bertie took his last chance to ask her about the Beast. "Do you know what happened to Jedson Barlow's old Beast pelt?"

She shook her head. "Can't say for sure. It's not in this town that I know. Rumors say it was seized by the crown. Or thrown in the bin, take your pick. Enjoy your meals."

Xav tucked into his stew like he hadn't eaten in days. "I really wanted to find out what was going on."

"I know," Bertie said, picking at the contents of his own bowl.

"We have to find out what's happening to the children."

Bertie bit his lip to keep from making a sarcastic remark. Obviously. It was the whole reason he'd ridden that flea-infested animal all the way to Barlow. "We should tell your parents before they find out."

Xav shook his head. "No. My father wants me to prove I'm responsible enough to take over Dunlock one day, and I told him that the orphanage was my way to show him that. I can't go to him after three months and admit I failed."

"We haven't failed. Clearly there's something bigger than us."

"Which we have to solve."

"How are they going to react if they find out we've been keeping this kind of a secret? What if they freak out?"

Xav was careful with his reply. "My parents aren't like yours. They won't do that."

Bertie grimaced. "So if that's not what you're worried about, what then? We're talking about magic. That's not forgetting to pay the candlemaker for this month's delivery."

There were times when Bertie forgot how stubborn Xav could be. He sighed, giving up on his stew all together. "What if this Caris Mourne person tells them?"

"Rob said all she did was talk nonsense about love potions. I doubt she'll leave the tower much while she's here."

"So what do we do? What's our next move?"

Xav pulled Bertie's discarded bowl toward him, wolfing down what remained. He didn't know what they should do next, but he acknowledged they weren't going to find it in Barlow.

# CHAPTER TWENTY-TWO
## Kira

***If given the option to eat glass or welcome her stepmother to Dunlock*** Castle, Kira would have gladly chosen the glass. But refusal to acknowledge the arrival of the Queen Regent would have embarrassed Prince Brandon and Princess Margo. Kira had always liked them. She had no wish to start gossip that could potentially hurt them. And so she dressed in one of her court dresses, as was expected of her, too-tight corset, cape, and all. The dress she'd brought with her for this occasion was at least slightly more comfortable than any of her others. It was made of a soft blue organza, complemented with bright blue ribbons that formed a border of cranes under the high waist and along the sweeping hem.

Because of the sheer size of Isadora's traveling party, only Kira, Prince Brandon and Princess Margo waited in the courtyard. The servants, except for those that would help unload the Queen Regent's carriages, were lined up behind the Herald on the ramparts. Xavier, Bertie, and all of the rest of the Moorelow children waited inside. Onlookers from the royal families already in Dunlock sat in window seats, or those unlucky enough not to be staying in the castle, lined the road outside the gates.

A series of triumphant horn blasts was followed by the Herald's announcement that the Queen Regent's party had been spotted on the road. Kira shifted her weight to her right foot. She'd been balancing on her left, because her shoe pinched her toes. She'd meant to have her maid send them to a cobbler for resizing, but her activities as the Beast had swallowed up a considerable amount of her time.

"Are you all right, Your Highness?" Princess Margo asked in a low voice.

"I'm fine, I seem to have worn the wrong shoes."

Princess Margo nodded, as if this were understandable. "I have my maid stuff the toes with paper to keep mine stretched out. My feet have not yet recovered from having my little Jenny."

"Oh, I'm so sorry," Kira said, trying to imagine what the Princess meant. What happened to a woman's feet in childbirth? Wasn't it enough that their midsections expanded?

Princess Margo smiled. "Don't tell my other children, who I love with all my heart, but right now Jenny is my favorite. She never fights with her siblings or tells me she's too busy for a good snuggle."

Kira was grateful for the horns blowing once again, because she had no idea how to respond.

"The Queen Regent approaches."

The gates were opened, and the first of the outriders, two dozen knights in sky blue tunics rode into the courtyard. They were followed by the first carriage, a pink and blue lacquered carriage that looked suspiciously like Sir Roderick's carriage. The members of the Kingdom Council were, of course, invited to attend the Festival, but as far as Kira knew, usually they didn't attend.

The carriage came to a halt, and Sir Roderick climbed out, as well as three other councilors Kira recognized, Madame Jenzi, Sir Fischer and Sir Torrance.

"Excellent," Prince Brandon said, as the men came up from their bows, and Madame Jenzi her rusty curtsey. "I trust the journey was comfortable."

The Councilors muttered their answers, looking around in awe at the scale of Dunlock Castle.

"We are pleased to have you," Princess Margo said. "If you would proceed inside. Our majordomo will show you all to your rooms."

While they had been greeting the Kingdom Council, another flank of outriders had come in, followed by the second and third carriages, some of the royals who'd been savvy enough to wait at the Palace until the Queen

Regent made her procession. Finally, the final flank of outriders, the knights who'd come to Corlea from the most prominent and the wealthiest houses, entered in a fluted formation, meant to look like the shape of a Corlea Crane from above.

"The Queen Regent arrives," said the Herald, as the horns played a jaunty tune, accompanied by drummers and flutes.

The Corlea ceremonial carriage rolled into the courtyard, resplendent in rose gold. Kira hadn't seen it since her mother's funeral. And then, pressed against the back wall, sobbing uncontrollably, trying to avoid her father's fit, she had no time to notice the details. All around the exterior, crisscrossed crane flowers molded in relief caught the light. The standard of Corlea rippled in the light wind from the front post. Footmen in their powdery pink and blue livery jumped down from their perches. One of them placed a set of gold steps on the ground, while the other opened the door and held his hand out to Isadora.

She wore black, of course. Not only because she was in mourning for her late husband, but because it was the color that made her look the most regal. Isadora may only have been only a duchess prior to her marriage to Kira's father, but she knew exactly how to dress to make herself look born for the throne. There was no adornment on her dress. She didn't need it. The dress was perfectly cut to her proportions, and the material had a matte sheen that said it was both costly and beautiful, even folded on the bolt. On her head Isadora wore the silver Regent's crown which looked exactly right on her.

Kira felt foolish in her flowered dress. Looking at her stepmother, her own attire seemed both dowdy and too young. Whereas it had seemed perfect when the maid dressed her, Kira could only think of it as the kind of gaudy thing made for an ugly child whose parents paid too much in hopes of distracting from her looks.

"Her Royal Highness, the Queen Regent, Isadora Cross-Vineland of Corlea and High Duchess of Zinnj."

The applause, from both inside and outside the gate, was thunderous. Kira tried to recall if the welcome she had received was anywhere near as loud. Even if so, it was certainly not as sustained. The royals seemed to love Isadora. Even the servants were cheering for her.

Did every one of them wish she were the Queen and not the Regent? Did they care if Kira ever got to take the throne that was rightfully hers?

Isadora approached, and Kira curtsied as low as her dress would allow. Prince Brandon followed her with his bow and Princess Margo curtsied. And then, Princess Margo bound forward and caught Isadora in a crushing hug.

"Oh, Dory, I've missed you," Princess Margo said.

"And I you," Isadora said.

"I can't believe you've been not two hours away all this time, and we haven't had one day together."

Kira felt a spurt of acid in her stomach crawl into her throat, unsure of what exactly was going on. Isadora was friends with Princess Margo? Since when?

The answer came soon enough, as Prince Brandon leaned close to Kira's ear and whispered. "They went to finishing school together. Thick as thieves when they were girls."

Isadora's only guests at the wedding had been her two sons, and a stray uncle. A handful of members of the Kingdom Council had been her father's only witnesses. Kira had been hiding in a closet.

"You always seem to be having babies when I can spare a moment." Isadora said with a smile.

Since when did Isadora actually smile? Sure, she made that pitying, serene smile at Kira all the time, but actual joy? That wasn't an expression Kira had seen before.

The four of them proceeded into the castle, with Princess Margo's arm wrapped firmly around Isadora. Like Kira had done, she went through the line of servants, greeting them all and earning their starstruck looks in return. She greeted the Moorelow children like a beloved aunt, seeming to know each of them by name. She spent considerable time pinching Xavier's cheeks and telling him he was, "Not so big he wasn't still her favorite Fairie godchild." When she moved on to bouncing baby Jenny, and placing kisses on her downy head, Kira pulled Xavier aside.

"You know her? How could you not tell me?"

"You don't exactly have perspective," Xavier said.

Kira fumed. Xavier rolled his eyes and said, "It would be a good time to start." He took both her and Bertie by the hand, and led them to one of the parlors off the main hall. The room had been used as a staging area for the meals in the great hall for the past two days. All around the furniture were stacks of plates, bowls, soup tureens and glassware. Dozens of tablecloths hung over the back of the chairs, and at least three folding tables were propped in front of the windows.

Xav sat on a plush settee, and Bertie leaned against one wall. but Kira was too agitated to sit still. She paced as much as her constricting dress would allow.

"Ki, are you going to wear a hole in the carpet, or can Xav and I tell you what we learned in Barlow?" Bertie asked.

"What could you have possibly learned in Barlow?" she said, turning carefully to walk back to the other side of the room.

"Well for one thing, the Beast of Barlow is 100% a made-up story."

"Obviously." Kira said.

"Not, just a story," Xav said. "The town of Barlow was founded by a guy who claimed to have killed a mythical creature and stolen its skin. Apparently, though, when he was dying, he recanted the whole story. There's never been a Beast. Ever."

Except for the fact that the magical skin of the Beast of Barlow was locked in her traveling trunk. "So basically, we're back at square one. I hate to say this but we're not very good at solving mysteries."

Kira continued her pacing. There was a connection she wasn't making. She wasn't the first person to show up in costume as the fearsome monster. There were sightings and bouts of hysteria about the appearance of the Beast all the time. It's why the costume was so effective.

Kira watched as Xav took a dark red flower from his pocket, absently twirling the stem between his fingers. If it was a crane she couldn't place where it had come from. And it seemed to give off a strong, sulfur smell. "What is that?"

Bertie shook his head. He'd picked up a soup ladle from one of the tables and was tapping it against his palm. "Nothing. In Barlow they're planted for luck."

"It smells awful. What kind of luck would that bring?"

"Nothing as far as I can tell," Bertie said.

Kira took the flower from Xav. A current, as if she'd touched a small bolt of lightning, traveled from her hand up her arm. She hissed in pain, and dropped it on the carpet.

Bertie picked it up. "It doesn't smell that bad." he

"No, it but it stings," Kira said.

"It's a flower," Xav said.

Kira picked up the bloom again. No current this time, not even a little buzz. Maybe she'd built-up static from pacing? Feeling foolish, Kira pushed that thought aside. Dwelling on ugly red flowers wasn't going to help. She went back to a safer topic. "And neither of you has heard from the witch?"

Xav took a stray soup ladle from Bertie before he could smack it against his palm and tucked it back into a large collection of serving spoons. Bertie rolled his eyes and picked up a spatula, slapping it lightly against his leg. "No. "

"And Sir Robert hasn't either?"

Xav and Bertie cracked identical, maniacal smiles. "You tell us," Bertie said. "You've spent more time with him than we have."

"I have not."

Bertie dropped the spatula back into the utensil jar. "Kira, seriously, you need to relax. We're teasing."

Kira blew out a breath, embarrassed at how easily she was provoked. "Can we focus, please? Robert has suggested we ask the Fairies, but I'm…."

Bertie wiggled his eyebrows. "Oh, did *Robert* suggest that? What else did *Robert* say?"

Kira rolled her eyes. "Must you do that? Do you have to make it weird?"

He feigned innocence. "What did I say?"

Disgusted, Kira resumed pacing. "If I can get away from the Queen Regent for a few hours, he and I will go to the Fairie chapel. Apparently you leave an offering and they'll tell you what you want to know."

Bertie gasped. "Why Kira Sabrina Stephanie, what a rendezvous you've planned."

Kira stared hard at her cousin. "Do you want my help or not?"

Bertie wiggled his eyebrows.

"I am the heir to the throne. I do not make "rendezvous" and if you don't shut up when I'm queen I will make you Earl of the Salt Mines. Pale redheads don't fare well in the desert."

"Wow," Xav said. "She's mean when you tease her."

Bertie nodded. "And she bites."

## Chapter Twenty-Three
### Kira

***Isadora had convened a meeting with the present members of the Kingdom*** Council in one of Dunlock's larger drawing rooms. A heavy wooden table big enough to seat a few dozen had been dropped in the center of the room, while the overstuffed settees and armchairs pushed to the sides. Flags from all of the regions had been tacked to the beams overhead, from the black and teal banner of Tull to the plain red of Rhymes.

Isadora had insisted Kira attend, because they would be speaking about the order of events at the Festival and how they wanted to proceed with the proposed hunt for the Beast of Barlow. But the four counselors in attendance were treating it as an extension of their usual meeting.

And that meant they spent most of the first hour talking about trash removal. Rubbish was apparently a subject that required careful thought, deliberation, and at times, Sir Roderick snoring quite loudly.

Kira had taken to biting down on her thumbnail to keep herself awake. She'd spent the first part of the meeting on tenterhooks, trying to figure out both what she could say to protect the children at Bertie's orphanage, and get time away to visit the Fairie chapel with Robert. All of it wasted energy in the face of so much refuse.

"Spire should obviously pay for their own services," Sir Torrance said. "Their Beech Crane crops bring in more money than all of the southern region crops combined."

He was vehemently berated by Madame Jenzi concerning the Corlea Compact, which stated that in exchange for sovereignty over the Known Kingdoms, all essential services were at the cost of the crown.

"Who is to say what is essential?" Sir Roderick said. He sat back in his chair with a little smile on his face, as if this question were somehow profound.

Kira would have to wear gloves for eternity. Her nails would never recover.

"Ladies, gentleman," Isadora said at long last, "As much as I appreciate the attention to procedure in discussing our old business, I would ask that we move on to the topic which prompted this meeting."

There was a murmur of discontent at the interruption. Sir Roderick cleared his throat. "Very good, Your Highness. I motion that we move onto the matter of the Beast of Barlow."

"Seconded," said Sir Fischer.

"So it be," said Sir Torrance, eager to move on after his chastisement at the hands of Madame Jenzi.

"If I may?" Isadora asked, and was then granted the floor to discuss her plans. She stood. Although she had changed from her traveling dress, she wore an equally long, sleek black dress that made her look taller and more elegant than Kira could ever hope to be.

Not that it mattered. In the woods she was a giant.

"As many of you know, I have arranged with Prince Brandon to address the problem of the Beast with an expediency which we might not have had with a celebration farther away. Some of the best hunters and most capable knights in the Known Kingdoms are in attendance. As we agreed upon, a hunt will take place the day after tomorrow."

"Indeed," Sir Roderick said with a dismissive wave of his hand. "I fail to see why we need to discuss it. Arrangements have already been made."

Isadora nodded serenely. "But we have yet to agree on a prize. I believe given the considerable threat posed by the Beast — and the limited time we have — a substantial reward must be offered."

"What kind of prize, Your Highness?" Kira asked. She had a vague vision of bringing back the cloak and claiming any prize for herself.

Isadora caught Kira's eye, with an almost regretful look. The hair on the back of Kira's neck stood up. For a wild heartbeat, she would have sworn Isadora was about to say, "The princess's hand in marriage," or something equally archaic. Instead, the Queen Regent looked up and said, "After expenses, and understanding that the workers must be paid, all profits from the year's Corlea Crane harvest."

Kira couldn't help but suck in a breath. The sum was staggering. Although the region grew several varieties, the Corlea Crane only grew within a few thousand yards of the Palace. Its rarity, combined with its many uses, made the flowers worth ten times the average harvest. A profit like that going to an individual was life-changing.

The Council went into an uproar.

"You'll bankrupt the kingdom!" Madame Jenzi said.

"Ridiculous!" said Sir Roderick.

Sir Torrance chose the more dramatic, "Suicide!" for his exclamation.

But Isadora hadn't come unprepared. She had numbers at the ready. "Corlea has enough in the treasury to cover all of our expenses for three years, provided we begin none of the infrastructure projects we'd hoped to begin. I propose that we postpone everything until we secure next year's profits. That way we keep a comfortable cushion in the vaults."

"Unacceptable," said Sir Torrance. "King Callum put off road improvements for 15 years. When you were appointed Regent it was with the understanding that this would no longer continue."

*Fifteen years?* How could her father have put off something so important for so long? That had to be a mistake.

"I am eager to make improvements to our roads, and to modernize our aqueducts, and all of the other projects that this esteemed body means to accomplish. But the threat of the Beast, whoever they are, is real. We face a greater risk if we begin infrastructure projects that then come under attack. There have been at least a dozen robberies."

No, that wasn't right. She'd only been the Beast for a few weeks. Her royal duties would never have allowed her to rob that many so fast. She did a silent tally, mentally cataloging the small personal items she'd taken along with the gold. Signet rings, pocket watches. The star-shaped eyeglasses. Little things kept safely in her trunk, away from any prying eyes.

But no, she couldn't have hit twelve carriages, that was impossible. And what made anyone believe that robberies would morph into the Beast destroying her own kingdom?

Isadora continued, calm as ever. "The prize money may be extreme, but Corlea can afford it in the short term. What we cannot afford is to wait, and let the threat from this creature grow."

There was a heavy silence in the room. All four councilors stirred in their seats, clearly uncomfortable. Sir Roderick stood and made a half-hearted motion to vote, but Madame Jenzi put a stop to it. She was an older woman with iron-gray hair and a dark complexion. She fixed Kira in her sights as she spoke.

"I must say my piece. Too long has this Council struggled in the face of royal neglect. King Callum failed Corlea and all of the Known Kingdoms in every way. We have seen the ruin and destruction of which you speak. By putting off improvements he failed his land and his people. You are now asking the Council to consider another year of that neglect. While the threat posed by the Beast of Barlow is extreme, I cannot agree to a plan that does not also address the systemic maleficence of the past. If this Council agrees to fund the hunt in this extreme manner, we demand that a plan be drawn up that would forbid any additional delays to our much-needed projects."

The rebuke was a gut check. Her father was seen as a failure? He'd been sick, but what Madame Jenzi was saying went far beyond the time he'd been ill. Kira felt foolish not to have known that. But then again, when had she seen her parents? They were gone so much. And after her mother died, she'd seen her father even less than before. Until his wedding to Isadora, she hadn't seen him more than in passing for close to six months.

There was some additional talk between the Councilors, as they voted to finalize a plan for the prize hunt, and disallow any further delays of the infrastructure projects.

Once it was done and signed, Isadora dismissed them and the four members departed.

"I'm sorry you had to hear that, Kira." Isadora gathered up the various papers she had brought to press her case.

Kira searched her face for some sign of truth. Did she really believe that the man she married was unworthy, that he'd shirked his duties as the council members suggested? Her face gave away nothing.

"Is it true?"

Isadora sighed. "I'm afraid it is, yes."

"Then tell me why the Council didn't make a rule about it when my parents were alive?"

"Bureaucracy and power are strange bedfellows. With your father's moods and his temper they were often cowed. I believe the Council feels emboldened to act now because you are young and have not yet assumed the throne."

Shame flooded into her chest. Her family had ruled Corlea for a thousand years. The Vineland line went back to the founding of the Known Kingdoms. Kira had been taught that her ancestors had seen the continent through all of its trials. The Vineland rulers loved their land, respected their people and brought peace. That was supposed to be her legacy. But her father was seen as a villain.

And what was she doing? Stealing the money from their pockets? Being the Beast made her feel powerful at a time when she had no power. Did that make her as bad or worse than her father?

"If my father was such a monster, why did you marry him?"

Isadora's dark eyes closed momentarily. Her expression went to pity, and Kira felt a fresh spurt of anger to mingle with the shame.

"Let us not pretend." She moved toward Kira, her hand extended. Kira stepped back, pulling her arms to her chest.

The Queen Regent drew back. Her words took on a new sharpness. "You know why I married your father. There was one reason, and one reason alone, and she is standing in front of me."

"Because you saw an opportunity to take what is mine."

Isadora got to her feet. "We are done here. I will see you at dinner."

"I will not be here," Kira snapped.

"You will."

"Go to the Fairies." She got as far as the door when Isadora's voice, calm and imperious, stopped her.

"Running away solves nothing, Kira. A princess will get her way with diplomacy, not impetuousness."

The mix of anger and embarrassment that roiled through Kira threatened to erupt. She fought to keep still; her back teeth clamped together with enough pressure to break her jaw. She wouldn't be surprised if sparks came shooting out of her fingers. "I'm not running away. I have plans. With a... friend."

She wasn't sure Robert was a friend, but if she couldn't explain it to herself, she wasn't going to try and say anything to her imperious stepmother.

Isadora, ever unruffled, continued. "Fine, but you will be in attendance for all of the other events of the Festival."

She nodded, with no words for a parting shot left.

## Chapter Twenty-Four
### Robert

**Kira didn't speak as they ambled their horses away from the castle.** A footman in the powder blue livery of Corlea trailed behind them and was likewise silent. Robert tried not to take it personally. He would have liked to talk about the plan for when they reached the little chapel in the woods, but whenever he brought his horse alongside hers, she urged her butterscotch pony forward, out of step with him.

It was a bright blue-sky day. No clouds obscured the sun, and with only the barest breeze to guide them. All along the road, they pass evidence of the crowds from the Queen Regent's arrival, discarded banners, folding chairs left behind, and empty flagons of ale tossed aside. The celebration had gone from the gates of the castle and at least a mile down the road. It had obviously been a merry party. Every now and then, a few people lingered, but whether they were picking over the remains or clearing out the mess, it was hard to say. A few of them spotted the Princess and waved, receiving an acknowledging incline of her head or a small wave from Kira in return, but most were too busy to glance up as they passed.

It was when they reached the forest that she slowed down enough for Robert to ride next to her. The trees created a low canopy. Branches from either side swept down to less than the height of a man in places, forcing them to lean into their horse's necks to pass. Kira seemed to be watching the forest for something, and Robert found himself doing the same. There was no evidence of the Beast being anywhere on the section of the Royal Route between Corlea and Dunlock, but that didn't mean it was advisable to let their guard down.

"The roads are bad here," she said, as they turned from the main route to a road that would take them directly to the chapel.

It was true. The path forward was marked with puddles from a weeks-ago rain, the rest of the way pitted with uneven ground and mud the consistency of tar.

"Not many people come down this way anymore. The chapels aren't as popular anymore."

He didn't need to tell her why. When Queen Clara had ordered the Fairie chapel on the Palace grounds burned, Fairie worship had fallen out of favor. Some still clung to the old ways, but it seemed to be less and less every year.

"This road goes to the town of Venter, doesn't it?" she asked.

It did.

"Then it should have been fixed. The citizens of even the smallest towns deserve easy passage." She guided her pony around a particularly large puddle, and Robert followed.

It didn't take them long to reach the Fairie chapel, which was tucked in a glen beyond the road. It was a small stone building, ringed by white columns, with three black doors across the front. Robert did his best to explain the purpose. While all three entered into the same room, the right would be used if their offering was for the Light Fairies, and the one of the left for the Dark Fairies. If their business might be for either, they'd enter through the center door.

"How would we know?"

"I guess people learn the different Fairies when they're young."

Kira colored at the gap in her education. "What do we do once we're inside?"

"Usually you first want to announce why you've come. Then you place whatever offering you have with the portrait of the Fairie who draws your eye. And if you can't decide, there's a central offering plate."

Kira neatly dismounted her pony, handed off the reins to her footman and went to stand in front of the center door. She hesitated. "Do I knock?"

"Three times."

She knocked three times in three different places on the door, and it swung open for her. Without having to be told, she curtsied low, as if an unseen Fairie might be watching.

The interior of the chapel was divided into three parts. A clever arrangement of sky tubes flooded one half of the chapel with sun, the beams catching on the golden frames of the Light Fairie portraits crowding the walls. On the opposite side of the chapel, the portraits were framed in obsidian and hung in the same fashion. On the altar in the center was the offering plate, evenly split between the light and the dark. It stood on an ornate gold and black pedestal, and was brimming with previous offerings, cigars, small bottles of liquor, child's toys, piles of sweets wrapped in colorful foil, and crane flowers gone dry and brittle.

Robert made his own bow, and took a gold coin from his pocket for the offering. Ahead of him, Kira stood to the left. In the dark half of the chapel, the emerald green riding outfit she'd worn took on a dark sheen, and her gold hair turned a shade of light brown.

"We've come with a petition," she said. She approached the altar and took her offering from the small case at her hip. She dropped three gold-wrapped chocolate bars on the plate, and then took out another for herself.

Robert did his best to ignore the uneasy feeling he got watching her peel off the wrapper in one narrow strip.

"If any Fairie is inclined to listen, we need information," she said.

Birdsong floated into the chapel, and the gentle noise of the horses waiting outside, but there was otherwise no answer. Kira took a visible breath, bit into her chocolate bar, swallowed hastily and then said, "We need to know if there is Fairie magic in place at the Dunlock Charity Orphanage."

Robert could have sworn he heard the far-away sound of gentle bells, but Kira didn't seem to notice.

"The house mother is terrified and the children, well, they're not themselves."

She moved around the chapel, taking in hundreds of portraits. The Fairies had been captured in profile to showcase the high points of their ears.

They varied in hair color and skin tone, but all of them, light and dark, had the same mischievous twinkle in their eye.

"She looks like she accuses the butcher of putting his thumb on the scale," Kira said, pointing to a severe gray-haired Fairie in a dark frame.

"Fairies don't eat," he said gently.

Kira shrugged. "Still," she said, with her own mischievous twinkle in her eyes. She moved to another grouping of portraits close to the altar, making up little stories.

"That one has a collection of human teeth." She pointed to a portrait of a particularly fierce looking Fairie. The points of their ears were so high their depiction touched the edge of the frame. Of another, with smaller ears but a shock of short, neon-yellow hair, she said, "This is Boris. He makes teapot mufflers."

Random portraits caught her eye and she gave them names and occupations, and hobbies such as, "Collects miniature spoons," and "raises baby goats, all of whom are called Rebecca."

Robert knew it was wrong, but he couldn't help but laugh. Perhaps because Kira had not grown up with Fairie worship, she had no reverence for the chapel. Robert had been taught that Fairie chapels were meant to be solemn spaces, but he thought he preferred Kira's method.

"What do you think of that one?" The picture she was looking at was of a Fairie with a full set of pointed teeth displayed. It was the only portrait in the chapel not done in profile.

"I think you'd better leave him his own chocolate."

Laughter bubbled up from within her, and Robert felt as if he'd won something. Whatever curse might fall on them for laughing in this place would be worth it.

Kira took another chocolate bar from her bag and balanced it on the edge of the grinning Fairie portrait. "Mr. Fang, I offer you the finest chocolate I've ever had. I have it shipped from Tull. If you would be so inclined, remove any spells from my cousin's orphans."

*It was a coincidence. Anyone can have chocolate shipped from a region hundreds of miles away.*

They waited without speaking for a few more minutes, but nothing seemed to be happening. The Fairies, even if they were present, did not always work quickly. They had made their petition and left their offerings. There was nothing left to do but go back to Dunlock. Robert followed Kira out of the chapel. They were within inches of the chapel doors when the center door slammed shut with a vicious bang.

"Let's hope that's not our answer."

Robert was struck momentarily mute. In the sunlight, Kira gleamed. Her laughter made her normally beautiful face so lovely that had the option been presented, he'd have gladly spent any money he'd ever made to get an artist to capture it.

A small pain in his wrist snapped him out of the reverie. He pulled back his glove, to see the angry mark, blood piercing the surface as red as when it was new.

"Something wrong, Sir Robert?" Kira asked, as the footman assisted her up into the saddle.

*"It's a claim," Caris Mourne had said.* Robert shook off a shiver.

"An old injury," he said. "It's nothing."

"Oh you're not going to be one of those old knights who spends all day in the tavern complaining about his old jousting wounds, are you?"

"Jousting is illegal. This was a different kind of injury." Robert hoisted himself into Amzi's saddle, drawing alongside her.

"Well what was it? Battle wound? Training mishap?"

"Bear attack," he said. He waited for a glimmer of recognition, but Kira merely scoffed.

"When you get to that tavern, make sure you make the bear at least twenty feet tall on his hind legs. And be sure to emphasize the sharpness of his claws. You don't want the other old men to think a cub got the better of you."

Her eyes sparkled with merriment. He realized that she was flirting with him. He should have been elated. A beautiful woman, royal and rich and fierce, wanted to flirt with *him*! It was winning the prize hunt without so much as venturing into the forest.

Three small drops of blood that escaped from his glove and fell onto Amzi's neck killed that notion.

"Oh my," she said, noticing the blood. She took an embroidered handkerchief with her initials on it and passed it to him. Grateful, Robert tended to Amzi, and then pressed the cloth to his wrist.

"That looks angry. How long ago did that bear go after you?"

"Fifteen years."

"What? That's ridiculous. You must have caught it on something as we left the chapel."

"Probably," he admitted, although he hadn't felt anything like that.

They rode in silence for several minutes, both watching the road for hazards. The sun was dipping low, dappling their surroundings in pink and orange light as they made the turn back to Dunlock Castle. In the gloaming, Kira shimmered. Robert willed his heart to stop beating.

"The first ball is tomorrow night."

The first dance of any Festival of the Flower was the Heir's Ball, meant for the express purpose of matching young royals. Robert's tongue went dry.

"I'll have to open the dancing. Will you be there?"

He knew what she wanted. As unbelievable as it was, she wanted to dance with him. It was on the tip of his tongue to ask her, but the words wouldn't come. The injury on his wrist pulsed, fresh blood staining her handkerchief.

"Umbrick."

"I'm sorry?"

"My uncle has an errand for me in Umbrick, I probably won't make it back in time."

"Oh," she said, her cheeks going rosy as the sunset.

*Melissa Constantine*

# CHAPTER TWENTY-FIVE
## Kira

**Kira brushed non-existent wrinkles from her dress.** The heavy blue fabric rustled, and she regretted the choice. It was impossible to be stealth when clad in quite so much shiny blue satin.

Then again, she wasn't supposed to fade into the wallpaper, was she?

She was the entertainment.

"Princess Kira, if you'll permit me?" Prince Brandon's foot tapped, ever so slightly against the marble floor.

Kira blinked, momentarily startled before remembering that the prince was supposed to introduce her to the assorted guests. She knew who many of them were, of course, but royals were like weeds, as soon as you thought you had them all so many more showed up.

"Of course," she murmured, and tried to summon a polite smile for the line of waiting Earls, Viscounts, and other minor royals.

"May I present the Duke of…"

A round young man with a fop of straw-colored hair bowed.

Kira had forgotten him before his name was off the Prince's lips. Robert stood by the punch bowl, bowing over the hand of the pretty redheaded girl Kira had met the other day. *How did he know her?* And also, *why the hell had he lied and said he'd be in Umbrick?* Was she that repulsive that he didn't even want to dance with her?

Kira bit the inside of her cheek to keep herself from calling out to him. How dare he lie to her? She was the future Queen of the Known Kingdoms, and what was he? The third son of a minor duke from nowhere?

Did he actually kiss that tacky girl's hand?

"May I say, Princess, that your eyes are like glittering stars?"

Kira turned back to the straw-colored Duke. "Glittering stars? I don't believe I've ever been so complimented."

"Yes, they are an extraordinary color, so, uh, purple."

How anyone got through a ball without getting a strain from the eye-rolling, Kira had no idea. "I thank you," she said, keeping her eyes downcast, less the Straw Duke believed he was winning with his generic praise.

"May I secure a dance for the opening set?"

"I am afraid I have already given the dance to…" she trailed off, watching Robert offer his arm to Diana Yarborough. Redheads should never wear pink. It was a law. Or it would be under her reign. Kira would make it a royal decree after her coronation, that and something about third sons being strung up by their thumbs to cure their impertinence.

Prince Brandon cleared his throat, and that little foot of his tapped against the floor again like he had a hummingbird trapped under his sole. "Princess, the Duke of Graff has a vested interest in the trade of all crane flowers. Perhaps you could discuss it on the dance floor."

Kira caught him in her icy glare and appropriately the man colored in a slight pink from the edge of his high collar upward. "In the second set, if you please, Your Grace. I am afraid I granted the first set of dances to Prince Travers."

"The first of the second set, then." The Straw Duke grabbed for the delicate fan at her wrist that served as her dance card and scribbled his name on the fourth blade. He didn't remove the fan from her wrist before he did, and so as he wrote, Kira's arm hung in the air, the ribbon strap eating into her flesh. She grimaced, but Graff took no notice. When he was done, he bowed deeply, his hair brushing the floor. Really, the ability to bow that low was impressive. Kira could curtsey with the best of them -she'd learned how before she could properly walk — but even she couldn't get that close to the ground.

After Graff, there were a dozen more introductions. The Earl of Pennyford, whose collar was so high the points bit into his cheeks. Baron Holt, whose coat was too tight, and Baronet Hill whose coat was too big. A few others whose names she promptly forgot and had no interest in knowing. Towards the end of the line, Kira was introduced to the Viscount Redmax, who had gorgeously long braided hair but also a sardonic expression on his face. His clothes were neither ill-fitting nor his compliments unoriginal, but she knew he would never do. He just wasn't... Robert.

When it seemed the line would never end, the orchestra struck the first notes for the dance. Grateful, Kira dropped the barest of curtseys to the Prince and the Viscount before excusing herself.

She couldn't see Travers, but all she had to do was follow the bellowing laugh echoing over the tuning violins. Sure enough, she followed the sound to the refreshment table, where Travers had a large tumbler of whiskey in his hand.

When she'd first met him half a dozen years ago, Kira had thought Travers handsome. He had rather nice shoulders, kind, almond-shaped eyes and lovely long blue-black hair. But there was something off about him now. Grief over losing his father had played havoc with his form.

"Come to claim me from the dragon, Fair Maiden?" His eyes were glassy from the booze, despite the ball being less than an hour old. He must have started early. March, maybe late February by the strong smell of the spirits coming out of his skin.

"As is my sacred duty."

Travers grinned. "You're a sport, Ki. Have a drink." He motioned to the attendant, who began to pour a deep garnet-colored liquid into a cut-crystal glass.

Kira shook her head at the attendant and held out her hand to Travers. "You owe me a dance, Trav."

Travers made an unpleasant face. "Is that strictly necessary?"

"If you don't dance with me for the first two dances, I will have you thrown in the Corlea dungeon for impertinence."

"Enough, you old shrew." His glass thumped against the refreshment table, the remaining liquid sloshing out and staining the white damask tablecloth.

Kira took his arm and led him to the dance floor. Only when she had taken her place did the orchestra begin the strains of the waltz.

"Oh, it has to be a twirly one," Travers groaned.

"I like the twirly ones. And I'm the guest of honor."

He made a noise that might have been some kind of pigeon being strangled. His hold on her might be best described as loosey-goosey, which matched his headless-chicken command of the simple steps. If Travers spouted a beak and wings before the ball was over she wouldn't be surprised. He twirled in the opposite direction of everyone else on the floor. As two of the most senior royals in the room, it was their right to twirl in whatever direction they chose and have everyone else catch up, but he wasn't making it easy for the rest of the dancers. He added a random step forward and jerked her backward when he should have done a graceful step sideways, crashing into the nearby couple, who went tumbling.

"Sorry, old chap," Travers said, with a grimace.

Kira bit her lip to keep from screaming. Of all the people that Travers could have banged into, it had to be the one person Kira did not want to see, because, of course, that was how the evening was going to go.

Robert and his dance partner detangled themselves from the heap that Travers had pushed them into and stood up.

"No apology necessary, Your Highness," Robert said. He didn't make eye contact with Kira.

"I'm afraid I'm going to have to sit this one out, Ki," Travers groaned. "Can't see straight at the moment."

Kira flushed with embarrassment. She could not sit out the opening dances during the Festival of the Flower. "Travers, that is unacceptable."

"Robby will dance with you, it's fine."

Diana's mouth dropped open slightly. "I'm committed to the first three dances with…"

"Oh, tosh," Travers said to her. "Kira will dance with Robby, and you'll come with me. I heard about your mother. She'll practically have kittens when she understands you ended up next to me, even if it's not to dance."

Diana, being a smart girl, took his offered arm, although given the state of his sobriety it was obvious she was supporting him as they made their way off the floor.

Robert held out his hand. "Your Highness, if I may."

The waltz had ended, and a country reel began. Kira gritted her teeth. At least there was less touching in the reel.

"Fine, if you're not too busy in Umbrick."

Robert didn't look chastised, to which Kira was abjectly disappointed. She would have to be more pointed with her insults.

"No," he said. He looked as if he would say more, but the words never passed his lips.

Kira wanted to shake him until he said something else but the first set of figures was a complicated series of steps that required concentration.

Around her, couples were missing the steps as they watched her dance with Robert. Gossip after the ball would probably start and end with the princess being pawned off on a third son. Thankfully, he was exceptionally handsome. That might mitigate some of the damage. The candlelight cast golden highlights into his brown hair. She was glad for the gloves she wore that would negate any chance she might reach up and run her fingers through it. Really, he should try not to be so handsome. It made it nearly impossible to be mad. She managed it, but it was an effort.

"You might have sent a note," she said, as the reel once again brought them face to face. He turned away with the steps of the dance, then back again, holding out his hand for the promenade.

Kira took it, keeping her touch light as they moved down the line of dancers.

"You wouldn't have read it," he said. They moved to the second set of figures, which was little more than stepping up and stepping back.

Kira couldn't really argue with that. After he'd said he wouldn't come, she'd been embarrassed about making the suggestion at all. Had he sent a note she'd likely have burned it without reading it. That he knew her so well on short acquaintance was a bit mortifying. She wanted to believe she wasn't so shallow.

She found she had nothing to say as the third set of figures began, with each couple separating and moving along the outside line of dancers until they reached the far end of the ballroom. When he took her hand again, his grip was considerably stronger.

"I am glad to see you," he said.

"I am your future queen," she said. "You should be."

"You've never pretended to be humble a day in your life, have you, Princess?"

"You've never pretended to be a high royal," she countered. "Tell me the difference?"

Robert said nothing, bowing as the dance finished.

There was a pause in the music as all of the couples sorted themselves back into pairs for the waltz that would close the first set. Kira looked about the room in order to avoid looking at Robert directly. He was so tall. She would decree against that too. Third sons must be ugly little ducklings, less they distract future queens from treating them like peasants.

He looped his arm around her as the waltz began, his hand across her back warm through the satin of her dress. It was a much slower dance than the opening waltz, and Robert held her much closer than Travers had ever done.

"You dance well," she admitted, as he maneuvered them through the couples in a seamless fashion.

"A dozen years of lessons," he said.

"A dozen years?"

"Four female cousins, all of whom needed dance partners."

"You have brothers."

He shrugged. "For a long time, I was small, fat, and easy for the dancing master to catch."

Kira couldn't help but smile. The image of a chubby little boy with Robert's thick, beautiful hair being press-ganged into dancing lessons was so oddly charming.

To his credit, Robert did not compliment or say anything so infuriating as "you should smile more," as so many men did when she smiled in their direction. He simply smiled back at her. Unaccountably, her heart beat faster.

# CHAPTER TWENTY-SIX
## Diana

**Travers's hand was clammy.** As he pulled her through a throng of people, Diana realized she shouldn't have taken off her gloves. Leaving them with her dance card had been an impulse, the desire to touch Robby's hand, and feel... something.

Sadly, all she felt was the obvious effects of Travers's drinking.

"Where are we going?"

The Prince let out something like a sigh. "Somewhere the music isn't."

"It's a ball!"

"It's a big castle, we'll find someplace."

Diana yanked her hand away. "No, thank you."

She turned and walked back toward the dance floor. Clumps of onlookers had grouped along the edge of the dancing, and a steady stream of chatter was quickly drowning out the musicians. Travers, despite his desire to leave, was on her heels as she found an open spot to watch the dancers, his breath humid on her neck.

There was only one couple twirling through the waltz. Robby and the Princess.

Neither of them seemed to notice they were the only ones dancing. Whatever conversation they were having was only for the two of them, and they looked into one another's eyes as if there was nothing else to see.

It was intense. Diana felt as if she were intruding, and was slightly ill.

Because one look at the two of them, smiling at one another, and she knew.

Robby wasn't hers.

Diana's skin heated. She shouldn't be seeing this, no one should.

Travers let out a low whistle. "Fairies be, he's got it bad."

Diana took a significant step sideways, out of Travers's reach. "You don't know what you're talking about."

"I've got eyes. And so does everyone in the room," he said, indicating the other onlookers. And it was true. The entire room had zeroed in on the couple. And it wasn't hard to see why.

They were radiant. Yes, objectively, they were both good looking on their own. But together? A handsome knight and the dainty blonde princess, twirling around the floor. Diana wanted to throw something.

"Oh relax. I told you; your mother is going to be glad you're with me. Lycette hasn't even got any property of his own. Third son."

"I've known Sir Robert since we were both in the cradle," she said, offended on her friend's behalf. Even if it was true.

Travers shrugged. "So you know he's not good enough for you."

Diana couldn't stop her mouth from falling open. "Robby is a good person."

Travers wasn't impressed. "And clearly he's in love with someone else, so what are you worried about?"

"Go away."

She tried moving, but the onlookers crowding the floor didn't make escaping the prince easy. Every time she tried to thread her way through a clump of people, others moved into her path, until she was lost in a forest of silk and satin.

Travers apparently thought that was hilarious. He chuckled. "Come on. Let's get out of here and let the happy couple inspire a thousand death stares on their own."

He took her by the hand again. Thankfully the sweat had dried off enough that she wasn't immediately disgusted at his touch. With a confidence she wouldn't have guessed he owned, he navigated them toward one of the open doors that lead out to the ballroom terrace.

The air was surprisingly cold, considering they were into the crane harvest. Diana shivered as the night wrapped around her, and like her missing gloves, she wished she'd thought to ask for sleeves on her gown. Her breath didn't snake out before her, but she suspected it wouldn't take much of a drop in temperature to have that happen.

Travers took a deep, bracing breath. He seemed taller out in the fresh air, although Diana had to admit that was probably her imagination. "I hate parties," he said.

"You seem to like to drink," she said, stepping toward the stone balustrade. In daylight, the view from the balcony was of the crane fields, but it was well after dark. Although plenty of light was being thrown from the castle windows, and the mostly-full moon, there was nothing to see in the distance. Diana looked out, only slightly afraid of what she might see if she looked back toward the ballroom.

"Parties aren't the only place a man can drink." Travers leaned against the stone; his arms crossed over his chest.

"Maybe they should be."

"You're a little bit mean," he said, smiling like a cat who caught the canary.

Diana rolled her eyes. She wasn't going to explain herself to the prince. It wasn't worth it.

Other couples had migrated outside, some taking advantage of the shadowy places. Diana noticed Xavier and Lord Albert talking by one of the far sets of the doors. She hadn't had a chance to catch up with Xavier since she arrived in Dunlock so she tried to wave to them, but they were too engrossed in their conversation. She couldn't be sure, but Lord Albert looked incredibly stressed, as evidenced by the flush to his face and neck. As a fellow redhead she could sympathize. Sometimes she felt like all of her emotions were written on her skin.

"Xav, don't let them," Lord Albert said. "Please."

"It's not a big deal."

Lord Albert looked stricken at that answer, and Diana began to feel as if she were eavesdropping.

"Another happy couple," Travers said disdainfully.

They certainly didn't look happy at that moment, but as far as she knew they'd been together for a few years. "Do you have something against happiness?"

She rubbed absently at her upper arms, trying to keep the cold at bay. Travers shucked off his elaborate coat and hung it over her shoulders. Reluctantly she murmured her thanks. It was a beautiful garment, a lightweight teal wool with a black silk lining. The breast was adorned with symbols of Tull — black silk thread embroidered into cranes with diamonds sewn in to look like stars. It was gorgeous and it was warm, but it belonged to the wrong person.

"Happiness is a myth," Travers said. He reached into the inner pocket of the coat, and took out a small flask. Diana startled at the casual way his hand brushed against her. It was brief contact, but decidedly not impersonal.

"We're here to make alliances."

"A good marriage should be both."

Travers snorted. "I'd like to see that."

"My parents have it. They made a great match and they're devoted to each other."

"And tell me, Lady Diana, where exactly is your father? Why isn't he in Dunlock?"

Diana's neck burned with indignation. "What does that have to do with anything?"

"Even if it's true that your parents are so in love it would make a grown man weep, he's not here is he? Couldn't be bothered to come see you married off. Probably because he knows it's all a scam."

"Why did you even come if you're so against the idea of marriage?"

"I'm not against the idea of marriage. In fact, the sooner I get a wife, the better."

"Charming."

Travers was unbothered. "You know I'm right. Keep the fuss to a minimum."

"Some women like fuss. Men too, for that matter."

Diana watched as Lord Albert followed Xavier back into the ballroom. Other couples followed. It was probably a good idea to head back inside, before anyone got any odd ideas about why she was out here with Travers in the first place. She shrugged off the coat and held it out to him.

"Thank you for the loan."

He shrugged, and tossed it over his shoulder. "I'll tell my aunt to speak to your mother."

"Why?"

"Why not?"

Travers's dark eyes were watery from all he'd drunk, but he held her gaze with an intensity that sent warning signals down her spine.

*Melissa Constantine*

## Chapter Twenty-Seven
### Robert

***Robert didn't know why he had lied to Kira.*** It had come out of his mouth like blackbirds bursting from a pie. Maybe he was a coward, or maybe it was a stupid lie. He'd already promised the first set of dances to Diana. Yes, Uncle Julius had sent him to Umbrick Castle, but it was a simple errand. He'd delivered a letter and had not had to wait for a reply.

After their return from the Fairie chapel, Robert tried to justify his words. She'd put the chance to dance with her out there, and it was the most terrifying thing he could imagine. Kira liked to have her way. She would run roughshod over and think less of him for hanging off her every word. Except that it was lousy to lie to her. Like whatever was between them was fragile and he'd broken it.

He should apologize to her. Knights did not lie. And when they did wrong, they made amends. He wouldn't hesitate to apologize to Diana. She was a great friend, and he felt bad that she was currently babysitting the drunken Prince of Tull. Not that Prince Travers's lack of sobriety was Robert's fault, but that he could not regret how it all turned out. He'd wanted to dance with Kira. To feel her in his arms, and spin her around the dancefloor.

"Kira, I..." he began, but his words were cut off by the sudden stop of the orchestra. Everyone in the ballroom turned as the dancers came to a halt.

Prince Brandon, Princess Margo, and all of their children stood on the dais in front of the musicians and were motioning for quiet. Xavier, and Bertie standing behind him, both looked embarrassed or perhaps guilty to be standing on the stage. The hair rose on the back of his neck. Something was off. He reached for Kira's hand, but she had folded her arms at her waist.

"Ladies and gentlemen," Prince Brandon said above the murmuring hush of the dancers. "I am pleased to welcome you all to Dunlock Castle and to the opening ball of the Festival of the Flower."

There was a round of applause.

"We are especially pleased to welcome our guest of honor, Princess Kira."

More applause. Beside him, Kira seemed to shrink from the attention. It had been easy to think on first meeting her that she would assume the notice was due to her. She was never shy about reminding him that she was to be queen. But something changed when she was front and center. She was a shell of her former self.

"We are especially pleased that the Princess has chosen to spend the festival with us, and to use the opportunity to support the charitable endeavors of our oldest son, Prince Xavier, and his partner, Lord Albert, in funding the Dunlock Charity Orphanage."

The giant doors to the ballroom opened, and a large, covered object at least ten feet tall was wheeled in by three servants in sparkling livery.

"I think we can all rejoice in knowing our future monarch takes such an interest in the welfare of the children of our kingdom. My wife and I were so touched by it, that we felt it was only appropriate to commemorate and celebrate this remarkable attitude with a tribute to the values that created such benevolence. To that end, we would like to present this statue, to be installed at the Dunlock Charity Orphanage so that all may see and appreciate it."

Two trumpeters stepped to the front of the dais and played as the covering over the statue was removed with a heavy snap of the fabric.

Queen Clara and King Callum, surrounded by dozens of long-stemmed crane flowers, with a baby lamb at the Queen's feet, all done in stunningly white marble. At the unveiling, there was an appreciative gasp from the crowd, followed by the loudest applause yet. The marble had the shimmer of crystal throughout that caught the light and dazzled.

Kira's face had drained of color. She dropped her arms to her side and drew her shoulders back to draw herself up to her full height. The smile that crossed her face was technically perfect and polite, but it wasn't hers. It didn't reach her eyes or have that hint of mischief that was so utterly Kira. She stepped to the dais and joined the Prince's family.

The voice she used when she spoke was meant to address a crowd. It had none of the exciting breathiness he'd heard her use in private. "What a beautiful monument," she said in such measured tones, it was as if Robert were seeing a new person emerge in front of his eyes. She drew a hand across her heart, "From the bottom of my heart, I thank you."

There was protracted applause, and then Kira waved to the crowd with a smile and stepped off the stage. A young royal with dull blond hair was pushing his way through the crowd toward her as the orchestra began the music for the next set of dances, but Robert couldn't say if he ever reached Kira. She disappeared into the mass of bodies.

****

Robert had stayed until all the candles had been extinguished and the last of the servants had swept away the remains of the refreshment table. It was only when the room was empty that he saw her at the foot of the statue.

Her dress was like the night sky. He hadn't noticed that before. It faded from a pale blue around her shoulders down to a deep, dark, almost black at her feet, and all along there were gems that caught the light from the Zephyr lamp she held. It cast swirls of yellow and pink light over the white marble of the statue of the King and Queen, in a way that made the figures look sickly.

Kira said nothing as he made his way across the darkened ballroom toward her, but as he approached, she said to him, "Do you love your parents?"

Of all the things that he might have expected her to say, whether or not he loved his parents was not one of them. "Yes, of course," he answered.

She kept her gaze on the immovable face of Queen Clara, who looked off in the distance. "I loved mine. I did."

"I'm sorry for your loss."

Kira shook her head. Her hair had come loose from the elaborate hairstyle she'd worn to the ball, and it brushed her cheek. She spoke in a whisper that made the hair on the back of his neck rise. "I'm not."

Any words he might have offered died in his throat.

"I'm so certain that makes me a bad, bad person. It must. I'm not sorry they're gone, even though I miss them."

Robert reached for her, but Kira took a half-step back. She held the lamp higher, and the pink swirls of light behind the glass darkened to red snakes, slithering across the queen's face.

"Do you want to know why?" Her voice cracked. Robert understood that it was not a question. As a knight and gentleman, he needed to remain silent. Even if he wanted to pull her into his arms and tell her that everything was going to be okay, he couldn't do that.

That would be a lie and he'd lied to her enough.

Kira took a visible breath and closed her eyes. "Because even though I loved them, I don't think they loved me. Not even a little bit. I don't think they knew how."

Kira's chin trembled, and she drew her free hand tight to her chest as if trying to hold herself together, but no tears fell. Perhaps she no longer had any left.

"I don't know if I'm right. Maybe... maybe they did. That's what people say, isn't it? *Every parent loves their children.* It's in all the stories. But I don't believe it."

She turned to him and held out the Zephyr lamp for him to take. She'd discarded her gloves at some point in the evening, and he saw that she'd bitten her nails down to the pads of her fingers.

He took the lamp from her. The trapped gas inside seemed to object to the transfer, it sputtered a strange, pale shade of green. He wanted to wish her good night, but his mouth felt like it was stuffed with cotton. He bowed to her, and she inclined her head. She left in no hurry. The starfield on her dress twinkled, and the satin rustled with each step that carried her farther away. It was only when the great double-doors to the ballroom closed behind her that Robert heard the first crack. It reverberated like a thunderbolt through the cavernous ballroom.

A vein deep in the marble statue burst open, and pieces of rock began to fall to the floor. Queen Clara's immovable face was cleaved in two, forcing him to jump out of the way as one of the chunks hit the floor right where he'd been standing.

The rest of the statue collapsed in the time between his frantic heartbeats. Clouds of dust rose, coating him from head to toe in fine, white powder. By the time he caught his breath, there was nothing left of the statue.

****

Robert took the steps to the Dunlock Witch's Tower two at a time. His legs ached and his breath hitched, but he kept running up. He left a trail of fine, choking dust from the collapse of the statue in his wake. Grit filled his lungs and he coughed and sputtered as he ran.

Despite the late hour, he pounded on the door, until Caris Mourne pulled it open, a pursed expression on her narrow face.

"Oh my," she said. "Come in, come in."

Robert shook his head. "It's Princess Kira," he gasped, his breath beating in an uncontrollable, nonrhythmic tattoo. "She's the source... she..."

The world went black. For half a heartbeat, Robert had the sensation that he'd stepped outside of his body and that he was looking at himself, crumpled on the floor.

"I am sorry, Sir Handsome," Caris Mourne said. "I promise I did it for a good reason."

And then, there was nothing.

# Chapter Twenty-Eight
## Kira

**Dunlock Castle was sweltering.**

Sweat had soaked her hair from root to the ends, dripped down her back, and ran in rivers down between her breasts. Disoriented and uncomfortable, Kira struggled to sit up in the lush bed. Her stubborn, recalcitrant eyes didn't want to open. She ground her palms into the sockets, pushing the crusty bits of sleep deeper into her eyelashes, and sending white sparks across her vision.

It wasn't yet dawn. Kira could hear Pamela gently snoring from the antechamber. The rest of the castle was silent. Not even the hot water pipes were squeaking.

The fire that had been stoked to ward off the chilly spring night had gone out. An anomalous spring heat must have snuck up on Dunlock Castle sometime after the ball. If it was this hot this early then the day wasn't promising. Every royal and retainer would spend the flower harvest marinating in their finery, like beef cooked too long in its own juice.

She could almost smell it, the stench of sweat and musty perfume, so strong it would make her mouth dry and leave a bitter taste on her tongue.

Although perhaps that was the need to brush her teeth.

Her toothbrush was on the washstand. As soon as she had the energy, Kira had every intention of brushing away the sticky sleep clinging to her teeth.

As soon as she didn't feel like the weight of the Known Kingdoms was coming down on her.

Stumbling out of bed, her feet hit the floor with a heavy thump.

If only all those royals who'd drummed up their generic praise about her grace and her light steps during the dancing could see her now.

The washstand was five, six, seven feet — no, an eternity — away. She couldn't see it, but she knew her alabaster-inlaid handle toothbrush sat next to the gold filigree pot of toothpaste. The whole set was fussy, but it did the job as well as a cheaper set. As soon as she dragged herself over to it, she wouldn't feel as if she'd swallowed every cotton ball in Dunlock.

She would have to wake Pamela, even though it was an obscene hour. The little towel and pathetically small bar of soap beside her toothbrush weren't going to cut it if it was this hot already. She would need a bath. She couldn't appear at breakfast as ripe as an old cheese.

Kira's eyes took their time adjusting to the dark. She would have to go back to that dippy witch Caris Mourne and ask for tonic if her vision remained this bad. Yes, all the candles had gone out but there was a disturbingly large amount of moonlight. It shone through the open window, hitting the gold frame of the mirror above the washstand. The shadow world reflected in it was somehow clearer than anything around her.

Close enough to reach for her toothbrush, Kira looked up, willing the world around her to be as sharp as the room reflected in the mirror, and stared deep into the eyes of the Beast of Barlow.

Her heart thudded painfully and her blood raced.

No, no, not the Beast, exactly.

But what was she doing wearing the cloak in bed?

She pulled at the hide, but it wouldn't budge. The hood had come down and was stuck to her face. She tried sliding a finger into the eyehole, but the leather wouldn't give. It weighed down on her shoulders with no wiggle room. Handfuls of fur pulled loose from the main body of the cloak but each yank felt as if the tuffs were coming out of her own skin.

She couldn't be seen. Not as the Beast of Barlow.

Pamela's sleepy voice came from the antechamber. "My lady, are you awake?"

Kira's voice caught in her throat. What came out was a deep rumble.

"My lady?"

Her riding boots were nearest. She grabbed them and sprinted toward the door. There was no time to do anything else before Pamela's blood curdling scream echoed through the castle.

## CHAPTER TWENTY-NINE
### Robert

*"He's prettier when he's sleeping."*

"Hush. You'll wake him."

Robert wanted to sit up and tell the voices that he was already awake, but his body refused to cooperate. Although the sensation of paralysis was unfamiliar, it wasn't uncomfortable. In fact, he was more relaxed than he had in days. He'd slept better than he had since he'd left Greater Miser three years ago for his training.

"Look at this hair," said the first voice.

Robert felt a small tug on his scalp.

"Can you give me hair like this?"

"No, I cannot."

The first voice huffed. "You're a witch, aren't you? Just a little of his curl and gloss."

"Neither my magic nor our marriage works like that," Caris Mourne said. "Leave him alone."

Caris Mourne was married? Witches didn't marry. They got old and got... cats? Robert wasn't sure. He should ask Kira. She'd know. Or she'd say something funny.

Kira was so funny.

Pretty and funny.

Not pretty. Beautiful.

No, he wasn't allowed to say that. She was going to be his queen.

Robert sat up, taking a giant gasp of crisp, cold air. "What happened?"

"Easy," said the voice that was not Caris Mourne. "Don't move too much."

Robert tried to stand up only to realize that it was the exact move he should have avoided. His head pounded and swirling lights swam in front of his vision. He fell back onto a small bed, set up on the fireplace hearth. Day broke through the giant windows that surrounded the tower, which were again open to the chilly air. Large bundles of multi-colored crane flowers that looked like they'd been conscripted from the ballroom's decorations sat in buckets and haphazard vases all around the circular room. Both Caris Mourne and her spouse watched him and both held delicate teacups.

Robert rubbed his eyes with the palms of his hands, not sure of what he was seeing. The person beside Caris Mourne did not seem to be a man or a woman. Although they had a bit of stubble across their high cheekbones, their dark hair went longer than their pointed chin, and many of their features seemed bent toward the feminine. Both they and Caris Mourne wore the white flowery dressing gowns as they had when she'd summoned him from his bed in the Corlea stables.

Robert had no wish to be rude, so he rose to his surprisingly shaking legs and bowed low. "I am pleased to make your acquaintance," he said to them.

"Oh, I like him." Long slim fingers tucked a lock of hair back, revealing high, pointed ears. Fairie ears.

"Enough, my love," Caris Mourne said. "Tea, Sir Robert?"

Exhausted from his bow, Robert could only nod.

The witch withdrew her silver watch from the dressing gowns pocket, twisted the top dial, and then raised her free hand and snapped. A teacup floated toward him, filled to the brim with mahogany-colored tea. Robert took it, grateful. The tea was fragrant and sweet, and Robert was restored to how he'd been before sitting up.

"Tea is wonderful stuff, isn't it?" Caris Mourne asked.

"Yes, thank you, My Lady."

"Do the manners come with the knighthood, or do you think they're native?"

Caris Mourne shot them a look and then turned back to Robert. "Sir Robert, may I introduce my consort, Jacobee."

"Good Morning," Robert said, inclining his head to the Fairie.

Jacobee smiled, revealing sharply pointed front teeth. "Definitely native to his species," they said and Caris Mourne laughed. Her laugh had a rusty, unused quality to it as if she had learned to do it too late in life.

"Enough with ogling our guest," Caris Mourne said. She snapped her fingers once again and the teacup in her hand disappeared.

"Mine too," said Jacobee, holding out their cup.

Caris Mourne snapped her fingers and their cup and Robert's own disappeared. "Now then," she said. "We have much to discuss."

Jacobee sighed. "Are you sure you can't give me hair like his?"

"I could give you his hair, but then he would be dead, and we'd be no closer to solving this mystery."

Robert found his hands sneaking into his hair. He was not vain, but he would rather start the day not dead.

"Sir Robert, you'd better tell me about your princess."

A rush of heat shot up his neck. "She's not my…"

"Are young humans always this blind?" Jacobee asked.

"I'm afraid so," said the witch.

Robert shook it off. He couldn't dwell on it. "I think Princess Kira is the source of the referred magic." He did his best to tell the story of the statue's demise, wondering how he'd missed obvious details. The claim on his wrist bleeding after so many years wasn't a coincidence. Nor was her insistence that the orphanage's sitting room was exactly thirteen steps across. He'd witnessed those things, but until he'd been covered in the statue's remains it hadn't even occurred to him — she had the magic. She was the future queen and the source of all the trouble.

Caris Mourne listened, and when Robert had laid all that he knew about Kira out before her she said, "I was afraid she might be."

Robert startled, unable to keep his voice in check. "Why didn't you say anything? What if she's in danger?"

Jacobee tisked at him; Caris Mourne shook her head at her companion and turned back to Robert. "Let me assure you she is not in danger. The princess likely has no idea that she's the cause of anything that's happening."

Robert opened his mouth, intending to ask a dozen questions at once, but he found that the words wouldn't form on his tongue.

Jacobee leaned toward Caris Mourne and said, "Magic this big is could be from Fairies. Do you want me to ask around the Court?"

The witch nodded. "Please."

Jacobee rose, gave their spouse a quick kiss on the cheek, and promptly disappeared.

"I know how it works, but I'll never get used to it. Blink and poof!"

Robert was trying to process and did not answer. Caris Mourne carried on. "Right, well, now that we know the princess is the source of the referral, we need to figure out the why and the how."

"What can I do? Kira...the princess she..." Robert hadn't felt this helpless since the age of nine when his brothers had locked him in the Greater Miser dungeons. "I think she might be the..." He bit back his suspicions. "She can't get hurt."

Caris Mourne gave him a rather pitying look. "She won't. I promise you."

But Robert didn't feel reassured. He'd missed the signs. He felt as if he were failing Kira, both as a knight and as her friend.

*Melissa Constantine*

## Chapter Thirty
### Robert

**The early morning air was frigid, a reminder that despite the beginning of** the harvest, spring had been a volatile season. Knights clapped their gloved hands together for warmth, while the gathered crowd bounced on the balls of their feet.

Queen Isadora sat atop her large black destrier, head to toe in matte black silk that soaked up the early morning light. The only color on her was the magnificent coronet perched in her thick hair, which sparkled with rich red rubies. She was flanked by two guards, carrying the banner of Corlea. Behind the riders, a royal box had been erected between two sets of grandstands for the Moorelow family and Lord Albert. It might have been the morning light or the late hours of the ball last night, but all of them looked a bit gray around the edges.

None of the knights spoke as Queen Isadora rode the length of the column, staring into the eyes of each of them she passed. Being acknowledged by the queen was an honor. Robert watched as one by one the knights fell under her spell. They sat up straighter in their saddles. A sense of purpose seemed to radiate from each man as she passed. He might be speculating, but he supposed each of them was falling a little in love with her.

Robert could appreciate that Queen Isadora was a beautiful woman, but to him, there was no one who could match Kira. Admitting that to himself felt like breaking a vow, and that left him feeling ill. That and a great deal of whisky he'd swiped from the flask Jordaan usually carried. After waking up in Caris Mourne's tower his courage had needed shoring up.

Last night, he'd held Kira in his arms for only a few moments yet he'd felt himself falling hard, even knowing nothing would come of it. He was a young knight from a nearly impoverished kingdom that produced next to nothing in exports. He had no tournament titles or battle victories to his name. There would never be a time when it would be appropriate to say anything to Kira. He was a knight. Sworn to Lower Miser, which had sworn fealty to Corlea. It was his job to protect her not to love her.

Caris Mourne and her companion's opinion be damned.

And then there was the whole matter of the unintended magic.

Amzi pranced nervously, snorting great puffs of hot breath into the cold air. Robert stroked his neck, but the usual gesture didn't calm the horse.

"Easy, easy."

But it was no good, Amzi was ready to run, though the queen had not finished her inspection. Robert tightened his grip on the reins.

Beside him, Jordaan scoffed. "Honestly, who taught you to ride?"

"Your father, if I remember it right."

Jordaan forced a laugh and made a rude gesture. He reached for the flask in his coat pocket and tipped his head back for a swallow before realizing that Robert had finished it off.

"You're an ass, Lycette."

Robert was too busy trying to control his agitated horse to respond.

The queen reached the end of the column and rode back to the center. A trumpeter stepped forward and played a short and sad tune to draw everyone's attention. It was then that the Queen Regent began speaking.

Her voice was not loud. But she sat tall in the saddle, and her voice projected well enough.

"When I proposed this hunt to the Kingdom Council, I had no idea how urgent the task would become."

Whispers whipped through the crowd and down the column of knights.

"Early this morning, the hunt took on a new dimension when it was discovered that Princess Kira had disappeared from her bed."

The ambient noise grew louder, forcing the Queen to raise her hands for silence.

"There are signs of a struggle. Blood and fur were found in her empty chamber. And at least one of the maids believes she saw the Beast of Barlow running from the castle."

Robert's stomach dropped. Despite the cold sweat broke out under his tunic. How was it possible? He'd seen Kira mere hours ago. She'd been melancholy but in no danger. He was a fool for even considering the idea that she was the Beast.

"Therefore, all participating in the hunt are to shift from the capture of the Beast, and instead focus on the safe return of the Princess. Bring her back and the rewards from the Corlea Crane harvest will go to your house. The one who brings back the princess unharmed will be given a royal title. Given the scope of this emergency, I have been given authorization by the Kingdom Council that this title shall include a deed to a parcel of property and that both shall pass down to the knight's oldest offspring."

The uproar through the crowd was deafening. New royal titles were strictly controlled. To also have that title come with land and the ability to pass on wasn't just a prize it was the gift of generations.

Servants had been sent running for the stables and the castle. Obviously, it would be more than knights taking to the woods to find the Princess if a royal title was on the line.

"May the Fairies bless you. I can only pray that the Princess is returned to us safely and quickly."

"Fairies be." Jordaan's voice boomed. "Do you believe that?"

Robert could only shake his head. He would be lying if he said it wasn't immediately tempting to give Amzi his head. He needed to be the first into the woods. He needed to be the one to rescue Kira.

A royal title would go a long way to bridging the gap between a knight and a princess.

Queen Isadora had finished speaking, but Prince Brandon had something to add. He stood at the ledge of the royal box waiting for the chaos of scurrying servants and fervent gossip to die down. When it didn't he was forced to signal for the trumpeter to call the crowd's attention.

"My wife and family and I want all members of the hunt to know that while you ride, all of the resources of Dunlock are at your disposal. All that matters is the safe return of Princess Kira. We offer our labor, our provisions, and any and all assistance you may need. If I may, I know that Fairie blessings are old fashioned, but it would make my family and I feel better. So if you will indulge me."

He called out the names of a dozen Fairies, invoking their various qualities. "...Brilla the Bloody, Gurr Tolf, Hardy the Fool, may their light shine the path in front of you. And may Baal Vick the Wizard bless you with insight. Light and Dark."

A half-hearted echo of "Light and Dark," went through the crowd, and dozens made the crook finger symbol to ward off curses.

The column broke, with groups of knights riding for the gates.

"Well, to each his own, huh?" Jordaan said. "I'll see you from the windows of my new castle." He spurred his horse forward and joined the departing band of knights leaving the courtyard.

Amzi was still too agitated, and Robert was forced to wait as the crowd broke up, doing what he could to calm his horse. Tempting as it was to make a beeline for the Royal Route where he'd encountered the Beast, if Amzi was hurt or injured, they wouldn't get far.

He dismounted to inspect Amzi's hooves. He'd checked each one, finding nothing but usual grit.

"So what is it then?" he asked the horse.

Amzi whinnied, throwing back his dark mane as the remaining crowd parted, and Caris Mourne stepped through.

The witch was given a wide berth. Instead of the traditional red robes that most witches wore when they descended from their towers, she wore her usual blue pants, this time held up by colorful suspenders over her billowy white shirt.

Robert couldn't help but notice that the morning sunlight wasn't in her favor. Her long, purple hair took on more of an artificial sheen, and her skin had an ashen texture that emphasized a slight beat of blue around her deep-set eyes. Ensconced in her tower she was a presence. Outside of it, she looked skinny and small and in need of sleep.

"Oh fantastic," she said, seeing him. "Sir Robert, I'll need your assistance."

Robert understood that it was a command, not a request. "My lady, I am at your service."

"Yes, that is best." She punctuated her sentence with a curt nod but didn't offer any other detail. Her eyes darted around to the crowd as if she weren't used to so many people at once.

"You've heard about the princess?"

Once again, she nodded. "That is why I hoped to find you."

He waited for her to say what she needed to say, but Caris Mourne remained tight-lipped. The crowd seemed to be drawn in tighter, with several of them openly craning their necks to get a look at the infamous witch.

"I must return to the tower." She patted the pockets of her pants as if she'd forgotten what she intended to take from them.

"My lady, is there something wrong?"

"Referred magic has run amuck and now the Princess Royal is missing, Sir Robert. There is most definitely something wrong."

Finally, she drew a small compass out of her pocket and handed it to him. It was a simple object, silver, with a slight inscription around the edge worn down by years of handling.

"It was my father's compass. If you are hurt or injured, you can use it to contact me. But it will only work once."

Robert turned the compass in his hands, allowing the needle to find north. It seemed to point true, if the rising sun was any indication. Caris Mourne pointed to a series of symbols among the inscriptions, and told him if he needed to use it contact him, with those symbols pointed toward the witch's tower at Dunlock.

"Speak my name, out loud, and I will hear."

"Thank you."

The witch drew herself up to her full but inconsiderable height. She seemed to square her thin shoulders. "Bring back Princess Kira. I fear we only have so much time to get this magic under control."

Given his marching orders, he remounted Amzi, who had calmed down considerably once the witch had disappeared back through the crowded courtyard.

"She's a tiny person. What has you so scared?"

Amzi bucked, as if to half-heartedly dislodge him. Used to his horse's oversized reactions, Robert was able to keep his seat. However, he wasn't able to leave with the last remaining knights.

Uncle Julius, astride what looked to be one of the Dunlock stable's oldest horses, was riding toward him. As far as he knew, it had been years since his uncle had ridden a horse. He was uncomfortable in the saddle and dressed much too finely for a hunt. Luckily for him, the horse was old and tired and apparently used to indifferent riders. He kept a steady seat thanks to the horse's tolerance and not much more.

"My boy! You brilliant young man, you've waited for me. I knew you would."

The dread and whisky that had been kerning in Robert's stomach had a new companion — defeat.

"Uncle, are you planning to ride?"

Uncle Julius pushed his already drooping wig back on his forehead. "Yes. Yes, of course."

"Is that…. Uncle I am sure you would no doubt be a fine tracker but…"

"There is a royal title on the line, Robby! This is my chance to secure Tobin's future."

Had it even been a fleeting dream having that royal title himself? No. Even if he hadn't given it conscious thought, he knew that Uncle Julius would have immediately decided to ride out. He'd been fighting his entire life to be able to pass a title to his son. If Robert did find the princess, Uncle

Julius was going to claim that title. It was just as well. What were the chances that a prize title was enough anyway? He'd do what he needed to do, and push those feelings down somewhere deep. That would allow him to focus on finding Kira.

If she was in the clutches of the Beast of Barlow, he needed to act like the trained knight he was, not an obsessed idiot.

"We'll start at the spot we saw him," Uncle Julius said, guiding his horse toward the gate. "That's the last time the Beast struck."

Jordaan probably had the same thought. He'd been there too, and was probably a handful of leagues ahead already. Robert said as much and the Duke's brow wrinkled, causing the towering white wig he wore to slip once again.

"Jordaan is not family," was Uncle Julius's only reply. Robert understood. Sworn to the kingdom of Lower Miser, Sir Jordaan might be, but he wasn't in the Lycette family tree. Which meant he wouldn't be obligated to hand over any titles that the Queen Regent might bestow if he found Princess Kira first.

"We should head toward Corlea. All of the attacks have been along the Royal Route, and every part of the Royal Route leads there. If we're going to find the Beast, it has to be there."

Uncle Julius smiled. "I knew you were the best of my nephews, Robby. So smart. Come."

The sun had fully risen by the time they made the main road back toward the Royal Route.

# Chapter Thirty-One
## Bertie

*Annabel Moorelow had the furry white doll Kira had given him in a death grip.*

"Mine!" she howled. "Xavvy gave it to me!"

"He said you have to share." Her sister tried once again to yank the doll away, only to have Annabel lash out and nearly hit her.

"Momma, make Violet stop touching my doll."

Was there a word for the wrong kind of nostalgia — the kind of memory that washed up and made you feel sick? Bertie felt like he should know a word like that, but he didn't. How many toys had he had that his parents had thrown out because they saw play as a weakness?

He reached over and pulled the doll away from the little girls. "Actually, Princess Kira gave me this doll, and I am the one who said you could play with it. But I'll take it back if you can't play nice."

"No fair!" Violet stuck her tongue out, and Annabel's little chin wobbled as she worked up some giant alligator tears.

"Enough, ladies." Princess Margo told her daughters. "Lord Albert is right. The doll belongs to neither of you."

"But Xavvy gave it to me!" Annabel said.

Princess Margo shooed both daughters toward one of the many mountains of toys piled around the family drawing room.

"I am sorry, Albert. I know it must be hard to see this silly squabbling when you're worried about Kira."

The family, save Prince Brandon who was meeting with the Queen Regent and the Kingdom Council, had retreated from the courtyard to their private space. The castle was so crowded because of the Festival, that it was one of the only rooms they could be assured of privacy. Someone was sure to come along and find them eventually, but for now the Moorelows were doing their best to hide. Later they would move among their guests, and try not to be identified as the royals who'd lost the heir to the throne.

"I'll take it upstairs. Out of temptation."

"Do you want me to come?" Xavier asked.

Usually if they were escaping his family, he and Xav would find a quiet and private place to retreat but Bertie found he wanted to be alone.

"No, I'll be back in a minute or two." He secured the doll under his arm, avoiding his boyfriend's confused look.

The castle halls were heaving with people. At every turn, servants were fighting their way through the throngs, carrying everything from tea trays to great trunks, as if their employers soon planned to depart. He wove his way through the mass of bodies, until he reached the staircase to his suite.

His room was as much a bedroom as it was a sanctuary. Bertie turned the key in the lock to prevent any unwanted visitors. He paused at the door to the doll closet, and said the small incantation to the Fairies he'd learned as a child in the Unknown Kingdoms.

"Light and Dark, protect me both."

He wasn't sure he really believed any of it. After all, Fairies were people — long-live people with pointy ears — but people. Accordingly, he didn't always invoke the incantation when he went to his collection, but something wasn't sitting right in his gut. On the off chance that such a feeling meant anything, he spoke the words. As he'd done since before he could remember consciously doing so, he needed to talk to Daniella.

Bertie knew it was silly. He was an adult. He probably should have grown out of it, put such a childish thing away, but no, he'd never been able to bring himself to do it. Kira was his best friend, but he hadn't met her until his family had returned to Corlea when he was six. Before that, his choice of playmates had been his much older brother or a cheap doll dressed like an old peasant. He'd chosen Daniella every time. Which was the only way he could explain why he kept her in a luxury wardrobe, complete with Zephyr lamps, and doll-sized furniture.

He lit the lamps, adjusting the color until they shone a pale pink. Usually when he showed off his collection he kept the light green to emphasize the grotesqueness of the dolls that had joined Daniella's enclave, but he had no wish to sit in the semi-dark. Besides, the closet that had been mostly emptied thanks to the little Moorelow girls and their lack of personal boundaries.

Daniella lay on her little bed, staring blankly at the ceiling. He laid the white monster doll next to her, tugging at the red ribbon tied around its horn until it came loose.

"Kira's missing."

Of course Daniella never actually spoke, but sometimes Bertie imagined that there was a little voice that answered for her. Not words, really, an "Hmm," or a "Ah," or something like that.

"I don't know what to do. I don't think there's anything I can do. Every knight in the kingdom is out looking for her."

The little voice seemed to agree.

He dropped his head into his hands, the red ribbon dangling from his fingers. He'd never been this worried. A maid had come running out of Kira's suite well before sunrise, screaming and showing what seemed to be a handful of dog hair to whomever came close to her.

"The Beast! The Beast is here!"

Bertie saw her running through the castle, hysterically crying. He'd never gone to bed. He hadn't slept after the ball because he knew that Kira had probably reacted badly to the statue of Aunt Clara and Uncle Callum. He'd seen it on her face. She'd disappeared after the statue's unveiling and he hadn't been able to find her.

He knew that the Moorelows hadn't meant any harm in gifting that monstrosity. He'd tried to tell Xavier that, to no avail. They didn't know that Auntie Clara and Uncle Callum were as bad if not worse than his own parents. Prince Brandon and Princess Margo had ten children and loved them so fiercely there was no way they could imagine a scenario like the one Kira had been through.

"No, I don't imagine they could."

Bertie startled. That was not Daniella's imaginary voice.

On the shelf next to her bed, the little horned monster sat up and extended a paw. "Do us a favor and return my ribbon."

He knew his mouth was hanging open, he knew the ribbon was still clutched in his hand, but Bertie couldn't seem to move.

"I say, are you all right?" asked the tiny monster.

Bertie nodded.

"Well then, return my ribbon. If those girls are coming for me again, I would hate to be conscious of any part of it."

"They don't mean any harm."

"Children never do, and yet." The doll held out one leg to show a good portion of its lower paw missing.

Bertie glanced at Daniella, who hadn't so much as blinked. Which was good as her eyelids were little more than paint.

"She has assured me you are quite revenant and I am not to fear from you."

*Oh, well that was a relief.* He would have hated to think Daniella didn't care for him after twenty-three years. Bertie shook himself. What was happening? He was being drawn into some kind of alternate reality with talking dolls. Which was not why he'd come.

"Am I dead?"

"No, but I would suggest you take me to that witch who has been hanging around here. Crazy Morning or whatever her name is."

"Caris Mourne?"

"Yes," said the monster. "Quickly please."

****

Xavier Moorelow was the best of boyfriends. Kind. Intelligent. Good in bed. He was all around loving and understanding. By that standard Bertie should have been able to say, "A doll spoke to me and told me to take him to see a witch," without much fuss, but, sadly, things hadn't worked out that way.

He'd had to extract Xav from the drawing room in a none-too-smooth fashion, and hadn't been able to form the necessary words to inform him where they were going. Instead he pulled him along the crowded corridors as Xav shared the gossip that had exploded through the castle during Bertie's retreat.

"You missed it. Dad came back and said Queen Isadora is furious. Only knights were supposed to be in the running for the prize title, but a bunch of royals had visions of gold, and they all went running into the woods on the hunt for Kira."

Bertie pulled up short. " Isn't it better that everyone is looking for my cousin?"

Xav shrugged in that particularly sexy way that showed off the breadth of his shoulders. "I guess. I don't know. Dad said that he thought the Queen was…"

"Queen Regent," Bertie corrected without thinking.

Xav scoffed. "Not you too."

"Sorry, this is stressful."

Xav leaned against one of the balustrades that overlooked the central hall. "I know it. Dad looks like he thinks he's going to be hanged for letting this happen under his roof."

Bertie felt bad for Prince Brandon, but not entirely. How did the Beast of Barlow even get into a castle during the Festival?

"What's in the bag?" Xav made a grab for the satchel Bertie held.

He sidestepped, and held it as a line of female servants, all carrying hot water for what seemed to be a dozen baths. When the parade had finally passed, Bertie grabbed Xav's arm and pulled him along once more.

"Where are we going?"

But that was obvious when they reached the winding staircase up to the witch's tower.

"Did you get an invitation?" Xav looked worried. "She came out of the tower today already today and from what I've heard, that means she's toast. Powerful but not really sociable."

"In a way, yes."

As they climbed the stairs, Bertie kept the bag tight to his chest. He was winded by the time they reached the door at the top.

Xav used part of his tunic to cover his hand and knock. They heard movement behind the door, but no one answered.

"Told ya, toast," Xav whispered.

"Knock again, please."

Once again, Xav shrugged. The door was answered.

Bertie had noticed the witch talking to Sir Robert in the courtyard. She'd looked small and slight and a bit crazy, if he were being honest. Up close, she was all of those things, but her eyes were sharp, boring into his own with a pointed glare.

"My lady, we've come, to…" Xav ran out of words, because he really didn't know why they were there.

"I was told to come show you something."

"And?" The witch folded her arms over her chest.

Taking the doll carefully from the satchel, Bertie held it up and yanked once again on the red ribbon tied around the horns.

"Coconut Mops!" said the doll.

"Anthony, you know my name," Caris Mourne said to the doll. She shook her head, and gestured them into the tower proper. "You'll have to pardon my brother-in-law; he thinks he's funny."

And with that, Xav fainted. He dropped so suddenly that Bertie hadn't any chance of catching him. All six feet of sexiness dropped like a stone to the floor.

"Such a useful person." Caris Mourne pulled a pocket watch from the high waistband of her trousers, and twisted the top gear as she spoke a gibberish-sounding spell. Xav's unconscious body rose a few feet in the air, and floated toward a small cot in front of a roaring fire inside the witch's tower.

The watch dinged before Xav was centered over the cot, and he fell in a heap, half on, half off, and entirely face down.

"Well, that was better than the last time. You wouldn't believe it, but that's the second time today I've had to do that."

"You can let me go," the doll in Bertie's hand said, wiggling away. Bertie set him down on the floor. The little monster yawned and stretched and touched his toes a half-dozen times.

"Anthony, how did you end up like that? And how bloody long have you been in Dunlock?"

"I don't know. I've been in and out of consciousness. A week? You get trapped in a musty old doll and tell me what time means."

Although he hadn't been invited to sit, Bertie was woozy. He took one of the arm chairs next to Xav's cot.

"Oh you poor dear, let me get you some tea," the witch said. She took out the watch again, and in half a heartbeat a tea cart let itself into the tower room.

Bertie looked at his boyfriend, currently snoring away, unconcerned. Maybe fainting wouldn't be so bad.

The teapot on the cart rose as though lifted by the invisible hands. Dark, steaming tea flowed into a delicate porcelain cup. Three sugar cubes followed, flying from their matching bowl and dropping one at a time into the tea. The cup and a small, dainty spoon floated toward him. Bertie found himself taking them with an expression of thanks. He had no more room left in his brain for wonder.

"Where's Jack?"

"Jacobee is at the Fairie Courts."

"Ugh. No place I want to be."

"But you would be a foot high and stuck in an old doll?"

"Well, no. But trust me, the Fairie Courts are the worst. Everything all day long is politics, politics, gossip, gossip, banquet, banquet. A man can only attend so many banquets before he decides he'd rather be at the mercy of wolves."

"I'm sure." Caris Mourne sighed and turned her attention back to Bertie. "Now, I imagine you're hoping to find some information about your missing cousin?"

Bertie cleared his throat. The tea had helped immensely. Its warmth seemed to run through his stomach and all his limbs like a balm. "Uhm, do you have any? My lady?"

"A bit. But I fear my erstwhile brother-in-law may know more than I do at this point."

They both looked to Anthony who had replaced toe touching with jumping jacks. Seeing them stare at him he said, "Well get me out of here, and I'll tell you what I know. Use your little watch to give me a head start. I can do the rest once I'm out of this wool prison."

"Very well," said the witch. The pocket watch made its reappearance, and in half a moment, a particularly tall Fairie with glossy black hair and high, pointed ears stood in place of the doll. The Fairie stretched, moving his head back and forth before staring at Bertie.

"Relax, child, your dolls don't actually speak."

Bertie turned to Caris Mourne who was frowning at her brother-in-law. "Am I having a stroke?"

"No my dear, but you may be witnessing fratricide if Anthony doesn't get his act in gear."

He should feel relieved. But whatever was happening, it was all a bit much.

****

"I was curious. You can hardly blame me! That chapel used to have quite a nice portrait of me before all that unpleasantness." The Fairie, Anthony, jumped on the balls of his feet, and wiggled his neck back and forth. "If I'd known, I wouldn't have.... Well that's not here or there."

Caris Mourne paced; her pale hands clasped behind her back. She took surprisingly long strides, despite her lack of height.

Xav had finally come around to consciousness, and thanks to a cup of the witch's healing tea, was following her progress with his eyes.

"What is happening?" Xav's whisper wasn't subtle, but was ignored.

"Please get to the relevant information," Caris Mourne said.

The Fairie scoffed. "What is relevant to you isn't necessarily relevant to me."

"How did you end up in the doll, Anthony?"

"I don't know," said the Fairie petulantly. "One minute I was in the chapel, and the next... well, I had fur."

Xav sipped his tea, and leaned, still sleepy, against Bertie's shoulder. His hair smelled like sage and honey. It was the only thing that felt normal. It was all too much. Kira was gone, the castle was in chaos, and an actual Fairie was striding about the Dunlock Witch's Tower like he owned the place.

"Kira will be found," Xav said in a low voice.

He threaded his fingers through Bertie's, and gave a reassuring squeeze.

"I don't think the Beast will keep her long. The sixth or seventh time she reminds him that she's the heir to the throne, he'll probably throw her back."

Bertie wanted to smile, but he couldn't. While it was true that if anyone could annoy a mythical creature to distraction it was his prickly, wonderful cousin, but he couldn't joke when she was in real danger. Why had the Fairie been in the chapel? Fairies had been banned for decades. Twenty years at least.

He'd been a toddler, living in the Unknown Kingdoms, when the crown tried to forbid magic in Corlea.

He was unclear of the exact story, but from what he'd pieced together from family history, Aunt Clara had had some kind of spell about the time Kira was born. He wasn't sure what exactly had happened, but the result was that the Fairie chapel was burned, and there hadn't been anyone with magic in residence in Corlea Palace since.

"Was there anything or anyone unusual?" Caris Mourne passed the silver watch between her palms in a jerky, nervous gesture.

Anthony's face wrinkled in disgust. "I don't waste my time learning human things."

"Charming manners as always, Brother," said the witch.

"I'm sorry," Bertie asked. "Did you see anyone or not?"

"Rude child," the Fairie snapped.

Caris Mourne's dark eyes stared past her brother-in-law. Bertie was almost sure she was going to speak again, but though her lips moved she didn't say anything.

Xav sat up. "Is there a spell or something you can do to find Kira? I mean, since you're magical?"

The Fairie laughed. "Finding spells? Please."

"So you can't?"

"Of course I could, but I won't. Spells like that are beneath me. That's human magic. It's silly and it's useless. The girl is not a lost handkerchief or a stray shoe."

"But if we could find her?" Xav said. "Wouldn't it be..."

"I said no. Haven't you been listening?"

Bertie had had enough of the preening Fairie. Despite what he knew about deference to magical creatures, he was done accepting the disrespect. He stood, and crossed the room and poked a finger into the Fairie's chest. "You were talking to the crown prince of Dunlock. And I am eighth in line for the throne of the Known Kingdoms. Stop speaking to either of us like we're stupid. The life of Princess Kira is at stake."

The Fairie rolled his eyes. "Honestly, such drama. This is why Fairies stay away from you."

"Can you do a spell to find her or not, you useless thing?"

Bertie wasn't sure what he expected taunting a Fairie, but whatever that was, it wasn't what happened. The Fairie's face took on a nasty expression, wrinkled brow, his black eyebrows nearly vertical, and the tips of his pointed ears blood red as he spit out. "I don't have enough power!"

A thick silence followed. And it was only broken by the subtle laughter of Caris Mourne. Her laugh was like a rusty hinge, so little used that it made a noise that sent a shiver down Bertie's spine.

"I suspected as much," she said, "when you showed up as you did."

The Fairie's nostrils flared, and he narrowed his eyes at Bertie. "Happy now? You've found me out!"

The witch took out her silver watch, and the Fairie's face drained of color. "Tell the boys what you saw, Anthony," she said, with no small amount of menace.

The Fairie let out a great sigh, before settling down into the window seat again. "She was walking around, asking who was there. But I don't know why she'd bother, because it was a mess. Has no one really cleaned up from the fire? That is terribly rude."

Unease set into Bertie's stomach like food poisoning, throwing around everything he'd eaten into an acidic storm. "Who?"

"Your "princess" that's who."

"So Kira was at the old chapel? She told me that."

Caris Mourne stood out the window, looking out into the low-hanging clouds. He didn't doubt she'd heard every word.

"Ma'am, I don't know if it's important, but the chapel is where Kira and I used to play."

She whipped around, her spun-candy purple hair catching the light. "In the burned-out chapel?"

Bertie nodded. "When we were kids. Really up until I left for the Royal Academy. That was our spot."

Caris Mourne dropped her watch. It clattered against the floor, but despite the thunderstruck nature of her expression, the witch only said. "Hmm."

"Is that relevant?"

"That remains to be seen, but it is interesting."

## Chapter Thirty-Two
### Diana

***"We're confirmed for a visit to Tull this summer. It's all arranged with the** prince's aunt."*

Diana had never seen her mother so happy. The Countess of Wills was too stately to bounce on the balls of her feet, but it wasn't hard to imagine.

"You've done so well, my dear. So well!"

Diana bit back her response. Telling her mother it was in bad taste to be happy about her new acquaintance with Prince Travers at a time when Princess Kira was missing would do her no good.

"I was worried when you agreed to dance the first set with Robby. He's a good boy, but I always knew you could do so much better."

"Mother, please." Diana would rather not think about Robby Lycette. The wound was too fresh.

The Countess plowed on, heedless of her daughter's plea. Once all this business at the Festival was over, they would head to Zinnj for fabric. There would be enough time to have a new wardrobe made before summer.

The great hall was crowded with royals, battered knights returned from the hunt, and servants tending to both. The remaining events of the Festival had been canceled, but with the search for the princess — and the incentive of a possible inheritable title as a reward — no one was leaving Dunlock. As a result, breakfast was chaos. By the time the servants fought through the crowds, the tea and coffee were practically cold.

"Perhaps we'll travel directly. I'll write to your father. He'll see no reason for us to return to Wills."

Diana kept her face impassive. She wanted to go home, but her mother wouldn't care. Not when there was a prince in her sights.

"Tull is lovely in the late spring, but I don't know about summer. I haven't been since…"

Diana willed her mother to stop talking. She even implored Bathsheba The Babbler for silence, but her prayer went unanswered.

The Countess was so absorbed in talking about the pleasures to be found in Tull that she kept ignoring the serving maid trying to put down her breakfast.

Diana motioned to the flustered girl. "You can put it here."

The maid hesitated, but as she was being hailed by yet another royal looking for breakfast, she placed all the dishes in front of Diana before hurrying off.

"We'll meet Prince Travers for tea today. Dunlock cannot object, despite all of this madness. Where is that girl with the food? I swear, it is taking ages."

Diana slid her mother's bowl over and cleared her throat significantly.

Her mother glanced down, tsked, and kept talking.

Diana cradled her coffee cup in both hands. It wasn't hot enough, but it would have to do.

"Ladies and Gentleman, if I may have your attention," said Prince Brandon from the head table.

Most eyes turned toward him, but the hush wasn't complete until the doors to the great hall opened and Caris Mourne walked into the room. Diana had only glimpsed her yesterday when the witch had come down at the beginning of the hunt.

She'd spoken to Robby. Diana would have once imagined that he would share such a momentous event as speaking to Caris Mourne and all of the details of that meeting with her, but no. The way the witch had spoken to him was an indication that it wasn't the first time they'd met. And yet, he'd said nothing about knowing her. More than his disregard, that hurt. How many times had they talked about the famous witch?

Caris Mourne's footsteps echoed through the hall. Diana had never imagined she was so tiny. The stories about her were so oversized, it seemed impossible that she was so insubstantial. With the brilliant sunlight streaming through the great hall's windows she looked rather sickly, to be honest. Her narrow face was ashen. Her clothing, including the red witch's shawl, seemed to swallow her whole.

The witch stepped up to the head table and spoke in a whisper to Prince Brandon.

"There has been news of the Princess. A shred of her nightdress was found in the woods outside Barlow."

"The Beast!" someone shrieked, and talk erupted throughout the great hall.

An older man in the pink and blue robes of the Kingdom Council stood, and shouted toward Prince Brandon but there was too much of a cacophony for his words to be heard.

Prince Brandon himself couldn't quiet the crowd, no matter how long he held up his hands for silence. Diana watched as Caris Mourne took what seemed to be a pocket watch from the waistband of her trousers and twisted the top dial.

In a heartbeat no sound came from the great hall, no voices, no chairs scraping against the stone floor, no clatter of bowls and silverware. People all around Diana seemed to realize they could no longer speak or make any noise, and panic took hold. They grabbed at their throats and opened and shut their mouths in quick succession with no luck.

The witch faced the crowd. "Your voices will return in a moment. I'm sorry for the spell, but needs must. Sir Roderick will speak, and then Prince Brandon will fill you in on the rest of the details of what the hunters have yet discovered."

She bowed her head toward Prince Brandon and Princess Margo, and took quick but soundless steps out of the great hall. Only when the doors closed once more did the uproar return, although the shock of having lost all ability to speak left a heavy dose of silence in its wake.

Sir Roderick, the Kingdom Council member spoke. "The Queen Regent has authorized me to direct that anyone who feels safe and is able to search — be it commoner or royal — please meet in the courtyard to be sorted into search parties."

"Are whole search parties to be given titles?" Someone shouted in an incredulous snit.

Sir Roderick colored. "The Kingdom Council will decide on the issue of the offered title when and if the Princess is found."

That went over about as well as might be expected in a room full of exhausted, hungry and power-mad royals. Diana couldn't hear distinctly afterwards, except for the man closest to her at the long trestle table who stood on his chair to shout, "So you're letting the Queen go back on her word?"

Sir Roderick was clearly over his head, because he sank back to his chair, and Prince Brandon was forced to speak once more.

"Our priority is finding the Princess Royal. Her welfare is paramount to the wealth and security of our lands."

But that wasn't the answer that anyone was looking to give. New royal titles were scarce. Because of the inheritance laws, most children of royals would lose their positions in society once their parents died. The chance for a new title, and one that could be passed down at that, was worth more than any Vineland princess.

"Please, if any of you could join the search, you would earn the never-ending generosity of my wife and I, and the entire Moorelow family."

Royals started streaming out of the halls. Diana spotted Sir Jordaan among the knights sporting bandages and more evidence of the previous day's hard ride. She didn't know him well, but he was a knight of Lower Miser which meant, despite her desire to forget all about Robby Lycette, she needed to speak with him.

Luckily, the Countess got caught up in a discussion with a woman the next table over, on the benefits of shoes from Spire, and Diana was able to slip away.

Sir Jordaan had a smirking, untrustworthy smile. It stretched across his face like a knife blade from the moment he realized she was approaching him.

"Well hello." He wiggled his eyebrows. He was definitely not her type. He was all-over sort of shaggy, from the rough cut of his blond hair to his rather thick eyebrows. And despite the wooden table and the unforgiving benches, he seemed to be sitting in recline.

"Do you have any news of Sir Robert," she asked. "I saw him ride out yesterday but he hasn't returned."

"Oh lord, you're the wife-to-be, aren't you?"

Pure embarrassment burned up Diana's face. "What?"

"What's your name, Deena-Something?"

"Diana Yarborough of Wills. And no, Robby I were never..." She bit back her words. Apparently everyone knew she was an idiot.

Jordaan waved his hand dismissively. "Relax. I'm teasing. Rob talks about you."

"I need to know if you've had word of him. He's my friend and I am worried about him."

Jordaan raised one shoulder. "Lycette's head over ass for the princess, so maybe save your worry."

That expression made no sense. Unless they were standing on their head, everyone was head over ass. "I'm not blind, Sir Jordaan. Nor am I deaf. I would appreciate a straight answer."

Jordaan shrugged. His tunic had a rather significant mustard stain on it, the lazy sod. She did feel rather bad about the bandage across his forehead that seemed to be covering a significant cut, but that wasn't enough to arouse enough sympathy to keep the conversation going much longer.

"I rode North yesterday. Hit a storm and had to turn back. I didn't see Lycette leave and I haven't heard of him since."

"Thank you." She turned to go, but Jordaan had one last parting shot.

"Don't be too worried. The crazy princess isn't going to marry our boy. He'll come crawling back to you eventually."

Diana clamped her back teeth together to avoid cursing and turned to fight her way back through the crowd. Even her mother's company was preferable to the humiliating Sir Jordaan.

"It's settled. Tea with Prince Travers and his aunt in the East sitting room at four," her mother said as Diana slunk back into her seat.

By four o'clock, Travers was likely going to be glassy-eyed and slurring his words. He was as likely to propose as he was to vomit in a potted plant. Not that she believed even for a moment that she would marry him, despite his leering at her during the ball. The man was a garbage fire unfit for matrimony.

Restless, Diana couldn't shake the feeling that it was all for naught. "Shouldn't we help look for Princess Kira?"

The Countess blanched. "You are not to go anywhere near the search. Trained knights are coming back in terrible shape. Apparently there was some kind of magic storm that resulted in injuries."

Diana looked back toward Sir Jordaan who was piling his plate high with eggs. His bandage wasn't small.

"Was anyone hurt badly?"

Mother didn't know how bad things, but she'd heard a few things that sounded ominous. "No one is leaving. It's not safe to travel. So as long as we're here, we might as well get on with the business at hand."

Which meant arranging tea with a potential suitor. Even if he was an ass.

"Fine, I'll wear the blue gown."

Her mother smiled, somehow wider and more predatory than seemed possible. "I knew you were my favorite child, Diana."

Diana forced a smile and tried not to think how stiff the competition was, given she was an only child.

## Chapter Thirty-Three
### Kira

***Kira pulled the bread from its place in the icebox.*** The mold hadn't bothered to contain itself to the bread. A blue-green bloom crawled over the towel that covered it.

*Damn.*

The other stores in her hut weren't much better. The marmalade jar had a broken lid, and the contents had gone hard and stuck to the glass. The butter had apparently sustained a family of rodents for some time. The pump, at least, brought in fresh, cold water, but a woman couldn't live on water alone.

She would need food until she figured out how to get out of the stupid cloak. It was hot and heavy and smelled like a wet dog.

Or perhaps that was her? It was a toss-up.

The weight of it was beginning to push down on her shoulders and pull on the muscles in her upper back. The hood was stuck to her face, and her peripheral vision was affected by the narrowness of the eye holes. It was a miracle she'd managed to make her way to the cottage. But then again, she'd run through the woods often enough wearing it.

Even taking the tunnels, it had taken her most of the day to reach her sanctuary. Night had long since fallen. She'd lit only one Zephyr lamp, and kept the flame an inconspicuous orange to avoid attracting too much attention.

She drank until her stomach was stretched. Hopefully that would keep her through the night. In the morning, she could take the tunnels the rest of the way to Corlea Palace. And with any luck, that nightmare would be over. The whole day would be nothing but a bad dream.

The bed groaned under her weight. One cloak shouldn't add that much. She stretched, but the unforgiving cloak wouldn't give. It was as if its fur of was growing out of her own skin. It itched and it stank. In the morning, she would bathe in the nearby creek. Maybe immersing herself in the water would loosen it.

The night wasn't quiet. Despite being tired in every fiber of her being, Kira couldn't shut out the noise. The creatures of the forest were too restless. Owls hooted, and bugs hit the window pane by the dozen. Trees swayed and twigs snapped. It was like trying to sleep with a party going on in the next room. She'd never been able to sleep during the events her parents threw at the Palace, much to the dismay of the nurses and governesses assigned to keep her confined to her chambers.

Perhaps she would take that dip in the creek before daylight. When her feet touched the stone floor, pain shot up from her legs. It was as if her boots were filled with crushed glass, and she struggled to pull them off.

Thick black nails grew out of her toes, and a coat of dense fur coated her foot. She hadn't time to examine her other foot before the talons broke through the boot's leather. Kira screamed, but instead of the high-pitch of her natural voice, a deep, ground-shaking rattle filled the room.

She pulled off the tatters of her second boot. Her feet were no longer dainty and small and fit for a princess. No glass slippers would ever fit the monstrous paws where they had once been. Kira reached for the Zephyr lamp to adjust the color and the brightness to see the damage, but as she did, talons, thick and sharp, grew rapidly from the ends of her fingers. The lamp tumbled to the floor, and the enchanted flame shot out of the casing. It pinged around the four corners of the cottage before finding an escape through the thin sliver of the open window.

The cottage was bathed in darkness. Which was probably why when the tea kettle began to speak, Kira didn't scream. It was too black to see the lid rise and fall like a mouth.

"Wasteful. Shamefully wasteful. Do you know, young lady, how much those lamps cost?"

Kira's eyes scanned the room, but the shadows were too long. It certainly didn't feel like anyone was here. Perhaps she was hallucinating.

The voice spoke again. "Two hundred pieces of gold! For one lamp. And now, you've got nothing more than glass."

The voice clucked his tongue in disapproval.

Kira suppressed a momentary spurt of irritation. She had been transformed into a hideous Beast. Who cared about a lamp? "I'm the Princess Royal. If I need another lamp, I'll buy a new one."

Another voice, female, joined the conversation. "And how, my dear, are you to do that in your current state?"

Kira sighed. There was no point in getting more upset, having a conversation with herself. "I'm going to bed. I shall figure it out in the morning."

"Leave the servants to do the work," said the woman. "Typical royal."

"Yes," Kira said, flopping back on the little bed. The bed springs snapped and collapsed, but what was one more tragedy for this terrible day? She circled like a dog, settling into the nest of feathers and torn bedding. "If you're really here, clean the cottage, fetch me some food, and wake me when this is all a terrible, horrid memory."

"Who are you to order us about?" said the first voice.

"The future queen of the Known Kingdoms," she said with a yawn. "And I've had a very bad day, so please shut up."

In the morning, or whenever her mind was her own again, she would examine why she was not more terrified. Perhaps because having been transformed into the image of the Beast of Barlow, what was left to fear?

****

Kira slept, dreamless and deep. She woke up in a pool of sunlight, her bones warmed, her terror at bay. She stretched, and used one of her deadly talons to detangle a small knot in the fur over her ear.

The cottage had the pleasant smell of bacon and toasted bread. She tried to breathe it all in, but was once again reminded too forcefully of her own stink.

"I need a bath." She spoke aloud for no reason other than she was lonely. For all her escapes to the cottage, that night's sleep was the longest she'd ever been by herself.

"Breakfast first," said the bossy female voice of the previous evening.

The smell of bacon hadn't been an illusion. A plate of neatly fried, crisp bacon sat on the dining table. A pile of thick, toasted country bread sat next to it, pots of butter and jam at the ready.

"Have I died?" Kira asked, but found she didn't care. She bounded to the table, scooping up the bacon in one paw and swallowing it whole. She hadn't eaten since before the ball and she was ravenous.

"And here I thought royals were supposed to have manners," said the tea kettle, as it emptied itself of boiling water into a waiting mug.

The broom took the trouble to answer her since the tea kettle wasn't inclined. "No dear, you're enchanted."

Well, that should have been obvious. Kira watched as the broom scurried about, kicking up dust from the corners of the cottage.

"Well, are you going to drink this tea or let it go to waste?" snapped the tea kettle.

Kira sat at the table, surprised the bench could hold her new, heavier weight. She reached for the rough-hewn mug, careful to take it in her paws so it didn't meet the same fate as the Zephyr lamp. The tea was hot, strong, and sweet, exactly as she liked it.

"More, please," she said when the mug was empty. "Of everything."

"Just so," said the tea kettle, hopping over to fill her mug once more. She watched as the handle detached from the side of the pot, and he used it to scoop tea into a diffuser.

"Are you enchanted as well?"

"Most certainly not," the tea kettle said.

"We were never human, if that is what you're asking," the broom said.

"Do you have names?"

The tea kettle scoffed, but the broom answered, "I have always wanted to be called Matilda. Isn't that a lovely name? Matilda Bristle."

"Lovely to meet you, Mrs. Bristle," Kira said. She couldn't curtsey from the bench, nor in the form she was in, but politeness seemed important. She'd been unaccountably rude last night. She looked at the tea kettle, who dropped the diffuser into the mug, and huffed in impatience when she reached for it.

"Not yet! Tea must steep."

And who could argue with that? Tea *did* need to steep.

"What shall I call you?" she asked the tea kettle.

"Kettle will do."

"Thank you for your service."

"Just so." The little kettle hopped off the table and returned to the fire. In no time more bacon was frying in the pan set above the flames.

"I really do need a bath," Kira said. "I'm frightfully disgusting."

"Yes, dear," said Matilda Bristle. "That is certain."

As Kettle served her a triple helping of bacon, the cottage door opened and a large copper tub floated to a spot in front of the fire. Bucket after bucket of steaming water followed. As it filled, a privacy screen scooted over and unfolded itself.

"In you go," said Kettle, taking the half-drunk tea from her paws.

Kira bounded over behind the screen. Neither Matilda Bristle nor Kettle had a face, much less eyes, but she was somehow reluctant to bathe in front of either of them.

The nightgown she'd been wearing when she fled Dunlock was little more than rags clinging to her fur. She shucked them off, but not before doing a quick survey of the room to make sure nothing else had come to life. It didn't seem so. The mantle clock and the candlesticks sat inert. She dropped the wretched remains of her clothing onto the floor and climbed into the tub.

The hot water was heaven although her larger body didn't have much room. Her paws stuck out over the edge. Kira examined them, marveling at their existence. Multi-colored fur, every shade from pure white to cream to beige to deepest, darkest black traveled from her wide, flat feet up her legs. Her whole body, it seemed, was coated in the same fur. In some places the colors clumped together, in others they spread out like the hair of a brindle dog.

The Beast of Barlow's cloak was the same. She'd worn the loose, heavy garment with a glad heart. She'd run through the woods, robbed the royals, and retreated to her little cottage. And this is where it had brought her.

"Am I to stay here?" she asked, sinking as much as she could under the shelter of the hot water.

"For a time, dear," said Matilda Bristle at the same time Kettle answered, "Most certainly not. Princesses don't live in the woods."

Kira had to wonder if she was still considered a princess. The Vineland women of the past had varied in looks, from stunning beauties to downright ugly old crones, but none had ever grown two short, curling horns out the tops of their heads. At least, not any of the ones on display in the portrait gallery.

"Clean yourself. Rest. Kettle will make more tea."

"And more bacon. And another loaf of toasted bread. Perhaps a rabbit?" Kira's stomach growled and pitched as if she would never get enough food.

"Ordering us about, bah," said Kettle. "Remind me never to be among royals again."

"Just so," said Matilda Bristle.

## Chapter Thirty-Four
### Robert

***Despite the old horse — and the wig he refused to take off — Uncle Julius*** was a surprisingly good hunting partner. He was eagle-eyed when it came to spotting tracks and identifying which animals were likely to have made them.

"A whole fleet of deer came through here. The last time the Beast was said to be on the loose, there were no deer in the woods at all."

They had spent most of the first day exploring the surrounding forest in the area between Dunlock and the Corlea border. The woods here weren't well-traveled and the trees dense. Robert hadn't seen the deer tracks at all.

"How is that possible? Isn't the Beast a bunch of old stories?"

"I suspect people would like it to be. The Beast of Barlow or something like it, turns up every twenty years or so. Runs wild, causes trouble."

"Does it usually rob carriages?"

Uncle Julius tipped his wig back into place for the 9th time. "Not that anyone would admit."

"Kidnapping, also new?"

His uncle nodded. "This is definitely something else, Robby."

Robert tried to work it out. Durrin's theory that the Beast was someone in costume didn't make sense with Kira missing. Was it even the same person? Or could someone pretending to be the Beast have been watching her or following her? Had they taken the gold wrapper as some kind of souvenir? Had all those carriage robberies been nothing more than a smoke screen to cover her eventual abduction?

"Fairies be, it's been a long time since I've gone on a hunt." Uncle Julius leaned back in his saddle and yawned.

An excellent hunter but not one of stamina. If they were going to find Kira, they were likely to be in the saddle for a long time.

"I think we should head to Corlea stables. Durrin, the Stablemaster had some interesting ideas about who might be behind it all."

Corlea stables meant Corlea Palace. Despite his usefulness of the trail, there was a good chance that Uncle Julius wouldn't be able to resist the lure of the comfortable Palace. With the princess missing and the Queen Regent in Dunlock, he'd practically have the place to himself.

"Excellent idea. Excellent."

They were another quarter of an hour from where the path cut back to the Royal Route when Uncle Julius pulled his horse up short. He held his finger to his lips. The brush around them seemed to rustle, as if cart loads of dry leaves had all been stirred up at once. No small animals emerged onto the path, but the forest around them seemed alive. A wave of debris — broken branches, leaves, pine needles, and fresh dirt — crashed out of the tree line and onto the path, causing both horses to spook and rear.

Robert was able to control Amzi, but the Dunlock job horse wasn't so easily reigned.

"This is beyond anything the Beast has ever done." Uncle Julius pulled hard on the bridle, but the horse, his legs covered by the forest wave, refused to be still.

A rumble like thunder shook the trees, and a rain of small branches started coming down on them.

"We need to keep moving!"

The job horse reared again. Uncle Julius slipped out of the saddle, but his grip on the bridle kept him from falling off. Unable to shake his rider, the horse bolted through the storm of brush. Robert spurred Amzi to follow.

Amzi whinnied, but charged after the fleeing horse and its dangling rider.

They were both breathless by the time they reached the Royal Route. Uncle Julius had somehow managed to keep hold of the horse, but his leg was badly bruised from the rough ride. Robert hadn't escaped unharmed either. At least one of the falling branches had scrapped his forehead, leaving a stinging cut behind.

"The forest had spoken." Uncle Julius's breath was short, his face ashen.

They made slow progress toward Corlea Palace. Neither of them seemed to want to speak after the unreal events they'd witnessed. Uncle Julius was clearly in pain and unable to carry on a conversation. By the time the gleaming pink and blue Palace emerged over the tops of the trees they were both in relief.

Uncle Julius didn't wait for the stable lads to come scurrying from the barn. Instead he dismounted as soon as they reached the open space of the yard. He limped as he led the horse toward shelter.

"I won't be able to go on."

Robert had known that was coming, had even counted on it, but he found he was sad to leave his uncle behind.

Durrin, cap pulled tight over his ears, emerged from the stables. A pipe was stuck between his teeth, and a cloud of smoke floated over his head.

"Sir Robby, back again."

"My uncle is hurt, I'm afraid we'll need to ask for your hospitality again."

Durrin's sharp eyes took in the state of the Duke of Lower Miser and whistled. A stable hand in too-short trousers came running at the summons. "Get up to the kitchen and tell Mrs. Barnbee to expect a healing."

The lanky young man took off at a run, and Durrin led them into his private quarters in the lush Corlea stables. Durrin occupied three rooms at the far end of the barn, and settled them in the first of them, a small sitting room stuffed with mismatched furniture. He pulled up a tufted ottoman, and helped Robert get Uncle Julius seated with his injured leg propped up.

"That ain't no wound from falling off a horse." Durrin hastily stuffed an escaped lock of curly hair under his cap.

"Perceptive as always, Master Durrin," Uncle Julius said. "We encountered some kind of storm in the woods."

Robert did his best to explain the swirl of debris that had seemed to attack them on the trail.

Durrin whistled. "Been a while since I've seen that."

Skeptical, Uncle Julius scoffed. "You're saying you've seen a mysterious dust storm go on the attack before?"

"Might have." Durrin bustled about the room, preparing a draft of whisky from an old flask. He handed the glass to the Duke, but Robert declined. He'd had enough whisky for a lifetime. "Lot of strange things in the forest."

"With the princess missing, it can't be a coincidence." Robert felt silly speaking, but Durrin was being unusually cagey, even for a half-Fairie.

"Missing, is she?"

Uncle Julius filled in the stable master with a few of the relevant details. "Stolen from her bed."

At the mention of the prize on offer, Durrin let out another long, high whistle. "The road will be crawling with folks."

Mrs. Barnbee arrived with a healing kit, and saw to clucking over the Duke as if he were a recalcitrant child and not a grown man. "Oh, Your Grace, *my my my*. Let Mrs. B get you all fixed up and then brought to the Palace. Queen Isadora will have our heads if she thinks we only put you up with these smelly old horses."

A frown cut into Durrin's elfin face. "Good enough for the likes of you, Aimee Barnbee."

"Oh hush," said the formidable Mrs. B, as she worked on the Duke's injured leg.

As much as he might have enjoyed the domestic teasing of the stablemaster and the housekeeper of Corlea Palace, Robert was impatient to go. Kira was out there somewhere with the Beast. It was still early, but with the tempestuous weather of late, and the chance of more mysterious storms emerging from the woods the danger was great.

Seeing his impatience, Mrs. Barnbee scolded Durrin for not offering him a drink.

"I offered," said Durrin, offended.

"Offer again. The poor boy is worried sick."

Robert wanted to protest, but that was the truth. He needed to be out in the woods. He wouldn't rest easy until Kira was found. Caris Mourne had said that the unintentional magic was getting stronger. Between that and the threat of the Beast, Kira was in real danger. Robert knew he had no claim to her, no right to feel protective other than his role as a knight of the realm, but somehow, somehow....

He loved her.

It was like jumping into a cold lake, fully clothed. Exhilarating, as if a thousand icy needles were waking up his skin all at once, but also terrifying. The water would weigh down his clothes and pull him toward the bottom. Acknowledging that he was in love with Kira — with the Princess Royal — was a heavy feeling. He had no right. He was a knight from an unimportant island in the Northern Sea.

Loving her would get him nowhere. Even if he was able to rescue her — to win the title granted by the Kingdom Council — he'd have to turn it over to his uncle. He was obligated to follow his lord. And if somehow he didn't, if he risked alienating his family and profession, a title and a castle weren't enough to elevate him to be anything close to worthy of her.

But he loved her.

Perhaps he should have taken that drink that Durrin offered, despite the lingering sourness in his stomach.

"You don't look well, Robby," Uncle Julius said. "Perhaps we should both stay here."

Sweat had broken out on Robert's forehead. His hands were clammy, and when he stood, the room swayed before him.

Mrs. Barnbee clucked and shooed him back into a seat. "Oh, Dear, dear. Sir Robby, are you all right?"

Robert tried to form words. To say that he was fine, that he only needed to see to Amzi and get back to the hunt. Uncle Julius stood, despite his bad leg, and put a hand to Robert's forehead. "Robby, my boy, why didn't you say you were hurt?"

"Not…" But even as he struggled to get the words out, Robert caught sight of the blood seeping from his wrist into the upholstery of Durrin's battered old armchair. The old bite mark — the claim — on his wrist was red and sticky with his blood.

Too woozy to do more than stare at it, Robert held up his arm. A drop of blood, as thick as pea soup, fell onto the floor as he watched.

"Oh my. Did you ever see such a thing?" Mrs. Barnbee asked.

Robert was almost sure he heard Durrin's spooked, "Might did," before the blackness took him.

# Chapter Thirty-Five
## Diana

**Prince Travers hadn't said much as he joined them in the East Room,** slipping into the seat beside her, smelling faintly alcoholic. Two days of patchy beard covered his chin, and his dark eyes were glassy. And that's what she'd expected, wasn't it? It was the moment he took the flask out of his coat pocket and tipped the contents into his teacup that got to her.

She wasn't shocked that he would do such a thing, it was the way that her mother and his aunt, Lady Passwood, were so determined to ignore it.

He noticed Diana's wild-eyed expression and tipped the flask toward her.

She took it. She didn't know why, but the whole situation was absurd. Maybe it would help.

He grinned. "I knew I liked you."

Even with the rumpled, misbuttoned state of his clothing and deep circles under his eyes, Travers was handsome when he smiled. It wouldn't last of course. Eventually he'd drink until the capillaries on his nose burst and his gut resembled uncooked dough. She supposed it was good that he was looking for a wife so young — before time and poor decisions slammed into him like a runaway horse. He'd have just enough charm and good looks to make the bargain look not so bad.

*Poor dear.*

Lady Passwood ignored the proceedings at the table, keeping up an endless chatter about the proposed visit to Tull Castle. "You'll arrive at the end of the crane season. You've never seen anything as beautiful as the teal cranes dropping over the Island's cliffs."

Every royal thought the cranes growing in their kingdom were special. Her father was particularly fond of telling people that the cranes in Wills were more fragile than any others. You could tell because the color was so pale a blush pink.

"Diana has always looked particularly good in shades of blue and green." Her mother's every attempt to turn the conversation back to her were admirable but like the spiked tea they were rebuffed with alacrity.

"We'll arrange a boat ride for the first day, and perhaps a trip on the royal yacht."

The whisky at least made the tea palatable. The repast sent by the Dunlock kitchens was both meager and tasteless.

"Diana is an excellent sailor."

"Mother, please."

Travers snickered.

Diana drained her cup and refilled it with what was left in the teapot. Travers supplied the whisky.

"Stop that." But she drank it anyway.

"After our stay in Tull, perhaps you'll join us in Wills this summer. The North Sea is particularly lovely then."

Travers gave a snort. "That's because it's bloody freezing the rest of the year."

Lady Passwood's only reaction was a subtle shift of her gaze. "I'm sure whatever little hospitality you can offer would be kind, but the Prince does travel with a large retinue."

Diana felt the color drain from her face. Had Lady Passwood implied they were poor?

The Countess forced a smile and soldiered on. "Wills Castle has 48 guest rooms. I'm sure we'll find a few that will accommodate the Prince's traveling parties."

Diana reached under the table and gave her mother's hand a squeeze. A small, sad smile flitted across the Countess's face, but only for a moment.

"Whatever does one do with four dozen guest rooms on the North Sea?" Lady Passwood had a mirthless laugh.

Diana rolled her eyes and drained the rest of her tea.

"Yarborough City Sea Port is the hub of all the crane imports for the northern territories. Royals are always coming and going."

In other words they were very well connected and very rich.

Lady Passwood dabbed her napkin at the corners of her mouth. She hadn't ingested a morsel. "The northern territories don't cover half the land of Tull all together."

Diana caught Travers' eye, hoping he'd pay attention and speak up before all hell broke loose. The Countess might want Diana to marry well but she wasn't going to sit here and be insulted.

"Including the unusable land, of course. But per capita, Wills crop production has far out-stripped all of the Known Kingdoms in the last decade. And if I remember, you had quite a difficulty with the Tull crane last year."

Pointing out the fallacy of the Tull crops was apparently a step too far for Lady Passwood. "Perhaps we were too hasty in our invitation."

"Well when one is trying to marry off poor goods, one does want to make hasty invitations."

Lady Passwood's over-powdered face went scarlet. The Countess didn't budge. She glared at the Prince's aunt, daring her to be the one to storm out.

Oddly it was Travers who managed to blow the tension to smithereens by breaking into a fit of laughter. He laughed so hard a tear slipped down his face.

"Oh this is good. Ten out of ten, I would definitely recommend this show to my friends."

"Travers, really," Lady Passwood said.

"I'm poor goods! You heard it, Auntie." He didn't bother pouring his whisky into his tea, but drank it straight from the flask.

"I think we're done here."

"No, by all means, please keep at it. Can we insult my dead father next? Maybe talk about Lady Diana's rather large feet?"

Her mother sprang to her defense. "Diana has a delicate step!"

"Diana trod on my feet three times before we were even off the dance floor. That's not the point, Countess."

All three women glared at him as they all waited for Travers to get to the point.

"You want me to marry her? Fine. Wills gets access to the southern and western territories for the crane trade and Tull gets a connected and wealthy princess. Seems like a fair trade to me."

"Really, Travers, you can do better," Lady Passwood said.

"No, I don't think I can."

Diana felt his eyes scan over her and had to resist the urge to shake like a dog expelling water from its coat. Her mother wasn't wrong. Travers was bad goods. Head of a massive territory that was, if the gossip were correct, facing financial trouble. Meanwhile, he was drinking his problems away.

There was an uneasy moment of silence as the two women stood down from their cold war.

Lady Passwood pushed away her undrunk tea and turned to Travers. "This is what you want?"

He nodded. "She'll do."

"Fine."

Diana gritted her teeth to keep from gasping. *She'll do?* That was what constituted a proposal from the Prince of Tull?

Lady Passwood swept from the room, and Prince Travers followed.

Her mother was still in high color. "When you marry him, Diana, give her title to your second cousin with the lazy eye."

"Merry wears corrective lenses now."

The Countess shrugged. "She can take them off for the investiture to stick to that awful…"

"Easy Tiger," Diana said, kissing her mother's cheek.

Her mother grabbed her hand. "I know he's not the man of your dreams, but so much good will come if you marry him."

She knew. Wills was prosperous, but if it were going to continue to grow, she needed to make an alliance with a larger kingdom. On that score, Tull was the biggest prize of all.

"He's still got time to grow up." At least, she hoped.

The Countess nodded. "I'll set your father on him."

"If I haven't told you lately, you are the best mother in the entire world."

"I am, aren't I? It's exhausting."

They laughed, and the Countess pushed away her own teacup. "I'm off to find some decent tea. This pot tasted of twice-washed leaves."

"Try it with whisky. I'm not sure it's better, but you won't care."

"We'll discuss that later." She dropped a kiss on the top of Diana's head.

Diana sagged in her chair. She was going to marry Prince Travers of Tull.

Maybe.

Because she'd "do," as if that meant anything at all. So far, he wasn't anything she'd hoped for in a partner. Travers was a mess, and he knew it. He also wasn't doing anything to fix it. He didn't seem to have any of Robert's inherent kindness. Or his shiny hair.

Not that Robert was such an ideal man. For years she'd been right in front of him, sharing confidences and first kisses and yet he didn't look at her as anything more than what she'd always been — a friend.

The pleasant buzz she had from drinking whisky-laced tea was short-lived. She needed to find some real food, and possibly another drink.

Something not watered down. She was on the point of leaving the East Room when Travers returned, sans his haughty aunt.

He grinned again. "My fair fiancé!"

"I haven't agreed to marry you." She went to move past him, but his big body blocked the only exit. He made no move to let her pass, but settled against the doorframe.

"It's a little late now, Sweetheart. Lady Passwood has given her blessing."

"That was giving a blessing? I hate to think what she does when she's displeased."

Travers snickered. "You'll get used to her."

Diana doubted it. Cousin Merry with the lazy eye might be in luck after all.

"Why are you here again?"

He shrugged. "I thought you might want to talk. Since we're going to marry and all."

"I'm sorry, did you not know the purpose of this tea was for us to speak?"

"With your mother squawking about your best colors and your ability to embroider orphan's underpants, or whatever that was?"

"Don't insult my mother."

"It's not insulting if I'm describing what happened."

"It's not being engaged if all you can say is, "She'll do," either."

His smirk went somehow deeper. He brushed his dark hair from his forehead. It was an action designed to draw attention to his eyes. Diana hated herself for looking. He was handsome. On the verge of certain and irreversible ruin, but handsome.

"Is that what has you in a snit?"

"Let me pass."

He wrapped his arms around her waist, pulling her close. He was big and solid — no bread dough in sight. "I should kiss you. To seal our engagement."

"Let go," she warned.

"Relax, Sweetheart."

He leaned in too close, and Diana reacted. She jerked her knee up between his legs and he cringed and dropped like a stone.

Diana pushed past him, only turning back when she was safely in the corridor. "You have to earn the right to call me anything other than Lady Diana, Asshole. In the meantime, clean yourself up."

Her dramatic exit would have been perfect if Sir Jordaan hadn't turned up like a bad penny. He was standing not two feet away from the door to the East Room looking between Diana and the collapsed Prince Travers.

"Fairies Be," he said. "Bravo." He clapped and whistled.

Diana rolled her eyes. "Save it."

He followed her as she made her way toward the great hall. "Honestly, that was excellent. Travers is a jackass."

"He's a drunk."

"They're not mutually exclusive."

Well, that was true. She took the stairs two at a time, but Jordaan kept up with her. "I'm not in the mood for flippant men at the moment. So can you take your assumptions and go away?"

"I'd offer to maim Travers for you, but you've already taken care of that."

She allowed him to open the doors to the great hall, where a buffet was kept up for the purpose of feeding all of the royals in attendance. The food on offer was more plentiful than the tea tray, but not by much. Servants watched over trays of sandwiches and bowls of fruit. A particularly stern footman was standing guard over the pastry tray, as if it were a precious commodity. Diana headed straight for the unwatched sideboard to pour herself a drink.

Sir Jordaan raised his eyebrows at her choice of beverage but wisely kept silent on that front.

"You said you saw Robby talking to Caris Mourne?"

She nodded and handed him a tumbler with a splash of whisky.

He took it but didn't drink. He gave her an assessing look. Unlike Travers' gaze, it didn't leave her feeling dirty. That was something. Still, she'd rather not have any man size her up like a prize pig at the fair.

"I asked Prince Brandon, and he didn't seem to know anything about it."

"I'm not sure how he missed her. Her hair is bright purple and she wears extremely interesting attire."

Jordaan brought the glass to his mouth, but once again, didn't drink. "She actually came out of the tower?"

Diana nodded. She'd said so this morning when Jordaan had brushed it off as nothing.

He gave up on the whisky. No sooner than he put it down, then a hovering footman whisked it out of view. Diana had to wonder if it would be poured back into a decanter when it reached the kitchens.

"Did you know he'd been in Dunlock since before the festival?"

"Was I supposed to know?"

Jordaan shook his head, as if there were a piece he couldn't quite work out. "We were on our way to Corlea for the Duke's inheritance petition when we were attacked by the Beast of Barlow. No sooner were we there then he rode out to Dunlock like the Fairies were after him."

"And now he's gone out again, only this time, no one has seen him in two days. Have you spoken to the Duke?"

"From all accounts, he tagged along with Robby."

Diana had known Lord Julius all her life. He was a sweet man but he wasn't exactly hearty. Jordaan apparently shared that assessment. "So maybe they stopped somewhere."

He nodded. "My guess is they're at Corlea. I'm going to ride out in the morning."

Diana got a rush of relief she wasn't prepared to acknowledge. Knowing someone would be looking for him lifted a weight she hadn't realized was sitting on her shoulders.

Jordaan's blue eyes narrowed. "You're not still pining for him, are you?"

"I do not pine. I told you, he's my friend."

Diana swirled the remaining liquid in her glass. The drink had helped some, but it was as if her insides had developed thorns, and her emotions were getting caught on them.

"He's an idiot, you know. I wouldn't be so stupid."

Startled, Diana looked up, caught by the momentary intensity in his eyes. It wasn't Travers' predatory look, but something else. Something like appreciation. There was a stutter of "Thank you," on the tip of her tongue, but no words came out. She wasn't ready to acknowledge anything of the kind.

"I'll send word if I find him." Jordaan bowed to her, and turned to go. Diana wondered if she should call out to him, wish him well on the journey, but honestly, she had no idea what to say.

The day had managed to chew her up and spit her out, and it wasn't quite five o'clock. She was going to be a walking vegetable by the time dinner was served if she didn't get some rest. She needed a quiet place. The suite she was sharing with her mother was no good. There would be questions from her lady's maid on the tea with the prince, and that was not a subject Diana cared to regurgitate. As spacious as Dunlock was, with all of the families in attendance for the Festival, and the search for the Princess, there was little chance she'd find a space in the castle itself.

She decided to try the gardens. There were at least a dozen follies scattered throughout the grounds. One of which was bound to have a reclining bench. It wouldn't be exactly comfortable, but that was okay. Alone — away from the men who plagued her — would be better.

The bitter cold of the morning of the hunt had worn off, and the sun was making its way over the grounds of Dunlock Castle. The gardens were a riot of greens and old statuary. It looked as if they had been designed by someone who only thought to make use of every old thing rather than any cohesive, planned designs. The path might lead to a Fairie fountain, or the giant marble bust of a long-dead Earl. The flowers followed suit. Rather than the manicured lanes of decorative cranes, there were unruly groups of anything that would grow – scraggly bushes, weedy daisies, stubby little star flowers all jammed into the same beds. It was all lovingly cared for, but without any rhyme or reason.

Most of the follies were unusable. Damp, lacking seating, or already crowded with royals seeking an escape from the castle. By the time she found a little rotunda both unoccupied and with a curvy little bench perfect for curling up with a book, Diana could feel the oppressive heat in her bones. Or maybe that was the weight of being all-but engaged to a letch with a drinking problem.

If she married him, she would be a princess. Wills would expand its trade far beyond its borders. Those were good things. She just wouldn't be happy.

Her parents were happy in their way. They loved each other, different as they were. Her mother loved to travel. She loved to visit and be social. Father was the opposite. He loved nothing better than to stay home and manage his land. Diana could count on one hand the number of times he'd left Wills Castle in her lifetime, and the number didn't take all of her fingers. And yet they were affectionate, loving and kind to one another. They shared a mutual respect.

She couldn't respect Travers as he was now. Unless he was hit upside the head with something heavy and completely changed his personality, it was hard to imagine him ever improving as a person. He'd looked at her as if she were cheap. As if he saw only enough to put in the least effort.

She deserved better.

Better than skeevy princes. Better than knights who couldn't get their head out of their ass. Just better.

"He demands payment, and then can't be bothered to answer…."

Diana startled, unsure of which direction the man's voice was coming from. It echoed around the dome of the folly.

"We've already paid," another answered.

Diana sat up, and peered out toward the garden. She didn't see anyone, but the two men continued talking.

"...demanding more. Ludicrous."

"Let me see the letter." It might have been another voice, but Diana couldn't be certain.

The voices weren't coming from outside. They were coming from an ornate grate set into the floor. A small shaft of light, probably from a Zephyr lamp, was visible in the darkness below, but nothing else. Whomever was speaking was in a room below the folly. She knelt down and put her ear close to the grate. The people must have been moving around, because their voices came in and out of sharpness.

Whatever was said next was muddled to her but caused multiple voices to raise objections.

Before Diana could figure out what was said, a clearer voice spoke. "Would he have sent the Beast?"

There was a pause but Diana had heard enough to make her heart pound. The last words made it all so much worse, because they weren't vague or unclear in the least.

"It's gone too far. We asked for a curse not a kidnapping."

Footsteps replaced the voices. She scrambled to her feet and darted out of the folly as the stone floor began to rise. Diana ducked around the far side and hid behind a flowering shrub. Through the tangle of blossoms, she watched as four people marched past. Three men and one woman, all of them wearing the pastel pink and blue robes of the Kingdom Council.

*Melissa Constantine*

# Chapter Thirty-Six
## Bertie

**Bertie looked through Mrs. Banes's notes on the children for the fourth** time, squinting at the woman's impossibly neat and tight handwriting. Nothing she'd written, until a couple of weeks ago, had any mention of the Beast.

*Vincent, aged 10, likes sweet bread and frogs. He is prone to getting out of bed at night and wandering around. Christopher, age 4, likes horses and his toys. Rose, age 7, likes all animals, and sneezes around most flowers.*

Not one of the records had any mention of horns, teeth, or mismatched ears.

In fact, the only mention of the Beast at all was written months ago. "*The littlest ones are scared of stories about the Beast. Recommend other Fairie Tales to staff.*"

And then came the fateful day the magic had hit the orphanage. The notes skipped the usual list of meals provided or classes held. Little Vincent didn't wander out of bed, or perhaps he did, but the only notation for the day was "Bad magic. Trouble. Children affected."

Mrs. Banes was apparently as reserved in her panic as she was in her style of dressing. Bertie wasn't sure one woman should own that many plain gray dresses, but that was neither here nor there. Someone — not Mrs. Banes by the handwriting — had added a note to the daily logs, describing the transformation.

"Happens outside. Once through the front door, the children change. Prince and Lord notified."

All of which he knew and none of it was helpful. None of this information was going to help him find Kira. Her rescue would have to come by the witch, or by the bevy of knights roaming around the Corlea and Dunlock border.

Bertie knew he shouldn't have spoken so harshly to the Fairie, but he had never experienced anger like that. He'd been mad plenty of times, miserable frequently thanks to his narcissistic parents, and lost during his early days at the Royal Academy. Yet he'd never like he felt anything as sharp and awful as trying to get the Fairie to give him a straight answer.

The truth he didn't want to admit to himself was that when it came to Kira's rescue he was helpless. He wasn't a hunter or an outdoorsman. He didn't have the skills to get on a horse like the knights the Queen Regent had sent off into the forest to look for his cousin. He'd have to continue to wait around like every other royal clinging to Dunlock Castle for dear life for a scrap of news.

Bertie gave up on the ledger, tossing the heavy book onto his desk.

Kira would find this whole situation hilarious. Assuming she wasn't terrified or hurt, the fact that most of the families of the Known Kingdoms had someone out looking for her would make her laugh. Her eyes would shine in pure delight, and the laugh would sputter out in gasps until it was so big it would practically burst from her.

After all, most of the royal families barely knew her, including her own parents. He'd watched as she'd been slighted and pushed aside by King Callum and Queen Clara. Like his own parents, the royal couple were always busy. When they were in residence at Corlea Palace, there were far more important people to fill their time. When they went on extended visits to far-flung territories she was left behind. Royal families knew not to ask about Princess Kira, because even her name upset them.

Sometimes, Bertie had to wonder if he was the only person who knew Kira. She loved chocolate and twirly dresses with pockets. And her mind was a kaleidoscope. Sometimes the ideas were colorful and intricate, but they never fixed for long. She darted between subjects, wherever fancy took her. Bertie knew that she clung to the idea of being Queen because it was the one constant in her life. Having grown up ignored and overlooked she was at least assured that one day she would rule. But if he knew all of these things, why wasn't he of any use in finding her?

Bertie wasn't much of a drinker, but he was beginning to see the appeal of losing himself in a bottle. He didn't want to lose Kira. She was his best friend, other than Xavier.

And lately, Xav hadn't been exactly enamored of him.

There was no fire in his suite, because the night was balmy for spring. Which was a shame, because staring into the flames in a broody manor would at least be something to salvage from these miserable feelings.

The door to the suite cracked open, and Xav stuck his head inside. "Anything?"

"No," Bertie admitted. "But I think we can at least be sure that Mrs. Banes wasn't hiding anything about the children. Other than which one of them liked porridge instead of eggs at breakfast."

Xav made no move to come fully into the room. He stayed with his hand on the doorknob. "Fine. I'm going to get some sleep."

"Aren't you coming in?"

"I'm…" Xav shook his head, as if the words weren't available to him.

"We haven't talked."

If there was a name to the feeling of a nerve being exposed to ice cold air, Bertie would have liked to have known it.

"I don't have anything to say."

"How is that possible? We're in the middle of an emergency. Surely there's something we can talk about."

"No," Xav said. "Maybe tomorrow."

"We're going to the orphanage tomorrow with your parents and Caris Mourne. Maybe we should talk about what's been happening? Or why you didn't want to bring your parents into it?"

Xav hit the palm of his hand so sharply against the door that it was like a thunder crack, echoing through the suite. Bertie paled.

"I don't want to talk. I hit my head when I fell in the Witch's Tower, and I feel like the Fairie Hells. So not now."

There should be instructions, or books maybe, in what lovers were thinking or not thinking at any given time. Because sorting it all out on his own was the worst. And at the moment, he had nothing to throw at his boyfriend to make the point that Xavier was being an ass.

"So that's it?"

"I'll see you in the morning," Xav said. He shut the door with another great bang. Bertie willed his heart to stop beating so fast.

They were in love. Fighting was part of that. His parents had fought like rival wolves. They may not have carried for Bertie or his older brother all that much but they loved each other.

It was normal.

He could only wish it wasn't occasionally terrible.

# Chapter Thirty-Seven
## Diana

*It was just a door.*

*A witch's door.*

*Caris Mourne's door.*

Diana brought her gloved hand to the door and hesitated. She needed a potion for the stuffy nose that had come on overnight. It was perfectly reasonable to visit the castle witch for that reason.

"Oh for goodness' sake." She was being silly. She raised her fist and knocked in short, insistent raps.

"Go away," said a masculine voice.

"I need to see…."

The heavy oak door swung open. A tall, menacing-looking Fairie answered. Diana didn't mean to stare, but she'd never seen a Fairie in the flesh before. The portraits in the chapels hadn't lied, his ears pointed up like knife blades on the side of his head. If she wasn't wrong, he was a member of the Dark Court, given that he was staring at her with nearly black eyes.

"Who are you?"

The Fairie startled. "Who am I? Who is the one knocking on this door like they own the place?"

"I'm Lady Diana Yarborough," she said. "I'm looking for Caris Mourne."

The Fairie made an exaggerated groan and called over his shoulder. "Coco Muppets, one of the pesky humans needs you." He stalked off. "It's like they've totally forgotten. Humans used to WORSHIP me!"

"It's your own fault," Caris Mourne said. She was wrapped in a floral dressing gown, despite the lateness of the afternoon, and her purple hair bound up in a messy topknot.

"My lady," Diana said, as she bobbed a curtsey. "I find I need a potion for…"

"Oh my dear, you are a mess, aren't you?" Caris Mourne had kind gray eyes. None of the books had ever mentioned that.

"I have a cold." Except that tears were springing to her eyes.

"Come in, I'll summon some tea."

An hour later, Diana tried to catch her breath. Never had she imagined that the day she met Caris Mourne she'd be crying while a scowling Fairie looked on.

Not only crying, but outright sobbing. All of the last few days came pouring out of her like a river.

"…And he's all shaggy. Like a dog. I hate dogs. I don't know when he last had a haircut. And why should I care? I don't know him, but he was all *"I won't make that mistake."* What's that supposed to mean? I can't turn off my heart from one man, get engaged to an absolute jackass, and then be expected to know how to react to him *LOOKING* at me!"

Caris Mourne rubbed her back in small circles. "Let it all out, dear. Every bit."

Diana sniffed. "It was supposed to be simple. See Robby, fall in love with him, live happily ever after. Except he's apparently in love with Princess Kira, because it's all anyone is talking about. Not that she's missing, but that she danced with him. Oh, and *and and*, apparently the Kingdom Council might have accidentally sent the Beast after her."

That seemed to be what Caris Mourne was waiting for her to say.

"And there it is," she said. The watch at her waist dinged.

Diana felt lighter, as if a led blanket had been lifted from her body.

"Don't mess with her Candy Mumbles!" The Fairie was lounging on the cushioned seat in the large, open window.

"Be quiet, Anthony," said the witch in a sharp tone.

Diana wiped her tears with the palm of her hand. Caris Mourne pulled a large, cotton handkerchief from the pocket of her dressing gown and pressed it into her hand.

"Tell me what you know about the Kingdom Council."

"I was trying to find a space to rest in the gardens yesterday. I ended up in one of the follies, except it's apparently it isn't a folly at all there's some kind of secret room underneath it. I kept hearing an argument. So I hid when I heard them coming up, and it was the whole damn Council. And when they came out, one of them said, 'How hard can it be to curse one Princess," or something."

Caris Mourne's foot tapped a frantic song against the stone floor. Diana thought she might have said something wrong, but for all the witch was rubbing small, comforting circles on her back, she had her sights dead on the Fairie. Diana thought about her offering to excuse herself, but before she could get the words out, Caris Mourne moved like a startled cat.

"Let me fetch you that potion." She said, hurrying over to a prep table where a dozen small cauldrons were bubbling away.

"Now Crispy Mutton gets around to helping the poor wretch," the Fairie said.

Diana's back stiffened. "I am not a wretch. I'm heir to the County of Wills."

"Human royalty, bah, what's that to me? I'm 348 years old."

Three hundred and forty-eight? That was remarkable. The Fairie didn't look a day over 30. Despite his intention to insult her, Diana felt compelled to say, "You look exceedingly well for your age."

"Yes, I do. It is about time you noticed."

"Anthony, do shut up," Caris Mourne said, bringing back a small vial of bright purple potion.

"You don't happen to be Ant the Argument of the Dark Court?" Diana asked, overcome with curiosity.

The Fairie beamed. "You've heard of me?"

"I've read about you."

"About my exploits in the mountains of Gruug? My excellent diatribe on the importance of ear care among elder Fairies?"

"Uh, no, not those things."

Realizing he may not be particularly enamored of what she'd read in the twelfth volume of *Dramatics of the Dark Court*, Diana took the potion Caris Mourne held out to her and drank it in one quick swallow. It tasted like a liquid lollipop. Immediately, the cool, sweet elixir seemed to cure her stuffy nose. Having cried her eyes out, there was nothing left for her to do. She handed back the handkerchief and the empty vial. "I should go."

"There is no rush," Caris Mourne said. "You need to give yourself time to address all that's going on."

"If the little human wants to leave, Cricket Meatballs, let her go. She's probably got to cry to her mother."

Caris Mourne gave him a glance so sharp, Diana thought she ought to check her own skin for residual cuts. She turned back to the witch. "Ma'am, do you think the Princess is in real danger?"

"I'm afraid so."

"Why would they want her cursed? You don't think she's actually crazy, do you?"

Caris Mourne tilted her head to the side, rather like Fritz. "Pardon?"

"I was hoping she was crazy. Because maybe Robby would… I'm sorry, I'm being mean."

"You're heartbroken, dear. Give yourself a bit of grace."

Was she heartbroken? Diana wasn't sure. She was confused more than anything. "I'm not."

"Don't bother protesting, wretch. My sister-in-law can feel all of your emotions. If she says you're heartbroken, you are."

Diana looked at her idol with new eyes. If she picked up the emotions of all the people around her, no wonder she was rarely seen. "How tiring that must be."

Caris Mourne actually blushed, as if she were embarrassed. "Please ignore him, Lady Diana."

The Fairie huffed. "I know what I know. I may not have the power I once had but I have eyes. My illustrious sibling has to nanny her back to health if she's around too many people. It's an odd relationship."

"You're married to a Fairie?" Diana felt silly as soon as the words were out of her mouth. A Fairie brother-in-law meant there had to be a Fairie spouse somewhere.

Caris Mourne smiled. "Yes. My spouse should return in a day or two. Hopefully they'll take their brother far, far away."

"Are you happy being married?"

Again, the head tilt, as if Caris Mourne were trying to work out a problem that hadn't been spoken aloud. "Jacobee is my great love. I wish all people would be as lucky as I am with them."

Would anyone ever call her their great love? Diana wasn't sure. But it was a nice thought. Even the most notorious witch in the world had found love. Surely it shouldn't be so hard for a redheaded future Countess with big feet, should it?

# CHAPTER THIRTY-EIGHT
## Robert

***Amzi danced away as Robert hoisted the saddle onto his back.*** Secured to the posts, there was little room for him to go, but his evasions caused the barely healed over skin at Robert's wrist to stretch and small drops of blood to come once again to the surface.

"Easy, easy," Robert cooed.

Amzi snorted.

"We have to find the Princess."

The horse didn't seem to have the same urgency. It was late, the moon like a wedge of lemon in the navy-blue sky. Robert had awakened in a small room inside Corlea Palace, his wrist bandaged, his fever broken. He'd hoped to hear some news from Dunlock, but there was no word on the Princess. She was missing, the Beast of Barlow was on the loose, and news on the knights and royals out on the search was sparse, despite the short distance and easy flow of gossip between Corlea Palace and Dunlock Castle. Robert had heard only that he and Uncle Julius were not the only ones to have been attacked in the woods. Knights were emerging from the Royal Route with all manner of wounds.

Robert tightened the girth of Amzi's saddle.

"We'll take the Royal Route back to the site of the robbery," he told the horse, if only to assure himself that he wasn't running off into the dark without a plan. Despite the late hour, there were still grooms moving about in the stables, and the warm glow of the white Zephyr lamps created a bubble of activity.

"Oy, Sir Robby, are you all right?" Durrin ambled up, still rubbing sleep from his eyes.

"Fine." He swayed on his feet as he said it, but carried on checking the buckles and reigns.

Durrin clucked. "You'll do yourself no favors, slinking out in the night."

"Princess Kira is out there with the Beast."

"Aye." Durrin's voice was neutral. He had no argument, and saw about as much urgency as Amzi.

"I have to save her." He had to go. He had nothing to give her, nothing to offer her, but he could and would do everything in his power to save her life.

"Aye."

"I must..." The words died on Robert's tongue as a wave of nausea hit him. The world went momentarily blurry, then black, as his eyes rolled back in his head.

Robert had enough consciousness left to hear Durrin's "That's enough of that."

\*\*\*\*

The Princess was in danger. He knew it. Everyone knew it.

They watched her running from the Beast. It was a horrid thing — all fur and teeth. It ran on all fours after her. The crowd watched. Some jeered. Children waved pink and blue flags with the Corlea crest. But no one interfered.

The Beast would catch her, and then they would all go on.

Robert tried to explain the dream to Uncle Julius. "It was real. She's in danger."

"Don't put too much stock in dreams, Robby. They're not mystic, but often confusing. Every able-bodied person in the Known Kingdoms is looking for her. Knights and nobles by the dozens. The Queen Regent sent out a dozen riders, summoning all the major houses to join the hunt."

Robert couldn't shake it off so easily. It was so real. He'd been watching her run. He'd seen the terror on her face. It lodged in a space behind his eyes and it wouldn't come out.

"The first thing is to get you better, Robby. You lost a lot of blood."

Robert shook his head. His wrist had scabbed over once again, but the healing was fragile. Mrs. B, the housekeeper, had dosed him with fever reducers and blood clotting potions but with no witch any closer than Dunlock, there was little more she could do.

He wasn't sure how long he'd been confined to bed, only that Uncle Julius had sat by his bedside for several hours in the bright, sunny little room.

Uncle Julius examined the wound. "Are those teeth marks? Did something bite you?"

"I don't know," he admitted.

"Something did."

He tried to explain. It was an old wound. It had been bleeding off and on for days.

"Old wounds don't reopen." Uncle Julius's face was drained of color.

Robert tried once again to rise from the bed, but his body was weak. He slumped against the headboard.

"I know you want to go, Robby, but our hunt is over. I'm too old for the saddle and you're too sick."

"I can't give up. If we find the Princess, you'll have a title to pass on to Tobin."

Uncle Julius shook his head. He went to adjust his wig, only remembering he wasn't wearing one when there was nothing to tip back into place. In the sunlight, devoid of face powder and the sartorial trappings of his dukedom, he looked older. "Even if you weren't my nephew, you are my sworn knight, Robby. And I will not risk your life for so little as a title."

Robert flushed. He'd been so used to thinking of his uncle as a fool, and he was humbled. "It's more than the title. It is my duty to save her."

His uncle chose his words carefully. "I know you feel for her."

His mouth was dry. How could anyone know? He'd said nothing, done nothing that might have given away his feelings.

The unasked questions hung in the air.

"The Heir's Ball has provided a fair bit of gossip."

He wondered if there was a name for feeling like he'd been kicked in the stomach, without actually anyone swinging at him. If there was gossip, despite the kidnapping, it wouldn't be good. Without meaning to, he'd have insulted her. Saving her might be the only way to atone for his too obvious feelings.

"I can't sit here." He could die of blood loss or humiliation, but not both.

Uncle Julius looked grave. "Rest, Robby. Please. You'll not solve any of it now."

"I know it sounds absurd, but, Uncle, I believe I have to find her."

Uncle Julius looked sad, as if he knew something Robert did not. "I'm leaving this afternoon and heading back to Dunlock to see what help Prince Brandon and the Queen need. We'll come through here on the way home to get you. Rest, please."

When he was gone, Robert was at a loss as to what to do. With no sign of the Princess, nearly all the Corlea servants had been organized into search parties and sent out into the woods. Many had come back, having encountered the same destructive debris storm that Robert and his uncle had encountered, but they'd been patched up and sent back out. Only the barest staff attended to the needs of the Palace. Although he'd been confined to bed, he'd been all too aware of the silence from so few people in residence.

He was too restless to sleep despite weakness. He needed something to do. There wasn't much to see in the room. The chair his uncle had occupied was pulled up to the single bed. His belongings — his tunic and his saddlebag — had been thrown over a small table. A shaggy green rug covered the marble floor. Nothing to keep him from going crazy.

He wasn't much for invoking the Fairies, but he figured it was worth a shot. He tried to remember which ones would have been a good one to summon to stave off boredom. Covi the Confused was... for trying to remember something. Hornus Bloodfire was for...

*Campfires?*

That was not useful at present.

Other than the visit to the chapel with Kira, his own practice had been a bit lax. There were a dozen names on the tip of his tongue, but none that seemed appropriate. Better to go with a general ask.

"Any Fairies who are inclined to listen, I humbly ask..."

"Rob,, don't tell me you've gone pious. It's only been like 3 days." Jordaan leaned against the doorframe, eyes narrowed at him.

Robert had never been so relieved to see anyone. "For Fairie's sake, help me get out of here."

Jordaan blew out a breath. "Like to help, buddy, but uh, I hear you're down for the count."

He pointed at Robert's wrist, where fresh blood was soaking through the bandages. Robert waved off his concern.

"I can't stay still. I've got to get out there."

Jordaan's shaggy blond eyebrows rose. "*You've* got to get out there? Everyone with freaking legs in the Known Kingdoms is out there, and you — Sir Robert of Greater Miser — *you* have to get out there?"

Robert heard the skepticism, but chose to ignore it. "Are you going to help me or not?"

"How close are you to dying?"

"We'll all die one day."

A sly smile crept across Jordaan's face. It was the same look he got when the suggestion to drink too much or flirt too heavily was on the table. "Now that's my boy."

He crossed to the table, and tossed Robert his saddlebag. As it landed on the bed, Caris Mourne's silver compass tumbled onto the bedding.

"What the heck is that?"

Robert picked up the elaborate silver object and flipped open the lid. A prism of light exploded from the quartz post in the center of cardinal directions. "Caris Mourne gave it to me."

The rainbow light sparked, and the pointed face of the witch appeared over the compass.

"Oh bother, you didn't intend to use it, did you?" The witch frowned.

Jordaan approached the bed, peering at the face of Caris Mourne. "Rob what is that?"

Robert ignored him. "I need help. I need to get out of Corlea Palace and go back out looking for the Princess."

The witch sighed. "Tell your inquisitive friend to take a step back. He smells like sage and I'm allergic."

Jordaan's eyes went wide and he took a significant step backwards.

"Better," said the witch. "Now, you're at the Palace are you?"

"Yes."

She made a little 'hm' and clicked her tongue.

"My uncle and I hit some kind of storm in the woods. We were injured."

"Injured how?"

"Cuts and bruises, but my old wound opened and I've been down with a fever."

Even though the image on the compass was barely 3 inches high, Robert could see the concern on Caris Mourne's face. There was something she wasn't saying.

"Put your hand over the quartz," she instructed.

Robert held his hand over it. Sharp pains shot through his hand and up his arm and nearly doubled with the force of it.

"Your injured hand, if you please."

Feeling like an idiot, Robert shifted the compass to his good hand, and did as he was told. This time when his palm crossed over the light, the feeling that shot through his hand was pleasantly warm. He could feel the wound closing, but as he did, the image of the witch lost color.

"I won't be able to do that again, not at a distance anyway. You should be well enough to travel, but please, take no unnecessary risks. Travel with company. When you find the Princess, bring her directly to the Witch's Tower at Dunlock. Understood?"

Robert agreed, and the prism from the quartz flickered out.

"Fairies be," Jordaan said, staring at the now ordinary compass. "What the hell have you been doing?"

****

"You're an ass, you know that Lycette?" Jordaan clicked his tongue and his horse surged forward.

"Why this time, specifically?" He spurred Amzi to catch up.

Jordaan turned his horse. "Are you really going to risk your own life to go after Crazy Kira?"

"Don't call her that!"

"Everyone calls her that! Answer the question. If what we saw wasn't enough to tell you these woods are dangerous, you're a bigger idiot than I thought. You're going to ride off to try and play hero for a woman who may not be worth it."

"She is the future queen and we are knights." Robert wasn't sure why that was unclear. It was their entire purpose as knights of the Known Kingdoms to serve and protect the royals, especially the queen.

"Rob you spent the last few days laid up in bed bleeding. I spent one day on the hunt and almost had my head blown off. Whatever is out there doesn't want company. There's no longer a title on the line, there's no reason to go."

"I love her." He hadn't meant to say that out loud. The words had simply tumbled out of their own accord.

"Then you're a greater ass than I thought."

"You don't understand. She's in danger. Caris Mourne said magic is collecting around her. And she doesn't know what it's going to do but so far it's been dangerous."

"Do you know you have a woman waiting in Dunlock who would probably tear down mountains for you?"

"What?" The sudden change in topic left Robert's head aching along with the pulsing pain in his wrist.

"Diana. She's beautiful and rich and oh yeah, you'd be an Earl if you married her. And yet you're chasing after the one you can't have."

"She's like a sister to me." It was unthinkable. He'd known her since they were in the cradle.

"She's not… " Jordaan stopped whatever it was he was going to say, shaking his head. Once again, he spurred his horse forward, away from the thick of the forest.

"I have to find the Princess. You heard Caris Mourne."

Jordaan wheeled around once more. "And that's the other thing. What the Fairies are you doing having secret conversations with a witch? We're friends and I didn't know anything about it."

Robert genuinely didn't have words. It was all too odd. Since when was Jordaan so sensitive? And why did he even care about Diana? The Princess Royal had been kidnapped. That trumped all. And yet, he was angry and hurt. What kind of knight left his friend in that position? A poor one. "I'm sorry."

Jordaan shook his head. "About damn time. Now tell me why I should be helping you, and save me all the noble bullshit."

They both dismounted and led their horses to a nearby stream. Amzi drank as if he'd never needed water so much in his life. Jordaan's horse wasn't as greedy, but still looked as if he'd drink until his stomach was round and bloated.

Robert did his best to explain about Xavier's request coming in as they arrived in Corlea and the children at the orphanage.

"You're telling me the Beast of Barlow is actually a group of pathetic orphans?"

"No, not exactly, I don't think they're capable of robbing anyone. They're small when they transform."

"But they get the ears and teeth and such?"

"No tails though."

"Well that's something. So when does the witch come into the story?"

Robert retraced what had happened. Meeting Kira, going to see Caris Mourne. He left out the part about the giant bird emerging from the book. Admitting that he'd been gun shy about anything that flew since his visit to the tower wasn't the kind of ridicule he wanted to hand his friend on a silver platter. But he filled him in on the visit to the Fairie chapel and the destruction of the statue.

"So you spent some time making googly eyes at each other trying to solve this mystery and now she's missing and you think you personally have to find her?"

"Yes."

"Well, Fairies take me."

They pulled their horses away from the stream. Amzi in particular seemed desperate to stay. Robert tried to soothe him, but his horse wouldn't be calmed.

"That horse won't go back there," Jordaan said. "If we're going into this part of the woods, we have to go on foot."

Robert knew he was right. Amzi wasn't a skittish horse, normally, but now, the slightest sound might make him bolt. He could be injured if he were tied down and tried to run.

"I can't leave him here."

"We'll take them back to Corlea stables. Then set out on foot."

They'd lose half a day's progress to go back, and more when they tried to return to the same area walking.

"If I'm going to babysit you on this quest, we go back. Now. Then I'll help you find her."

There was no time to marvel at the depth of friendship in that offer. Besides, Jordaan would simply call him an ass again for making anything of it.

"You're right."

Jordaan's smirk went on for days. "Keep saying it, Lycette. It sounds good coming from you."

Robert flashed him a rude gesture. "Let's go before we lose any more time."

A bank of black clouds crowded the sky and a crack of thunder caused both horses to rear. The storm had emerged from the woods and was advancing toward them at an unnatural speed. Another crack of thunder preceded an outbreak of heavy rain. Jordaan managed to gain his seat on his horse, but Amzi was still too unsettled. The reins were slippery in his hands and Robert lost his grip.

"Easy, boy, easy." But the rain and the lightning were too much. Amzi bolted.

"I'll go after him. Find shelter as close to here as you can. I'll bring him back," Jordaan said. He spurred his horse and took off through the rain. He was out of sight before Robert had the chance to object.

He had nothing but the clothing on his back, and that was already soaked. He took off for the nearest clump of trees. The leaf canopy provided some cover, but not enough. He'd never seen rain this torrential. The ground around him was quickly filling with pooled water. His boots were good, but had their limits. He needed to find more than trees for shelter.

Anything that might keep the sheeting rain off him would do. There was a glimmer of light in the distance, and with no other option except to drown where he stood, Robert ran toward it. With luck it would be a cottage or a hunting cabin. The rain drummed down relentlessly as he ran toward the orange glow. Too late Robert realized the light itself was moving, drawing him deeper into the forest.

The smell of smoke was faint, muddled by the heavy musk of the rain on the forest floor, but it was there. He'd find some respite from the weather. The light zipped in excited circles as he broke into a clearing where a small, stone cottage stood. There was light inside and despite the rain thick plumes pumped out of the chimney.

He pounded on the thick oak door. "Hello? Hello? Open, please."

Beside him, the little light, barely bigger than a butterfly, danced like a dog welcoming its master home.

Robert knocked again, pleading for shelter.

The door swung open.

"Well, that's that then," said a female voice.

A broom moved of its own accord, carrying the empty glass of a Zephyr lamp. Which was impossible, because brooms didn't have hands. Rather, the lantern floated in front of the broom, and when it reached the doorway, the light zoomed forward into the glass enclosure.

"Come in, Deary, come in," said the broom.

In shock, Robert stepped into the warm, snug cottage. The door shut behind him.

"Kettle, a towel if you please."

There was a deep sigh of a grumpy man, and the tea kettle jumped from the table to the floor. Using its handle, the kettle unearthed a large, fluffy white towel, which sailed across the room and landed on Robert's shoulders.

"Sit, sit," said the broom. "Take off your boots. I'm afraid the mistress is sleeping, but she'll be sure to greet you when she awakes."

Robert sat, still trying to take in that inanimate objects were serving him. The cottage was lit by a fire, had a small table, two chairs, and a series of hooks over the fire where various pots were hung. A curtain hung at the far end, blocking the only window. Over the cracking of the fire, Robert realized he could hear a none-too-gentle snore.

Kettle hopped from the trunk of linens and came over to assist him with his wet boots. In no time, they were drip-drying by the fire irons.

"Tea, I should think," said the broom.

"And that'll be me, I suppose?" said the tea kettle.

"Do you see another tea pot in this place?" snapped the broom.

Robert dropped his head into his hands. "Pardon me, Sir, Ma'am, but…"

The broom laughed. "Such manners!"

"Yes, a young fellow displays basic politeness, and we fall all over ourselves," said Kettle, nevertheless jumping toward the pump to fill itself with water.

"I wondered if…" Robert stopped, unsure of what he was wondering. It was all a bit too fantastic, although he should have expected it shouldn't he? Birds coming out of books, wigs rolling through dark corridors, and now talking household objects. Next, he'd find Amzi sitting cross-legged behind the curtain having a whisky with his dead grandmother.

"As we explained to the mistress," said the broom. "It's all an enchantment."

"Who's enchantment?"

The tea kettle laughed with bitterness. "What an excellent question."

One he made no move to answer, given that he was busy making tea.

The broom came to stand in front of him. "Now, we have decided that I am called Matilda Bristle, and this rude fellow is Kettle."

Robert bowed his head. "A pleasure to meet you."

Matilda Bristle giggled.

A broom giggled. Robert decided he would ask Caris Mourne for a potion when he returned to Dunlock. Something that would cure a wild imagination.

With a little sigh, the broom moved to the curtain and leaned around the edge to check on the snoring person. "Still sound asleep. She sleeps rather a great deal, I'm afraid."

"Will she mind that I'm here?"

Kettle hopped up to the table, pouring hot water into a waiting mug. "Hard to say. She's prickly as a hedgehog, that one."

A rumbling snore, followed by a cough echoed through the little cabin.

"The mistress is not so bad," Matilda Bristle said, nudging the curtain closed. "Her heart is good, even if her head is often in the wrong place."

Robert accepted the mug of tea, thankful for the warmth that sank into his stomach. It was exceptionally sweet and strong tea, as he liked it.

"Is your mistress also under an enchantment?"

"I'll say," said Kettle.

"She has her troubles," Matilda Bristle said.

"Oh do stop talking," said a smoky rumble of a female voice.

Robert rose, preparing to bow to his host.

The curtain snapped back. A massive beast with mismatched ears, curling horns coming out of her head, and a coat of a hundred colors stood glaring at him. Sharp teeth protruded from the corners of her wide mouth, and thick black talons protruded from her paws.

But those purple eyes he'd recognize anywhere.

If he wasn't dreaming or dead, Kira, the Princess Royal, the woman he loved, was the Beast of Barlow.

## CHAPTER THIRTY-NINE
### Bertie

***Surely there were laws against being up so early.*** If not, he would ask Kira to make one. She was fond of that kind of nonsense. Bertie yawned, nearly falling out of the carriage in the process. He wasn't opposed to getting up with the sun if it meant a few hours to lie in bed with tea and scones, but to be up and out before such a thing was inhuman. Xavier caught him before he hit the gravel.

"It's almost ten."

"I'm a creature of habit and I've been denied my habits. I barely had time for tea."

"You're a lazy sod is what you mean."

Normally, Bertie would have smiled, laughed at Xav's gentle teasing, but there was something cold there. It had been that way since last night. Bertie hadn't wanted to fight, and turned away, which made Xav angrier, and he hadn't felt like being anywhere near him.

Apparently he hadn't slept off his bad mood.

"That's uncalled for," Bertie said, running his fingers through his hair to try and control the red nest of curls. Hair care had also gone by the wayside in his quest to meet the carriages on time for their trip to the orphanage.

"You missed breakfast with my parents."

"So?"

"They don't ask much of you. A family meal. Show up at the occasional afternoon tea."

Well, what did that have to do with the price of scones? So what if he missed cozying up to Xavier's parents? They had plenty of children, they didn't need one more. Especially not an adult child. Besides, spending time with the Moorelows was a lot. They were so nice to one another. Even when the littles were fighting, they never left a room without hugs and kisses.

It was unnerving.

"You don't even care do you?" Xav snapped.

"How is not showing up to breakfast equated to not caring?"

There was no time for the fight to continue, but the Dunlock royal carriage, led by a team of six perfectly matched gray horses, was pulling into the drive. Bertie watched as the Prince, Princess, and Caris Mourne all stepped onto the gravel. Prince Brandon and Princess Margo were all smiles, their faces happily beaming. The witch, however, looked ill, as if sunlight did not agree with her. The spring sun seemed to soak into her candy-floss colored hair, turning it a darker shade that only served to make her already pale face all but translucent. Prince Brandon and Princess Margo's good mood, however, was immediately ruined as they caught sight of the guards standing on either side of the orphanage's front door. Their normally robust complexions went ashen, their mouths slack as they took in the absurdity of the charming timbered house with its outsized security.

"Boys?" Prince Brandon questioned. "I thought we were here for a tour?"

"I'm afraid not," said the witch. "We don't have that much time."

Bertie was grateful when she took charge, taking her watch from her blue trousers, and turned the dial. "Ten minutes."

Bertie had sent a note ahead to warn Mrs. Banes, and to ask her to have the children lined up and ready. He wasn't sure of the exact order of events, but he suspected it would all unfold fast and furious. Which, given how frustrating every single event had been in the last few days, might be a nice change.

Xav signaled to the guards, who in tandem removed the lock.

Whatever magic Caris Mourne had worked seemed to include a barrier. Bertie could see the children, all scrubbed up and in their best uniforms, frantically looking toward the open door with the intent to bolt on their little faces. A worried Mrs. Banes stood with them, twitchy as always.

"Mrs. Banes, if you please," Caris Mourne said, motioning her through the invisible shield. Hesitantly, the house mother stepped through the doorway.

"Your highnesses," she said as she bobbed clumsy curtsey to the royal couple, and one to the witch. "Madame."

"It's good to see you, Mrs. Banes," Bertie said.

Mrs. Banes was tense to a degree that Bertie had never seen on a person before. Every limb, facial feature and hair on her head seemed to tighten. "Lord Albert, I know this is important, but the children...."

Bertie shook his head. "Don't worry. This is Caris Mourne. She's the best. She'll have them fixed in a hurry."

As if summoned, Caris Mourne spoke up, "I believe there is no time like the present."

He nodded, not sure of what else was required of him. He didn't know enough about how a witch's magic worked, or how it was any different from that of a Fairie. The ban of the witches and Fairies from Corlea had meant his only memories of such things were from his early childhood in the Unknown Kingdoms.

"What do we do?" asked Xav.

"You stay still," said Caris Mourne, as if it were the most obvious thing in the world.

And with that, there was a loud bang, and the front of the orphanage was engulfed in a cloud of opaque blue smoke. As expected, the children came screaming through the doorway, one by one transforming into their beastly forms as they broke through the haze.

Caris Mourne's thin lips were moving, though Bertie couldn't tell if she spoke as the children's buoyant laughter became deep, rumbly growls.

Princess Margo screamed, and clung to her husband. The transformed children didn't run, to Bertie's surprise. They started to form a circle around the lawn, moving closer as if hunting their prey like a pack of wolves.

"Son?" Prince Brandon said, with a significant look at Xav. "What are we seeing here?"

Xav had to admit, they didn't know. "It's been happening since before the Festival started."

"Why didn't you tell us, dear?" Princess Margo asked, slowly letting go of Prince Brandon's tunic. "You know you can tell us anything."

Bertie had to wonder if that was true. There had to be a reason beyond "the stress of the Festival," that Xav had wanted to keep this from his parents. But maybe it was, if the expression on Xav's parent's faces was any indication. It was something like concern, or sad but not fatal disappointment. Bertie wasn't sure which. It wasn't the cold look his own parents had given him when he turned down the heiress from Spire, that was for sure.

"Enough!" Caris Mourne said in a booming voice. Bertie startled, only to realize she was talking to the children. "One by one, you will come to me."

The little furballs, amazingly, did as she bade them. They lined themselves up, smallest to largest, and one by one, scampered up to the witch. To each she gave a piece of yellow candy, and all of the children looked at her with extreme adoration, as if they'd never seen a sweet before.

Bertie was almost sure he was offended. He always made sure that Mrs. Banes had plenty of money in the budget for treats. No orphan under his care would grow up deprived.

The candy, however, had another purpose. As soon as the last of the orphanage's dozen children had been given one she took out her watch again. And with one big bang, each of the beasts was a child again.

One covered in copious amounts of green goo, but a child nonetheless.

"What is going on here?" Princess Margo gasped.

Caris Mourne turned toward her. "No time to explain. Lord Albert, if you please," she said, beckoning Bertie to her side.

Afraid of getting green goo on his best waistcoat, but more afraid of the kind of power the witch had expelled, he hurried toward her.

In time to catch her as she collapsed.

****

Mrs. Banes took charge of the newly restored children, ushering them all back into the house for baths, while Princess Margo had headed to the kitchens to arrange tea. Xav and Prince Brandon helped Bertie carry the witch into the orphanage's snug sitting room. It seemed a lifetime ago he and Xav had sat in this room with Kira and Rob, trying to come up with a plan. Had it really been only a few days ago?

They settled Caris Mourne on the sofa, and Prince Brandon tucked a pillow under her head.

"I must say," he said, "This is not how I expected today to go."

Xav wouldn't make eye contact with his father, so Bertie did his best to explain. "We didn't have much of a choice."

"I understand that. I wish the two of you would have come to me. We are a family, and there shouldn't be anything you two can't tell me about."

Bertie wished he believed that, but he had little experience with loving families.

Xav colored. "You and mother were so busy with the Festival; we couldn't add one more thing. I knew how much of a big deal it was that it went well."

"Festivals be damned," Prince Brandon said. "You are my son, Xavier. And that trumps all. Besides, after we managed to lose the Princess Royal, there isn't much else that could go wrong."

"Kira was helping us," Bertie said. "Before she was kidnapped she was trying to help us figure out what was happening. I'm afraid she might have learned something or gotten too close to the Beast."

Prince Brandon turned his kind eyes to Bertie. "It is not your fault, Albert. No matter what we find, I want to make sure you know that."

Bertie nodded, not trusting himself to speak. Maybe it was true, but he didn't believe it. It was all too much to think about it.

"Come," Prince Brandon said. "Let's go have some tea, and we can talk about it."

"Give Bertie and I a minute," Xav asked.

"Fine, but I expect you both to join us in the dining room."

"Of course," Xav said.

He waited until his father left the room, his footsteps retreating down the hall with soft echoes. The silence after his exit was thick as molasses, and Bertie was tempted to make a joke, but his mouth didn't seem to want to form words.

Perhaps because he knew what was coming, and making any noise would hasten the inevitable.

"We have to break up," Xav said.

Bertie looked at the sleeping witch. She needed tending to. No doubt the magic she'd used had taken a toll on her. He would have preferred to have this conversation with Xav without an audience — even an unconscious one — but actually, he was glad of the distraction her presence caused. She gave him something else to think about as the thing he'd feared most had come to pass. "What will we do about the orphans?"

"That's what you're going to say?"

"We can't abandon them, they're children."

"And they have Mrs. Banes, who doesn't need us interfering. I never should have gone along with the stupid idea of yours that we could run this place. We have no idea what we're doing."

That was unfair. Running the orphanage wasn't stupid. Bertie had loved the whole process, from finding the building, to picking out the text books and designing the blue and purple uniforms for school and play. "We're the royal patrons, we…"

"Fairies be, I'm breaking up with you and all you can think about? Royal patrons aren't meant to be so involved. We show up to official functions and fundraise. That's all we have to do. So forget it. Say something else."

"I don't know what else you want me to say," Bertie admitted.

"You're not fighting for me. You fought with that stupid Fairie, but you won't fight with me."

That had been different. His cousin's life was in danger. Fighting with Xav now would be useless, and Bertie didn't get into useless fights. Not if he could help it. Xav should know that. "I won't cause a scene. Let's go have tea. We'll figure it out later."

"There's nothing to figure out," Xav said.

There was a lot to figure out, but contradicting Xav wasn't worth the effort, so Bertie kept quiet.

"You're not going to say anything?" Xav prodded. "Fine. Typical Bertie."

Bertie supposed it was. It was one of those things about him that seemed unlikely to change. He was Albert Todd Vineland, eighth in line to the Corlea throne. Without proper tea he was cranky. His body was sturdy, but he wasn't built to run long distances or carry heavy objects. And after a childhood subject to his parent's volatile marriage, he knew to back away slowly from arguments. So that was what he was going to do.

Except that didn't seem to be what Xav wanted him to do. But when it came to Prince Xavier Moorelow, Bertie was often out of his element. He'd spent the past two years trying to figure out how a man that gorgeous and that kind would want to be with him. He'd assumed that when Xav finally came to his senses and broke up with him, life would make sense again.

Except that now that it was a reality, that the break-up he'd been anticipating since the beginning of their relationship was happening, he didn't understand it at all.

## Chapter Forty
### Kira

*Kira stared at Sir Robert, grateful for the fur that hid the embarrassed* blush burning her face.

Why did it have to be him?

Of all the people who could have found her hiding spot, it had to be him? With his shiny hair and his blue eyes and his stupid muscles and his infuriating, impeccable manners. He'd obviously been caught in the storm, and yet even dripping wet he was gorgeous. Which was massively unfair. Anyone else, herself included, would've been a drowned rat after all that rain. But no, Sir Ridiculously Handsome had to be the one standing in her cottage, drinking tea made by an anthropomorphized kettle.

Kira saw the moment recognition dawned; his face went pale. He bowed, as if it were all perfectly ordinary. "Your Highness."

During the Heir's Ball he'd held her in his arms on the dancefloor, and he'd looked into her eyes; she'd felt beautiful and cherished. She'd hoped to hold onto that memory. When she was on her throne and married to whomever was the most politically advantageous, she'd remember being spun around the ballroom by this man. She would remember the hope that surged within her, the sense that anything was possible.

But now? Milk curdled in her stomach. He was disgusted by her. She'd seen the momentary look of revulsion in his eyes. He'd done his best to school his features, to divert his gaze, and lean back on his knightly training, but it was too late.

Was this punishment? It felt like punishment. She'd messed with magic. She'd sought revenge on the royals who'd ignored her and shoved her to the side and for that she was caught in a hulking fur prison, mortified as the most beautiful man she'd ever seen could no longer meet her eye.

"Go away." Her voice was unfamiliar, a deeper, animalistic growl. She'd pulled the curtain closed and fumbled back toward the broken bed. She burrowed into the thick pile of quilts, trying to catch her breath. To her own ears, she sounded like a pig sniffing out mushrooms, but what was one more mortifying thing?

She would sleep. She would shut her eyes and sleep and make this nightmare all go away.

Although, she was hungry. Her stomach had a deep hollowness, as if she'd never eaten, though Kettle had served her a fully roasted rabbit not an hour before Sir Robert's arrival. She'd practically eaten the thing whole, the bones melting under her sharp teeth. And she suspected that the other occupants of the cottage — both human and not — could hear the rumbling.

"No use hiding, Young Lady," said Matilda Bristle.

"Be quiet and let me have a breakdown in peace."

"Rude," snapped Kettle. "Come greet your guest."

"He is an intruder, not a guest."

"Your Highness, I'm here to help you."

She didn't need help. She needed to be left alone to deal with the repercussions of her actions. Or maybe she needed more toast and jam. And bacon. She did love bacon. It had a way of making a lot of terrible things better. Surely it might work on extreme mortification?

"I'll put on the frying pan," Kettle said with a sigh.

"No," she snapped in Sir Robert's direction. "You can't help me. You lied to me."

"About the ball, I …"

"About being my friend. You wouldn't be standing here, being all…knightly again if you were ever my friend. So I can't trust you and you need to go. Immediately."

Preferably before he saw her disgusting table manners. She might be a beast but she was also the Princess Royal and she would not embarrass herself any more.

"I'm only trying to make this less awkward."

Kira snorted. The sound was unsettling. "That is not possible."

Her stomach, unwilling to be ignored, chimed in. "I'm hungry, so I need you to go away."

Kettle hoped about arranging the pans at the hearth. "Stop complaining, it interrupts my work."

"No use fighting, dear," said Matilda Bristle. "We have been waiting for Sir Robert to arrive."

Kira sat up. What did that mean? How could they know he'd be here? She whipped back the curtain once again. By the look on his face, Sir Robert was also confused. Although he wasn't any less lovely for the befuddlement. The light from the fire had turned Sir Robert's cheeks rosy, and bounced off his quickly drying hair like sparkling diamonds.

"I have no use for him." She turned to him, daring him to contradict her.

He gave her such a pitying look; Kira couldn't help the low growl that roared through the cottage.

His face paled a bit, but he said, "My lady, the kingdom is worried you've come to harm. I have to bring you back."

"You can go back and tell them I am fine. I am safe and fed and..." Her stomach growled at such an audible level; Kira's skin heated with fresh embarrassment.

Matilda Bristle swept forward, moving the curtain out of the way. She spoke with a little sigh, as if remembering something bitter sweet. "I'm afraid not, my dear. Kettle and I are only temporary. We can't keep you hidden forever."

Well she didn't see why not. If magic had condemned her it should certainly cosset her a little bit longer? At least another day.

"By morning, no more bacon." Kettle slapped the meat into the hot pan and sizzle and smoke filled the cottage. Kira's mouth watered. She was tempted to eat it raw to kill the gnawing hunger inside her.

No more bacon. No more refuge.

She was surely being punished.

"Caris Mourne will help you. She's told me to bring you directly to the Witch's Tower."

"NO!" Her words shook the cottage with greater force than the crack of thunder overhead.

She had to run. She had to get out and get away and hide a little longer. She wasn't helpless, she needed time.

"Kira, please, let me help you."

His words struck her, an arrow directly to the heart. Why him? Why did he have to see her as a monster? Why couldn't she fool him as she fooled everyone else?

"You'll go with him," Kettle said.

"Oh, fine." She roared in displeasure. She flopped back down on the bed. Already broken, the bed timbers splintered to dust.

"We'll go as soon as the storm clears," Sir Robert said, looking out the window where the rain pounded relentlessly.

"Just so," said Matilda Bristle. Outside the windows, the storm dried up instantly. Clouds rolled back, and weak spring sunlight filled the cottage yard. Even the puddles that had flooded the yard dried up as if all the moisture were being carried away by the retreating storm.

Kettle put the bacon on two plates, one piled significantly higher than the other. He added what appeared to be a whole loaf of toast to a basket on the table and gestured with his handle to the seats. "Sit, eat. Then go."

Kira pulled one of the thick white quilts with her to the table. It was large enough that it wrapped her in a shroud of cotton, mismatched ears to paws. She slunk into a seat. The plate of food was within her reach and every instinct she had wanted to pull it toward her and shove it into her mouth.

She was shaking with the effort of using her manners, taking one strip of bacon between her talons and bringing it to her mouth.

Oh Fairies take her, it was heavenly. She grabbed a dozen slices, but stilled as Sir Robert's eyes went wide.

"If you ever felt anything for me, please look away."

He nodded, took his plate and turned his back.

Kira demolished the rest of her food in seconds. It wasn't nearly enough, but at least it filled up a little of the emptiness.

She caught her breath, and willed Kettle to cook more. Bless him, he hopped to the task without her having to ask. Before Sir Robert had managed to eat his one slice of toast and pathetically small portion of bacon, her plate was magically refilled.

"Thank you." She sighed from the effort of keeping herself in check. She was so tired.

"So you do have manners." Kettle hoped back to the hearth.

Perhaps it was right that she was leaving. How long she could be lectured on her behavior by a disagreeable tea kettle was probably not a limit she needed to test.

Sir Robert rose and went back to the single window. The day was as fresh and sunny as any day in spring beyond the mottled glass. "The storms have to be part of the referred magic."

"The what?" Kira asked. She used a portion of the quilt to wipe the grease and bread crumbs from her face.

"Caris Mourne believes that you are the victim of…"

"I'm not a victim of anything."

He turned back, the deep skepticism evident in his expression. "You've been transformed."

She nodded. There was no denying what they could both see. But, she refused to be a casualty. Not for her current state, not for anything. She was the future queen. She was from a long line of nobility who had ruled for a millennium. And while she might be currently indisposed, she was not a quitter or a coward. She meant to speak, to tell him that for once and for all, she wasn't cursed, but the only thing that came out of her mouth was a low and menacing growl. His mouth opened, a bit like a fish. It was, thankfully, his most unattractive face. Kira felt a bit better knowing he at least had a less than perfect moment.

## Chapter Forty-One
### Robert

**Robert paced the courtyard, holding the compass up to the clear sky.** Nothing. The dial spun, unable to find true north. Caris Mourne hadn't exaggerated, the compass had only been good for one use. It didn't spark when he spoke her name. The crystal in the center had gone gray.

This cottage seemed to exist without a fixed location. If he stepped into the woods he was never in the same place twice. Different trees, different brush, different skyline. How he was supposed to get Kira back to Dunlock when the world seemed to be spinning like a child's toy top, he had no idea.

Not to mention, keeping her safe wouldn't be easy. She was the Beast of Barlow, and there were knights all over the forest looking for her.

But was she the one who robbed all those carriages? And why? The one who knights from all over the kingdom were looking to capture.

There was little chance Jordaan would catch up with them and have both horses fit to travel, and that meant walking. If they stepped away from the cottage where would they end up? Was the Royal Route through the woods as it should have been or would they be on the far side of Corlea altogether?

"Are you coming or not?" Kira stood in the doorway. She'd exchanged the quilt for what appeared to be dark blue trousers and a shapeless butter-yellow top. Nothing quite fit, as if even the magic that surrounded this place didn't know what to make of her new body.

"I'm trying to find which way we should go. There's something wrong with the compass."

"We aren't going that way. Come."

She beckoned him back toward the tidy cottage.

Neither the broom nor the tea kettle greeted him this time, though the Zephyr lamp's little ball of light danced behind the glass. The rest of the objects remained still and lifeless. Whatever enchantment had brought them to life was done.

Kira had cleared away the broken pile of timber that had once been a bed. The quilts and the pillows were packed away. No pots hung over the hearth, the embers in the hearth appeared cool. The little table where they'd eaten and the two chairs covered in a large white dust cloth. Any traveler coming across this place might never know how recently anyone had been here.

"The tunnel entrance is behind the bookcase," she said, moving the empty shelf to reveal a rough gap in the stone wall. Darkness as deep as any he'd seen lay past it.

Awareness tickled the back of his neck. He swiped at it, hoping it was an insect. "Where does it lead?"

"Everywhere."

They entered the tunnel, and the bookcase slid closed behind them. For a moment they were in total, low-ceilinged darkness. Robert's eyes hadn't had time to adjust when the Zephyr lamp sparked pale green, illuminating the dirt packed walls.

"The tunnels run all through Corlea. I haven't explored most of them, but they cut the distance to at least one point on every border."

So in theory, they could take the tunnels all the way back to Dunlock. It was also, in all probability, the way the Beast of Barlow had avoided detection all these months. Secret tunnels were as good a hiding place as any. If she could stand to be in the tunnels, then surely he could do the same. But the darkness stretching out before them had a heaviness he didn't trust.

"Which way?"

One taloned hand pointed into the longest, darkest section ahead. "That way. I think."

She thought that Dunlock was that way? That didn't seem promising, but as Robert had nothing to guide him, he didn't have a better option.

He took the Zephyr lamp, adjusting the dial from the brilliant green to warmer white. The beam wasn't as strong, but the color change made the tunnel feel less menacing.

\*\*\*\*

The tunnel narrowed to a passage barely big enough for a rabbit to pass. Kira was forced to hunch over, her shoulders brushing against the walls, the dirt collecting in her fur. Robert himself still didn't feel entirely comfortable with either the dark or the close confines. It was like one of those dreams that goes all night long, a series of mini horrors without end. Muck and worms and so much dirt. They would have to go topside.

"How far do you think we've come?" he asked. They'd reach an intersection where tunnels branched off in three directions, none of them promising, though at least they could stand upright for the moment. He raised the lantern toward the unfathomable blackness burrowed into the earth.

Kira wasn't sure. She'd taken the tunnels often enough to know the general direction they lay, but the only time she'd taken them all of the way between Dunlock and Corlea, she'd been on the run. It had been a few hours since they left the cottage, but time, she'd found, wasn't a good indicator for distance when it came to the tunnels. They'd reached a point where the tunnel was so small, there was no going on, only up the series of footholds and hand notches carved into the dirt.

"You'll have to go first," she said, when he hesitated.

"You're a royal. You proceed me."

"We're not at tea."

Humbled, Robert hoisted himself up the wall. There wasn't much purchase. He ascended a dozen feet high before he saw a sliver of sunlight.

He had to use his shoulder like a battering ram to push through the old wooden door at the top.

In mere seconds, Kira followed, leaping out of the tunnel exit like a gazelle.

They emerged into the forest with the looming specter of Corlea Palace over the trees.

Robert clenched his jaw, keeping back a curse. How had they gone in the wrong direction? They should have been miles from Corlea by now.

Kira growled.

Robot felt it like a punch in the gut. Anger surged through him. He wanted to scream, or hit something. He tensed every muscle in his body, doing his best to hold back. He was a knight. Knights didn't have fits in the middle of the forest because things didn't go their way.

He had to be better than the instinct to swear until he was blue in the face.

Kira was counting on him.

She paced the area around the door. Her back was hunched and she walked more like an animal then he'd anticipated. In the tunnel, he'd assumed that she walked like that because of the low ceiling. He watched her with fascination. Whatever magic had transformed her was thorough. Except for her eyes, he'd have never known the Beast of Barlow was the Princess Royal.

He held up the compass, searching for North. Dunlock was south of the Palace by horseback. But as he took a step in what he presumed was the right direction, the needle spun in dizzying circles around the dial.

"Damn it!"

Kira turned to him, eyes wide. "What was that?"

"Nothing." He tucked the compass back into his tunic. "We need to go…" The sun was in the west, sinking toward the horizon. If they kept it to their right, they could be headed in the right direction.

"I'm tired, Sir Robert. Don't lie to me."

She dropped in a heap at the base of a birch tree. It couldn't have been a comfortable position. Her knees were drawn up, her face against the white, powdery bark.

"Go back to Dunlock by yourself and tell them I'm...." She yawned, showing a considerable amount of teeth. Her eyes closed, and she let out a noisy exhale. "Go away."

This time, Robert failed to bite back the curse that came roaring out of his throat. He wasn't entirely sure of what he said, but it was a long, and detailed string of frustrations. He was barely conscious enough to see Kira's eyes go wide.

How did she still not understand? He was a knight of the Known Kingdoms. He couldn't go back and pretend that everything was fine when the heir to the throne was hiding out in the woods, clearly under some kind of spell. He'd never be able to do his job again. "I will not leave you."

"I am the Princess Royal. You're supposed to do what I say."

"That's not how it works!"

Kira sat up. Her eyes looked especially large amid all of the dark, speckled fur. "You yelled at me."

A deep flush crept up his neck. He was hot, and tired, and he had no idea how to help, but dammit, why did Kira have to be the most frustrating person he'd ever met? "I did not mean…"

"Oh you can't take it back."

She didn't succeed in keeping a little giggle from her voice. It hit right at the base of Robert's spine. His shoulders tensed, and he fought to reign himself in.

She got to her pawed feet, and slowly moved closer. "It's okay, you know."

"What is *okay*, Your Highness?"

"To have emotions. Fairies know, I have a lot of them. All the freaking time. It's a little exhausting, but I also can't imagine trying to have none."

"A knight's personal feelings aren't important."

"Yes they damn well are! I don't know who made these rules, but when I'm queen, they're out the window."

Robert dropped his head into his hands. "You can't decide to change the code of knighthood. It's been in place for a thousand years."

"And my family has been in charge of knights for all that time. And I will do what I want when I am queen."

"You say that a lot, but do you even know what it means? You can't change everything and expect people to be okay with it because you think it's a good idea. That's what your parents did and look how that turned out."

Kira took a step back. Her face was too coated in fur to see if she went pale, but Robert found he didn't actually need to see it to know he'd said something unintentionally cruel. Shame washed out all traces of his anger.

"I didn't mean that."

Kira turned away. "Clearly, what you mean you didn't actually intend to say the quiet part out loud." She dropped again at the base of the birch tree.

"The King and Queen were…."

"Reckless? Thoughtless? Terrible people in general? Tell me something I don't know."

"I'm sorry. I don't know what else to say."

She shook her head, and leaned her face into the bark once more. The silence that stretched between them was a physical weight that pressed into Robert's chest. It seemed to block out the noise of the surrounding forest.

"We need to return to Dunlock. There's nothing we can do here."

She shook her head. Her violet eyes seemed fixed on some distant point behind him. "I can't go back there looking like one of the scullery maid's old mops. Why do you think I ran away in the first place?"

"I have to assume you were scared."

She rolled her eyes.

"If it's okay for me to have emotions, it's okay to admit you're scared. Especially if you're under a spell or a curse of some kind."

Kira laughed, but unlike the mischievous, irritating giggle he knew, this was a joyless sound.

"Caris Mourne is powerful. She knows things. She'll be able to help."

"No witches. No witches, no fairies, no magic, I can't."

"Clearly, something is affecting you. You can't ignore magic."

She growled, a low and guttural rumble that raised the hair in his inner ear. It was more beast than woman. "I am not ignoring magic. I am the consequence of it!"

A flight of birds rose at once from the trees, cawing in thunderous disharmony. Their shadows blocked what little light filtered into the forest.

Kira let out a deep breath. "I did this. It was me."

Robert, bless his shiny boots, was definitely confused.

It wasn't pretty.

Not that Kira had any room to lament a loss of beauty, considering her current predicament.

"Why would you say that?" He swallowed, as if the taste of the truth were bitter.

Kira couldn't bring herself to say any more. She'd thought admitting the truth would help her feel less awful, but apparently the stories weren't true. Saying the bad thing out loud didn't lessen the gut punch feeling one bit.

"Kira, you couldn't have done this to yourself. Caris Mourne said that the magic is around you, somehow."

Whether consciously or not, Robert was pacing. His long stride made short work of the small clearing and he circled back, hands clasped behind his back. A deep crease ran down the middle of his forehead.

"I may not know much about either, but I do know my own faults. At least credit me with that."

Robert's mouth opened, as if he were about to say something. He shook himself and continued his long-limbed pacing.

"Would you please be still? I'm getting a headache watching you."

"Yes, of course, Your Highness."

He was dressed too well to sit on the forest floor. The blue and gold tunic he wore was pristine, despite how far they traveled. He took a seat on a tree stump a yard from her. Kira regretted not choosing that spot for her pity party. But the bark of the birch had been cool against her cheek.

"Do you actually want to hear the story?"

"Yes. Especially if it will help us fix your situation."

He thought he could fix her. That was endearing.

He was wrong, but she didn't have the energy to tell him that was well.

The beginning was too far away. There were plenty of traumas she'd continue to keep to herself. It was bad enough that he saw her now as the Beast of Barlow.

"You know about how I grew up." She kept it as a statement of fact. He was well-mannered enough to leave it that way. Everyone in the kingdom knew about the feral princess, running wild through Corlea Palace while her parents destroyed the Known Kingdoms willy-nilly.

"I didn't know there was anything wrong with me. Until my uncle came back from his post in the Unknown Kingdoms, I didn't think it was weird at all that I was one my own almost all the time."

Something like nostalgia passed over Robert's face. It lessened the look of abject befuddlement, and brought back some of his gorgeous features. Whatever he was thinking about, it must have been a kind memory to soften him. Kira tried staring past him.

"Thankfully, Bertie helped me a lot. I calmed down. A bit. I learned to be a royal alongside him. But then a few years ago he left. And in quick succession my mother died and my father he…."

Kira inhaled deeply, but as she exhaled the sound rumbled through the forest.

"It was the worst kept secret in the kingdom, I imagine, my father's illness?"

Robert nodded. She'd known that word of the King's condition had spread beyond the palace walls. How could it not? In the first three months after the Queen's death, over 100 new laws had been issued on everything from what color a duke might wear to dance, to what a lady-in-waiting might say to the kitchen maid. It was mostly nonsense, but even nonsense had consequences. On a whim King Callum had ordered all of the Crane flowers in Corlea Palace Gardens plowed under, wasting millions in revenue from their sale.

"He was manic, most of the time. It was awful. And no one really did anything to stop it. Everyone was so accustomed to giving him everything he wanted. And then one day he decided he needed a new wife."

Royals had come from all over. The palace had been stuffed full of people day and night, all doing the most ridiculous things to gain his favor."

"Is that how he ended up married to Isadora?"

It was a fair question. The wedding had been shrouded in secrecy. But Sir Robert was getting ahead of the story.

"A bit. Um, Isadora was um…" Why was talking about any of it, even the acceptable part, so damn hard to say? "She was the only one who spoke up and said that what was happening wasn't right. But there was only so much she could do. Everyone else was so desperate to join the royal family."

"Anyway, I couldn't take it. Bertie was gone, I didn't have anyone who could talk me out of it."

"Out of what?"

Kira pulled her arms to her chest. It was a lame attempt to hold herself together.

"Revenge."

*Melissa Constantine*

## Chapter Forty-Two
### Robert

**The story came out of Kira in fits and starts.** Whether she realized she was glossing over large chunks of the narrative or not, Robert couldn't say. He pieced together what she said with what he knew.

After the death of the Queen, Corlea Palace was in disarray. King Callum had gone mad, though no one would say that for fear of reprisal.

It was only when the King had married Isadora of Zinnj that things in the Known Kingdoms had begun to calm down. After the King's untimely death some four months later, the Kingdom Council went about repelling dozens of edicts and superfluous decrees. The order of succession should have meant that Kira became Queen on her father's death, but things hadn't gone that way. Isadora had been installed as Regent. Kira wasn't crowned.

"All those royals. All those people in the Palace. They watched, and they plotted, and they never helped. Not when the King, when he tried to…"

Robert's stomach dropped. He had a bad feeling that whatever Kira was trying to say, it wasn't pretty.

"He was determined to get married, but he wouldn't say to whom. He had the palace staff plan a secret wedding. He'd announce the bride after the deed was done. All those fools in the palace, they all thought it was going to be their candidate. I didn't even know when it was supposed to happen, but then one night I was pulled out of bed and marched to the chapel. I didn't know that I was supposed to be…. But when I got there my father announced that he was going to appease the Fairies that had cursed him by marrying the changeling that they'd left in place of his real daughter."

Robert felt sick. *The king wanted to marry his own daughter.* It was unbelievable and upsetting as a story. For Kira it had to have been a living nightmare.

"I don't know how Isadora knew what was happening. At the time, I was so upset I didn't question why she was there. She took the veil they'd put on me, hid me in a closet, and took my place without my father knowing."

"Kira, I'm so sorry."

"Don't say that." She shook her head, and looked down at the forest floor. He was beginning to understand something about her. She didn't want pity. She couldn't take it. Kindness was such a rarity in her life that gestures of it were met with suspicion.

"Afterwards, everyone made a big deal about Isadora. She'd saved the kingdom. She was the savior. And no one gave a damn about me, or what had almost happened. So I decided I would do something."

"The Beast of Barlow?"

She gave the barest nod. "I wanted a way to make myself invincible. And the cloak was magical. I could tell."

Her chin quivered. Despite her size and the fearsome points of her teeth, she looked vulnerable. Robert had to resist the urge to go and gather her in his arms. It wasn't right. Knights were supposed to protect, not touch.

"I read somewhere that the Beast of Barlow's cloak was an incredibly powerful thing. No one was sure if it was real or not, because it looked like it was made from all kinds of animals. I was only going to use it a handful of times. But it turns out I was so good at running through the woods and robbing the rich. And it was fun."

She paused, as if trying to judge the impact of her words. Robert kept his face as neutral as he could. He needed her to tell him as much of the tale as possible. If he gathered enough information, Caris Mourne might be able to untangle the mess and restore Kira to herself.

"I knew I was using magic, but I didn't think I'd get stuck like this." She slammed her hand against her chest. A hundred different colors of fur spilled through her taloned finger.

Robert tried to imagine how hard it had been for her to admit that she had grown up unloved. That wasn't anything like his own experience. His parents weren't perfect. His mother was often short-tempered and frustrated by their relative poverty, but he knew she would have died for him or any of his siblings. His father was often easily distracted, but had nonetheless taught him to love and to protect his family and friends with every part of himself. Even Uncle Julius had played a parental role, guiding him to knighthood and offering him a job. No, none of the parents in his life were perfect, but Robert had never had to doubt they loved him.

It was the saddest thing he could imagine. Yet she was here. Brave and funny and fierce. Which was remarkable.

"It's not your fault, Kira. Any of it."

"Magic doesn't give a damn about fault. Why do you think there are so many children's stories about princes who look sideways at a Fairie and end up cursed with goat horns and purple spots?"

Caris Mourne had said that whatever unintended magic was coming from her she would be unaware of it. Except that she wasn't unaware. Not totally. But there had to be more to it than Kira simply putting on a magical cloak. How could that simple act transform the orphans, or take down statues, or send objects rolling through Dunlock Castle in the middle of the night? They needed to get back to Dunlock and speak with the witch. She was their best chance of solving the problem.

While they'd been talking the sun had dipped lower and an encroaching gloom had spread through the trees. He'd been about to suggest they get moving when a flock of birds in the woods took flight all at once. They squawked as if in fear as they flew upward.

"Someone is here." Kira got to her feet, moving between the trees as she searched.

Robert drew his sword. He listened, trying to discern any sounds of movement beyond their own. He motioned for Kira to stop.

A twig snapped, and a shadow moved in the distance. "Who's there?"

An agonizing moan was the only answer.

"Are you hurt?"

Whomever it was, they were definitely closer, and in pain.

Kira gave him a worried look. "A hunter?"

Robert wasn't sure, but he called out again. The detritus on the forest floor cracked under the approaching footsteps. The figure burst from a dense patch of brush, collapsing at Kira's feet.

The bandage on Jordaan's head was damp with blood, and his clothes were torn and dirty.

She gasped, despite her larger size. "What in the Fairies?"

"It's okay, I know him."

Kira knelt down and turned his unconscious body face up. "Who is he?"

"He's a friend. He's a knight in my uncle's household."

"What happened to him?" She cradled his head in one taloned paw.

Robert could only guess. "We were both looking for you. We got separated by the storm." Robert felt for a pulse at Jordaan's neck. It beat, but it was weak.

"Jordaan, you ass, wake up."

Nothing.

"I will drink all of your whisky; I swear to the Fairies."

"He needs a healer, Sir Robert."

If they couldn't rouse him, they would need a way to get him to the nearest place where a healer or a witch could find them. If he didn't wake up, they would have to find a way to carry him. Perhaps they could fashion a stretcher from branches, or...

Robert hadn't realized he was speculating out loud until Kira picked up the unconscious knight as if he were no more than a new puppy. "Pick a direction. I'm not sure how long I'll be able to hold him."

"You can't carry him all the way back to Dunlock."

"I don't know that I will, but for now I can." Jordaan's blank face hung over her shoulder.

He should say something. He should offer to carry Jordaan himself. Even as a Beast, Kira wasn't meant to carry heavy burdens. And yet, he said nothing. He simply checked the position of the last of the sunlight and pointed their way South.

# Chapter Forty-Three
## Kira

**Kira struggled under Jordaan's weight.** When she was queen, knights would be put on a restricted diet. They should not be allowed to get this heavy.

*Well, perhaps some of them.*

Sir Robert filled out his tunic nicely, and he was a fair bit bigger than Sir Jordaan.

Maybe the rule ought to be something else. Something about looking nice all the time and definitely not turning up half-dead in the woods. Kira shifted the unconscious Sir Jordaan on her shoulder, unable to stop a soft grunt from the effort.

Kira could only hope Robert hadn't heard it. She doubted her luck was that good. It hadn't been so far. For goodness sake, she had tusks!

Bertie would probably piss himself laughing when he saw her. She could only imagine how many more jokes he'd have about kissing behind potted plants now. She shook her head, trying to expel the picture she'd accidentally conjured of trying to steer Robert behind a palm with her giant paws.

"Is something wrong?"

Kira startled. If there was any justice in the world, he'd have no idea what she'd been thinking about. "It's not important."

An uneasy silence hung between them as they continued their trudge. Kira was perfectly fine with that, but Robert apparently was not.

"We should talk about what to do when we get back to Dunlock."

Kira did not want to think about it. Her sole focus was putting one foot in front of the other and keeping Sir Jordaan on her shoulder.

"Caris Mourne wants to see you right away."

Kira gave a low growl. "Wants to insult me to my face no doubt."

"She understands the magic that's surrounding you."

"Stop talking, please," she said. "I know what's around me."

"Kira, she's your best bet to change back."

*No. No.* She would not have this particular conversation. Because there was a real possibility that she was never going to change back. She'd used a powerful magical object. It had been locked away in the archives for a reason. Using it for her petty reasons meant she'd taken a risk. And now she was paying the price.

She shifted the inert Jordaan again. "I don't know how much longer I can carry him. My legs will give out."

Kira had only wanted to change the subject, but she realized it was true. Exhaustion swamped her, along with the realization that they'd been walking for hours. Sticking to the Royal Route they should have arrived in Dunlock already. It wasn't above two hours from Corlea Palace to Dunlock Castle by horseback, three by a slower carriage. Even at a third of the pace, skirting the road, they should have arrived at the gates hours ago. Instead it was as if there was nothing but trees and an inconsistently winding path ahead of them. With the sun going down, they would need to find a place to camp for the night.

As if the forest were listening to her, a dozen lights beckoned out of the darkness ahead. The lights came from a row of neatly thatched cottages, perched on the edge of a creek where the road widened.

Unease pricked at Kira. She'd run all over these woods and she hadn't seen anyone living on the road between Corlea and Dunlock. "Where are we?"

"I don't know," Robert said. "But some of them must be home, there's smoke."

Kira huffed. It didn't matter if anyone was home or not. There shouldn't be anyone out here at all. As far as she knew, they were in Corlea woods. Miles from the Palace, yes, but within the crown's land all the same.

She stopped, needing to stretch out her long, furry limbs. The crouched gait the beast's body demanded didn't lend itself well to long walks hefting man-sized burdens. It was an awkward business, trying to get Jordaan down to the ground without stabbing him with her claws. She couldn't say that his already-ripped tunic hadn't sustained more damage.

"There are no towns out here. What if it's some kind of trap?"

Robert didn't seem to believe it. "It's a settlement. It's not unusual. We may be able to get some food, maybe shelter for the night."

Kira shook her head. "These are my woods."

The light was fading, but her eyesight was good enough to see the look of utter confusion on the knight's face. "Lots of people live between towns, some of them in the forests. The world is more than royals in castles."

"That's not what I mean."

Robert rubbed at the back of his neck. "I'm sure it's fine."

Kira tried to sit, doing her best not to squat like some kind of large dog. Sadly sitting, like walking and putting things down, was definitely not a smooth action. She stumbled, and barely caught herself before she ended up on the ground in an ungainly heap.

Robert reacted as if he would help her but Kira pulled away. He couldn't touch her, not in this body.

"It's fine, I promise," he said. "They're houses. There's nothing scary about ordinary people."

That was a giant lie, although beside the point.

*Fairies be.* Did he really think she was so shallow?

"We should ask for help," he said.

"No!"

Robert's expression was incredulous. "You're the future queen. No one in this kingdom would refuse to help you."

Panic built like steam in her gut. "I can't be seen like this!"

A woman in a homespun dress had emerged from one of the cottage doors ahead of them. "Is someone out there?" she called in a gruff voice.

Kira's breath came out in frantic snorts. She shook her head at Robert, imploring him to keep quiet.

"If someone's out there, better come in. Things in these woods aren't safe."

Robert pointed to the woman, whispering. "See?"

"I am the thing in the woods!" Kira growled.

The woman's scream left no doubt she'd heard. It pierced the air, sharp as a knife. The thud of the slamming door followed, along with the extinguishing of all the lights in the little collection of homes.

Robert's mouth opened, as if he wanted to scream, but couldn't get the words out. "Kira! We can't keep wandering around lost. Jordaan needs help if nothing else."

"Don't you think I know that?"

The panic had a hold of her, gripping her from the inside. No amount of strength in this new, enormous body could tear it away. Her heart pounded furiously, the blood rushing through her veins so loudly that any surrounding noise was drowned out. She swayed, unable to stay upright.

"I can't. I can't."

Air seemed to be in short supply. She rubbed at her chest, her claws raking through the dense fur. It itched, so badly she thought she might rip her skin apart trying to scratch it.

Robert started toward her, as if he might try to hold her but Kira pushed out the magic that seemed to be living in her chest. It burst out of her in an array of sharp, white stars, lethal as cut glass.

She fell, her body hitting the forest floor with such force that her bones felt as if they slipped out of place. She tried for one more breath before the world went black at the edges.

# Chapter Forty-Four
## Diana

***If she lived to be one hundred, Diana was sure she'd never forget the scene*** in the courtyard when Robby reappeared with the Princess.

At best, she hoped that the memory of it wouldn't hurt.

Her mother and Lady Passwood, despite their mutual animosity, had decided to arrange a twilight carriage ride for her and Prince Travers. To her everlasting shock, Travers had been sober enough to drive the open-top carriage, and the two of them had set off at golden hour for a drive through the crane field. The night air had been cool but comfortable, with the last of the sun making swirls of pink and orange watercolor overhead. Diana had tried to enjoy the evening.

It went downhill faster than even she imagined.

"So you'll marry me." Travers said. Not a question. "We'll get this done."

Aghast, she shook her head. "I've agreed to no such thing."

"You're here."

"That's not an acceptance because there has been no proposal." Diana didn't like the sharpness in her own voice, but she couldn't help it.

"What's got you so riled up?" he had the nerve to ask.

And that was all it took to bring out her own simmering anger.

"How about when you tried to force yourself on me? Is that enough to be angry about?"

Travers had the sense to look embarrassed, or perhaps it was the memory of her knee making contact that caused him to go pale. "It's not a big deal."

"You say that because you weren't the one being attacked."

"I didn't attack you! If anything you attacked me. I couldn't stand up for an hour."

"It's no less than you deserve. You don't try to maul a woman you're supposed to be getting to know."

Travers scoffed. "If you're going to hold it over my head for the rest of our lives we might as well forget the whole thing."

"Fine with me," Diana said. She shifted as far from him as she could on the carriage's single seat.

She had assumed Travers would turn the carriage back toward the castle, but instead, he drove deeper into the fields. She kept her mouth shut her arms folded across her chest.

Travers huffed, but said nothing for a long stretch.

"Why aren't you taking me back?" she finally asked, when he once again directed the horse pulling them in a direction that was decidedly not Dunlock Castle.

"Because then my aunt would ask questions, and I don't feel like answering them before I've had whisky."

"Of course, how silly of me not to remember your utter dependence on drink."

Travers snorted in a way that might have been laughter. "Careful, Yarborough, you might actually make me like you."

"You wouldn't be so gauche."

"Probably not," he admitted. "Liking one's future wife. Disgusting."

They skirted the edge of the main section of fields, where a series of conical evergreens lined up by the dozens like a massive natural fence. While the trees appeared narrow from a distance, in the fading light they cast long, dark shadows.

"I thought we had established I am not your future wife."

"I can change my mind. I'm a prince."

"You're an ass."

They gave up trying to talk to one another, until the sun had finally set, and Travers brought the carriage back to the Dunlock courtyard. It was after dark, but there was a considerable amount of activity in the courtyard. Grooms and other servants were still at work; a large party of knights had returned from the hunt for Princess Kira. As Travers brought the carriage up to the wide steps at the front, Diana watched the men dismount. It was easy to tell they were frustrated from the lack of progress. The dozen men seemed fine, although bruised and exhausted.

Travers climbed out of the carriage, and had crossed over to help her down. She had reluctantly taken his hand when bright, blinding light exploded through the courtyard. Her vision went white, and her hearing drowned out by a great, reverberating roar.

In its wake, there was mayhem. Someone screamed, "It's the Princess!" and a host of voices began screaming, so many she could no longer make out the words.

Diana inadvertently gripped Travers's hand tighter, only to shake off his grip when her sight returned.

Everyone was transfixed by the scene in front of them. Travers summed it up, "Damn the Fairies, what is that?"

Squarely in the middle of the courtyard, Robert sat on the ground, the unconscious Princess in his arms. He was holding her so tightly, rocking back and forth, imploring her to wake up.

"Kira, Kira, please, Kira," he said, pleading and plaintive. Diana's heart cracked like glass.

Princess Kira didn't stir.

Something had to be done. Diana turned to Travers. "We have to do something," but the Prince wasn't moving.

"Is she dead?" he asked, his voice low. He looked ashen, as if the idea of death was somehow unacceptable.

"No, don't say that. We have to help them for Fairie's sake!"

Giving up on Travers, Diana ran toward Robert. Only when she was close enough to see his trembling hands did she notice that Sir Jordaan also lay on the ground, unconscious.

"What happened?" She asked Robert. She bent down, checking Jordaan for injuries. He seemed to be unharmed, and breathing, his eyes moving furiously behind the lids.

Robert shook his head, and continued imploring the Princess to wake up.

Diana was aware that the people were coming from all directions, but in the chaos, nothing was happening. She could feel the shift and sway of the crowd, and the sweat pool down her back.

Robert's face was covered in small cuts, as if glass had shattered only inches from his face.

"Robby, you're bleeding," Diana said. "You have to get up and get some help."

"I can't leave her!" Tears were gathered in his eyes.

Diana gathered up the hem of her skirt and ripped a large strip from her petticoat. "Hold this to your cheek," she said as sternly as she could.

He took it, but used the material to dab at the dirt on Kira's face. The Princess was covered in what looked like a ragged yellow bed sheet over a heavy, multi-colored fur cloak. Dirty bare feet stuck out from beneath it.

"Robby, please. You have to get up."

"I won't leave her."

"That's fine. Tell me what you need," Diana said. "I will help you."

"Go tell Caris Mourne. We were on our way, and… and…" His breath was coming so short that words no longer seemed possible.

He didn't have to say more. Diana got to her feet and ran for the witch's tower.

*Melissa Constantine*

# Chapter Forty-Five
## Kira

**The voices were at once far away and uncomfortably close.**

"My love, you must turn him back."

There was a sharp snort in return. "He came to me in this condition, he might as well stay that way."

"My brother may be an ass, but he is a Fairie. The Dark Court will not take well to sending him back in this current state."

"If he calls me Coco Miserable or Canary Mulberry one more time, I swear he'll spend eternity as a dust mop."

Kira groaned. It might have been a dream, waking up in her own body again. She wasn't sure she could trust the feeling of her limbs, hairless and smooth. She rubbed her hands over her face, surprised at the lack of claws. The feeling that she'd slept with her mouth open was all too real. She grimaced from the sourness on her tongue.

As the world came into focus, she saw Caris Mourne in the arms of a tall, black-haired Fairie wrapped in a floral dressing gown.

How had she gotten to the Dunlock witch's tower?

"Be easy," said the Fairie to the witch, kissing her on the forehead.

Kira watched as they handed over a bright yellow potion in a long, skinny vial. Caris Mourne swallowed the contents in one long drink, and calm seemed to seep through the tower room. Kira struggled to sit up on the small bed. It was only as her eyes adjusted to the dim firelight that she noticed Robert asleep at the foot of the bed. He looked as if he hadn't so much as had a chance to wash since they arrived back in Dunlock. He was disheveled and travel-worn, a streak of dirt across his cheek. Kira longed to reach out and rub it away for him, but she couldn't do such a thing with an audience.

Caris Mourne and the regal looking Fairie watched her. Kira pulled the covers up over her chest, as if sheets of soft cotton were any protection at all.

"It is good to see you awake."

"How long have I been here?"

"About a day."

The massive windows outside the witch's tower showed a navy blue, starlit sky. A cool wind whipped around the circular confines of the room, battled by a massive fire roaring in the hearth.

"Has Sir Robert…"

The Fairie with Caris Mourne rolled his eyes. "He finally fell asleep about an hour ago. Before that he was pacing. Would barely sit still to let us bandage his wounds."

Kira's body stiffened. Robert had been hurt when she'd had her fit? What was he doing laying at the foot of her bed, and not in one himself?

"Relax," Caris Mourne said. "He'll be fine. Stubborn but fine."

"What about Sir Jordaan? Is he going to be okay? He was with us in the woods."

"He's safely in the knight's quarters."

"Is he awake?"

The Fairie and witch hesitated. Finally, the Fairie said cautiously, "That remains to be seen. For now he's safe."

Kira's head and heart pounded. "How did we get here?"

"Ah, that is something even I'm not sure of," Caris Mourne admitted. "One moment you were simply here. It was quite shocking."

Kira's head hurt. There was a pitcher of water beside the bed, and she fumbled for a glass in hopes it would stop the relentless pounding. "How does that happen?"

"Jacobee, perhaps you could give our guest a dose of the potion? I believe that should do a great deal for her recovery."

The Fairie's thick eyebrow curled up, but they nodded. A similar vial to the one they'd given Caris Mourne was placed in her hands.

"What is it?"

"An elixir to bring down your emotions."

Kira took it, though her hands were clumsy from the memory of larger paws. The substance was cold and almost sweet as it trickled down her throat. As the Fairie had said, she felt as if the tide of emotions within her ebbed. It left her feeling empty and calm. The absence felt like a blessing. She had to wonder how long it would last. Her emotions had plagued her for the whole scope of her life. They were too wild, too undisciplined. Perhaps if she suppressed them, she might be better off.

The Fairie seemed to understand the direction of her thoughts. "Humans must learn to control their emotions on their own. No Fairie draught will help forever."

Kira swung her legs over the side of the small bed. At some point, she'd been cleaned up and put in a simple white nightgown. She was careful not to disturb Robert.

"So," said Caris Mourne. "There are things we should discuss." She gestured to where the Beast of Barlow's cloak was strung up over a clothes line that ran between two of the tower's large open windows.

Kira shook her head. She wasn't sure she would repeat what she had managed to say to Robert in the woods. "Does everyone know I'm back?"

"I'm afraid so," said the witch. She bustled about the room, pulling books from large stacks. "But I've assured them you're under my care. And that there is a perfectly good explanation for your reappearance."

The witch raised her purple eyebrows expectantly, but Kira kept her secrets locked tight. She wasn't sure she could explain it anyway.

"Sir Robert had some things to say, though I must admit, he was a bit incoherent."

Curiosity peaked through the veil the yellow potion had brought down inside of her. It was an odd thing, to feel the bud of emotion pressed against her chest when she was otherwise numb. It quickly faded. It was as if the witch herself had reached into her chest and physically moved it aside. "So what is everyone in the castle saying?"

The Fairie seemed to cast a sympathetic look at her, but quickly turned to Caris Mourne. "Darling, perhaps I should inform the Queen Regent about our friend here?"

"Please, Love," the witch agreed, and the Fairie bowed to them both before disappearing.

Kira wasn't sure she wanted anyone to know she was awake. She wanted to crawl into a hole and hide for a while longer. Because not knowing how she landed back in her own body left her terrified she might shift back at any moment.

"Will I change back?"

"I can't say," the witch admitted. "You seem to have quite a bit of chaos swirling around you."

Robert was drooling on the white blanket. She wanted to laugh, but the numbness would allow it. "What about Bertie's orphans, are they…"

"I was able to give them something to keep their transformations under control. But we will need to work out what type of magic is affecting you in order to restore them permanently."

The numbness inside her took over, chilling any desire to know. She sagged back on to the bed. Sir Robert snored a bit, snuggling deeper into the blanket. It was odd to look at him and feel nothing. It was perhaps a starker absence of feeling than anything else. For the first time she was able to look at him without the haze of attraction. He was objectively beautiful. Even dirty, his hair was a shiny riot of soft, touchable curls.

"He's far too pretty," said the witch.

"It makes it hard to like him."

She smiled. "No, it doesn't."

Well, that was true. "Should we leave him there?"

"I will take care of him. You've had quite a day."

Also true. Kira moved to a chair and the witch got to work, turning the dial on the silver watch, and reciting a short spell that had the unconscious knight rising from his spot at the end of the bed. A tangle of sheets surrounded Robert creating a modesty screen, and soap and a bucket of water went flying. In no time, he was scrubbed, changed into a similar garment to what she wore and settled into a cot that had walked itself up the stairs.

When Caris Mourne finished the spell, she put away her silver watch and asked Kira to follow her to the sitting area. "I understand you may wish to avoid saying certain things, but if you're well enough, I have some questions for you."

Kira nodded. The potion zinging around in her blood seemed to surge, as if it knew that she needed protection from the conversation.

"Sir Robert mentioned that before you appeared back in the castle, you got angry."

Kira blushed. Angry wasn't the word. "I was scared."

"How scared?"

The witch had spoken it like a question, but Kira had no doubt she knew exactly what happened in the woods.

"I could feel it in my chest and my limbs. It hurt, and I thought it would burst out. And it did. There was a village nearby, and I may have…I don't know what I did, but, it was bad."

She tried to describe the light, how the shards of it had seemed to surround her, and how before she'd blacked out, she felt as if the earth under her feet were being blown apart.

The witch looked sad, as if she were about to deliver bad news. "That is definitely magic."

"Why?"

"The better question is what kind. We know you have something around you. And if I am correct, there's more than one type. The collision between them is causing them both to spin out, causing all sorts of havoc."

Kira felt her stomach drop, and the effects of potion seemed to drain out of her. It was as if she had been dropped off a tall building. "So it's my fault? Bertie's orphans and...."

"Fault and blame are not subjects I like much. What I like to do is fix things. There's work to do to determine the full impact. There's a lot of magic in the Known Kingdoms, and there are many enchantments competing to claim responsibility for all that has happened to you."

Kira looked at Robert. He'd come to find her. Sick, chased off his horse, bleeding. He'd done his best to get her back here. How could she ever repay him?

"He'll recover. I promise."

Kira shook, all of her emotions surging, as if ever having been held back they needed to rush out like a dam had been broken. "I can't have any more people dying. Not after my parents, I can't... I can't...." Her head felt heavy in her hands. "They died because of me."

Kira had felt grief before. She knew the weight that it carried, and had felt the pressure on her chest and shoulders. This wave was nothing like that. It was so much worse, as if she might be crushed by giant boulders with no place to escape.

Caris Mourne got up from her chair and stood beside her. Kira felt the unexpected warmth of a small hand press her upper back.

"You have never caused anyone's death. Ever." Unlike the whimsical, quirky tone she had been used to hearing from Caris Mourne, the statement she made was spoken with a brisk finality.

"I wished my father dead. I did. I wanted him gone after it all happened."

"Your father was ill. Because he refused the help of witches and healers, an infection likely affected his mind."

"You don't know, you weren't there. You don't understand."

Kira did not ever remember crying. Not after her mother's funeral. Not after the sham wedding, or her father's funeral either. What she'd felt then was rage. It had seemed to come pouring out of her, shimmering in the air around her like summer heat. The sobs that tore through her showed no mercy. Every part of her, from the tips of her toes to the last hair on her head had its own set of tears, and she wouldn't be finished until they were all out.

Through it all, the witch let her cry, kept that warm, comforting hand on her back, and murmured in a soothing, inaudible whisper.

Only when the tears stopped did she speak again, handing Kira a clean handkerchief to replace the dozen she'd already soaked. "There is no timeline on grief. Even in the best of circumstances."

"I loved them. But I also hated them."

"Now that is a feeling I know well."

"How?"

"A story for another time. Let us say that families are complicated. Sometimes, they don't treat us as we deserve."

"I don't want to cry," Kira said, unable to stop the sobs that once again filled the circular room.

Caris Mourne brushed a loose strand of hair from Kira's forehead. "Crying is good for the soul."

Tiredness was like a blanket settling over her whole body, and tears seemed to stream down her face and into the neck of her nightdress. It was wonderful and it was awful. She wasn't sure when the crying actually stopped, only that her whole body was wrung out like an old rag.

"Well," said the witch, "Now that is done, we are expecting a visitor."

There was no pause between her words and the knock on the door that admitted the Queen Regent.

# Chapter Forty-Six
## Kira

*Kira found it hard to make eye contact with her stepmother, whose* appearance in the cavernous space made the room feel smaller. Perhaps that wasn't fair, and what she felt was the physical signs of all the mistakes she'd made. Either way, she wanted nothing so much, when Isadora stood there looking regal and patient, then to slink away and hide. But that wasn't going to help.

She tried to get to her feet to curtsey, but Isadora waved her off. "You're still in recovery. We have no need for the formalities."

*Didn't they?* Kira wasn't sure. She had so often been disrespectful with her stepmother that it seemed the polite formality was the only way to begin to treat her with the reverence she deserved.

"I'm very happy you're back," the Queen Regent said.

Kira murmured her thanks, because it was one thing to be aware of her own short-comings and another to correct herself so entirely.

There was a pop like a champagne cork, as the Fairie, Jacobee, returned to the tower. Although they had left in a frilly sort of dressing gown, on return they wore an elaborate red coat decorated in gold silk braid that covered them from ears to toes.

"Ah, I take it the mission was successful?" Caris Mourne said to her spouse.

"It was," they agreed. Kira was almost certain she remembered the Fairie having only gone to fetch Isadora, but she had no time to wonder.

The witch and the Fairie touched their foreheads together in a loving way, the witch's eyes closing as if the feelings between them were so strong that adding sight would have been too much. It was such a small gesture, but Kira felt as if she shouldn't be there to bear witness. What was between the two was meant to be private, and in turn she glanced nervously at Isadora, who had a sad look, as if she'd lost something.

Kira realized that the affection between Caris Mourne and her spouse was love. It was the kind of thing her parents should have had, that her father might have had with Isadora if things had been different.

"Please, all, sit," the witch said, breaking up the tableau. More chairs joined them by the fire, although Kira couldn't say where the extras had come from.

"I am hopeful that you have some answers for me about what has been happening," Isadora said.

Caris Mourne made a non-committal noise. "I suspect we're in for a bit of a long road on that front. But, my love has been able to bring a document to us that should begin this particular narrative."

There was another pop, and a large scroll appeared in the Fairie's elegant hand. "I found this in the Dark Court archives."

They passed the scroll to Caris Mourne who unfurled the document with a crisp efficiency. Her eyes zipped over the language, and she frowned, significantly. "Well, this does begin to shed some light on the matter."

She handed the document next to Isadora, whose beautifully sculpted face took on a similar look of shock. "Would this explain everything that's been happening?"

"No," said the witch. "There are far too many layers to the magic here."

Her bright gaze caught Kira, who felt her pulse tick upward. Her new resolve to be polite crumbled under the unspoken accusation. "Would someone tell me what it says?"

The Fairie cleared their throat. "This document is the terms of a Covenant, brought between King Callum the Third, and Queen Clara, of the Known Kingdoms, and my father, ruler of the Dark Court of Fairie."

Her parents had gone to the Fairies? Why? They hated all magical practitioners, especially Fairies. Kira tried to shake off a looming sense of something being wrong, but she couldn't. "But they…"

Isadora saved her from speculation. "I have to assume that the terms of the Covenant were significant?"

Kira wanted to sink into the chair's cushions and never come out. She wasn't sure she wanted to know what the Covenant said. But she had to ask, because not knowing left her feeling as if she'd been put on a raft and pushed out into the cold Northern Sea. "What did they ask for?"

Isadora reached over and took Kira's hand. Her touch was warm, her hand strong. Kira wished she had another dose of the yellow potion because her stepmother being so unfailingly kind was making the impending sense of doom so much worse.

"An heir to the throne," Isadora said.

A thousand emotions threaten to burst out of Kira like shards of glass. She tried for a bracing breath, but found her chest too tight to make such a big move. "Me?"

"And it seems," the Fairie said carefully, "that soon after the bargain was struck, the King and Queen violated the terms of the Covenant."

"They burned the Fairie chapel," Kira said, filling in the answer to an unspoken question.

"Yes, the Dark Court specified that the chapel be maintained in perpetuity, and that the child be…" Caris Mourne stopped speaking mid-sentence.

Kira was glad of it. She didn't need the words spoken. The witch had already witnessed her tearful confession, and that was enough. "They thought I was … They burned the chapel because I was a changeling. Not their daughter."

"Yes," Jacobee said simply. "That appears to be the case."

Isadora gave Kira's hand another reassuring squeeze before withdrawing and turning her attention to the magical couple. "Given all that's happened, that Kira has apparently displayed signs of magic, could she be a changeling?"

Jacobee shook their head. "Our kind do not give away their children. The Princess is the rightful heir to the throne."

"Where does that leave us in trying to sort out what happened to Kira?" Isadora asked.

"We'll need to gather more information," Caris Mourne said. "I believe what we've learned about the Kingdom Council's movements recently may be the beginning."

"Perhaps I should speak to Prince Brandon about holding an inquest. We can gather all of the royals, as well as the Council, and try to piece together what has taken place."

The words tumbled out of Kira before she could stop them. "You can't." Panic rose in her chest. She wanted to bolt from the tower room, but she wasn't sure her legs would carry her. "You can't tell them anything about this."

"Kira, we must find out what has happened to you."

"No." She frantically shook her head back and forth. "You can't go in front of the people I'm supposed to lead one day and tell them my parents didn't love me. They can't know about the wedding and the…"

Isadora rose from her chair and gathered Kira in a tight hug. The panic ebbed as Kira breathed in the comforting scent of crane flowers, basking in the sunshine. "We only tell them what is needed. It will all be all right."

Kira wished she could be sure. She wished she could lean into the hug and squeeze every bit of reassurance from it, but she couldn't.

An inquest meant questions. And those questions couldn't help but lead from the broken Covenant to her own actions. And no one was going to allow her to be queen once they knew she was both unlovable and a monster.

## Chapter Forty-Seven
### Robert

**Robert had no dreams.** All of the terrifying things had played out, and there was nothing left. Or perhaps it was the potion that had been poured into his mouth when he wouldn't stop pacing the tower, needing Kira to wake up. He could taste the lingering minty-ness of it on his tongue, and he hadn't quite lost the feeling that it was zinging around in his blood, burning him from the inside out.

He knew he'd fallen asleep at the foot of Kira's bed, desperate to have her whole and alive. He couldn't say when in the last two days they'd switched places, but there she was; her blonde hair spilled every which way over his feet. The tower room was empty, the light from the crackling fire illuminating her flushed face.

He reached for her, shaking her shoulder gently.

She came awake with a start, as if her own sleep hadn't been so peaceful. She clutched her chest as if her heart were beating too quickly. After a moment, she turned, her eyes still dazed with sleep. "How are you?"

"I'm all right."

Her pinched expression said that she didn't really believe that, and Robert couldn't be certain himself. But it felt right to assure her. "I swear."

She nodded, and seemed to realize she was sitting on the stone floor in her nightgown. She pulled back, wrapping her arms around her chest. "I don't know how to thank you."

"You don't have to thank me. I did what anyone would do."

A strawberry-colored flush rose up from her neck. "Except that no one else did. You risked everything to find me and bring me back here."

He hadn't meant to make her feel bad. "It was my duty."

"No, I have thousands of knights, but you're the one that saved me. I'll never be able to thank you."

"You're under no obligation to me."

Her lips parted as if she were going to speak, but there was a heavy moment where only the wind through the tower room windows could be heard. Unease pricked at the back of Robert's neck. He saw his mistake in that eerie quiet.

He'd only meant to make sure she knew he expected nothing in return, but she reacted as if his refusal was personal. She got to her feet, holding her head high. It was as if in that instant she summoned all the strength and bearing of a thousand years of noble ancestors.

"I'll bid you good day then."

She left the tower room and Robert immediately felt the loss of her presence. He didn't know what he was supposed to have said. She was the future queen. He was sworn to protect her. He'd done exactly what he promised to do on the day she'd touched that ceremonial sword to his shoulders and made him a knight.

Robert slumped forward, catching his head in his hands. He would only be fooling himself if he said aloud that his only thought had been duty. He'd been terrified for her. Not the future queen, but Kira.

He should go after her. But his legs felt weak, as if he'd walked for legions. In fact, his whole body felt tired.

The Fairie, Jacobee, came in with a tray, motioning for him to sit up so he could give him a nourishing meal. "Hard day?"

Robert had no words. He shook his head. How did one explain that he'd insulted the future queen and the woman he might love?

Jacobee passed him a large mug full of steaming yellow liquid that smelled oddly sweet. "Drink up."

Robert thanked him and brought the mug to his lips. The mug's contents tasted like a strongly brewed tea with a note of citrus. Whether it was tea or something stronger he couldn't say. But the more he drank, his appetite increased. He traded the tea for a bowl of soup and a heel of crusty bread.

Jacobee smiled. "Good to see you eat. My wife was worried."

"I'm grateful," he said between bites.

Jacobee watched him for a beat longer than Robert could comfortably stand, their head tilted to the side, the firelight emphasizing the slightly elongated features that marked them as not human. "Something is bothering you."

Robert shrugged. He tried concentrating on his food, but the awkwardness caused him to look at the Fairie again, waiting for them to say something else.

Jacobee scratched one of the long, pointed ears. "I don't pretend to be empathic. I watch Caris struggle enough for that, but I do see… confusion? Ugh, humans are so opaque."

"It's been a strange few days, is all."

Immediately, Jacobee shook their head. "No."

"I'm sorry?"

"You've been on a journey. You're hurt. You're tired. But that's not it. Look my patience is thin, why don't you tell me whatever is bothering you so we can move on."

"I don't know what you mean."

Jacobee's eyes narrowed. They reached out and took Robert's hand, pulling his arm up for close inspection. The mark on his wrist began to throb.

"What's this?"

"Caris Mourne said it was a magical claim."

The Fairie scoffed, releasing him. "Unlikely. Do you know where it came from?"

"The Princess. She bit me," he said, hurrying to add, "It's not recent."

"And Caris told you what exactly?"

Not much, Robert had to admit. He told them of the odd aside, and how it seemed like every time after when they were together the wound had opened again. Jacobee stayed silent for a moment, and then said, "And you're afraid that this means something?"

When said out loud it did sound a bit ridiculous. "I thought it might be influencing how I thought about her."

Jacobee smirked and snapped their fingers. There was a flutter of clothing, and Robert watched one of his new gloves he'd bought to replace the ones he lost to Kira sail through the air and landed in the Fairie's hands. Despite the days-long trek through the woods, the glove's leather was still remarkably stiff. Jacobee turned it over, their mouth set in a thin line. They turned the cuff out, where Robert's blood stained the lining. "Seems to me the problem might be a little more practical than all of that." Robert caught the glove. A seam had split through the interior fabric. Where the leather was joined the edges were extremely sharp.

"I feel like a fool."

"Don't be too hard on yourself. Caris may well have had a good reason for letting you believe it. Eighty years of marriage has not given me enough context to parse out all of her motives."

Jacobee left him for the remainder of his meal, disappearing with a sudden snap. Robert finished it as Xavier was admitted to the tower room.

Xav looked miserable. His hair stood out in several directions, and looked as if he hadn't slept. "Please tell me you're not going to die."

"Not that anyone has told me."

Xav released a breath. He fetched a stool and pulled it up to the side of the bed. "You scared the hell out of me."

"I'm sorry."

The prince shook his head. "There's nothing to be sorry about. Just don't do it again."

They sat there a long time, neither of them saying anything. Robert could tell Xav wanted to tell him something, but he let him come to it in his own time.

The tower room was once again a contrast in temperatures — the cold wind from the large open windows competing with the fire in the large hearth. Sweat had gathered at Xav's hairline before he spoke. "Bertie and I broke up."

"Do you want to talk about it?"

He did not. He hung his head. "With everything going on, I can't be with him."

The excuse sounded weak. If Xav loved Bertie why would he give up so easily? They were the same age, both royal, and from what he'd seen, affectionate. But what did he know? He was equally an idiot when it came to love.

"No one teaches you how to deal with this stuff," Xav said.

No, it definitely hadn't been part of his squire training. "You'd think it'd be important. Reading, writing, handling your love life."

"It feels like that's a big omission."

"Should we tell someone?"

Xav nodded, his gaze fixed on the starry night beyond the tower. "I'll get right on that."

They lapsed into silence again, until Robert's injuries caught up with him, and Xav left him to sleep it off.

****

Robert tucked a small flask of whisky next to Jordaan, deliberately trying to keep it out of the nursemaid's sight. He'd been well enough to leave the witch's tower after dawn, but his friend wasn't so lucky. Jordaan had been up in a small, sunny room in the knight's quarters, with a cadre of caregivers around the clock. No one was entirely sure what was happening, but he'd been coming in and out of consciousness since their return. Robert could only imagine the hangover Jordaan would have when he woke up for good, and so he'd come prepared.

"I know I said we all die one day, but I was being an ass. I'd rather you didn't."

No response from his unconscious friend.

"If you wake up, I could tell you how badly I mucked up with Princess Kira."

There might have been a snore, but Robert wasn't sure.

"You would probably find it funny."

It hurt like a paper cut, but he'd endure it if his friend would wake up. Besides, Robert suspected that was how it was supposed to feel. He wasn't sure exactly what he should have said to her and wasn't sure how to make it up to her.

"I'll stop back before we leave the Festival," he said, careful to hide the flask in the folds of Jordaan's blanket.

He was halfway back to the castle when he saw Amzi being led across the courtyard to the stables. Relief flooded him, and he took off at a run, catching up with the man leading his horse.

"When did he arrive?"

The groom wasn't sure, only adding, "Came with Master Durrin from Corlea."

"Is he still here?"

"Yeah, yacking it up with whoever will listen," said the groom affectionately.

Robert gave Amzi a quick scratch behind the ears, and promised him a bushel of apples before leaving the groom to finish exercising the horse.

The Dunlock stables weren't as elaborate as the ones at Corlea Palace, but neither were they as tumbledown as the ones on Greater Miser. No gold plating or expensive Zephyr lamps, just plain wood and candles. The space was clean and bright and massive. It had stalls for something like fifty horses, everyone filled. Even with the sheer size of the place, it wasn't hard to find Durrin. Robert only had to listen for the sound of excited conversation taking place outside one of the tack rooms.

Durrin had a handful of the grooms in thrall. Robert wasn't quick enough to catch more than what appeared to be the punchline of an old joke.

"...And he says, he said, *did you really think I asked for a pony?*" which caused the stable hands to roar with laughter.

"All right, I've kept you from your work long enough," Durrin said, dismissing his audience. "Afternoon, Sir Robby."

"Thank you for bringing Amzi back."

Durrin nodded; his arms crossed over his chest. "He and that one over there turned up at my stables the other day. Scared of everything and anything." He pointed to Jordaan's horse, Bull, who was lazily chewing on a bunch of hay.

"It's a relief to have them back."

Durrin scratched at his ear under the rim of his cap, a merry twinkle in his eye. "I could bring him back now that the Beasty isn't running around." He paused and then added with a little laugh, "Is she?"

Words died on Robert's tongue. Durrin knew. *Of course he did.*

"She's safely out of the forest," he said carefully.

Durrin smiled a broad grin with a hint of teeth. Robert suppressed a shiver. It was the first time he'd looked at the Corlea Stable Master and seen a Fairie, but it was undeniable.

"I suspect that we'll have no more trouble along the Royal Route, eh? We'll let all these stuffy royals and their pampered horses head home."

Robert nodded, keeping his tone neutral. "Yeah, I suppose so."

"Just one more bit of business. Time to get the Queen involved, no?"

"I heard she's holding an inquiry to figure out what happened."

"Useful," Durrin said with a smirk. "Be sure to tell the Princess I said hello, Sir Robby."

Robert promised he would, and Durrin sauntered off, no doubt looking for someone else to strike up a conversation. As he walked away he stuck his hands in his pockets, whistling out a jaunty tune. Other grooms in the stables picked it up, adding melody and words, until the song filled the giant space.

## Chapter Forty-Eight
### Kira

**The antechamber off the ballroom had been cleared of the stacks of plates** and soup tureens that had crowded it a few days previously, but was by no means empty. It was rammed with items — vases with dying crane flowers and stacks of spindly gold chairs swept from the edges of the dance floor. The old flowers created a powerful, sweet scent that burned Kira's nostrils. She cracked open the door, watching as royals took seats facing the stage, where Queen Isadora and Prince Brandon sat stone faced.

She needed to calm her raging anxiety and get out there, but for the life of her she couldn't make herself move into the ballroom. She closed the door again, retreating to the far corner. She leaned against the wall, putting her palms flat against the wallpaper. It was slightly sticky to the touch, as if it had been dusty far too long.

Kira took several deep breaths. They didn't calm her as she hoped. She supposed that was appropriate. Although Isadora had assured her again that the meeting was, "a gentle inquest," she knew. They were going to take her crown away.

How could they not? As they began to peel back the layers to her "kidnapping" the truth would be there. Every ugly piece of it. She wasn't a victim. She was the villain. Try as she might to hide it, to conceal her previous activities in the woods, it would come out. There was no kidnapping without the Beast, and there was no Beast without her. Once that was known there was no way that she was ever going to be queen.

The door hinges creaked, and a tall figure slipped inside the antechamber with her. Carefully, he closed the door as if making any noise would draw attention. Only then did Sir Robert turn to her. For a long moment, he stared at her, his blue eyes dark in the low, pale flame from the room's lone Zephyr lamp.

"Princess, you must come into the ballroom."

She knew that, but her heartbeat had yet to return to normal.

"How did you know I was here?"

"I saw you slip away," he said.

So much for her ability to be stealth.

"Are you alright?" His voice had a low register that snuck along her nerves. He'd said he never wanted her to think about him, so what was he doing following her into a glorified closet?

She shook her head. "I'm scared."

Robert stepped closer, until he was close enough that his body blocked some of the inadequate light. She could feel the subtle heat of him. And it was so massively unfair that he didn't love her, that she had no right to sink into him and try and ring comfort from him like water from a scullery maid's mop.

"What can I do to help?"

There were a dozen things she might have said. She could have asked to borrow some of his courage or his sense of right and wrong. She might have told him he could march right out of the antechamber and never give her any false hope ever again.

But she didn't say any of that. Instead the words that slipped from her mouth seemed to belong to someone else who was infinitely braver. "Would you kiss me?"

"I have no right."

Kira cursed herself for her stupidity. He was never going to see her as anything but a monster. She was thankful for the low light that hid her blush. There was an uneasy silence between them that made Kira want to scream.

"Princess..."

"You used to call me Kira. You said you wanted to be my friend."

"I do. I do, but you're the Princess Royal."

It sounded like an excuse to her. Having seen her with fangs and claws, he could not see her as she really was, as a woman.

"Not for long. They might take away my crown."

"They can't do that."

"They can and they should. Even if it is the only thing I have."

"You're so much more than your title."

She shook her head, wrapping her arms around her chest. "I'm not. And they're not wrong, I don't deserve it. I haven't served my kingdom as I should. I have lied and I have stolen. When the royals in that room take everything I have away from me, it will be justified."

She'd never been one of those women who cried at small children or adorable animals. She wasn't sentimental. But being the future queen was everything to her, and she couldn't stop the tears pricking at the corners of her eyes. She tried to hastily wipe them away.

Robert took a handkerchief from inside his tunic. He pressed it to her check. The contact was a brief brush of summer lightning.

She wanted him to touch her, and to touch him in turn. She wanted to run her hands along his strong arms, rest her head against his chest and listen to his heartbeat. She wondered if it had ever thumped as fast as her own. It wouldn't now, obviously, but it would have been nice to imagine.

"You need to come into the ballroom. Caris Mourne has something important."

"What could she say that would excuse what I've done?"

Robert didn't know, but urged her again to go back and face the assembled.

"When I do, will you tell them what you know?"

She didn't know what she expected him to answer. She'd put in a position that was unwinnable. Stay loyal to her or to his own moral code.

"Do you want me to say something?"

She had to wonder - did she? If Robert were the one to stand up and say, "The princess is the Beast" would that make anything better? Would it would be easier in the moment to have to face the Queen Regent and the Council and the assembled royal families? She wouldn't have to make her voice heard among all of the noise. And that was tempting. But it would prove what she already knew deep in her heart. She wasn't ready to be queen.

She might want it, badly, but that didn't mean she was anywhere near prepared.

Kira took a bracing breath, willing her spine to straighten. "I'll do it. You'd be far less attractive if you were a tattletale."

She thought she detected a smile, but the light wasn't enough to really say. Robert pressed the handkerchief into her hand, and then offered her his arm.

They entered the over-bright ballroom to an impossible hush, as if the inhabitants were physically prevented from speaking. There were at least two hundred people in the room, including the four members of the Kingdom Council in their pink and powder blue robes. Sir Roderick tried to make eye contact, but Kira ignored him.

At the front of the room, the Queen Regent and Prince Brandon sat with Caris Mourne and her spouse, Jacobee. They were an odd couple, the tiny witch and her slim Fairie companion. Her concession to her post as Castle Witch was a red stole over her unusual garb of wide-legged trousers and striped waistcoat that cinched in a voluminous white blouse. The Fairie, by contrast, still wore their regalia, the richly-embroidered red coat that covered them floor to the tips of their ears.

There was only one other plush chair on the stage, the one meant for her. From that angle and the height, no one in the room would fail to see her. The thought made Kira vaguely uncomfortable. She had been on display many times — in the throne room at Corlea Palace, chiefly — but this felt different.

Robert guided her through the rows of chairs, leaving her at the stage steps. He slipped into the crowd and was immediately lost to her among the throngs of royals. She supposed he would take up space with the other knights at the edges of the gathering, their array of brightly-colored tunics like standards on display. It was good that she could no longer see him. She didn't need to be reminded of another of her foolish choices.

She curtsied to the four people on stage, and took her seat.

"Excellent," said the purple-haired witch. "Now we can begin."

Caris Mourne took out the silver watch and pressed the stopper. Around the room there was a great exhale, as if everyone had been instructed to hold their breath at the same time. It wasn't that they were afraid to speak, Kira realized, it was that they couldn't. Such a spell would be extremely useful during the royal audiences if she could ever learn it. But, she suspected like the yellow potion she'd been given, there was some catch or caveat that would prevent its usefulness.

"My love," Jacobee said to her in a low voice, "perhaps we should refrain from enchanting so many people at once?"

The witch shrugged, as if it were no matter. Chatter in the room picked up, but many seemed too afraid to speak. Several people tugged at their collars, or rubbed their throats.

Queen Isadora rose and walked to the center of the stage, where soft, golden light from the overhead chandeliers illuminated her fine brown skin and lustrous hair. She waited a beat, staring out among the crowd until she had their full attention. And when she began to speak, she didn't raise her voice above normal conversation, so that some at the back had to pay particular attention to hear her. Kira couldn't help but admire her sense of command.

"Ladies, gentlemen, and distinguished beings, thank you for attending today's inquiry. Our goal for the day is to discover what we can about the strange happenings of the last week. I am sure many of you have noticed the return of previously stolen sentimental items, the destruction of the statue of King Callum and Queen Clara, and, of course, the disappearance of the Princess Royal."

*Disappearance* was such a nice way to put it. Escape was better, but Kira suspected Isadora was being circumspect with her words.

"I've asked the castle witch, Caris Mourne, to begin our inquiry with what she has learned since her arrival. Ms. Mourne, if you please."

The witch rose, but not before touching her forehead to that of the Fairie beside her. It was such a simple gesture, but Kira could feel the energy behind it, the simple, emotional pull between them.

The witch thanked Isadora, and stood at center stage, although the candlelight wasn't as kind to her. She looked small and silly standing there, much like Kira felt.

"Some months ago," Caris Mourne began, "I created a new hybrid variety of crane flower. I did so by splicing two distinctly different flowers together, the hearty Dunlock crane, and the beautiful but delicate flower that grows only on the Misery Islands. And if you'll permit me, I'd like to bring in some examples for all of you."

She indicated to a footman staged at the back of the room, and the ballroom doors swung open. Servants in the elaborate lavender livery of Dunlock poured inside, all bearing large buckets full of oddly gray and green-speckled cranes. The buckets were dropped at the ends of each aisle, and then gathered up to be passed to the royals, one stem for each of them. A single bloom was brought to Caris Mourne, who twirled it between her small fingers.

Kira wasn't sure why, but the sight made her palms sweat. She stuck her hands into the pockets of her gown, where she found Robert's handkerchief. She shouldn't have kept it, but her distress had made her focus narrow, and brought out her selfish desires. She was glad to have it, the simple linen like a mooring line.

Caris Mourne sniffed at the ugly petals, and laughed. "Not very pretty, is it?"

There was a general murmur of ascent. Most of the royals didn't seem to know what to do with the long, reedy blossom they held.

"You may wonder why I've grown so many of these, given they are likely the most vomitous color? And what I think you'll find is that the answer lies in what each of the two parent flowers brings to the table. The Dunlock cranes are some of my favorites. They are extremely useful, and the fibers made from their stems are unmatched. By contrast the Misery cranes are not so useful. They are a beautiful array of pale colors, their petals nearly transparent. But nothing, so far as I know, has ever been made from them?"

She looked out at the crowd expectantly, as if one of them might have an answer for her. No one did, and she resumed her speech, using the flower a bit like a magician might use a wand or a conductor wave his baton.

"But one of the tenets of the magic I practice says that there is power in contrast. The space between the differences in the two flowers allows for something to be produced. Something useful and helpfully transparent."

"My lady," said Prince Brandon carefully. "I'm afraid I'm not seeing how this is related to the matter at hand."

Kira couldn't help but notice the poor man looked as if he'd rather keep quiet than speak. His courage was heartening, and more in the crowd seemed to appreciate him putting words to the confusion they felt.

"Ah, yes, that is a roundabout way of getting us back to the point, Your Highness. If you'll give me another moment?"

Prince Brandon looked to the Queen Regent for permission, and then nodded hastily.

"Excellent. As to the events of this week. I had not been in residence a day when I had a visit from the Princess, and her companion, a young knight. They brought me an interesting issue. Magic on the loose in Dunlock! If you can believe it, they said children were being turned into little copies of the Beast of Barlow!"

She said it as if it were a joke, and there were several hesitant laughs. Her tone abruptly shifted as spoke again, harsher this time. "That is magic afoot. Big magic. The kind that has to come from somewhere. So now I ask all of you? Where did the magic that was affecting those children come from?"

Kira mirrored the uncertainty among the assembled. What did ugly flowers have to do with magic on the loose? Even having been amidst the sorcery, she couldn't have confidently said what any of it had to do with anything.

There was an awkward silence, augmented by the scraping of chair legs and delicate coughs. It seemed as if no one would speak, until one voice from the middle of the crowd shouted. "It was a charm! A simple hex to make her hiccup!"

There was no time to gasp at the silliness of that statement before some other royal was saying, "I paid that sorcerer good money! He was supposed to turn her into a newt!"

"I left an offering at the Fairie chapel in Killmarn," said a particularly morose Duchess. "A small token, a little request for her to be gone. I could have done so much more!"

Her confession was followed by a parade of increasingly ugly requests for magical actions. Kira had to marvel at what she'd done to earn such ire from her people. Maybe they knew about her scandal before she did? Because it seems when it came to removing her from the ascension to the throne, there was no magical being unworthy of being petitioned. Witches, Fairies, Pixies, and even an abandoned well noted for wish-granting.

An old Earl, ears bursting with wiry white hair, began a long diatribe about a wizard he'd met in the Unknown Kingdoms. "I told him, get her out of the way. My son will be a wonderful king. So smart that boy. Numbers absolutely sing for him. He revolutionized the books in Renson. So I asked the old fool, I said, "Can't you give her gout or the pox or something?" and do you know what he told me? "No!" I was willing to pay, at least enough to get him a new pointy hat — his own was a disgrace — and he told me, *The affairs of the Known Kingdoms are not my responsibility."* Rude."

Kira wasn't sure if she should laugh or cry, and was somewhere between both when Sir Roderick stood up. He cast his watery eyes out over the crowd and said with a surprising amount of vigor, "All I know is that whatever I did, *whatever WE did*," he indicated with fellow council members, "she deserved it!"

He pointed an accusatory finger at Kira. She startled at the force of his dislike. It was thick as molasses, sticky and uncomfortable.

Sir Roderick continued "I don't like her. Never have. She bit me once. Little bitch."

There was an audible gasp among the royals, as Madame Jenzi jumped in, "She did not."

Indignity practically bursting out of him, Sir Roderick leaned toward his fellow council member, pointing that accusing finger at each of them. "On the leg! Came running out of a cupboard during a Council meeting, chomped into my calf, and had the nerve to tell the King it was all my fault."

"You scraped your leg on a splintered bit of the table, you old fool!" Madame Jenzi shouted. "I told you not to make it personal, Roddy. The

Fairie warned you not to make it personal, but here you are, listing out your imaginary grievances time and again."

Caris Mourne gave a small indication to her spouse, who rose from their chair. The Fairie joined her at the center of the stage, and took a doll from inside their red coat.

The doll she'd given to Bertie last week, the horned creature with the shaggy white fur.

"Perhaps, Madame Jenzi," Caris Mourne said, "you mean this Fairie? Forgive me a moment if you don't recognize him."

The doll was placed at center stage, and Caris Mourne took out her silver watch. With a twist of the dial, where the doll had once stood was a frighteningly tall Fairie with a thatch of thick black hair, high, pointed ears, and scowl that could curdle milk.

"Cagey Muckworm, I've had enough of you!" the Fairie yelled.

Caris Mourne simply twisted the dial of her watch and the Fairie, for all his gesturing and gesticulating, was silent. "I'm afraid anyone who created a bargain with my esteemed brother-in-law made a bad bargain. He's been exiled from the Dark Court, and has little magic."

The Fairie looked mortally offended, his mouth hanging open.

"And you should all know better than to go to the Fairies," the witch added.

Madame Jenzi and the two other members of the Council had the sense to look guilty, but Sir Roderick was adamant. He bellowed for the whole room to hear. "So what if we created a bargain with the Fairies? It's only right! The whole Vineland family is corrupt. Corrupt and unfit to rule!"

In the resulting chaos, Kira saw a path forward. One where she wouldn't have to admit to anything. She could hide behind all the vitriol and magic in this room. The hope that she would never have to admit her own crimes flared hot and bright in her chest.

And died just as quickly.

She couldn't do it. She couldn't pretend that she wasn't a part of the magical mess. She was the very center of it. Not admitting what she had done would leave so many unanswered questions.

Caris Mourne walked toward her, extending the ugly green and gray flower. "Something you'd like to add?" she asked in a low voice.

Kira waved away the magical truth-telling flower. She stood up, and walked to the front of the stage. She took a deep breath, trying to summon courage she didn't feel. It was no good. She would have to say it. Let the truth come out.

"You can all stop your confessions and your accusations," she said, stopping when her voice cracked. She cleared her throat and started again. "I'm to blame. I'm the Beast of Barlow."

\*\*\*\*

Kira wasn't sure she understood the meaning of the word chaos until the ballroom erupted.

Royals screamed. Some stormed out. Others blustered and seethed. A few of them fainted. And they did it all at once. It took several minutes for the Queen Regent to restore order. Enough quiet to continue the inquest was only achieved after Caris Mourne took out her pocket watch, as if she were about to cast another hushing spell on them. Thankfully she didn't need to, as the mere threat was enough to restore some semblance of order.

Kira willed her heartbeat to slow down. It had spent weeks running a never-ending race.

"When my mother died, I was angry. But my father was bereft. Although even that seems too kind of a word for his grief. They had been madly in love, to the exclusion of everyone. Including me."

"I spent much of my childhood alone. Yes, there were nannies and governesses and nurses running after me, but the King and Queen were not there. And I was so mad that no one had ever stepped in and fixed it. No one had ever told them to love me."

Kira heard a few pitying gasps, but did her best to ignore them. She would tell as much of the story as she could. She had been holding her secrets for so long, but now it was time to let some of them go.

"When the queen died, my father got sick. Not physically, but, in his heart and his mind. His illness was wicked and it was pernicious. And none of you seemed to care. He slipped into madness so quickly. And all I saw was a fight to make one of your own the new queen. And then he too died."

Grief, Kira realized, was not a defined period of time. The storm of feelings ebbed and flowed. But while a tide might be reliably calculated, grief never could. She mourned her mother and father. They had not cared for her as they should, but they were the only parents she'd known. Their loss had changed her in an indelible way.

"My whole life, I was told that one day, I would be queen. It was the thing that defined me. I would rule the Known Kingdoms. Except that when my father died, the crown did not land on my head. And I was so angry."

There was an odd calm in telling her story. She told them about finding the cloak, and how she had staged her robberies along the Royal Route. "Everyone is afraid of the Beast. It's a legend for a reason. And in my grief, I wanted to be the biggest, meanest thing I could imagine."

"I used the magic of the Beast's cloak."

Kira felt a hand on her back, but did not look up to see the source. She had spotted Robert in the crowd, steady as a beacon guiding her to some unknown place. She kept her eyes on him. He knew the story she was telling. He knew the details she didn't dare share with a larger audience. It was one of the many reasons he didn't want to be with her.

"A little while ago, Sir Roderick said that I wasn't fit to rule. And I'm afraid that's true. I have acted in a way that no sovereign should. The story you've heard probably tells you that. But I want to rule. I want to make the Known Kingdoms better than they are. Perhaps that isn't enough for any of you. Apparently it wasn't enough for the Kingdom Council. I have so much to learn. I know that now, but I fear it is too late. I can only apologize and ask for your forgiveness."

# Chapter Forty-Nine
## Kira

*Sir Roderick was not taking well to his dismissal.*

While the rest of the members of the Kingdom Council had accepted Isadora's decision to disband, slinking away from the inquest with their proverbial tails between their legs, Sir Roderick had apparently not. Kira could hear him shouting at the Queen Regent as she approached the sitting room Isadora had taken as her presence chamber.

"She admitted being the Beast! And I don't see that we have any choice but to bar her from ever taking the throne."

Kira hesitated at the door, waiting for Isadora's response, her heart beating frantically. She knew she should knock and make herself known, but she couldn't resist the chance to hear Isadora's true opinion.

"Do you suppose that was before or after you took the treasonous action of looking to have her cursed?"

A shiver traveled down Kira's spine. She knew not to hang her hope on anything she overheard, but perhaps it was a sign that she wasn't going to be deposed?

Sir Roderick sputtered, but it seemed he would not be deterred by a little matter of fact. "I have always acted in the best interest of the Known Kingdoms."

The door was open a fraction, and Kira could see glimpses of Sir Roderick pacing back and forth.

"Sir Roderick, I have no doubt that you believe that. In the two years since I married King Callum, I depended on your insight and knowledge. Apparently, however, you took that to mean you had carte blanche to make decisions based on your own feelings."

"Princess Kira is an undisciplined, impulsive, and a terrible representative of the Vineland family! From the time she was little..."

"Yes," Isadora interrupted with a sharp, "So I've heard you say."

Kira suppressed a small spurt of hope, and knocked quickly on the door. Isadora had barely had time to acknowledge the knock before Kira pushed her way inside.

Sir Roderick had stopped his pacing, and she thought she detected a flare of color in his face that might indicate he knew she'd heard him. However, if he felt any remorse for his actions, he wasn't backing down. When Kira dipped a curtsy, he rolled his eyes and turned back toward the Queen Regent.

"The Known Kingdoms deserve better than someone who would seek to deceive!"

"In that we are agreed."

"Then what do you plan to do? I would remind you that the Kingdom Council was created to keep the royals from running roughshod over the commoners. The system of checks and balances is obliterated if there is no Council."

"The Council will meet again when the people select new members. Ones who have not been compromised by their own prejudices."

Kira did not know if dismissing the members of the council was the right move, but she didn't dare contradict Isadora in front of Sir Roderick. Palms sweating, she waited for the scene between them to conclude.

Sir Roderick straightened his back, his nostrils flaring with a certain drama. "I have served on the Council for 36 years."

"And the crown thanks you. But you have also acted against a member of the royal family in a way that could have caused irreparable harm. And for that you are dismissed."

"This is not the end!" Sir Roderick said, drawing himself up to his full height. "I will be back."

And with that, he swept out of the room, taking all his fire and rage with him. Kira held her tongue, giving Isadora a chance to reset after his dramatic exit. Isadora's eyes closed briefly, and she took a bracing breath. Kira watched in awe as her iron-like composure snapped back into place. Someday she would need to learn that skill.

If she ever got the chance. Finally, when the Queen Regent spoke, "Sir Roderick and the other members of the Council are dismissed, but I urge you to be wary. A man like that does not go quietly. Snakes will hide in tall grass."

"I understand."

"I hope that's true."

Indignation roared in Kira's chest like a lion denied prey, but she held back her retort. She was trying to be humble, for Fairie's sake! Her hands were clenched into tight fists, tension thrumming from her whole body.

"I'm trying to…"

Isadora got that pitying look she used with Kira sometimes, and Kira shut her eyes to avoid acknowledging it any farther.

"I owe you an apology," Kira managed to say. "A few of them."

There was a significant pause. Kira opened her eyes to see Isadora leaning over the desk, her fingers steepled in front of her. "And what has brought this about?"

"There's nothing like being turned into the Beast you were pretending to be to teach one humility."

Isadora smiled sadly. "That must have been quite an ordeal."

Isadora indicated the seat across from her, and Kira sat.

"I feel it is time we had a frank conversation," Isadora said. "There are many things that need to be said. Without innuendo or spite."

Chastised, Kira nodded. "Without blaming you for taking my crown, you mean?"

"Among other things."

Kira bit her lip, until it felt like the words exploded out of her. "If you could just tell me how you knew about the wedding! I didn't even know. I was roused from my bed, marched down to the great hall, and next thing I know my father is telling everyone in the room the most horrible…."

"And you were there. With your whole family! It made no sense."

Kira wasn't sure what she had intended to say, and she definitely hadn't intended to start with the thorniest issue, but once the words were out she felt as if a crushing weight had been lifted.

Isadora's kind expression made Kira feel about two inches tall.

"For two years, I have been trying to teach you to rule."

Kira's brow creased. "I know that."

"Tell me, what was the first lesson?"

Kira's mouth went slack as she tried to remember the tedious lessons she'd done her best to ignore. "I guess, it was… to treat your servants well."

The Queen Regent nodded. " They are a wealth of knowledge about the workings of any castle."

Light dawned "Vendell?"

"You may not like him, but he is a remarkably capable majordomo. The man knows how to collect secrets."

"Well, not every secret," Kira said carefully.

"True. But he was the one who told me about your little cottage in the woods, and how you'd been disappearing from the castle for hours at a time."

Vendell had saved her. Vendell and Isadora. "Thank him for me?"

"Thank him yourself when we return to the Palace."

Tea service was brought in, and they were silent as the maids arranged the table with a porcelain teapot and a tiered platter of delicate pastry. Only when they were alone again, and the sitting room door shut tight did either of them speak.

"What are you going to do about me?" Kira asked, sipping at her tea to avoid saying too much.

Isadora had to admit she had no decision. "I need to think about it. I will meet with Prince Brandon and Princess Margot, and some of the other high royals and we will have a discussion. There is much to go over. I would ask, however, if there's anything else you need to tell me, now would be a good time."

Kira chewed her bottom lip as she gathered her thoughts. Her hands began to shake. She put down her teacup to avoid spilling. "I'm genuinely sorry for what I did. I know now that there were a dozen other ways I might have addressed it and I chose the wrong way entirely. I can't make up for it, but I promise, I will try. Every day for the rest of my life."

Isadora nodded. "Thank you, Kira. That means a great deal."

Kira had the insane urge to run. Her legs wanted to jump up and carry her as far from the sitting room as she could get. It was as if her body wanted to be in motion. However, Isadora wasn't finished with her, and Kira kept herself tense

" I would like you to work with Caris Mourne to figure out the magic surrounding you. You should know what kind of abilities you possess, and if they're the kind that would require you to be trained."

"You want me to train as a witch?"

"No, I simply want you to know what you are dealing with. If Caris Mourne believes this magic is something that will stay with you, we will find you an acceptable tutor when we return to Corlea Palace."

Kira got to her feet. "I think I might do best to stay out of sight for the rest of the day. If you need me I shall be in my cousin's suite."

Isadora agreed that it was best if she lay low. "Kira, I hope you know that whatever happens, I have never been your enemy."

Kira blinked back tears. "I know."

She stood and made a final curtsey, leaving Isadora to work out her fate.

*Curtsies & Consequences*

# Chapter Fifty
## Bertie

***Tea made things better.***

The measurable amount was infinitesimal, but better was better. Given all that had happened, Bertie would take what he could get.

He and Kira had barricaded themselves in his suite, only opening the door for a laden tea tray.

Kira was slumped into one of the chairs, balancing her tea cup on her chest. Kira had made no bones about hiding until the Queen Regent decided her fate. She'd sought him out after the inquest, and said simply, "You might be stuck with me."

Bertie was concerned his cousin might be crying and inconsolable, but Kira was mostly numb. Which was good, because Bertie wanted to be the one to be an unholy mess. His breakup was like a splinter pushed under his fingernail — a nagging, constant reminder of his broken heart.

"What you did, standing up like that, was remarkable and mature and I hated every second of it," he told her.

Kira gave a weak smile, her gaze not quite fixed on anything. "They're going to take my crown away."

"Well, you never really had it, so think about it — all the perks, none of the crushing responsibility. Might be the best thing that ever happened to you."

Kira put her cup aside, curling forward to catch her head in her hands. "But I want to be queen, Bertie. I know that's what I am supposed to do with my life. And there's a real chance now that it will never come to pass. And I have no one but myself to blame."

"Whatever happens, you'll be okay."

Kira didn't look like she believed it. She shook her head and changed the subject. "How are you holding up?"

It was his time to shine, to let out all the agony that had built up since his break up with Xavier. He bit into a biscotti, trying to decide where to start his rant. His mouth was oddly dry, however, and he found the words weren't coming out. He settled for the one constant — the thing that hadn't changed in the whirlwind of the last 48 hours. "I don't know what to do."

Kira sighed. She didn't know either. They kicked around ideas for a few minutes, each more absurd than the last. Taking up knitting. Running away with the circus. Staging a rebellion based on the belief that the only decent scones contained chocolate chips and never, ever raisins.

"What if we built a blanket fort and refused to come out?" Kira suggested.

It wasn't the worst idea but it was, considering his own situation, extremely impractical. He was going to have to decamp from Dunlock. The Moorelows would let him stay — they were kind like that — but he couldn't be around Xavier and not love him. It would hurt, and Bertie knew he wasn't strong enough to handle it.

"A thousand years our family has ruled the Known Kingdoms. How did we end up this pathetic?"

Kira didn't care to speculate. "Perhaps we should go hide in your doll closet and lick our wounds?"

He turned to her, momentarily confused as to why she didn't know. "I've given it up."

"Why? You love your collection."

Bertie shrugged. He had been delighted with the collection. But when the dolls had disappeared into the hands of Xavier's sisters, he hadn't missed them. The Moorelow girls were welcome to them. Even baby Jenny and her sharp teeth. Besides, after the doll Kira had brought him had turned out to be a disdainful Fairie, he wasn't sure he'd look at a doll the same way. "You missed a few things while you were... busy."

"Like what?"

Bertie blew out a long breath before launching into the story of the talking doll and his disconcerting trip to Caris Mourne's tower.

"That's unbelievable."

"You spent the last several days as a mythical Beast, and that's unbelievable?"

Kira bristled. "I was under an enchantment!"

"That you caused!"

Kira was on her feet, pacing furiously. "Well, you weren't around. I didn't have anyone to stop me."

Guilt flooded him. He knew Kira didn't really blame him, but he also knew that he had abandoned her. He'd been so miserable before he'd left for the Academy. He'd only wanted to leave Corlea Palace and get far away from his parents and their ridiculous demands about his future. They'd have married him off to anyone with enough clout and coin. But Kira was not like his parents. She was his best friend.

"Would you have told me about the Beast, if I was there?"

Kira stopped, pivoting to face him. Her face crumpled. "I don't know."

He put down his cup and got to his feet to pull her into a hug. "Let's get all this misery out of our systems. I'm exhausted."

"Deal." Kira pressed her face against his shoulder, her arms snaking around him with an iron-like grip. "But are you sure we can't have a blanket fort?"

## Chapter Fifty-One
### Kira

**Caris Mourne was a crazy person.** Kira was sure she'd known that. Their first meeting had been one of the more bizarre afternoons of her life. Yet, after the witch had cared for her, let her cry and offered comfort, Kira was sure she'd imagined all of that chaotic energy.

But, no she definitely had not imagined any of it.

There had been no decision yet from the inquest. Kira had waited all day, hiding in Bertie's suite and helping him pack up his belongings. She'd slept restlessly, only losing consciousness before dawn. Kira had awoken on what would have been the last morning of the Festival of the Flower to an invitation from the witch.

Or rather, the invitation had woken her up.

A large scroll of paper had been poking her in the arm. She hadn't seen it at first, only felt the sharp jab. Her maid, Pamela, had been flattened against the wall, eyes as big as saucers.

"My lady, what do I do?"

Well what was there to do but open it? Kira sat up and reached for the scroll which helpfully unfurled at her touch. "First, coffee, then we decide to figure out what this summons is about."

Pamela was all too eager to run to the kitchens for a tray.

The scroll, mercifully, didn't speak on its own or make any demands of her. In simple script it gave a time for her to show up at the witch's tower, and an admonition to "wear comfortable shoes and clothing."

Well, at least that was practical. Kira put aside the scroll, which took it on itself to roll up, and blink into oblivion.

And thus, after consuming her weight in coffee, and dressing in a clean pair of riding trousers, a fitted blouse, and the requisite shoe choice, Kira found herself climbing the spiral stairs. She wasn't sure what she expected to find at the top, but it was not the constant ringing of small, tinkling bells and the bellow of trumpets, flutes, and trombones played by persons unseen. In the middle of the mele, the witch was sending small sparks up to the high, steepled ceiling of the tower room. Kira put her hands over her ears, grimacing as the discordant music clanged like mad.

"Do us a favor," Caris Mourne said. "Put a stop to it."

"What?"

The witch sent several colorful sparks from her fingertips up to the ceiling, where they exploded in a shower of light.

"Try, if you please."

Kira had no idea what she was meant to do. She had never purposely done magic before. The few times before it had come out of her in sudden and furious bursts. She had no way to summon it that she knew.

"How?"

Caris Mourne sighed, and all at once the symphony shut down. She took out her pocket watch, clicked the stopper on top, and the instruments, bells, and the fireworks disappeared.

"I'm afraid you'll have to do better if we are to get any of this under control."

Kira shivered. As usual the windows of the tower room were wide-open, but unlike her previous visits there was no fire in the hearth. The little beds she and Robert had occupied were likewise gone, as were all the contents of the room. There were no chairs or tables or piles of books.

Caris Mourne paced in a tight circle. "We'll need a way to bring out the magic so that we can poke at it, see what form it takes."

Kira crossed her arms against a sudden gust of wind. "I would prefer not to be poked."

"Yes, well, that is not an option. There are many kinds of magic in the world. And the sooner we know what kind you have, the sooner we can clear it all up. Fairie magic — which is awfully messy for humans to possess — is my leading candidate."

An unseen weight pressed Kira into the wooden floor. "If I'm a human, how could I have Fairie magic? It seems contradictory."

"Yes, I suppose it does," she answered. Before Kira realized what the witch was doing, she'd taken out her watch again, and Kira found herself surrounded by a swarm of buzzing insects.

Kira screamed, swatting at the mass and doing her best to cover her head from potential stings. She ran toward the windows, hoping that if the little beast sensed they had an escape route they would leave her alone. But no, they dived toward her face. The magic burst out of her in one blinding green flash that surrounded Kira like a bubble. It kept the bugs at bay, and one by one they disappeared in bursts of glitter.

Caris Mourne stepped forward holding a glass jar she used to collect the magical refuse.

Breathless, Kira wanted to tuck her head between her knees or at the least sit down until the world stopped spinning. Unfortunately, there was no place to recover.

With all the green matter in the jar, Caris Mourne took a long, thin, twisted stick from the pocket of her loose trousers. She tapped the stick twice against the glass, and the substance inside swirled like a tornado. "Now that is something."

Aghast, Kira found herself shrieking, "How? What is that?"

Caris Mourne held out the jar. "Take it."

"I don't want it! I want to know what's going on!"

The witch extended the jar, and Kira had no choice but to take it. It was warm to the touch, as if the whirlwind inside were producing its own heat. As she looked inside, the color deepened to a darker green, with swirls of teal at the edges.

"It's like a Zephyr lamp," Kira found herself saying.

Caris Mourne took the jar back, holding it up to the light coming in through the windows. "So it is."

"What does that mean?"

The witch made a vague but gesture that somehow grated on Kira's nerves. "Let's find out."

She put the jar down on the bare floor and stepped back, motioning for Kira to do the same. The watch made another appearance, and the jar began to rise in the air.

"Turn it into a duck."

"Why a duck?"

"Why not?" Caris Mourne handed her the twisted stick. "You might as well turn the jar into waterfowl as anything else."

"I don't like ducks," Kira muttered. Unsure of how she was supposed to go about using transformational magic, she concentrated on the jar. The color inside might have changed again, perhaps to something like the color of a mallard's wing, but that might have been wishful thinking.

"Point the wand," Caris Mourne said. "It may help concentrate things."

Kira pointed the stick, but beyond a few slight changes in color, nothing much happened. She growled in frustration and threw the stick down. There was a green flash, and the jar was no longer a jar.

It wasn't a duck.

A small black kitten with large green eyes had taken the place of the jar. It was almost immediately scooped up by the witch.

"Excellent. I've always wanted a cat." She cradled the small, furry thing under her arm. "It always struck me as such a cliche — witches with cats as familiars — but honestly they're wonderful companions."

Kira felt as if the air around her had been replaced with something else entirely. She was light-headed, watching Caris Mourne place small kisses on the kitten's head.

"What shall we name it? I've always been fond of the name Veronica."

It was a pretty thing; Kira could admit that much. She stepped forward, scratching the cat behind the ears. The cat allowed that for exactly three seconds before it hissed at her. She jumped back out of fear of being bitten.

Caris Mourne held up the animal, and spoke to it. "Go and find Jacobee. They will care for you until I am done."

Impossibly, the cat seemed to nod. In a blink, it was gone.

She turned back to Kira. "So, let's review." She used her watch to summon the arm chairs that had occupied the room on Kira's first visit, dropping them in the middle of the room with a definitive thump. She gestured to one for Kira to sit. Exhausted, Kira complied. She wasn't sure if the magic was responsible or it was yet another consequence of having an exceptionally strange week.

Caris Mourne sat tucking her feet underneath her as if she were about to curl up and read a book. "We know that your magic isn't strictly Fairie magic," she said, ticking off the item on her fingers.

"How do we know that?"

"Color," Caris Mourne said, as if it weren't the most obvious of things. "Fairie magic is always a particular shade of yellow."

*How silly of her not to know.*

Undaunted, the witch continued, ticking up a second finger. "We know it isn't Nature magic. Your inability to use a wand is proof of that."

"And as you've no training at the Coven in Fairie City, we can easily conclude that whatever type of magic you possess, it isn't any of the learned varieties. Unless there's something you haven't told me?"

Kira shook her head. She yawned. She didn't remember being this tired since her last robbery. When she used too much of the cloak's magic she could sleep for six or seven hours at least. She felt as if she could easily do the same now, if not longer.

"One simple hex should not make you drowsy," Caris Mourne noted.

"It always does," Kira said, with another great yawn. The chair underneath her was insanely comfortable, and she felt as if she might drift off to sleep right here.

"Brought out by anger and frustration. Green in color. Leaves you sleepy," Caris Mourne repeated, as if to herself. "Wait here." She got up, and raced across the room.

Kira was sure the room had been empty before, but Caris Mourne dashed to a large table set up in the center of the room, bearing various potions in strange-shaped containers, bubbling over lit candles. She grabbed a handful of sea glass green crane flowers from the table, pulling the petals off with a dramatic yank. "When you took the emotion dampening draught, it worked at first, didn't it?"

Kira nodded. For a short time she'd been blissfully numb. But it was far too short lived.

"Let's try something," said the witch. She stuck the green petals into mortar, tamping them down into a paste. She swiped her finger into the mixture, bounding back over to Kira. Before she could object, the witch had dabbed her forehead with four blobs of the mixture. She asked Kira to stand, and then herself retreated several feet across the room. Kira went to follow her, but the witch held up a hand to stop her.

"I want you to think of something you want. It can be anything. A dress, a lemon tart, a shiny gold medal, anything."

"Is that all?"

"Yes. Concentrate. Fill your mind with something that you want."

She hadn't had chocolate in days. When she'd fled Dunlock, there hadn't exactly been time to pack her satchel. She concentrated on the chocolate bars she had specially sent to her from a chocolate maker in Tull. If there was anything she wanted it was a simple bit of chocolate and five minutes of peace to eat it.

Another green flash filled the room, this one bigger, although it disappeared much quicker than the one she'd summoned earlier. What was left afterwards was also much bigger.

Robert stood in front of her chair.

*Melissa Constantine*

## Chapter Fifty-Two
### Robert

***Caris Mourne prodded him in the chest.*** "You are the actual Sir Robert, are you not?"

"The last I checked," he said, patting his chest to make sure his form was solid. One second he'd been in the stables and the next he was standing in front of the fireplace in the witch's tower. The sudden travel had left him dizzy, as if his head had been plunged into a whirlpool. He supposed with all that had happened he should have been used to the pull of magic, but he wasn't, and he doubted he ever would be.

Kira stood with the witch. She was pale and clearly horrified. "I thought about chocolate," she said.

Caris Mourne nodded. "And instead you got what you needed."

A deep red flush crept up Kira's face. "I don't…"

But the witch was on a roll and didn't hear. "I gave you the draught to stop your emotions but you needed to cry."

Kira turned an even deeper shade of red. "I do not cry."

"But you needed to!" Caris Mourne said with obvious delight. "And whatever magic you have was stronger than my potion. And I make strong potions."

"My ladies, am I needed here?" Robert sensed that despite the moment they'd shared in the antechamber, Kira was uncomfortable with his presence.

Caris Mourne blinked, as if it hadn't occurred to her that he was more than a prop. Or perhaps that was his resentment at believing he'd been somehow enchanted. "Why would you need him?" she asked Kira.

Kira was too startled to answer. Robert couldn't do much about how things were between them, but he could answer that to save her any embarrassment. "Perhaps it's because the Queen Regent has called the inquest back to order? Everyone is to meet in the main hall in the next hour. I understand she's made a decision."

Caris Mourne laughed in a rusty, yet decidedly gleeful way. "You see, it's exactly what you needed to hear."

But Kira didn't look as if that news was welcome. She said she was afraid, and that didn't seem to have changed since yesterday. He wanted to reach for her. There were things he should have said before they went back to the ballroom. There were things he meant to say when they were last in the tower room. If he didn't say them soon, he might never get the chance.

"If the inquest is meeting again, I must change," she said, going to move past him.

Without thinking about it, Robert caught her hand. "Let me walk you to your suite."

"I am perfectly capable of…" but her words petered out as he caught her gaze. He'd never get over how extraordinary her eyes were — the violet color like gems. He should have told her. That and a hundred more small things. He'd never be worthy of her, but he could try.

"Please." He didn't want to beg, but he would if it meant ten more minutes in her company he'd do it.

"Yes, yes, go," Caris Mourne said, dashing over to her potions. "I must run another experiment."

Kira nodded, slipping her hands around his offered arm. For several long moments as they ascended the stairs, Robert felt time slipping away, as if it were nothing more than sand slipping through his clenched fingers.

"Don't think because I took your arm that I think it means anything," she said.

"No, My Lady, of course not."

"You've made it perfectly clear that you don't want anything to do with me, and I understand that. I'm not pining for you."

"I wouldn't presume."

Kira growled with an almost animalistic sound, and released his arm with a force that might have sent a smaller man tumbling down the winding staircase. "Why not?"

Confused, Robert stopped and turned. "Your Highness, I…."

She huffed, working up a head of steam. "You're a knight but I'm a princess! I practically threw myself at you time and time again and you can't even bother to assume I might have feelings for you?"

"Do you want me to think you do?"

"Of course I do, you silly man!"

"You want me to think that you have feelings for me, and also acknowledge that you don't have any?"

"If it's not too much to ask!"

She really was adorable. A bit insane, but in a good way. "I could do that," he said, failing to hold back the laughter that bubbled up in him.

"Why are you laughing? It is literally the least you can do."

She was standing a step above him on the spiral stairs, which meant despite their considerable height difference, they were face to face He cradled her cheek in his hand.

"For the sake of argument, if I were to kiss you now, would that be presumptuous enough?"

"It would be a start."

He leaned in, and then pulled back, coming away with a pale green petal that had been stuck in her hair.

"You had this in your hair."

Kira practically sprang forward, crashing her lips into his. It took him a half of a moment to realize what was happening, and to tilt his head enough to properly kiss her. Her lips were so soft, and she tasted, somehow, like strawberries. He could have stood there forever, but sadly, they didn't have much time before the inquest began again.

Her breath caught as they broke apart. "Robert, why don't you want to be with me? I know you've seen me at my worst, but.... As I am now, am I not pretty enough? Not smart enough? It can't be because I'm not funny, people laugh at my jokes all the time. So why would you not want to be with me?"

He wasn't sure how to tell her she couldn't be more wrong. "I'm not royal. I'm a third son from an island that barely qualifies as part of the Known Kingdoms. All I have is my knighthood, and that means nothing compared to what others could offer you. I'm so far below you it's comical."

Kira brought her hand up to his jaw. "How could you ever believe you're less than me? You've proved your worth ten of me every day I've known you. You drop everything to help your friends. Not to mention you put yourself in danger to save me. And you're so nice it's disgusting."

He colored under the praise. "I'm not special."

Kira pressed a quick kiss to his cheek. "I am the future queen, and I get to make that decision. If I say you're special, you're special. Now, come on, I have to change. If they decide to toss me out of Corlea altogether, I should dress for the occasion."

****

Robert was reluctant to let her go, but Kira was right. He left her at the door to her suite. With all the maids, footmen, and royals late for the inquest running about all he could do little but leave her with a chaste kiss on the hand.

On his way to the ballroom he ran into Diana.

"Congratulate me, Robby," she said, slipping her arm through his. "I'm getting engaged."

Diana engaged? Little Diana who used to push him in the mud? "Congratulations. Who is the lucky person?"

"Prince Travers of Tull."

Robert felt his stomach drop. The man who'd been too drunk to dance with Kira at the Heir's Ball? That made no sense whatsoever. Robert didn't realize he'd said it out loud until Diana gasped. "Excuse me, Mr. Lycette, but I am perfectly capable of making my choices based on factors of which you are not aware."

Robert knew Travers. For a brief time, before he'd inherited the throne of Tull, they'd both been enrolled in the same squire training in Spire. Travers wasn't a bad person, but he was lazy. And a drunk. "Diana, the rumor is he drinks himself to the point of blacking out every day."

Being a redhead, Diana couldn't hide the color of outrange in her face. "Tull is the largest coastal territory on the continent. Joined with the County of Wills, we'll increase our shipping capabilities exponentially."

"But do you love him?"

He'd known Diana all his life, and her face couldn't hide her emotions. The space between her freckles lost color, and her eyes were sad. No, not sad. *Disappointed?*

"You might not understand but marrying Travers will be what's best."

He was no expert on women, if his interactions with Kira were any indication. And he could tell he'd hurt Diana by responding the way he had. And so Robert did the only thing he could. He apologized. "I'm sorry. If it's what you want, then I'll support you and wish you well."

A little of the color returned to her face as they took their seats in the ballroom. "Thank you. I hope I can always count on your friendship."

"Always."

Neither the Queen Regent nor of the high royals had yet entered the room, but all the seats below the dais were filled. The pitch of voices created a tide, advancing and retreating as the anticipation for the decision built. Robert heard several people offering wagers as to the outcome, but no one seemed to be confident enough to take the bet either way.

The voices only quieted with Kira's arrival. The doors to the ballroom were opened, and she made her way through the crowd with a wide berth, all eyes on her. She'd chosen a gold dress in a lustrous, heavy satin. The gown left her shoulders bare, except for a loop around each arm. It hugged her waist, and then fell like molten sunshine down to her feet.

Robert didn't know much about clothing. He wore what he was given. But Kira clearly knew something about how to dress. She looked radiant, and somehow like the future queen. Who could dispute her place on the throne when she looked that regal?

Diana watched him watch Kira. Keeping her voice low, she asked. "Do you love her, Robby?"

"I think so," he answered honestly, his eyes still on the princess.

"Tell her. No matter what happens, tell her."

He'd never seen her so serious before. Diana was always a bright light. But now, she was dimmed, as if part of her had been covered up and snuffed out. Had it happened in the three years they'd been apart, or if it was more recent? Robert couldn't say. Diana was strong and she was capable. He had to trust that she would know how to get herself out of whatever funk she was in.

"I will," he said.

"Good. Invite me to your wedding."

He and Kira were a long way from getting married, but he knew that wasn't what she meant. "You'll get the first invitation." He squeezed her hand, hoping to convey all of the things he couldn't otherwise say.

There was an even greater hush among the royals as the doors to the ballroom opened again. Prince Brandon, Princess Margo, and the Queen Regent had arrived. It was time for everyone to learn their fate.

*Melissa Constantine*

## Chapter Fifty-Three
### Kira

*Her cloak glimmered under the elaborate chandeliers of the Dunlock* ballroom. Among its many colors of fur, the silver, gold, and copper strands danced with the flickering light. It had been strung up over the dais where the musicians had been playing only a handful of nights ago so that everyone might see it and understand her crimes.

Kira kept her eyes forward as she made her way to the front of the room and took her seat. She was no calmer than she'd been yesterday, but she resigned herself to hearing what was to be said. At least after the meeting, some of the upheaval she felt would be over.

Hiding in a blanket fort with Bertie remained her preferred future. She waited as the high royals, Isadora, Prince Brandon and Princess Margo, Caris Mourne, and a handful of others filled into the seats around her. Isadora caught her eye and gave her a small nod. A small flicker of hope ignited in Kira. She kept her expectations low, but the gesture meant it couldn't be all bad.

*Could it?*

Isadora stood, staying silent until all eyes in the room were on her. Really, it was remarkable how well the woman commanded attention. The inhabitants of the ballroom were hers to command. Perhaps Kira should have paid more attention to her lessons after all.

When the last murmurs had died down, Isadora spoke. "Yesterday we learned some disturbing information, both about the actions of many of the people entrusted with the care of this kingdom, as well as the princess herself."

"This leaves the Known Kingdoms in a precarious position. One that I believe requires more study. On that note, I've asked Caris Mourne to work with Princess Kira to determine the scope of the magic that surrounds her."

She ceded the floor to the witch, who stood for an awkward moment looking out onto the crowd. Kira gritted her teeth. She didn't know what Caris Mourne was going to say, but something about the way she looked out into the sea of royals made her vaguely ill. Finally, the witch took out her watch and twisted the dial. An exaggerated image of Kira in the witch's tower rose above the crowd. "This morning, through some experimentation with the princess, I was able to pinpoint she possesses a kind of magic that can be said to be *Needful Magic*. As the name suggests, it comes to people, particularly children, who need it most. It is a protective force, often volatile, and very powerful."

Kira watched the image as the witch summoned the bees, the bees then turned to the giant green cloud, and the cloud was gathered into a jar and the jar turned into the cat. Thank the Fairies, the magical lookback shifted before she'd summoned Robert.

"Princess Kira should have had little ability to control it. Yet somehow when she started to masquerade as the Beast of Barlow, she was unintentionally tapping into a portion of that magic. My working hypothesis is that when the Council and others tried to hex her, the protective nature of the Needful Magic expanded outward. It had to go somewhere. And so it did. Namely to the transformation of the children of the Dunlock Charity orphanage."

For a brief moment, the image hanging above the crowd was that of the front of the orphanage, a cloud of smoke obscuring the door. Caris Mourne let the image linger long enough for the assembled royals to watch the children tumble out and transform. There were a few gasps as the little beasts appeared and then disappeared along with the lookback.

Kira's head went from throbbing to threatening to split open. Isadora rose once again, thanking Caris Mourne for her insight. "As you see, the situation here is complex. There is no one neat answer or person to blame. And given that, I have decided that it is in the realm's best interest to work on restoring calm and cleaning up the mess that has been created."

The crowd seemed to anticipate Isadora's next words, if the increase in chatter were any indication. Isadora signaled for calm, but that only quieted the crowd so much.

"Princess Kira is as much a victim as an instigator of the problems we face. However, she has proven herself remorseful of her actions and willing to dedicate herself to the Known Kingdoms. Given that, I have decided that she will continue to learn at my side, until such time as the new members of the Kingdom Council decide on a date for her coronation. I propose a time table of one year."

She was aware of the voices around her being raised, but it was as if cotton wool had been stuffed in her ears. None of it felt quite real.

Despite everything, she would be queen.

Eventually.

## Chapter Fifty-Four
### Robert

**It seemed impossible that the closing ball of the Festival of the Flower** would take place after everything that had happened, but Robert found himself in his formal wear, watching couples spin and twirl around the dance floor like oak seeds pitched to the wind. Prince Brandon had asked that everyone come together to salvage what had likely been the most eventful Festival on record. He'd given a nice speech about new days and new ways as the inquest had wrapped up, promising that the Festival of the Flower would always endure. Everyone seemed pleased with that idea, and had thrown themselves into enjoying the evening.

Thus, the same room where all of the furor of the inquest had taken place was now adorned with giant displays of purple and lavender Dunlock cranes. The giant chandeliers had been given fresh candles, which seemed to glow with a brighter and warmer light. The flames danced with the crystals adorning the chandeliers, making the room sparkle with refracted rainbows. A group of musicians were set up on the dais, playing with a gusto that matched the smiles of everyone on the floor. Because the final ball was open to anyone in the kingdom, kitchen maids dancing with knights, and stable hands with ladies.

Everyone seemed determined to be in a good mood, but Robert still felt as if the ground underneath him were made of soup. His equilibrium pitched and the room spun. Or maybe that was being around Kira. She'd opened the dancing with him, despite protocol that said she should have sought out Travers or Xavier. He knew it had caused more than one comment, but he didn't care.

In the candlelight, her gown shone as if it were made of moonglow. It fell in graceful swoops as if bands of pure silver swirled around her. Everything about her said that she was so high above him he had no business even looking at her.

He couldn't look anywhere else.

As they finished the opening set of dances, they made their way to the refreshment table. She was waiting for him to say something, but words left him. He concentrated on handing her a cup of punch without spilling it all over her.

Finally, she spoke. "I suppose you'll be headed back to the Misery Islands?"

He nodded. "My uncle wants to leave in the morning. Since Prince Brandon bought all of this year's crane crop, he wants to oversee the shipment himself."

"So does that mean you'll come back this way?"

He had the urge to take her hand. To slip his fingers in between hers, and never let go. "I hope so."

She picked up the folds of her skirt, stepping so close he could pick up the subtle hint of floral perfume. "If I asked you to come see me, would you?"

"It would be my honor."

"Is that all?"

That uneven ground feeling hit again. How was it he never knew the right thing to say?

She blushed. "I'm the future queen. Of course it's your honor to come see me. I'm not asking you to marry me or anything. I want to know if you want to see me. Specifically. For reasons."

Robert smiled. She was spiraling, in her adorable, very wordy way.

"I want to come see you. Specifically."

"Good," she said, straightening her spine. "That's good."

He held out his hand. "Dance with me again?"

She stepped into his embrace as the music in the ballroom swelled. They moved together effortlessly, twirling through the other couples crowding the floor.

"Are you going back to the Palace tomorrow?"

"Yes. Queen Isadora and I have a lot to do in preparation for the vote on new members of the Kingdom Council. And starting the restoration of the Fairie chapel."

"That sounds... not fun."

"It won't be, but it's what I have to do. And Bertie is coming with me, so at least I'll have him."

"I was sorry to hear he and Xav broke up."

"Me too. Bertie is devastated."

Robert wished he had some insight to share that would help, but he didn't. He knew that his friend seemed to be carrying a great weight on his shoulders, but beyond that, he wasn't sure what would make him think he couldn't be with the man he loved. "Give him my best, please."

"I will. You know, he's the one who... well, it's silly but he said I should flirt with you and try and snog you behind a potted plant. As if you'd ever want to do that."

If he'd chosen the moment, Robert wouldn't have kissed her in the middle of a crowded ballroom, with the eyes of every royal house on them, but he wouldn't pass on his chance. He pulled her closer, cradling her cheek in his palm. Maybe a kiss wasn't going to transform them into different people. It wouldn't break the magic in her or make him anything other than a knight from the smallest territory. But as his lips touched hers he knew that something was different.

"I love you," he said, keeping his voice deliberately low because the words were only for her.

"When I'm queen I'll make a law that you're never allowed to say that to anyone else."

"So you love me too?"

She nodded, her cheeks burning red. "Yes. Please don't break my heart."

"When you're queen will you make a law that says you're never allowed to break my heart?"

"As soon as they put that crown on my head."

The music picked up tempo, and their chance to speak was lost. All too soon, official duties would pull her away. The dance would end, eventually. The music would cease, the candles would burn down to nothing, the ball would be a memory. But for now, he would hold her and look into her eyes, the luckiest man in the Known Kingdoms.

# Epilogue
## Diana

**The day they'd arrived in Dunlock, the courtyard had been set up for a** ceremony — full of waving banners and hundreds of thousands of crane flowers. The day after the Festival it was a much more practical space. Carriages pulled up to the front steps, and an army of servants ushered the royal families and their luggage inside of them. Diana stood with her mother, waiting for the Wills carriage to be brought round.

"I wish you'd gone to the ball last night. I know we can't officially announce your engagement but it would have been nice to see you dance with Prince Travers." Her mother had a far too wistful tone for so early in the morning.

"Travers isn't much of a dancer."

"But think of it. You two are well matched. You'd have made a lovely couple taking a turnabout the floor."

Diana didn't bother to respond. Mother wasn't unaware of Travers' habits. She knew he likely wouldn't have been well enough to speak, much less remember the steps to a dance.

A cool wind blew through the courtyard, and Diana breathed deeply. They had a long journey back to Wills, and the carriage was likely to be stuffy. The presence of Fritz, who was currently being walked by one of the Dunlock footmen, wouldn't help that.

She had run into Robert at breakfast. They were parting as friends, but she would always be a little sad that her childish infatuation was over. She didn't begrudge him his newfound love, but she could acknowledge her jealousy. Everyone had been talking about his kiss with the Princess on the dancefloor. Over breakfast, she'd heard at least a dozen other women talking about it as if it were the most romantic kiss in the history of kisses.

And Fairies be damned, that was annoying.

She'd have to console herself with the fact that if she married Travers she'd be a princess from the second most powerful territory. It wasn't an inconsiderable incentive. She could do a lot of good with that kind of clout.

Mother sighed. "Margo told me this morning she's expecting another baby. Can you believe it? Eleven children."

Diana knew a plea for solidarity when she heard one, and she answered appropriately. "Imagine, she'll still be raising young children when you're a grandmother."

Her mother smiled, and kissed her on the cheek. "You remain my favorite child."

"Oh thank the Fairies. I thought I might have some competition."

A line of carriages lurched toward the gate, and six new ones lined up in the space they'd occupied. The Countess offered goodbyes to the families she knew in the form of polite acknowledgement and small waves. Diana knew she wanted to say more, especially about the potential engagement. Her mother wore a smile on her face that said she had a lovely little secret, and couldn't wait to tell each and every one of them.

Politically, and socially, it would be a triumph.

If only Travers weren't such an unrelenting ass.

"This is much more organized than I expected after all that's happened. I am glad to be done with the chaos," her mother said, as another of her acquaintances left the courtyard.

Diana wasn't as sure. Chaos had its advantages. The mele surrounding Princess Kira had cemented some important things for her. For one, she was good in a crisis. And for another that her heart was more definitely broken.

Robert hadn't hurt her intentionally. He'd fallen in love with someone else. She couldn't blame him for that no matter how much it stung.

The next group of carriages included the party from Lower Miser. The great ceremonial carriage rolled up, clanging its obnoxious buoy bell. There was a pang in Diana's chest as Robert held a hand up in acknowledgement before climbing inside. No romantic, lingering goodbye for her. A wave, a half-smile, and he was gone.

"Have you heard about their knight?" Mother asked. "Apparently he's been in and out of consciousness since he came back with Robby and Princess Kira. He's going to stay in the care of the witch, Caris Mourne, until she can figure out what's keeping him from healing."

"Sir Jordaan?" Diana's heartbeat increased, though she didn't want to speculate as to why.

Mother happily scooped up Fritz from the beleaguered footman, kissing the little dog on the head. "I think that's the one. He's apparently slumbering away like a storybook princess in the knight's quarters."

Diana had never considered herself an impulsive person, but she found herself making a hasty excuse for why she absolutely needed to head back inside the castle. "I'll be a few moments, Mother, I promise," she said, taking off at an unladylike run. "I think I left my handbag in our suite."

"Send a servant, Diana!" Mother called after her.

She took the stairs two at a time, before realizing that the knight's quarters weren't in the castle proper. She turned and sprinted back past her mother at full speed.

"Our carriage is in the next group!"

But Diana was too preoccupied to answer.

The knight's quarters were alongside the stables. Diana couldn't say where she was going. She'd had no reason to be in the knight's quarters before, and she wasn't familiar with the layout. But her feet carried her into the long corridor, and she found herself in the small, sunny room where Sir Jordaan lay unconscious, watched by one of the Dunlock maids.

"Miss, you shouldn't be here," the little maid said. "They don't know what's wrong with him."

Jordaan's eyes moved furiously underneath his lids, and sweat had dampened his shaggy blond mane.

Diana reached tentatively for his hand. She wasn't sure what she expected, perhaps that it would be lifeless and cold. Instead, his hand was overly warm and alive.

"Give me a moment, would you. I'd like to say goodbye."

The maid hesitated, but eventually edged her way out. "Be careful, Miss. I'll be down the hall if you need me."

With the maid gone, and Jordaan obviously sound asleep, she wasn't sure what she expected. They'd had that moment after her disastrous tea with Prince Travers, when he'd looked at her and seemed to imply… something.

"I hope you heal," she told him. "You are impertinent and entirely too sure of yourself to be like this."

Of course he didn't answer, and Diana began to feel silly for having sprinted here so thoughtlessly.

"I do want to thank you for what you said. Goodbye, Sir Jordaan."

She leaned down to press a kiss to his cheek, but as she did, Jordaan turned. Her lips grazed his, with the barest whisper. As if the kiss wasn't shocking enough, Sir Jordaan also seemed to be awake.

"Why did you do that?" she demanded, backing away as quickly as she could.

Jordaan sat up, a lazy smile on his face. "It was a true love's kiss. You've cured me."

"You are full of yourself. I don't even know why I came here," she said, turning to go.

"You'll figure it out," he said with a yawn.

# The End

*Melissa Constantine*

## Author's Note

My very initial idea for this book (and the series to come) started with an episode of the *Jim Henson's The Storyteller*. Specifically the "Sapsorrow" episode, which is a version of Cinderella where the princess dresses up in an old fur cloak, passes herself off as a lowly servant, and wins the prince anyway. I saw it randomly on my dorm's cable TV, one too-warm afternoon; one of those days when nothing except staying in the air-conditioning is remotely appealing. It was probably a decade old when I saw it. Regardless, something about it lived in my head rent-free for almost twenty years afterward. That led me to the Grimm's version, "Allerleirauh" and other versions such as "All Kinds of Fur" and "Donkeyskin." A lot of them are weird, I'm not going to lie. Lots of gold tokens put in food, which is just… unhygienic. But the gist is a princess in disguise, taking her destiny into her own hands. I knew I wanted to do something with that story, it just took a lot longer than I anticipated to build this world.

And while we're talking about story inspirations, I've always been a sucker for the Disney versions of Beauty and the Beast (both animated and live-action). In many ways this book also owes inspiration to them, hence the enchanted cottage and it's inert mantle clock and candlesticks. I couldn't resist the nod.

Anyhow, I hope you enjoyed this book, and that you'll consider reviewing it on your platform of choice (Amazon, Goodreads, B&N, etc). It came together after years of workshops, writer's groups, good friends (especially Erin who read an early draft), and my ever-supportive sister Jamie. Never let anyone tell you writing is a solo activity. Like most things it takes a lot of people to do something by yourself.

## About The Author

Melissa Constantine drinks too much coffee. It's not a problem, it's a choice. She is the author of the self-published book *Smashing*, a young adult contemporary, available on Amazon. She is busy writing at least 3 more books in this series (possibly 4), as well as other projects in fantasy, sci-fi, romance, and possibly historical fiction. It really just depends on how much coffee she drinks.

Printed in the USA
CPSIA information can be obtained
at www.ICGtesting.com
JSHW020910180924
69820JS00001B/3